A PLACE TO BELONG

NEW YORK TIMES BESTSELLING AUTHOR

RaeAnne Thayne

Previously published as *A Cold Creek Homecoming* and
Coming Home to Crimson

ISBN-13: 978-1-335-40987-4

A Place to Belong

Copyright © 2021 by Harlequin Books S.A.

A Place to Belong
First published as A Cold Creek Homecoming in 2009.
This edition published in 2021.
Copyright © 2009 by RaeAnne Thayne

Coming Home to Crimson
First published in 2018.
This edition published in 2021.
Copyright © 2018 by Michelle Major

Recycling programs for this product may not exist in your area.

For questions and comments about the quality of this book, please contact us at CustomerService@Harlequin.com.

Harlequin Enterprises ULC
22 Adelaide St. West, 40th Floor
Toronto, Ontario M5H 4E3, Canada
www.Harlequin.com

Printed in Lithuania

MIX
Paper from responsible sources
FSC® C021394

CONTENTS

New York Times bestselling author **RaeAnne Thayne** finds inspiration in the beautiful northern Utah mountains, where she lives with her family. Her books have won numerous honors, including six RITA® Award nominations from Romance Writers of America and Career Achievement and Romance Pioneer Awards from *RT Book Reviews*. She loves to hear from readers and can be reached through her website at raeannethayne.com.

Books by RaeAnne Thayne

HQN

The Cliff House
The Sea Glass Cottage
Christmas at Holiday House
The Path to Sunshine Cove

Haven Point

Snowfall on Haven Point
Serenity Harbor
Sugar Pine Trail
The Cottages on Silver Beach
Season of Wonder
Coming Home for Christmas
Summer at Lake Haven

Hope's Crossing

Blackberry Summer
Woodrose Mountain
Sweet Laurel Falls
Currant Creek Valley
Willowleaf Lane
Christmas in Snowflake Canyon
Wild Iris Ridge

Visit the Author Profile page
at Harlequin.com for more titles.

A COLD CREEK HOMECOMING

RaeAnne Thayne

In memory of my dear aunt, Arlene Wood,
for afghans and parachutes and ceramic frogs.
I only wish I'd dedicated one to you before!
And to Jennifer Black, my sister and hero, for
helping her pass with peace and dignity.

Chapter 1

"You're home!"

The thin, reedy voice whispering from the frail woman on the bed was nothing like Quinn Southerland remembered.

Though she was small in stature, Jo Winder's voice had always been firm and commanding, just like the rest of her personality. When she used to call them in for supper, he and the others could hear her voice ringing out loud and clear from one end of the ranch to the other. No matter where they were, they knew the moment they heard that voice, it was time to go back to the house.

Now the woman who had done so much to raise him—the toughest woman he had ever known—seemed a tiny, withered husk of herself, her skin papery and pale and her voice barely audible.

The cracks in his heart from watching her endure the long months and years of her illness widened a little more.

To his great shame, he had a sudden impulse to run away, to escape back to Seattle and his business and the comfortable life he had created for himself there, where he could pretend this was all some kind of bad dream and she was immortal, as he had always imagined.

Instead, he forced himself to step forward to the edge of the bed, where he carefully folded her bony fingers in his own much larger ones, cursing the cancer that was taking away this woman he loved so dearly.

He gave her his most charming smile, the one that never failed to sway any woman in his path, whether in the boardroom or the bedroom.

"Where else would I be but right here, darling?"

The smile she offered in return was rueful and she lifted their entwined fingers to her cheek. "You shouldn't have come. You're so busy in Seattle."

"Never too busy for my best girl."

Her laugh was small but wryly amused, as it always used to be when he would try to charm his way out of trouble with her.

Jo wasn't the sort who could be easily charmed but she never failed to appreciate the effort.

"I'm sorry to drag you down here," she said. "I…only wanted to see all of my boys one last time."

He wanted to protest that his foster mother would be around for years to come, that she was too tough and ornery to let a little thing like cancer stop her, but he couldn't deny the evidence in front of him.

She was dying, was much closer to it than any of them had feared.

"I'm here, as long as you need me," he vowed.

"You're a good boy, Quinn. You always have been."

He snorted at that—both of them knew better about that,

as well. "Easton didn't tell me you've been hitting the weed as part of your treatment."

The blankets rustled softly as her laugh shook her slight frame. "You know better than that. No marijuana here."

"Then what are you smoking?"

"Nothing. I meant what I said. You were always a good boy on the inside, even when you were dragging the others into trouble."

"It still means the world that you thought so." He kissed her forehead. "Now I can see you're tired. You get some rest and we can catch up later."

"I would give anything for just a little of my old energy."

Her voice trailed off on the last word and he could tell she had already drifted off, just like that, in mid-sentence. As he stood beside her bed, still holding her fingers, she winced twice in her sleep.

He frowned, hating the idea of her hurting. He slowly, carefully, released her fingers as if they would shatter at his touch and laid them with gentle care on the bed then turned just as Easton Springhill, his distant cousin by marriage and the closest thing he had to a sister, appeared in the doorway of the bedroom.

He moved away from the bed and followed Easton outside the room.

"She seems in pain," he said, his voice low with distress.

"She is," Easton answered. "She doesn't say much about it but I can tell it's worse the past week or so."

"Isn't there something we can do?"

"We have a few options. None of them last very long. The hospice nurse should be here any minute. She can give her something for the pain." She tilted her head. "When was the last time you ate?"

He tried to remember. He had been in Tokyo when he

got the message from Easton that Jo was asking for him to come home. Though he had had two more days of meetings scheduled for a new shipping route he was negotiating, he knew he had no choice but to drop everything. Jo would never have asked if the situation hadn't been dire.

So he had rescheduled everything and ordered his plane back to Pine Gulch. Counting several flight delays from bad weather over the Pacific, he had been traveling for nearly eighteen hours and had been awake for eighteen before that.

"I had something on the plane, but it's been a few hours."

"Let me make you a sandwich, then you can catch a few z's."

"You don't have to wait on me." He followed her down the long hall and into the cheery white-and-red kitchen. "You've got enough to do, running the ranch and taking care of Jo. I've been making my own sandwiches for a long time now."

"Don't you have people who do that for you?"

"Sometimes," he admitted. "That doesn't mean I've forgotten how."

"Sit down," she ordered him. "I know where everything is here."

He thought about pushing her. But lovely as she was with her delicate features and long sweep of blond hair, Easton could be as stubborn and ornery as Jo and he was just too damn tired for another battle.

Instead, he eased into one of the scarred pine chairs snugged up against the old table and let her fuss over him for a few moments. "Why didn't you tell me how things were, East? She's withered away in the three months since I've been home. Chester probably weighs more than she does."

At the sound of his name, Easton's retired old cow dog

that followed her or Jo everywhere lifted his grizzled gray muzzle and thumped his black-and-white tail against the floor.

Easton's sigh held exhaustion and discouragement and no small measure of guilt. "I wanted to. I swear. I threatened to call you all back weeks ago but she begged me not to say anything. She said she didn't want you to know how things were until…"

Her voice trailed off and her mouth trembled a little. He didn't need her to finish. Jo wouldn't have wanted them to know until close to the end.

This was it. For three long years, Jo had been fighting breast cancer and now it seemed her battle was almost over.

He *hated* this. He wanted to escape back to his own world where he could at least pretend he had some semblance of control. But she wanted him here in Cold Creek, so here he would damn well stay.

"Truth time, East. How long does she have?"

Easton's features tightened with a deep sorrow. She had lost so much, this girl he had thought of as a sister since the day he arrived at Winder Ranch two decades ago, an angry, bitter fourteen-year-old with nothing but attitude. Easton had lived in the foreman's house then with her parents and they had been friends almost from the moment he arrived.

"Three weeks or so," she said. "Maybe less. Maybe a little more."

He wanted to rant at the unfairness of it all that somebody like Jo would be taken from the earth with such cruelty when she had spent just about every moment of her entire seventy-two years of life giving back to others.

"I'll stay until then."

She stared at him, the butter knife she was using to spread mustard on his sandwich frozen in her hand. "How can you possibly be away from Southerland Shipping that long?"

He shrugged. "I might need to make a few short trips back to Seattle here and there but most of my work can be done long-distance through email and conference calls. It shouldn't be a problem. And I have good people working for me who can handle most of the complications that might come up."

"That's not what she wanted when she asked you to come home one more time," Easton protested.

"Maybe not. But she isn't making the decisions about this, as much as she might think she's the one in charge. This is what I want. I should have come home when things first starting spiraling down. It wasn't fair for us to leave her care completely in your hands."

"You didn't know how bad things were."

If he had visited more, he would have seen for himself. But like Brant and Cisco, the other two foster sons Jo and her husband, Guff, had made a home for, life had taken him away from the safety and peace he had always found at Winder Ranch.

"I'm staying," he said firmly. "I can certainly spare a few weeks to help you out on the ranch and with Jo's care and whatever else you need, after all she and Guff did for me. Don't argue with me on this because you won't win."

"I wasn't going to argue," she said. "You can't know how happy she'll be to have you here. Thank you, Quinn."

The relief in her eyes told him with stark clarity how difficult it must have been for Easton to watch Jo dying, especially after she had lost her own parents at a young age and then her beloved uncle who had taken her in after their deaths.

He squeezed her fingers when she handed him a sandwich with thick slices of homemade bread and hearty roast beef. "Thanks. This looks delicious."

She slid across from him with an apple and a glass of milk. As he looked at her slim wrists curved around her glass, he worried that, like Jo, she hadn't been eating enough and was withering away.

"What about the others?" he asked, after one fantastic bite. "Have you let Brant and Cisco know how things stand?"

Jo had always called them her Four Winds, the three foster boys she and Guff had taken in and Easton, her niece who had been their little shadow.

"We talk to Brant over the computer every couple weeks when he can call us from Afghanistan. Our webcam's not the greatest but I suppose he still had front-row seats as her condition has deteriorated over the past month. He's working on swinging leave and is trying to get here as soon as he can."

Quinn winced as guilt pinched at him. His best friend was halfway around the world and had done a better job of keeping track of things here at the ranch than Quinn had when he was only a few states away.

"What about Cisco?"

She looked down at her apple. "Have you heard from him?"

"No. Not for a while. I got a vague email in the spring but nothing since."

"Neither had we. It's been months. I've tried everything I can think of to reach him but I have no idea even where he is. Last I heard, he was in El Salvador or somewhere like that but I'm not having any luck turning up any information about him."

Cisco worried him, Quinn had to admit. The rest of

them had gone on to do something productive with their lives. Quinn had started Southerland Shipping after a stint in the Air Force, Brant Western was an honorable Army officer serving his third tour of duty in the Middle East and Easton had the ranch, which she loved more than just about anything.

Cisco Del Norte, on the other hand, had taken a very different turn. Quinn had only seen him a few times in the past five or six years and he seemed more and more jaded as the years passed.

What started as a quick trip to Mexico to visit relatives after a stint in the Army had turned into years of Cisco bouncing around Central and South America.

Quinn had no idea what he did down there. He suspected that few of Cisco's activities were legal and none of them were good. He had decided several years ago that he was probably better off not knowing for sure.

But he *did* know Jo would want one more chance to see Cisco, whatever he was up to south of the border.

He swallowed another bite of sandwich. "I'll put some resources on it and see what I can find out. My assistant is frighteningly efficient. If anyone can find the man and drag him out of whatever cantina he calls home these days, it's Kathleen."

Easton's smile didn't quite reach her eyes. "I've met the redoubtable Kathleen. She scares me."

"That makes two of us. It's all part of her charm."

He tried to hide his sudden jaw-popping yawn behind a sip of water, but few things slipped past Easton.

"Get some sleep," she ordered in a tone that didn't leave room for arguments. "Your old room is ready for you. Clean sheets and everything."

"I don't need to sleep. I'll stay up with Jo."

"I've got it. She's got my cell on speed dial and only has to hit a couple of buttons to reach me all the time. Besides, the hospice nurse will be here to take care of things during the night."

"That's good. I was about to ask what sort of medical care she receives."

"Every three hours, we have a home-care nurse check in to adjust medication and take care of any other needs she might have. Jo doesn't think it's necessary to have that level of care, but it's what her doctors and I think is best."

That relieved his mind considerably. At least Easton didn't have to carry every burden by herself. He rose from the table and folded her into a hug.

"I'm glad you're here," she murmured. "It helps."

"This is where I have to be. Wake me up if you or Jo need anything."

"Right."

He headed up the stairs in the old log house, noting the fourth step from the top still creaked, just like always. He had hated that step. More than once it had been the architect of his downfall when he and one of the others tried to sneak in after curfew. They would always try so hard to be quiet but then that blasted stair would always give them away. By the time they would reach the top of the staircase, there would be Guff, waiting for them with those bushy white eyebrows raised and a judgment-day look on his features.

He almost expected to see his foster father waiting for him on the landing. Instead, only memories hovered there as he pushed open his bedroom door, remembering how suspicious and belligerent he had been to the Winders when he first arrived.

He had viewed Winder Ranch as just another prison,

one more stop on the misery train that had become his life after his parents' murder-suicide.

Instead, he had found only love here.

Jo and Guff Winder had loved him. They had welcomed him into their home and their hearts, and then made more room for first Brant and then Cisco.

Their love hadn't stopped him from his share of trouble through high school but he knew that without them, he probably would have nurtured that bitterness and hate festering inside him and ended up in prison or dead by now.

This was where he needed to be. As long as Jo hung in, he would be here—for her and for Easton. It was the right thing—the *only* thing—to do.

He completely slept through the discreet alarm on his Patek Philippe, something he *never* did.

When he finally emerged from his exhausted slumber three hours later, Quinn was disoriented at first. The sight of his familiar bedroom ceiling left him wondering if he was stuck in some kind of weird flashback about his teenage years, the kind of dream where some sexy, tight-bodied cheerleader was going to skip through the door any minute now.

No. That wasn't it. Something bleak tapped at his memory bank and the cheerleader fantasy bounced back through the door.

Jo.

He was at the ranch and Jo was dying. He sat up and scrubbed at his face. Daylight was still several hours away but he was on Tokyo time and doubted he could go back to sleep anyway.

He needed a shower, but he supposed it could wait for a few more moments, until he checked on her. Since Jo had always expressed strongly negative feelings about the boys going shirtless around her ranch even when they were mowing the lawn, he took a moment to shrug back into his travel-wrinkled shirt and headed down the stairs, careful this time to skip over the noisy step so he didn't wake Easton.

When he was a kid, Jo and Guff had shared a big master suite on the second floor. She had moved out of it after Guff's death five years ago from an unexpected heart attack, saying she couldn't bear sleeping there anymore without him. She had taken one of the two bedrooms on the main floor, the one closest to the kitchen.

When he reached it, he saw a woman backing out of the room, closing the door quietly behind her.

For an instant, he assumed it was Easton, but then he saw the coloring was wrong. Easton wore her waterfall of straight honey-blond hair in a ponytail most of the time but this woman had short, wavy auburn hair that just passed her chin.

She was smaller than Easton, too, though definitely curvy in all the right places. He felt a little thrum of masculine interest at the sight of a delectably curved derriere easing from the room—as unexpected as it was out of place, under the circumstances.

He was just doing his best to tamp his inappropriate interest back down when the woman turned just enough that he could see her features and any fledgling attraction disappeared like he'd just jumped naked into Windy Lake.

"What the hell are you doing here?" he growled out of the darkness.

Chapter 2

The woman whirled and grabbed at her chest, her eyes wide in the dimly lit hallway. "My word! You scared the life out of me!"

Quinn considered himself a pretty easygoing guy and he had despised very few people in his life—his father came immediately to mind as an exception.

But if he had to make a list, Tess Jamison would be right there at the top.

He was about to ask her again what she thought she was doing creeping around Winder Ranch when his sleep-deprived synapses finally clicked in and he made the connection as he realized that curvy rear end he had been unknowingly admiring was encased in deep blue flowered surgical scrubs.

She carried a basket of medical supplies in one hand and had an official-looking clipboard tucked under her arm.

"*You're* the hospice nurse?" His voice rose with incredulity.

She fingered the silver stethoscope around her neck with her free hand. "That's what they tell me. Hey, Quinn. How have you been?"

He must still be upstairs in his bed, having one of those infinitely disturbing dreams of high school, the kind where he shows up to an advanced placement class and discovers he hasn't read a single page of the textbook, knows absolutely none of the subject matter, and is expected to sit down and ace the final.

This couldn't be real. It was too bizarre, too surreal, that someone he hadn't seen since graduation night—and would have been quite content never to have to see again—would suddenly be standing in the hallway of Winder Ranch looking much the same as she had fifteen years earlier.

He blinked but, damn it all, she didn't disappear and he wished he could just wake up, already.

"Tess," he said gruffly, unable to think of another thing to say.

"Right."

"How long have you been coming here to take care of Jo?"

"Two weeks now," she answered, and he wondered if her voice had always had that husky note to it or if it was a new development. "There are several of us, actually. I usually handle the nights. I stop in about every three or four hours to check vitals and help Jo manage her pain. I juggle four other patients with varying degrees of need but she's my favorite."

As she spoke, she moved away from Jo's bedroom door and headed toward him. He held his breath and fought the instinct to cover his groin, just as a precaution.

Not that she had ever physically hurt him in their turbulent past, but Tess Jamison—Homecoming Queen, valedictorian, and all-around Queen Bee, probably for Bitch—had a way of emasculating a man with just a look.

She smelled not like the sulfur and brimstone he might have expected, but a pleasant combination of vanilla and peaches that made him think of hot summer evenings out on the wide porch of the ranch with a bowl of ice cream and Jo's divine cobbler.

She headed down the hall toward the kitchen, where she flipped on a small light over the sink.

For the first time, he saw her in full light. She was as lovely as when she wore the Homecoming Queen crown, with high cheekbones, a delicate nose and the same lush, kissable mouth he remembered.

Her eyes were still her most striking feature, green and vivid, almond-shaped, with thick, dark lashes.

But fifteen years had passed and nothing stayed the same except his memories. She had lost that fresh-faced innocent look that had been so misleading. He saw tiny, faint lines fanning out at the edges of her eyes and she wore a bare minimum of makeup.

"I didn't know you were back," she finally said when he continued to stare. "Easton didn't mention it before she went to bed."

Apparently there were several things Easton was keeping close to her sneaky little vest. "I only arrived this evening." Somehow he managed to answer her without snarling, but it was a chore. "Jo wanted to see all of us one more time."

He couldn't quite bring himself to say *last* instead of *more* but those huge green eyes still softened.

She was a hospice nurse, he reminded himself, as tough as he found that to believe. She was probably well-trained to pretend sympathy. The real Tess Jamison didn't care about another soul on the planet except herself.

"Are you here for the weekend?" she asked.

"Longer," he answered, his voice curt. It was none of her business that he planned to stay at Winder Ranch as long as Jo needed him, which he hoped was much longer than the doctors seemed to believe.

She nodded once, her eyes solemn, and he knew she understood all he hadn't said. The soft compassion in those eyes—and his inexplicable urge to soak it in—turned him conversely hostile.

"I can't believe you've stuck around Pine Gulch all these years," he drawled. "I would have thought Tess Jamison couldn't wait to shake the dust of podunk eastern Idaho off her designer boots."

She smiled a little. "It's Tess Claybourne now. And plans have a way of changing, don't they?"

"I'm starting to figure that out."

Curiosity stirred inside him. What had she been doing the past fifteen years? Why that hint of sadness in her eyes?

This was Tess, he reminded himself. He didn't give a damn what she'd been up to, even if she looked hauntingly lovely in the low light of the kitchen.

"So you married old Scott, huh? What's he up to? All that quarterback muscle probably turned to flab, right? Is he ranching with his dad?"

She pressed her lips into a thin line for just a moment, then gave him another of those tiny smiles, this one little more than a taut stretch of her mouth. "None of those things, I'm afraid. He died almost two years ago."

Quinn gave an inward wince at his own tactlessness. Apparently nothing had changed. She had *always* brought out the worst in him.

"How?"

She didn't answer for a moment, instead crossing to the coffeemaker he had assumed Easton must have forgotten to turn off. Now he realized she must have left a fresh pot for the hospice worker, since Tess seemed completely comfortable reaching in the cabinet for a cup and pouring.

"Pneumonia," she finally answered as she added two packets of sweetener. "Scott died of pneumonia."

"Really?" That seemed odd. He thought only old people and little kids could get that sick from pneumonia.

"He was…ill for a long time before that. His immune system was compromised and he couldn't fight it off."

Quinn wasn't a *complete* ass, even when it came to this woman he despised so much. He forced himself to offer the appropriate condolences. "That must have been rough for you. Any kids?"

"No."

This time she didn't even bother to offer a tight smile, only stared into the murky liquid swirling in her cup and he thought again how surreal this was, standing in the Winder Ranch kitchen in the middle of the night having a conversation with her, when he had to fight down every impulse to snarl and yell and order her out of the house.

"Jo tells me you run some big shipping company in the Pacific Northwest," she said after a moment.

"That's right." The third biggest in the region, but he was hoping that with the new batch of contracts he was negotiating Southerland Shipping would soon slide into the number two spot and move up from there.

"She's so proud of you boys and Easton. She talks about you all the time."

"Does she?" He wasn't at all thrilled to think about Jo sharing with Tess any details of his life.

"Oh, yes. I'm sure she's thrilled to have you home. That must be why she was sleeping so peacefully. She didn't even wake when I checked her vitals, which is unusual. Jo's usually a light sleeper."

"How are they?"

"Excuse me?"

"Her vitals. How is she?"

He hated to ask, especially of Tess, but he was a man who dealt best with challenges when he gathered as much information as possible.

She took another sip of coffee then poured the rest down the sink and turned on the water to wash it down.

"Her blood pressure is still lower than we'd like to see and she's needing oxygen more and more often. She tries to hide it but she's in pain most of the time. I'm sorry. I wish I had something better to offer you."

"It's not your fault," he said, even as he wished he could somehow figure out a way to blame her for it.

"That's funny. It feels that way sometimes. It's my job to make her as comfortable as possible but she doesn't want to spend her last days in a drugged haze, she says. So we're limited in some of our options. But we still do our best."

He couldn't imagine *anyone* deliberately choosing this for a career. Why on earth would a woman like Tess Jamison—Claybourne now, he reminded himself—have chosen to stick around tiny Pine Gulch and become a hospice nurse? He couldn't quite get past the incongruity of it.

"I'd better go," she said. "I've got three more patients to check on tonight. I'll be back in a few hours, though, and Easton knows she can call me anytime if she needs me. It's…good to see you again, Quinn."

He wouldn't have believed her words, even if he didn't see the lie in her vivid green eyes. She wasn't any happier to see him than he had been to find her wandering the halls of Winder Ranch.

Still, courtesy drilled into him by Jo demanded he walk her to the door. He stood on the porch and watched through the darkness until she reached her car, then he walked back inside, shaking his head.

Tess Jamison Claybourne.

As if he needed one more miserable thing to face here in Pine Gulch.

Quinn Southerland.

Lord have mercy.

Tess sat for a moment outside Winder Ranch in the little sedan she had bought after selling Scott's wheelchair van. Her mind was a jumble of impressions, all of them sharp and hard and ugly.

He despised her. His rancor radiated from him like spokes on a bicycle wheel. Though he had conversed with at least some degree of civility throughout their short encounter, every word, every sentence, had been underscored by his contempt. His silvery-blue eyes had never once lost that sheen of scorn when he looked at her.

Tess let out a breath, more disconcerted by the brief meeting than she should be. She had a thick enough skin to withstand a little animosity. Or at least she had always assumed she did, up to this point.

How would she know, though? She had never had much opportunity to find out. Most of the good citizens of Pine Gulch treated her far differently.

Alone in the quiet darkness of her car, she gave a humorless laugh. How many times over the years had she thought how heartily sick she was of being treated like some kind of venerated saint around Pine Gulch? She wanted people to see her as she really was—someone with hopes and dreams and faults. Not only as the tireless caretaker who had dedicated long years of her life to caring for her husband.

She shook her head with another rough laugh. A little middle ground would be nice. Quinn Southerland's outright vilification of her was a little more harsh than she really wanted to face.

He had a right to despise her. She understood his feelings and couldn't blame him for them. She had treated him shamefully in high school. Just the memory, being confronted with the worst part of herself when she hadn't really thought about those things in years, made her squirm as she started her car.

Her treatment of Quinn Southerland had been reprehensible, beyond cruel, and she wanted to cringe away from remembering it. But seeing him again after all these years seemed to set the fragmented, half-forgotten memories shifting and sliding through her mind like jagged plates of glass.

She remembered all of it. The unpleasant rumors she had spread about him; her small, snide comments, delivered at moments when he was quite certain to overhear; the friends and teachers she had turned against him, without even really trying very hard.

She had been a spoiled, petulant bitch, and the memory of it wasn't easy to live with now that she had much more wisdom and maturity and could look back on her terrible behavior through the uncomfortable prism of age and experience.

She fully deserved his contempt, but that knowledge didn't make it much easier to stomach as she drove down the long, winding Winder Ranch driveway and turned onto

Cold Creek Road, her headlights gleaming off the leaves that rustled across the road in the October wind.

She loved Jo Winder dearly and had since she was a little girl, when Jo had been patient and kind with the worst piano student any teacher ever had. Tess had promised the woman just the evening before that she would remain one of her hospice caregivers until the end. How on earth was she supposed to keep that vow if it meant being regularly confronted with her own poor actions when she was a silly girl too heedless to care about anyone else's feelings?

The roads were dark and quiet as she drove down Cold Creek Canyon toward her next patient, across town on the west side of Pine Gulch.

Usually she didn't mind the quiet or the solitude, this sense in the still hours of the night that she was the only one around. Even when she was on her way to her most difficult patient, she could find enjoyment in these few moments of peace.

Ed Hardy was a cantankerous eighty-year-old man whose kidneys were failing after years of battling diabetes. He wasn't facing his impending passing with the same dignity or grace as Jo Winder but continued to fight it every step of the way. He was mean-spirited and belligerent, lashing out at anyone who dared remind him he wasn't a twenty-five-year-old wrangler anymore who could rope and ride with the best of them.

Despite his bitterness, she loved the old coot. She loved *all* her home-care patients, even the most difficult. She would miss them, even Ed, when she moved away from Pine Gulch in a month.

She sighed as she drove down Main Street with its darkened businesses and the historic Old West lampposts somebody in the chamber of commerce had talked the town into putting up for the tourists a few years ago.

Except for the years she went to nursing school in Boise and those first brief halcyon months after her marriage, she had lived in this small Idaho town in the west shadow of the Tetons her entire life.

She and Scott had never planned to stay here. Their dreams had been much bigger than a rural community like Pine Gulch could hold.

They had married a month after she graduated from nursing school. He had been a first-year med student, excited about helping people, making a difference in the world. They had talked about opening a clinic in some undeveloped country somewhere, about travel and all the rich buffet of possibilities spreading out ahead of them.

But as she said to Quinn Southerland earlier, sometimes life didn't work out the way one planned. Instead of exotic locales and changing the world, she had brought her husband home to Pine Gulch where she had a support network—friends and family and neighbors who rallied around them.

She pulled into the Hardy driveway, noting the leaves that needed to be raked and the small flower garden that should be put to bed for the winter. Mrs. Hardy had her hands full caring for her husband and his many medical needs. She had a grandson in Idaho Falls who helped a bit with the yard but now that school was back in session, he didn't come as often as he had in the summer.

Tess turned off her engine, shuffling through her mental calendar to see if she could find time in the next few days to come over with a rake.

Her job had never been only about pain management and end-of-life decisions. At least not to her. She knew what it was like to be on the other side of the equation and how very much it could warm the heart when someone showed up unexpectedly with a smile and a cloth and window spray to wash the winter grime she hadn't had time to clean off because her life revolved around caretaking someone else.

That experience as the recipient of service had taught her well that her job was to lift the burdens of the families as much as of her patients.

Even hostile, antagonistic family members like Quinn Southerland.

The wind swirled leaves across the Hardys' cracked driveway as she stepped out of her car. Tess shivered, but she knew it wasn't at the prospect of winter just around the corner or that wind bare-knuckling its way under her jacket, but from remembering the icy cold blue of Quinn's eyes.

Though she wasn't at all eager to encounter him again—or to face the bitter truth of the spoiled brat she had been once—she adored Jo Winder. She couldn't let Quinn's forbidding presence distract her from giving Jo the care she deserved.

Chapter 3

Apparently Pine Gulch's time machine was in fine working order.

Quinn walked into The Gulch and was quite certain he had traveled back twenty years to the first time he walked into the café with his new foster parents. He could clearly remember that day, the smell of frying potatoes and meat, the row of round swivel seats at the old-fashioned soda fountain, the craning necks in the place and the hot gazes as people tried to figure out the identity of the surly, scowling dark-haired kid with Jo and Guff.

Not much had changed. From the tin-stamped ceiling to the long, gleaming mirror that ran the length of the soda fountain to the smell of fried food that seemed to send triglycerides shooting through his veins just from walking in the door.

Even the faces were the same. He could swear the same old-timers still sat in the booth in the corner being served by Donna Archuleta, whose husband, Lou, had always manned the kitchen with great skill and joy. He recognized Mick Malone, Jesse Redbear and Sal Martinez.

And, of course, Donna. She stood by the booth with a pot of coffee in her hand but she just about dropped it all over the floor when she looked up at the sound of the jangling bells on the door to spy him walking into her café.

"Quinn Southerland," she exclaimed, her smoker-husky voice delighted. "As I live and breathe."

"Hey, Donna."

One of Jo's closest friends, Donna had always gone out of her way to be kind to him and to Brant and Cisco. They hadn't always made it easy. The three of them had been the town's resident bad boys back in the day. Well, maybe not Brant, he acknowledged, but he was usually guilty by association, if nothing else.

"I didn't know you were back in town." Donna set the pot down in an empty booth to fold her scrawny arms around him. He hugged her back, wondering when she had gotten frail like Jo.

"Just came in yesterday," he said.

"Why the hell didn't anybody tell me?"

He opened his mouth to answer but she cut him off.

"Oh, no. Jo. Is she…" Her voice trailed off but he could see the anxiety suddenly brim in her eyes, as if she dreaded his response.

He shook his head and forced a smile. "She woke up this morning feistier than ever, craving one of Lou's sweet rolls. Nothing else will do, she told me in no uncertain terms, so she sent me down here first thing so I could pick one up and take it back for her. Since according to East, she hasn't been hungry for much of anything else, I figured I had better hurry right in and grab her one."

Donna's lined and worn features brightened like a gorgeous June morning breaking over the mountains. "You're in luck, hon. I think he's just pullin' a new batch out of the oven. You wait right here and have yourself some coffee while I go back and wrap a half-dozen up for her."

Before he could say a word, she turned a cup over from the setting in the booth and poured him a cup. He laughed at this further evidence that not much had changed, around The Gulch at least.

"I think one, maybe two sweet rolls, are probably enough. Like I said, she hasn't had much of an appetite."

"Well, this way she can warm another up later or save one for the morning, and there will be extras for you and Easton. Now don't you argue with me. I'm doing this, so just sit down and drink your coffee, there's a good boy."

He had to smile in the face of such determination, such eagerness to do something nice for someone she cared about. There were few things he missed about living in Pine Gulch, but that sense of community, belonging to something bigger than yourself, was definitely one of them.

He took a seat at the long bar, joining a few other solo customers who eyed him with curiosity.

Again, he had the strange sense of stepping back into his past. He could still see the small chip in the bottom corner of the mirror where he and Cisco had been roughhousing and accidentally sent a salt shaker flying.

That long-ago afternoon was as clear as his flight in from Japan the day before—the sick feeling in the pit of his gut as he had faced the wrath of Lou and Donna and the even worse fear when he had to fess up to Guff and Jo. He had only been with them a year, twelve tumultuous months, and had been quite sure they would toss him back into the foster-care system after one mess-up too many.

But Guff hadn't yelled or ordered him to pack his things. Instead, he just sat him down and told one of his rambling stories about a time he had been a young ranch hand with a little too much juice in him and had taken his .22 and shot out the back windows of what he thought was an old abandoned pickup truck, only to find out later it belonged to his boss's brother.

"A man steps up and takes responsibility for his actions," Guff had told him solemnly. That was all he said, but the trust in his brown eyes had completely overwhelmed Quinn. So of course he had returned to The Gulch and offered to work off the cost of replacing the mirror for the Archuletas.

He smiled a little, remembering Lou and Donna's response. "Think we'll just keep that little nick there as a reminder," Lou had said. "But there are always dishes around here to be washed."

He and Cisco had spent about three months of Saturdays and a couple afternoons a week after school in the kitchen with their hands full of soapy water. More than he cared to admit, he had enjoyed those days listening to the banter of the café, all the juicy small-town gossip.

He only had about three or four minutes to replay the memory in his head before Lou Archuleta walked out of the kitchen, his bald head just as shiny as always and his thick salt-and-pepper mustache a bold contrast. The delight on his rough features matched Donna's, warming Quinn somewhere deep inside.

Lou wiped his hand on his white apron before holding it out for a solemn handshake. "Been too long," he said, in that same gruff, no-nonsense way. "Hear Seattle's been pretty good to you."

Quinn shook his hand firmly, aware as he did that much of his success in business derived from watching the integrity and goodness of people like Lou and Donna and the respect with which they had always treated their customers.

"I've done all right," he answered.

"Better than all right. Jo says you've got a big fancy house on the shore and your own private jet."

Technically, it was the company's corporate jet. But since he owned the company, he supposed he couldn't debate semantics. "How about you? How's Rick?"

Their son had gone to school with him and graduated a year after him. Tess Jamison's year, actually.

"Good. Good. He's up in Boise these days. He's a plumbing contractor, has himself a real good business. He and his wife gave us our first granddaughter earlier this year." The pride on Lou's work-hardened features was obvious.

"Congratulations."

"Yep, after four boys, they finally got a girl."

Quinn choked on the sip of coffee he'd just taken. "Rick has five kids?"

His mind fairly boggled at the very idea of even one. He couldn't contemplate having enough for a basketball team.

Lou chuckled. "Yep. Started young and threw in a set of twins in there. He's a fine dad, too."

The door chimed, heralding another customer, but Quinn was still reeling at the idea of his old friend raising a gaggle of kids and cleaning out toilets.

Still, an odd little prickle slid down his spine, especially when he heard the old-timers in their regular booth hoot with delight and usher the newcomer over.

"About time you got here," one of the old-timers in the corner called out. "Mick here was sure you was goin' to bail on us today."

"Are you kidding?" an alto female voice answered. "This is my favorite part of working graveyard, the chance to come in here for breakfast and have you all give me a hard time every morning. I don't know what I'll do without it."

Quinn stiffened on the stool. He didn't need to turn to

know just who was now sliding into the booth near the regulars. He had last heard that voice at 3:00 a.m. in the dark quiet of the Winder Ranch kitchen.

"Hey, Miss Tess." Lou turned his attention away from bragging about his grandkids to greet the newcomer, confirming what Quinn had already known deep in his bones. "You want your usual?"

"You got it, Lou. I've been dreaming of your veggie omelet all night long. I'm absolutely starving."

"Girl, you need to get yourself something more interesting to fill your nights if all you can dream about is Lou's veggie omelet," called out one of the women from a nearby booth and everybody within earshot laughed.

Everybody but Quinn. She was a regular here, just like the others, he realized. She was part of the community, and he, once more, was the outsider.

She had always been excellent at reminding him of that.

He couldn't put it off any longer, he knew. With some trepidation, he turned around from the counter to the dining room to face her gaze.

Despite the mirror right in front of him, she must not have been paying attention to the other patrons in the restaurant. He could tell she hadn't known he was there until he turned. He saw the little flash of surprise in her eyes, the slight rise and fall of her slim chest as her breathing hitched.

She covered it quickly with a tight smile and the briefest of waves.

She wasn't pleased to see him. He didn't miss the sudden tension in her posture or the dismay that quickly followed that initial surprise.

Join the club, he thought. Bumping into his worst nightmare two times in less than six hours was twice too many, as far as he was concerned.

He thought he saw something strangely vulnerable flash

in those brilliant green eyes for just an instant, then she turned back to the old-timers at the booth with some bright, laughing comment that sounded forced to him.

As he listened to their interaction, it was quickly apparent to him that Tess was a favorite of all of them. No surprise there. She excelled at twisting everybody around her little finger. She had probably been doing the very same thing since she was the age of Lou Archuleta's new granddaughter.

The more the teasing conversation continued, the more sour his mood turned. She sounded vivacious and funny and charming. Why couldn't anybody but him manage to see past the act to the vicious streak lurking beneath?

When he had just about had all he could stomach, Donna returned with two white bakery bags and a disposable coffee cup with steam curling out the top.

"Here you go, hon. Didn't mean to keep you waiting until Christmas but I got tied up in the back with a phone call from a distributor. There's plenty of extra sweet rolls for you and here's a little joe for the road."

He put away his irritation at Tess and took the offerings from Donna with an affectionate smile, his heart warmer than the cup in his hand at her concern. "Thanks."

"You give that girl a big old kiss from everybody down here at The Gulch. Tell her to hang in there and we're all prayin' for her."

"I'll do that."

"And come back, why don't you, while you're in town. We'll fix you up your favorite chicken-fried steak and have a coze."

"It's a date." He kissed her cheek and headed for the door. Just as he reached it, he heard Tess call his name.

"Wait a minute, will you?" she said.

He schooled his features into a mask of indifference as

he turned, loathe for any of the other customers to see how it rankled to see her here still acting like the Pine Gulch Homecoming Queen deigning to have breakfast with all of her hordes of loyal, adoring subjects.

He didn't want to talk to her. He didn't want to be forced to see how lovely and perky she looked, even in surgical scrubs and even after he knew she had been working all night at a difficult job.

She smelled of vanilla and peaches and he didn't want to notice that she looked as bright as the morning, how her auburn curls trailed against her slender jawline or the light sprinkle of freckles across her nose or the way her green eyes had that little rim of gold around the edge you only saw if you were looking closely.

He didn't want to see Tess at all, he didn't want to feel like an outsider again in Pine Gulch, and he especially didn't want to have to stand by and do nothing while a woman he loved slipped away, little by little.

"How's Jo this morning?" she asked. "She seemed restless at six when I came to check on her."

As far as he remembered, Tess had never been involved in the high-school drama club. So either she had become a really fabulous actress in the intervening years or her concern for Jo was genuine.

He let out a breath, tamping down his antagonism in light of their shared worry for Jo. "I don't know. To me, she seems better this morning than she was last night when I arrived. But I don't really have a baseline to say what's normal and what's not."

He held up the bakery bag. "She at least had enough energy to ask for Lou's sweet rolls this morning."

"That's excellent. Eating has been hard for her the past few weeks. Seeing you must be giving her a fresh burst of strength."

Was she implying he should have come sooner? He frowned, disliking the guilt swirling around in his gut along with the coffee.

Yeah, he should have come home sooner. If Easton and Jo had been forthright about what was going on, he would have been here weeks ago. They had hid the truth from him but he should have been more intuitive and figured it out.

That didn't mean he appreciated Tess pointing out his negligence. He scowled but she either didn't notice or didn't particularly care.

"It's important that you make sure she doesn't overdo things," Tess said. "I know that's hard to do during those times when she's feeling better. On her good days, she has a tendency to do much more than she really has the strength to tackle. You just have to be careful to ensure she doesn't go overboard."

Her bossy tone brought his dislike simmering to the surface. "Don't try to manage me like you do everybody else in town," he snapped. "I'm not one of your devoted worshippers. We both know I never have been."

For just an instant, hurt flared in her eyes but she quickly blinked it away and tilted that damn perky chin up, her eyes a sudden murky, wintry green.

"This has nothing to do with me," she replied coolly. "It's about Jo. Part of my job as her hospice nurse is to advise her family regarding her care. I can certainly reserve those conversations with Easton if that's what you prefer."

He bristled for just a moment, but the bitter truth of it was, he knew she was right. He needed to put aside how much he disliked this woman for things long in the distant past to focus on his foster mother, who needed him right now.

Tess appeared to genuinely care about Jo. And while he wasn't quite buying such a radical transformation, people could change. He saw it all the time.

Hell, he was a completely different person than he'd been in high school. He wasn't the angry, belligerent hothead with a chip the size of the Tetons on his shoulder anymore, though he was certainly acting like it right now.

It wasn't wholly inconceivable that this caring nurse act was the real thing.

"You're right." He forced the words out, though they scraped his throat raw. "I appreciate the advice. I'm…still struggling with seeing her this way. In my mind, she should still be out on the ranch hurtling fences and rounding up strays."

Her defensive expression softened and she lifted a hand just a little. For one insane moment, he thought she meant to touch his arm in a sympathetic gesture, but she dropped her arm back to her side.

"Wouldn't we all love that?" she said softly. "I'm afraid those days are gone. Right now, we just have to savor every moment with her, even if it's quietly sitting beside her while she sleeps."

She stepped away from him and he was rather horrified at the regret suddenly churning through him. All these conflicting feelings were making him a little crazy.

"I'm off until tonight," she said, "but you'll find Cindy, the day nurse, is wonderful. Even so, tell Easton to call me if she needs anything."

He nodded and pushed past the door into the sunshine.

That imaginary time machine had a few little glitches in it, he thought as he pulled out of the parking lot and headed back toward Cold Creek Canyon.

He had just exchanged several almost civil words with Tess Jamison Claybourne, something that a dozen years ago would have seemed just as impossible as imagining that someday he would be able to move past the ugliness in his past to run his own very successful company.

Chapter 4

"Do you remember that time you boys stayed out with the Walker sisters an hour past curfew?"

"I'm going to plead the fifth on that one," Quinn said lazily, though he did indeed remember Sheila Walker and some of her more acrobatic skills.

"I remember it," Jo said. "The door was locked and you couldn't get back in so you rascals tried to sneak in a window, remember that? Guff heard a noise downstairs and since he was half-asleep and didn't realize you boys hadn't come home yet, he thought it might be burglars."

Jo chuckled. "He took the baseball bat he kept by the side of the bed and went down and nearly beaned the three of you as you were trying to sneak in the window."

He smiled at the memory of Brant's guilt and Cisco's smart-aleck comments and Guff's stern reprimand to all of them.

"I can't believe Guff told you about that. It was supposed to be a secret between us males."

Her mouth lifted a little at the edges. "Guff didn't keep secrets from me. Don't you know better than that? He used to say whatever he couldn't tell me, he would rather not know himself."

Jo's voice changed when she talked about her late husband. The tone was softer, more rounded, and her love sounded in every word.

He squeezed her fingers. What a blessing for both Guff and Jo that they had found each other, even if it had been too late in life for the children they had both always wanted. Though they married in their forties, they had figured out a way to build the family they wanted by taking in foster children who had nowhere else to go.

"I suppose that's as good a philosophy for a marriage as any," he said.

"Yes. That and the advice of Lyndon B. Johnson. Only two things are necessary to keep one's wife happy, Guff used to say. One is to let her think she is having her own way. The other, to let her have it."

He laughed, just as he knew she intended. Jo smiled along with him and lifted her face to the late-morning sunshine. He checked to make sure the colorful throw was still tucked across her lap, though it was a beautiful autumn day, warmer than usual for October.

They sat on Adirondack chairs canted just so in the back garden of Winder Ranch for a spectacular view of the west slope of the Tetons. Surrounding them were mums and yarrow and a few other hardy plants still hanging on. Most of the trees were nearly bare but a few still clung tightly to their leaves. As he remembered, the stubborn elms liked to hang on to theirs until the most messy, inconvenient time, like just before the first hard snowfall, when it became a nightmare trying to rake them up.

Mindful of Tess's advice, he was keeping a careful eye on Jo and her stamina level. So far, she seemed to be managing her pain. She seemed content to sit in her garden and bask in the unusual warmth.

He wasn't used to merely sitting. In Seattle, he always had someone clamoring for his attention. His assistant, his board of directors, his top-level executives. Someone always wanted a slice of his time.

Quinn couldn't quite ascertain whether he found a few hours of enforced inactivity soothing or frustrating. But he did know he savored this chance to store away a few more precious memories of Jo.

She lifted her thin face to the sunshine. "We won't have too many more days like this, will we? Before we know it, winter will be knocking on the door."

That latent awareness that she probably wouldn't make it even to Thanksgiving—her favorite holiday—pierced him.

He tried to hide his reaction but Jo had eyes like a red-tailed hawk and was twice as focused.

"Stop that," she ordered, her mouth suddenly stern.

"What?"

"Feeling sorry for me, son."

He folded her hand in his, struck again by the frailty of it, the pale skin and the thin bones and the tiny blue veins pulsing beneath the papery surface.

"You want the truth, I'm feeling more sorry for myself than you."

Her laugh startled a couple of sparrows from the bird feeder hanging in the aspens. "You always did have a bit of a selfish streak, didn't you?"

"Damn right." He managed a tiny grin in response to

her teasing. "And I'm selfish enough to wish you could stick around forever."

"For your sake and the others, I'm sorry for that. But don't be sad on my account, my dear. I have missed my husband sorely every single, solitary moment of the past five years. Soon I'll be with him again and won't have to miss him anymore. Why would anyone possibly pity me?"

He would have given a great deal for even a tiny measure of her faith. He hadn't believed much in a just and loving God since the nightmare day his parents died.

"I only have one regret," Jo went on.

He made a face. "Only one?" He could have come up with a couple dozen of his own regrets, sitting here in the sunshine on a quiet Cold Creek morning.

"Yes. I'm sorry my children—and that's what you all are, you know—have never found the kind of joy and love Guff and I had."

"I don't think many people have," he answered. "What is it they say? Often imitated, never duplicated? What the two of you had was something special. Unique."

"Special, yes. Unique, not at all. A good marriage just takes lots of effort on both parts." She tilted her head and studied him carefully. "You've never even been serious about a woman, have you? I know you date plenty of beautiful women up there in Seattle. What's wrong with them all?"

He gave a rough laugh. "Not a thing, other than I have no desire to get married."

"Ever?"

"Marriage isn't for me, Jo. Not with my family history."

"Oh, poof."

He laughed at the unexpectedness of the word.

"Poof?"

"You heard me. You're just making excuses. Never thought I raised any of my boys to be cowards."

"I'm not a coward," he exclaimed.

"What else would you call it?"

He didn't answer, though a couple of words that came immediately to mind were more along the lines of *smart* and *self-protective*.

"Yes, you had things rough," Jo said after a moment. "I'm not saying you didn't. It breaks my heart what some people do to their families in the name of love. But plenty of other people have things rough and it doesn't stop them from living their life. Why, take Tess, for instance."

He gave a mental groan. Bad enough that he couldn't seem to stop thinking about her all morning. He didn't need Jo bringing her up now. Just the sound of her name stirred up those weird, conflicting emotions inside him all over again. Anger and that subtle, insistent, frustrating attraction.

He pushed them all away. "What do you mean, *take Tess*?"

"That girl. Now *she* has an excuse to lock her heart away and mope around feeling sorry for herself for the rest of her life. But does she? No. You'll never find a happier soul in all your days. Why, what she's been through would have crushed most women. Not our Tess."

What could she possibly have been through that Jo deemed so traumatic? She was a pampered princess, daughter of one of the wealthiest men in town, the town's bank president, apparently adored by everyone.

She couldn't know what it was like to have to call the police on your own father or hold your mother as she breathed her last.

Before he could ask Jo to explain, she began to cough—

raspy, wet hacking that made his own chest hurt just listening to it.

She covered her mouth with a folded handkerchief from her pocket as the coughing fit went on for what seemed an eon. When she pulled the cloth away, he didn't miss the red spots speckling the white linen.

"I'm going to carry you inside and call Easton."

Jo shook her head. "No," she choked out. "Will pass. Just...minute."

He gave her thirty more seconds, then reached for his cell phone. He started to hit Redial to reach Easton when he realized Jo's coughs were dwindling.

"Told you...would pass," she said after a moment. During the coughing attack, what little color there was in her features had seeped out and she looked as if she might blow away if the wind picked up even a knot or two.

"Let's get you inside."

She shook her head. "I like the sunshine."

He sat helplessly beside her while she coughed a few more times, then folded the handkerchief and stuck it back into her pocket.

"Sorry about that," she murmured after a painful moment. "I so wish you didn't have to see me like this."

He wrapped an arm around her frail shoulders and pulled her close to him, planting a kiss on her springy gray curls.

"We don't have to talk. Just rest. We can stay for a few more moments and enjoy the sunshine."

She smiled and settled against him and they sat in contented silence.

For those few moments, he was deeply grateful he had come. As difficult as it had been to rearrange his schedule and delegate as many responsibilities as he could to the other executives at Southerland, he wouldn't have missed this moment for anything.

With his own mother, he hadn't been given the luxury of saying goodbye. She had been unconscious by the time he could reach her.

He supposed that played some small part in his insistence that he stay here to the end with Jo, as difficult as it was to face, as if he could atone in some small way for all he hadn't been able to do for his own mother as a frightened kid.

Her love of sunshine notwithstanding, Jo lasted outside only another fifteen minutes before she had a coughing fit so intense it left her pale and shaken. He didn't give her a choice this time, simply scooped her into his arms and carried her inside to her bedroom.

"Rest there and I'll find Easton to help you."

"Bother. She…has enough…to do. Just need water and… minute to catch my breath."

He went for a glass of water and returned to Jo's bedroom with it, then sent a quick text to Easton explaining the situation.

"I can see you sending out an SOS over there," Jo muttered with a dark look at the phone in his hand.

"Who, me? I was just getting in a quick game of solitaire while I wait for you to stop coughing."

She snorted at the lie and shook her head. "You didn't need to call her. I hate being so much of a nuisance to everyone."

He finished the text and covered her hand with his. "Serves us right for all the bother we gave you."

"I think you boys used to stay up nights just thinking about new ways to get into trouble, didn't you?"

"We had regular meetings every afternoon, just to brainstorm."

"I don't doubt it." She smiled weakly. "At least by the middle of high school you settled down some. Though there was that time senior year you got kicked off the baseball team. That nonsense about cheating, which I know you would never do, and so I tried to tell the coach but he wouldn't listen. You never did tell us what that was really all about."

He frowned. He could have told her what it had been about. Tess Jamison and more of her lies about him. If anyone had stayed up nights trying to come up with ways to make someone else's life harder, it would have been Tess. She had made as much trouble as she could for him, for reasons he still didn't understand.

"High school was a long time ago. Why don't I tell you about my latest trip to Cambodia when I visited Angkor Wat?"

He described the ancient temple complex that had been unknown to the outside world until 1860, when a French botanist stumbled upon it. He was describing the nearby city of Angkor Thom when he looked down and saw her eyes were closed, her breathing regular.

He arranged a knit throw over her and slipped off her shoes, which didn't elicit even a hint of a stir out of her. That she could fall asleep so instantaneously worried him and he hoped their short excursion outside hadn't been too much for her.

He closed the door behind him just as he heard the bang of the screen door off the kitchen, then the thud of Easton's boots on the tile.

Chester rose from his spot in a sunbeam and greeted her with delight, his tired old body wiggling with glee.

She stripped off her work gloves and patted him. "Sorry it took me a while. We were up repairing a fence in the west pasture."

"I'm sorry I called you in for nothing. She seems to be resting now. But she was coughing like crazy earlier, leaving blood specks behind."

Easton blew out a breath and swiped a strand of hair that had fallen out of her long ponytail. "She's been doing that lately. Tess says it's to be expected."

"I'm sorry I bugged you for no reason."

"I was ready to break for lunch. I would have been here in about fifteen minutes anyway. I can't tell you what a relief it is to have you here so I know someone is with her. I'm always within five minutes of the house but I can't be here all the time. I hate when I have to leave her, but sometimes I can't help it. The ranch doesn't run itself."

Though Winder Ranch wasn't as huge an operation as the Daltons up the canyon a ways, it was still a big undertaking for one woman still in her twenties, even if she did have a couple ranch hands and a ranch foreman who had been with the Winders since Easton's father died in a car accident that also killed his wife.

"Why don't I fix you some lunch while you're here?" he offered. "It's my turn after last night, isn't it?"

She sent him a sidelong look. "The CEO of Southerland Shipping making me a bologna sandwich? How can I resist an offer like that?"

"Turkey is my specialty but I suppose I can swing bologna."

"Either one would be great. I'll go check on Jo and be right back."

She returned before he had even found all the ingredients.

"Still asleep?" he asked.

"Yes. She was smiling in her sleep and looked so at peace, I didn't have the heart to wake her."

"Sit down. I'll be done here in a moment."

She sat at the kitchen table with a tall glass of Pepsi and they chatted about the ranch and the upcoming roundup in the high country and the cost of beef futures while he fixed sandwiches for both of them.

He presented hers with a flourish and she accepted it gratefully.

"What time does the day nurse come again?" he asked.

"Depends on the nurse, but usually about 1:00 p.m. and then again at five or six o'clock."

"And there are three nurses who rotate?"

"Yes. They're all wonderful but Tess is Jo's favorite."

He paused to swallow a bite of his sandwich then tried to make his voice sound casual and uninterested. "What's her story?" he asked.

"Who? Tess?"

"Jo said something about her that made me curious. She said Tess had it rough."

"You could say that."

He waited for Easton to elucidate but she remained frustratingly silent and he had to take a sip of soda to keep from grinding his back teeth together. The Winder women—and he definitely counted Easton among that number since her mother had been Guff's sister—could drive him crazy with their reticence that they seemed to invoke only at the most inconvenient times.

"What's been so rough?" he pressed. "When I knew Tess, she had everything a woman could want. Brains, beauty, money."

"None of that helped her very much with everything that came after, did it?" Easton asked quietly.

"I have no idea. You haven't told me what that was."

He waited while Easton took another bite of her sandwich before continuing. "I guess you figured out she married Scott, right?"

He shrugged. "That was a foregone conclusion, wasn't it? They dated all through high school."

He had actually always liked Scott Claybourne. Tall and blond and athletic, Scott had been amiable to Quinn if not particularly friendly—until their senior year, when Scott had inexplicably beat the crap out of Quinn one warm April night, with veiled references to some supposed misconduct of Quinn's toward Tess.

More of her lies, he had assumed, and had pitied the bastard for being so completely taken in by her.

"They were only married three or four months, still newlyweds, really," Easton went on, "when he was in a bad car accident."

He frowned. "Car accident? I thought Tess told me he died of pneumonia."

"Technically, he did, just a couple of years ago. But he lived for several years after the accident, though he was permanently disabled from it. He had a brain injury and was in a pretty bad way."

He stared at Easton, trying to make the jaggedly formed pieces of the puzzle fit together. Tess had stuck around Pine Gulch for *years* to deal with her husband's brain injury? He couldn't believe it, not of her.

"She cared for him tirelessly, all that time," Easton said quietly. "From what I understand, he required total care. She had to feed him, dress him, bathe him. He was almost more like her kid than her husband, you know."

"He never recovered from the brain injury?"

"A little but not completely. He was in a wheelchair

and lost the ability to talk from the injury. It was so sad. I just remember how nice he used to be to us younger kids. I don't know how much was going on inside his head but Tess talked to him just like normal and she seemed to understand what sounded like grunts and moans to me."

The girl he had known in high school had been only interested in wearing her makeup just so and buying the latest fashion accessories. And making his life miserable, of course.

He couldn't quite make sense of what Easton was telling him.

"I saw them once at the grocery store when he had a seizure, right there in frozen foods," Easton went on. "It scared the daylights out of me, let me tell you, but Tess just acted like it was a normal thing. She was so calm and collected through the whole thing."

"That's rough."

She nodded. "A lot of women might have shoved away from the table when they saw the lousy hand they'd been dealt, would have just walked away right then. Tess was young, just out of nursing school. She had enough medical experience that I have to think she could guess perfectly well what was ahead for them, but she stuck it out all those years."

He didn't like the compassion trickling through him for her. Somehow things seemed more safe, more ordered, before he had learned that perhaps she hadn't spent the past dozen years figuring out more ways to make him loathe her.

"People in town grew to respect and admire her for the loving care she gave Scott, even up to the end. When she moves to Portland in a few weeks, she's going to leave a real void in Pine Gulch. I'm not the only one who will miss her."

"She's leaving?"

He again tried to be casual with the question, but Easton had known him since he was fourteen. She sent him a quick, sidelong look.

"She's selling her house and taking a job at a hospital there. I can't blame her. Around here, she'll always be the sweet girl who took care of her sick husband for so long. Saint Tess. That's what people call her."

He nearly fell off his chair at that one. Tess Jamison Claybourne was a saint like he played center field for the Mariners.

Easton pushed back from the table. "I'd better check on Jo one more time, then get back to work." She paused. "You know, if you have more questions about Tess, you could ask her. She should be back tonight."

He didn't want to know more about Tess. He didn't want anything to do with her. He wanted to go back to the safety of ignorance. Despising her was much easier when he could keep her frozen in his mind as the manipulative little witch she had been at seventeen.

Chapter 5

"You haven't heard a single word I've said for the past ten minutes, have you?"

Tess jerked her attention back to her mother as they worked side by side in Ed Hardy's yard. Her mother knelt in the mulchy layer of fallen leaves, snipping and digging to ready Dorothy Hardy's flower garden for the winter, while Tess was theoretically supposed to be raking leaves. Her pile hadn't grown much, she had to admit.

"I heard some of it." She managed a rueful smile. "The occasional word here and there."

Maura Jamison raised one delicately shaped eyebrow beneath her floppy gardening hat. "I'm sorry my stories are so dull. I can go back to telling them to the cat, when he'll deign to listen."

She winced. "It's not your story that's to blame. I'm just…distracted today. But I'll listen now. Sorry about that."

Her mother gave her a careful look. "I think it's my turn to listen. What's on your mind, honey? Scott?"

Tess blinked at the realization that except for those few moments when Quinn had asked her about Scott the night before, she hadn't thought about her husband in several days.

A tiny measure of guilt niggled at her but she pushed it away. She refused to feel guilty for that. Scott would have wanted her to move on with her life and she had no guilt for her dealings with her husband.

Still, she didn't think she could tell her mother she was obsessing about Quinn Southerland.

"Mom, was I a terrible person in high school?" she asked instead.

Maura's eyes widened with surprise and Tess sent a tiny prayer to heaven, not for the first time, that she could age as gracefully as her mother. At sixty-five, Maura was active and vibrant and still as lovely as ever, even in gardening clothes and her floppy hat. The auburn curls Tess had inherited were shot through with gray but it didn't make Maura look old, only exotic and interesting, somehow.

Maura pursed her lips. "As I remember, you were a very good person. Not perfect, certainly, but who is, at that age?"

"I thought I was. Perfect, I mean. I thought I was doing everything right. Why wouldn't I? I had 4.0 grades, I was the head cheerleader, the student body president. I volunteered at the hospital in Idaho Falls and went to church on Sundays and was generally kind to children and small pets."

"What's happened to make you think about those days?"

She sighed, remembering the antipathy in a certain pair of silvery blue eyes. "Quinn Southerland is back in town."

Her mother's brow furrowed for a moment, then

smoothed again. "Oh, right. He was one of Jo and Guff's foster boys, wasn't he? Which one is he?"

"Not the army officer or the adventurer. He's the businessman. The one who runs a shipping company out of Seattle."

"Oh, yes. I remember him. He was the dark, brooding, cute one, right?"

"Mother!"

Maura gave her an innocent sort of look. "What did I say? He *was* cute, wasn't he? I always thought he looked a little like James Dean around the eyes. Something in that smoldering look of his."

Oh, yes, Tess remembered it well.

After leaning the rake against a tree, she knelt beside her mother and began pulling up the dead stalks of cosmos. Every time she worked with her hands in the dirt, she couldn't help thinking how very much her existence the past eight years was like a flower garden in winter, waiting, waiting, for life to spring forth.

"I was horrible to him, Mom. Really awful."

"You? I can't believe that."

"Believe it. He just… He brought out the absolute worst in me."

Her mother sat back on her heels, the gardening forgotten. "Whatever did you do to the poor boy?"

She didn't want to correct her mother, but to her mind Quinn had never seemed like a boy. At least not like the other boys in Pine Gulch.

"I don't even like to think about it all," she admitted. "Basically I did whatever I could to set him down a peg or two. I did my best to turn people against him. I would make snide comments to him and about him and started unsubstantiated rumors about him. I played devil's advocate, just for the sake of argument, whenever he would express any kind of opinion in a class."

Her mother looked baffled. "What on earth did he do to you to make you act in such a way?"

"Nothing. That's the worst part. I thought he was arrogant and disrespectful and I didn't like him but I was... fascinated by him."

Which quite accurately summed up her interaction with him in the early hours of the morning, but she decided not to tell her mother that.

"He was a handsome boy," Maura said. "I imagine many of the girls at school had the same fascination."

"They did." She grabbed the garden shears and started cutting back Dorothy's day lily foliage. "You know how it is whenever someone new moves into town. He seems infinitely better-looking, more interesting, more *everything* than the boys around town that you've grown up with since kindergarten."

She had been just as intrigued as the other girls, fascinated by this surly, angry, rough-edged boy. Rumors had swirled around when he first arrived that he had been involved in some kind of murder investigation. She still didn't know if any of them were true—she really couldn't credit Jo and Guff bringing someone with that kind of a past into their home.

But back then, that hint of danger only made him seem more appealing. She just knew Quinn made her feel different than any other boy in town.

Tess had tried to charm him, as she had been effortlessly doing with every male who entered her orbit since she was old enough to bat her eyelashes. He had at first ignored her efforts and then actively rebuffed them.

She hadn't taken with grace and dignity his rejection or

his grim amusement at her continued efforts to draw his attention. She flushed, remembering.

"He wasn't interested in any of us, especially not me. I couldn't understand why he had to be so contrary. I hated it. You know how I was. I wanted everything in my life to go exactly how I arranged it."

"You're like your father that way," Maura said with a soft smile for her husband of thirty-five years whom they both missed dearly.

"I guess. I just know I was petty and spiteful to Quinn when he wouldn't fall into line with the way I wanted things to go. I was awful to him. Really awful. Whenever I was around him, I felt like this alien life force had invaded my body, this manipulative, conniving witch. Scarlett O'Hara with pom-poms."

Her mother laughed. "You're much prettier than that Vivien Leigh ever was."

"But every bit as vindictive and self-absorbed as her character in the movie."

For several moments, she busied herself with garden shears. Maura seemed content with the silence and her introspection, which had always been one of the things Tess loved best about her mother.

"I don't even want to tell you all the things I did," she finally said. "The worst thing is, I got him kicked off the baseball team when he was a senior and I was a junior."

"Tessa Marie. What on earth did you do?"

She burned with shame at the memory. "We had advanced placement history together. Amaryllis Wentworth."

"Oh, I remember her," her mother exclaimed. "Bitter and mean and suspicious old bat. I don't know why the school board didn't fire her twenty-five years before you were even in school. You would think someone who chooses teaching as an avocation would at least enjoy the company of young people."

"Right. And the only thing she hated worse than teenage girls was teenage boys."

"What happened?"

She wished she could block the memory out but it was depressingly clear, from the chalkboard smell in Wentworth's room to the afternoon spring sunlight filtering through the tall school windows.

"We both happened to have missed school on the same day, which happened to be one of her brutal pop quizzes, so we had to take a makeup. We were the only ones in the classroom except for Miss Wentworth."

Careful to avoid her mother's gaze, she picked up an armload of garden refuse and carried it to the wheelbarrow. "I knew the material but I was curious about whether Quinn did so I looked at his test answers. He got everything right except a question about the Teapot Dome scandal. I don't know why I did it. Pure maliciousness on my part. But I changed my answer, which I knew was right, to the same wrong one he had put down."

"Honey!"

"I know, right? It was awful of me. One of the worst things I've ever done. Of course, Miss Wentworth accused him of cheating. It was his word against mine. The juvenile delinquent with the questionable attitude or the student body president, a junior who already had offers of a full-ride scholarship to nursing school. Who do you think everybody wanted to believe?"

"Oh, Tess."

"My only defense is that I never expected things to go that far. I thought maybe Miss Wentworth would just yell at him, but when she went right to the principal, I didn't know how to make it right. I should have stepped forward when he was kicked off the baseball team but I...was too much of a coward."

She couldn't tell her mother the worst of it. Even she couldn't quite believe the depths to which she had sunk in her teenage narcissism, but she remembered it all vividly.

A few days later, prompted by guilt and shame, she had tried to talk to him and managed to corner him in an empty classroom. They had argued and he had called her a few bad names, justifiably so.

She still didn't know what she'd been thinking—why this time would be any different—but she thought she saw a little spark of attraction in his eyes when they were arguing. She had been hopelessly, mortifyingly foolish enough to try to kiss him and he had pushed her away, so hard she knocked over a couple of chairs as she stumbled backward.

Humiliated and outraged, she had then made things much, much worse and twisted the story, telling her boyfriend Scott that Quinn had come on to her, that he had been so angry at being kicked off the baseball team that he had come for revenge and tried to force himself on her.

She screwed her eyes shut. Scott had reacted just as she had expected, with teenage bluster and bravado and his own twisted sense of chivalry. He and several friends from the basketball team had somehow separated Quinn from Brant and Cisco and taken him beneath the football bleachers, then proceeded to beat the tar out of him.

No wonder he despised her. She loathed that selfish, manipulative girl just as much.

"So he's back," Maura said. "Is he staying at the ranch?"

She nodded. "I hate seeing him. He makes me feel sixteen and stupid all over again. If I didn't love Jo so much, I would try to assign her to another hospice nurse."

Maura sat back on her heels, showing her surprise at her daughter's vehemence. "Our Saint Tess making a selfish decision? That doesn't sound like you."

Tess made a face. "You know I hate that nickname."

Her mother touched her arm, leaving a little spot of dirt on her work shirt. "I know you do, dear. And I'll be honest, as a mother who is nothing but proud of the woman you've become and what you have done with your life, it's a bit refreshing to find out you're subject to the occasional human folly just like the rest of us."

Everyone in town saw her as some kind of martyr for staying with Scott all those years, but they didn't know the real her. The woman who had indulged in bouts of self-pity, who had cried out her fear and frustration, who had felt trapped in a marriage that never even had a chance to start.

She had stayed with Scott because she loved him and because he needed her, not because she was some saintly, perfect, flawless angel.

No one knew her. Not her mother or her friends or the morning crowd at The Gulch.

She didn't like to think that Quinn Southerland might just have the most honest perspective around of the real Tess Jamison Claybourne.

That evening, Tess kept her fingers crossed the entire drive to Winder Ranch, praying she wouldn't encounter him.

She had fretted about him all day, worrying what she might say when she saw him again. She considered it a huge advantage, at least in this case, that she worked the graveyard shift. Most of her visits were in the dead of night, when Quinn by rights should be sleeping. She would have a much better chance of avoiding him than if she stopped by during daylight hours.

The greatest risk she faced of bumping into him was probably now at the start of her shift than, say, 4:00 a.m.

Wouldn't it be lovely if he were away from the ranch or busy helping Easton with something or tied up with some kind of conference call to Seattle?

She could only dream, she supposed. More than likely, he would be right there waiting for her, ready to impale her with that suspicious, bad-tempered glare the moment she stepped out of the car.

She let out a breath as she turned onto the long Winder Ranch access drive and headed up toward the house. She could at least be calm and collected, even if he tried to goad her or made any derogatory comments. He certainly didn't need to discover he possessed such power to upset her.

He wasn't waiting for her on the porch, but it was a near thing. The instant she rang the doorbell of Winder Ranch, the door jerked open and Quinn stood inside looking frazzled, his dark hair disheveled slightly, his navy blue twill shirt untucked, a hint of afternoon shadow on his cheeks.

He looked a little disreputable and entirely yummy.

"It's about time!" he exclaimed, an odd note of relief in his voice. "I've been watching for you for the past half hour."

"You…have?"

She almost looked behind her to see if someone a little more sure of a welcome had wandered in behind her.

"I thought you were supposed to be here at eight."

She checked her watch and saw it was only eight-thirty. "I made another stop first. What's wrong?"

He raked a hand through his hair, messing it further. "I don't know what the hell I'm supposed to do. Easton had to run to Idaho Falls to meet with the ranch accountant. She was supposed to be back an hour ago but she just called and said she'd been delayed and won't be back for another couple of hours."

"What's going on? Is Jo having another of her breathing episodes? Or is it the coughing?"

Tess hurried out of her jacket and started to rush toward her patient's room but Quinn grabbed her arm at the elbow.

Despite her worry for Jo, heat scorched her nerve endings at the contact, at the feel of his warm hand against her skin.

"She's not there. She's in the kitchen."

At her alarmed look, he shook his head. "It's none of those things. She's fine, physically, anyway. But she won't listen to reason. I never realized the woman could be so blasted stubborn."

"A trait she obviously does not share with anyone else here," she murmured.

He gave her a dark look. "She's being completely ridiculous. She suddenly has this harebrained idea. Absolute insanity. She wants to go out for a moonlight ride on one of the horses and it's suddenly all she can talk about."

She stared, nonplussed. "A horseback ride?"

"Yeah. Do you think the cancer has affected her rational thinking? I mean, what's gotten into her? It's after eight, for heaven's sake."

"It's a bit difficult to go on a moonlit ride in the middle of the afternoon," she pointed out.

"Don't you take her side!" He sounded frustrated and on edge and more than a little frazzled.

She hid her smile that the urbane, sophisticated executive could change so dramatically over one simple request.

"I'm not taking anyone's side. Why does she suddenly want to go tonight?"

"Her window faces east."

That was all he said, as if everything was now crystal clear. "And?" she finally prompted.

"And she happened to see that huge full moon coming up an hour or so ago. She says it's her favorite kind of night. She and Guff used to ride up to Windy Lake during the full moon whenever they could. It can be clear as day up in the mountains on full moons like this."

"Windy Lake?"

"It's above the ranch, about half a mile into the forest service land. Takes about forty minutes to ride there."

"And Tess is determined to go?"

"She says she can't miss the chance, since it's her last harvest moon."

The sudden bleakness in the silver-blue of his eyes tugged at her sympathy and she was astonished by the impulse to touch his arm and offer whatever small comfort she could.

She curled her fingers into a fist, knowing he wouldn't welcome the gesture. Not from her.

"She's not strong enough for that," he went on. "I *know* she's not. We were sitting out in the garden today and she lasted less than an hour before she had to lie down, and then she slept for the rest of the day. I can't see any way in hell she has the strength to sit on a horse, even for ten minutes."

Her job as a hospice nurse often required using a little creative problem-solving. Clients who were dying could have some very tricky wishes toward the end. But her philosophy was that if what they wanted was at all within reach, it was up to her and their family members to make it happen.

"What if you rode together on horseback?" she suggested. "You could help her. Support her weight, make sure she's not overdoing."

He stared at her as if she'd suddenly stepped into her old cheerleader skirt and started yelling, "We've got spirit, yes we do."

"Tell me you're not honestly thinking she could handle this!" he exclaimed. "It's completely insane."

"Not completely, Quinn. Not if she wants to do it. Jo is right. This is her last harvest moon and if she wants to enjoy it from Windy Lake, I think she ought to have that opportunity. It seems a small enough thing to give her."

He opened his mouth to object, then closed it again. In his eyes, she saw worry and sorrow for the woman who had taken him in, given him a home, loved him.

"It might be good for her," Tess said gently.

"And it might finish her off." He said the words tightly, as if he didn't want to let them out.

"That's her choice, though, isn't it?"

He took several deep breaths and she could see his struggle, something she faced often providing end-of-life care. On the one hand, he loved his foster mother and wanted to do everything he could to make her happy and comfortable and fulfill all her last wishes.

On the other, he wanted to protect her and keep her around as long as he could.

The effort to hold back her fierce urge to touch him, console him, almost overwhelmed her. She supposed she shouldn't find it so surprising. She was a nurturer, which was why she went into nursing in the first place, long before she ever knew that Scott's accident would test her caregiving skills and instincts to the limit.

"You don't have to take her, though, especially if you

don't feel it's the right thing for her. I'll see if I can talk her out of it," she offered. She took a step toward the kitchen, but his voice stopped her.

"Wait."

She turned back to find him pinching the skin at the bridge of his nose.

"You're right," he said after a long moment, dropping his hand. "It's her choice. She's a grown woman, not a child. I can't treat her like one, even if I do want to protect her from…the inevitable. If she wants this, I'll find a way to make it happen."

The determination in his voice arrowed right to her heart and she smiled. "You're a good son, Quinn. You're just what Jo needs right now."

"You're coming with us, to make sure she's not over-doing things."

"Me?"

"The only way I can agree to this insanity is if we have a medical expert close at hand, just in case."

"I don't think that's a good idea."

"Why not? Can't your other patients spare you?"

That would have been a convenient excuse, but unfortunately in this case, she faced a slow night, with only Tess and two other patients, one who only required one quick check in the night, several hours away.

"That's not the issue," she admitted.

"What is it, then? Don't you think she would be better off to have a nurse along?"

"Maybe. Probably. But not necessarily this particular nurse."

"Why not?"

"I'm not really much of a rider," she confessed, with the same sense of shame as if she were admitting stealing heart

medicine from little old ladies. Around Pine Gulch, she supposed the two crimes were roughly parallel in magnitude.

"Really?"

"My family lived in town and we never had horses," she
said, despising the defensive note in her voice. "I haven't
had a lot of experience."

She didn't add that she had an irrational fear of them
after being bucked off at a cousin's house when she was
seven, then later that summer she had seen a cowboy badly
injured in a fall at an Independence Day rodeo. Since then,
she had done her best to avoid equines whenever possible.

"This is a pretty easy trail that takes less than an hour.
You should be okay, don't you think?"

How could she possibly tell him she was terrified, especially after she had worked to persuade him it would be
all right for Jo? She couldn't, she decided. Better to take
one for the team, for Jo's sake.

"Fine. You saddle the horses and I'll get Jo ready."

Heaven help them all.

Chapter 6

"Let me know if you need me to slow down," Quinn said half an hour later to the frail woman who sat in front of him astride one of the biggest horses in the pasture, a rawboned roan gelding named Russ.

She felt angular and thin in his arms, all pointed elbows and bony shoulders. But Tess had been right, she was ecstatic about being on horseback again, about being outside in the cold October night under the pines. Jo practically quivered with excitement, more alive and joyful than he had seen her since his return to Cold Creek.

It smelled of fall in the mountains, of sun-warmed dirt, of smoke from a distant neighbor's fire, of layers of fallen leaves from the scrub oak and aspens that dotted the mountainside.

The moon hung heavy and full overhead, huge and glowing in the night and Suzy and Jack, Easton's younger cow dogs, raced ahead of them. Chester probably would have enjoyed the adventure but Quinn had worried that, just like Jo, his old bones weren't quite up to the journey.

"This is perfect. Oh, Quinn, thank you, my dear. You have no idea the gift you've given me."

"You're welcome," he said gruffly, warmed despite his lingering worry.

In truth, he didn't know who was receiving the greater gift. This seemed a rare and precious time with Jo and he was certain he would remember forever the scents and the sounds of the night—of tack jingling on the horses and a great northern owl hooting somewhere in the forest and the night creatures that peeped and chattered around them.

He glanced over his shoulder to where Tess rode behind them.

Among the three of them, she seemed to be the one *least* enjoying the ride. She bounced along on one of the ranch's most placid mares. Every once in a while, he looked back and the moonlight would illuminate a look of grave discomfort on her features. If he could see her hands in the darkness, he was quite certain they would be white-knuckled on the reins.

He should be enjoying her misery, given his general dislike for the woman. Mostly he just felt guilty for dragging her along, though he had to admit to a small measure of glee to discover something she hadn't completely mastered.

In school, Tess had been the consummate perfectionist. She always had to be the first one finished with tests and assignments, she hated showing up anywhere with a hair out of place and she delighted in being the kind of annoying classmate who tended to screw up the curve for everybody else.

Knowing she wasn't an expert at everything made her seem a little more human, a little more approachable.

He glanced back again and saw her shifting in the saddle, her body tight and uncomfortable.

"How are you doing back there?" he asked.

In the pale glow of the full moon, he could just make out the slit of her eyes as she glared. "Fine. Swell. If I break my neck and die, I'm blaming you."

He laughed out loud, which earned him a frown from Jo.

"You didn't need to drag poor Tess up here with us," she reprimanded in the same tone of voice she had used when he was fifteen and she caught him teasing Easton for something or other. He could still vividly remember the figurative welts on his hide as she had verbally taken a strip off him.

"She's a big girl," Quinn said in a voice too low for Tess to overhear. "She didn't have to come."

"You're a hard man to say no to."

"If anyone could do it, Tess would find a way. Anyway, we'll be there in a few more moments."

Jo looked over his shoulder at Tess, then shook her head. "Poor thing. She obviously hasn't had as much experience riding as you and Easton and the boys. She's a good sport to come anyway."

He risked another look behind him and thought he heard her mumbling something under her breath involving creative ways she intended to make him pay for this.

Despite the lingering sadness in knowing he was fulfilling a last wish for someone he loved so dearly, Quinn couldn't help his smile.

He definitely wouldn't forget this night anytime soon.

"She's doing all right," he said to Jo.

"You're a rascal, Quinn Southerland," she chided. "You always have been."

He couldn't disagree. He couldn't have been an easy kid

to love when he had been so belligerent and angry, lashing out at everyone in his pain. He hugged Jo a little more tightly for just a moment until they reached the trailhead for Windy Lake, really just a clearing where they could leave the horses before taking the narrow twenty-yard trail to the lakeshore.

"This might get a little bit tricky," he said. "Let me dismount first and then I'll help you down."

"I can still get down from a horse by myself," she protested. "I'm not a complete invalid."

He just shook his head in exasperation and slid off the horse. He grabbed the extra rolled blankets tied to the saddle and slung them over his shoulder, then reached up to lift her from the horse.

He didn't set her on her feet, though. "I'll carry you to Guff's bench," he said, without giving her an opportunity to argue.

She pursed her lips but didn't complain, which made him suspect she was probably more tired than she wanted to let on.

"Okay, but then you'd better come back here to help Tess."

He glanced over and saw that Tess's horse had stopped alongside his big gelding but Tess made no move to climb out of the saddle; she just gazed down at the ground with a nervous kind of look.

"Hang on a minute," he told her. "Just wait there in the saddle while I settle Jo on the bench and then I'll come back to help you down."

"I'm sorry," she said, sounding more disgruntled than apologetic.

"No problem."

He carried Jo along the trail, grateful again for the pale

moonlight that filtered through the fringy pines and the bare branches of the aspens.

Windy Lake was a small stream-fed lake, probably no more than two hundred yards across. As a convenient watering hole, it attracted moose and mule deer and even the occasional elk. The water was always ice cold, as he and the others could all attest. That didn't stop him and Brant and Cisco—and Easton, when she could manage to get away—from sneaking out to come up here on summer nights.

Guff always used to keep a small canoe on the shore and they loved any chance to paddle out in the moonlight on July nights and fish for the native rainbow trout and arctic grayling that inhabited it.

Some of his most treasured memories of his teen years centered around trips to this very place.

The trail ended at the lakeshore. He carried Jo to the bench Guff built here, which had been situated in the perfect place to take in the pristine, shimmering lake and the granite mountains surrounding it.

He set Jo on her feet for just a moment so he could brush pine needles and twigs off the bench. Contrary to what he expected, the bench didn't have months worth of debris covering it, which made him think Easton probably found the occasional chance to make good use of it.

He covered the seat with a plastic garbage bag he had shoved into his pocket earlier in case the bench was damp.

"There you go. Your throne awaits."

She shook her head at his silliness but sat down gingerly, as if the movement pained her. He unrolled one of the blankets and spread it around her shoulders then tucked the other across her lap.

In the moonlight, he saw lines of pain bracketing her mouth and he worried again that this ride into the mountains had been too much for her. Along with the pain, though, he could see undeniable delight at being in this place she loved, one last time.

He supposed sometimes a little pain might be worthwhile in the short-term if it yielded such joy.

As he fussed over the blankets, she reached a thin hand to cover his. "Thank you, my dear. I'm fine now, I promise. Go rescue poor Tess and let me sit here for a moment with my memories."

"Call out if you need help. We won't be far."

"Don't fuss over me," she ordered. "Go help Tess."

Though he was reluctant to leave her here alone, he decided she was safe with the dogs who sat by her side, their ears cocked forward as if listening for any threat.

Back at the trailhead, he found Tess exactly where he had left her, still astride the mare, who was placidly grazing on the last of the autumn grasses.

"I tried to get down," she told him when he emerged from the trees. "Honestly, I did. But my blasted shoe is caught in the stirrups and I couldn't work it loose, no matter how hard I tried. This is so embarrassing."

"I guess that's the price you pay when you go horseback riding in comfortable nurse's shoes instead of boots."

"If I had known I was going to be roped into this, I would have pulled out my only pair of Tony Lamas for the occasion."

Despite her attempt at a light tone, he caught something in her stiff posture, in the rigid set of her jaw.

This was more than inexperience with horses, he realized as he worked her shoe free of the tight stirrup. Had he really been so overbearing and arrogant in insisting she come along that he refused to see she had a deep aversion to horses?

"I'm sorry I dragged you along."

"It's not all bad." She gazed up at the stars. "It's a lovely night."

"Tell me, how many moonlit rides have you been on into the mountains around Pine Gulch?"

She summoned a smile. "Counting tonight? Exactly one."

He finally worked her shoe free. "Let me help you down," he said.

She released the reins and swiveled her left leg over the saddle horn so she could dismount. The mare moved at just that moment and suddenly his arms were full of warm, delicious curves.

She smelled of vanilla and peaches and much to his dismay, his recalcitrant body stirred to life.

He released her abruptly and she wobbled a little when her feet met solid ground. Out of instinct, he reached to steady her and his hand brushed the curve of her breast when he grabbed her arm. Her gaze flashed to his and in the moonlight, he thought he felt the silky cord of sexual awareness tug between them.

"Okay now?"

"I...think so."

That low, breathy note in her voice had to be his imagination. He was almost certain of it.

He couldn't possibly be attracted to her. Sure, she was still a beautiful woman on the outside, but she was still Tess Claybourne, for heaven's sake.

He noticed she moved a considerable distance away but he wasn't sure if she was avoiding him or the horses. Probably both.

"I'm sorry I dragged you up here," he said again. "I didn't realize how uncomfortable riding would be for you."

She made a face. "It shouldn't be. I'm embarrassed that it is. I grew up around horses—how could I help it in Pine

Gulch? Though my family never had them, all my friends did, but I've had an…irrational fear of them since breaking my arm after being bucked off when I was seven."

"And I made you come anyway."

She mustered a smile. "I survived this far. We're halfway done now."

He remembered Jo's words suddenly. *You'll never find a happier soul in all your days. Why, what she's been through would have crushed most women. Not our Tess.*

Jo thought Tess was a survivor. If she weren't, could she be looking at this trip with such calm acceptance, even when she was obviously terrified?

"That's one way of looking at it, I guess."

She didn't meet his gaze. "It's not so bad. After the way I treated you in high school, I guess I'm surprised you didn't tie me onto the back of your horse and drag me behind you for a few miles."

His gaze narrowed. What game was this? He never, in a million years, would have expected her to refer to her behavior in their shared past, especially when she struck exactly the right note of self-deprecation.

For several awkward seconds, he couldn't think how to respond. Did he shrug it off? Act like he didn't know what she was talking about? Tell her she ought to have *bitch* tattooed across her forehead and he would be happy to pay for it?

"High school seems a long time ago right now," he finally said.

"Surely not so long that you've forgotten."

He couldn't lie to her. "You always made an impression."

Her laughter was short and unamused. "That's one way of phrasing it, I suppose."

"What would you call it?"

"Unconscionable."

At that single, low-voiced word, he studied her in the moonlight—her long-lashed green eyes contrite, that mouth set in a frown, the auburn curls that were a little disheveled from the ride.

How the hell did she do it? Lord knew, he didn't want to be. But against his will, Quinn found himself drawn to this woman who was willing to confront her fears for his aunt's sake, who could make fun of herself, who seemed genuinely contrite about past bad behavior.

He liked her and, worse, was uncomfortably aware of a fierce physical attraction to her soft curves and classical features that seemed so serene and lovely in the moonlight.

He pushed away the insane attraction, just as he pushed away the compelling urge to ask her what he had ever done back then to make her hate him so much. Instead, he did his best to turn the subject away.

"Easton told me about Scott. About the accident."

She shoved her hands in the pocket of her jacket and looked off through the darkened trees toward the direction of the lake. "Did she?"

"She said you had only been married a few months at the time, so most of your marriage you were more of a caregiver than a wife."

"Everybody says that like I made some grand, noble sacrifice."

He didn't want to think so. He much preferred thinking of her as the self-absorbed teenage girl trying to ruin his life.

"What would you consider it?"

"I didn't do anything unusual. He was my husband," she said simply. "I loved him and I took vows. I couldn't just abandon him to some impersonal care center for the rest of his life and blithely go on with my own as if he didn't exist."

Many people he knew wouldn't have blinked twice at responding exactly that way to the situation. Hell, the Tess he thought she had been would have done exactly that.

"Do you regret those years?"

She stared at him for a long moment, her eyes wide with surprise, as if no one had ever asked her that before.

"Sometimes," she admitted, her voice so low he could barely hear it. "I don't regret that I had that extra time with him. I could never regret that. By all rights, he should have died in that accident. A weaker man probably would have. Scott didn't and I have to think God had some purpose in that, something larger than my understanding."

She paused, her expression pensive. "I do regret that we never had the chance to build the life we talked about those first few months of our marriage. Children, a mortgage, a couple of dogs. We missed all that."

Not much of a sacrifice, he thought. He would be quite happy not to have that sort of trouble in his life.

"I'll probably always regret that," she went on. "Unfortunately, I can't change the past. I can only look forward and try to make the best of everything that comes next."

They lapsed into a silence broken only by the horses stamping and snorting behind them and the distant lapping of the water.

She was the first to break the temporary peace. "We'd better go check on Jo, don't you think?"

He jerked his mind away from how very much he wanted to kiss her right this moment, with the moonlight gleaming through the trees and the night creatures singing an accompaniment. "Right. Will you be okay without a flashlight?"

"I'll manage. Just lead the way."

He headed up the trail toward Jo, astonished that his most pressing regret right now was the end of their brief interlude in the moonlight.

Though Tess loved living in the Mountain West for the people and the scenery and the generally slower pace of life, she had never really considered herself a nature girl.

As a bank manager and accountant, her father hadn't been the sort to take her camping and fishing when she was younger. Later, she'd been too busy, first in college and then taking care of Scott, to find much time to enjoy the backcountry.

But she had to admit she found something serene and peaceful about being here with the glittery stars overhead and that huge glowing moon filtering through the trees and the night alive with sounds and smells.

Well, it would have been serene if she weren't so intensely aware of Quinn walking just ahead of her, moving with long-limbed confidence through the darkness.

The man exuded sensuality. She sighed, wishing she could ignore his effect on her. She disliked the way her heart picked up a beat or two, the little churn of her blood, the way she couldn't seem to keep herself from stealing secret little glances at him as they made their way toward the lake and Jo.

She hadn't missed that moment of awareness in his eyes back there, the heat that suddenly shivered through the air like fireflies on a summer night.

He was attracted to her, though she had a strong sense he found the idea more than appalling.

Her gaze skidded to his powerful shoulders under his denim jacket, to the dark hair that brushed his collar under his Stetson, and her insides trembled.

For a moment there, she had been quite certain he wanted to kiss her, though she couldn't quite fathom it. How long had it been since she knew the heady, exhilarating impact of desire in a man's eyes? Longer than she cared to remember. The men in town didn't tend to look at her as a woman with the very real and human hunger to be cherished and touched.

In the eyes of most people in Pine Gulch, that woman had been somehow absorbed into the loving, dutiful caretaker, leaving no room for more. Even after Scott's death, people still seemed to see her as a nurturer, not the flirty, sexy, fun-loving Tess she thought might still be buried somewhere deep inside her.

Seeing that heat kindle in his eyes, replacing his typical animosity, had been both flattering and disconcerting and for a moment, she had been mortified at her little spurt of panic, the fear that she had no idea how to respond.

She just needed practice, she assured herself. That's why she was moving to Portland, so she could be around people who saw her as more than just Pine Gulch's version of Mother Teresa.

They walked the short distance through the pines and aspens, their trail lit only by pale moonlight and the glow of a small flashlight he produced from the pocket of his denim jacket. When they reached the lake a few moments later, Tess saw Jo on a bench on the shore, the dogs at her feet. She sat unmoving, so still that for a moment, Tess feared the worst.

But Quinn's boot snapped a twig at that moment and Jo turned her head. Though they were still a few yards away, Tess could see the glow on her features shining through clearly, even in the moonlight. Her friend smiled at them and for one precious instant, she looked younger, happier. Whole.

"There you are. I was afraid the two of you were lost."

Quinn slanted Tess a sidelong look before turning his attention back to his foster mother. "No. I thought you might like a few moments to yourself up here."

Jo smiled at him as she reached a hand out to Tess to draw her down beside her on the bench. When she saw the blankets tucked around Jo's shoulders and across her lap, everything inside her went a little gooey that Quinn had taken such great care to ensure his foster mother's comfort.

"Isn't it lovely, my dear?"

"Breathtaking," Tess assured her, her hand still enclosed around Jo's thin fingers.

They sat like that for a moment with Quinn standing beside them. The moon glowed off the rocky face of the mountains ringing the lake, reflecting in water that seethed and bubbled as if it was some sort of hot springs. After several moments of watching it, Tess realized the percolating effect was achieved by dozens of fish rising to the surface for night-flying insects.

"It's enchanting," she said to Jo, squeezing her fingers. She didn't add that this moment, this shared beauty, was almost worth that miserable horseback ride up the mountainside.

"This is such a gift. I cannot tell you how deeply it touches me. I have missed these mountains so much these past weeks while I've been stuck at home. Thank you both so very much."

Jo's smile was wide and genuine but Tess didn't miss the lines of pain beneath it that radiated from her mouth.

Quinn must have noticed them as well. "I'd love to stay here longer," he said after a moment, "but we had better get you back. Tess has other patients."

Jo nodded, a little sadly, Tess thought. A lump rose in her throat as the other woman rose, her face tilted to the huge full moon. Jo closed her eyes, inhaled a deep breath of mountain air, then let it out slowly before turning back to Quinn. "I'm ready."

Her chest felt achy and tight with unshed tears watching Jo say this private goodbye to a place she loved. It didn't help her emotions at all when Quinn carefully and tenderly scooped Jo into his arms and carried her back toward the waiting horses.

She pushed back the tears as she awkwardly mounted her horse, knowing Jo wouldn't welcome them at all. The older woman accepted her impending passing with grace and acceptance, something Tess could only wish on all her patients.

The ride down was slightly easier than the way up had been, though she wouldn't have expected it. In her limited experience on the back of a horse, gravity hadn't always been her friend.

Perhaps she was a tiny bit more loose and relaxed than she had been on the way up. At least she didn't grip the reins quite so tightly and her body seemed to more readily pick up the rhythm of the horse's gait.

She had heard somewhere that horses were sensitive creatures who picked up on those sorts of things like anxiety and apprehension. Maybe the little mare was just giving her the benefit of the doubt.

As she had on the way up the trail, she rode in the rear of their little group, behind the two black and white dogs and Quinn and Jo, which gave her the opportunity to watch his gentle solicitude toward her.

She found something unbearably sweet—disarming, even—at the sight of his tender care, such a vivid contrast to his reputation as a ruthless businessman who had built his vast shipping company from the ground up.

That treacherous softness fluttered inside her. Even after she forced herself to look away—to focus instead on the rare beauty of the night settling in more deeply across the mountainside—she couldn't ignore that tangled mix of fierce attraction and dawning respect.

As they descended the trail, Winder Ranch came into view, sprawling and solid in the night.

"Home," Jo said in a sleepy-sounding voice that carried across the darkness.

"We're nearly there," he assured her.

When they arrived at the ranch house, Quinn dismounted and then reached for Jo, who winced with the movement.

Worry spasmed across his handsome features but she watched him quickly conceal it from Jo. "Tess, do you mind holding the horses for a few moments while I carry Jo inside and settle her back in her bedroom?"

This time, she was pleased that she could dismount on her own. "Of course not," she answered as her feet hit the dirt.

"Thank you. I'll trade places with you in a few moments so that you can get Jo settled for bed while I take care of the horses."

"Good plan."

She gave him a hesitant smile and was a little astonished when he returned it. Something significant had changed between them as a result of one simple horseback ride into the mountains. They were working together, a team, at least for the moment. He seemed warmer, more approachable. Less antagonistic.

They hadn't really cleared any air between them, other than those few moments she had tried to offer an oblique apology for their history. But she wanted to think perhaps he might eventually come to accept that she had become a better person.

Chapter 7

After Quinn carried Jo inside, Tess stood patting the mare, savoring the night before she went inside to take care of Jo's medical needs. Quiet moments of reflection were a rare commodity in her world.

She had gotten out of the habit when she had genuinely had no time to spare with all of Scott's medical needs. Perhaps she needed to work at meditation when she moved to Portland, she thought. Maybe yoga or tai chi.

She was considering her options and talking softly to the horses when Quinn hurried down the porch steps a few moments later.

"How's Jo?"

"Ready for pain meds, I think, but she's not complaining."

"You gave her a great gift tonight, Quinn."

He smiled a little. "I hope so. She loves the mountains. I have to admit, I do as well. I forget that sometimes. Seattle is beautiful with the water and the volcanic mountains but it's not the same as home."

"Is it? Home, I mean?"

"Always."

He spoke with no trace of hesitation and she wondered again at the circumstances that had led him to Winder Ranch. Those rumors about his violent past swirled through her memory and she quickly dismissed them as ridiculous.

"I'm sorry. Let me take the horses." He reached for the reins of both horses and as she handed them over, their hands brushed.

He flashed her a quick look and grabbed her fingers with his other hand. "Your fingers are freezing!"

"I should have worn gloves."

"I should have thought to get you some before we left." He paused. "This was a crazy idea, wasn't it? I apologize again for dragging you up there."

"Not a crazy idea at all," she insisted. "Jo loved it."

"She's half-asleep in there and I know she's in pain, but she's also happier than I've seen her since I arrived."

She smiled at him, intensely conscious of the hard strength of his hand still curled around her fingers. Her hands might still be cold from the night air but they were just about the only thing not heating up right about now.

He gazed at her mouth for several long seconds, his eyes silvery-blue in the moonlight, and for one effervescent moment, she thought again that he might kiss her. He even angled his head ever so slightly and her gaze tangled with his.

Her pulse seemed abnormally loud in her ears and her insides jumped and fluttered like a baby bird trying its first awkward flight.

He eased forward slightly and her body instinctively rose to meet his. She caught her breath, waiting for the brush of his mouth against hers, but he suddenly jerked back, his expression thunderstruck.

Tess blinked as if awakening from a long, lovely nap as cold reality splashed over her. Of course he wouldn't kiss her. He despised her, with very good reason.

With ruthless determination, she shoved down the disappointment and ridiculous sense of hurt shivering through her. So what if he found the idea of kissing her so abhorrent? She didn't have time for this anyway. She was supposed to be working, not going for moonlit rides and sharing confidences in the dark and fantasizing about finally kissing her teenage crush.

Since he now held the horses' reins, she shoved her hands in the pockets of her jacket to hide their trembling and forced her voice to sound cool and unaffected.

"I'd better go take care of Jo's meds."

"Right." He continued to watch her out of those seductive but veiled eyes.

"Um, good night, if I don't see you again before I leave."

"Good night."

She hurried up the porch steps, feeling the heat of his gaze following her. Inside, she closed the door and leaned against it for just a moment, willing her heart to settle down once more.

Blast the man for stirring up all these hormones she tried so hard to keep contained. She *so* did not want to be attracted to Quinn. What a colossal waste of energy on her part. Oh, he might have softened toward her a little in the course of their ride with Jo, but she couldn't delude herself into thinking he was willing to forgive and forget everything she had done to him years ago.

She had work to do, she reminded herself. People who needed her. She didn't have time to be obsessing over the

past or the person she used to be or a man like Quinn Southerland, who could never see her as anything else.

She did her best the rest of the night to focus on her patients and not on the little thrum of desire she hadn't been
able to shake since that almost-kiss with Quinn.

Still, she approached Winder Ranch for her midnight
check on Jo with a certain amount of trepidation. To her
relief, when she unlocked the door with the key Easton had
given her and walked inside, the house was dark. Quinn
was nowhere in sight, but she could still sense his presence in the house.

Jo didn't stir when Tess entered her room, which worried
her for a moment until she saw the steady rise and fall of
the blankets by the glow of the small light in the attached
bathroom that Jo and Easton left on for the hospice nurses.

The ride up to the lake must have completely exhausted
her. She didn't even wake when Tess checked her vitals and
gave her medicine through the central IV line that had been
placed after her last hospitalization.

When she was done with the visit, she closed the door
quietly behind her and turned to go, then became aware
that someone else was in the darkened hallway. Her heart
gave a quick, hard kick, then she realized it was Easton.

She wasn't sure if that sensation coursing through her
was more disappointment or relief.

"I hope I didn't wake you," Tess said.

The other woman's sleek blond ponytail moved as she
shook her head. "I've still got some pesky accounts to finish. I was in the office working on the computer and heard
the door open."

"I tried to be quiet. Sorry about that." She smiled at her

friend. "But then, Jo didn't even wake up so I couldn't have been *too* loud."

"You weren't. I'm just restless tonight."

"I'm sorry."

Easton shrugged. "It sometimes knocks me on my butt if I think about what things will be like in a month or so. I'm trying to get as much done now on ranch paperwork so I have time to…to grieve."

Tess placed a comforting hand on her arm and Easton smiled, making a visible effort to push away her sadness. "Quinn told me about your adventure tonight," she said.

Tess made a rueful face. "I'm nowhere near the horse-woman you are. I felt like an idiot up there, but at least I didn't fall off."

"Jo was so happy when I checked on her earlier. I haven't seen her like that in a long time."

"Then I suppose my mortification was all for a good cause."

Easton laughed a little but her laughter quickly faded. "It won't be much longer, will it?"

Tess's heart ached at the question but she didn't pretend to misunderstand. "A week, maybe a little more. You know I can't say exactly."

Her friend's blue eyes filled with a sorrow that was raw and real. "I don't want to lose her, Tess. I'm not ready. What will I do?"

Tess set her bag on the floor and hurried forward to pull Easton into her arms. She knew that ache, that deep, gnawing fear and loss.

"You'll go on. That's all you can do. All any of us can do."

"First my parents, then Guff and now Jo. I can't bear it. She's all I have left."

"I know, sweetheart."

Easton didn't cry aloud, though Tess could feel the quiet shuddering of her shoulders. After a moment, the other woman pulled away.

"I'm sorry. I'm just tired."

"You need to sleep, honey. Everything will seem a little better in the morning, I promise. Midnight is the time when our fears all grow stronger and more vicious."

Easton drew in a heavy breath, then stepped away, swiping at her eyes. "Brant called from Germany earlier. He's hoping to get a flight any time now."

She remembered Brant Western as a tall, serious-minded boy who had always seemed an odd fit to be best friends with both Quinn, the rebellious kid with the surly attitude, and Cisco Del Norte, the wild, slightly dangerous troublemaker.

"Jo will be thrilled to have him home. What about Cisco?"

Easton's mouth compressed into a tight line and she focused on a spot somewhere over Tess's shoulder. "No word yet. We think he's somewhere in El Salvador but we can't seem to find anything out for sure. He's moving around a lot. Seems like everywhere we try, we just keep missing him by a day or even a few hours. It's so aggravating. Quinn has his assistant in Seattle trying to pull some strings with the embassy down there to find him."

"I hope it doesn't take much longer."

Easton nodded, her features troubled. "Even if we find him, there's no guarantee he can make it back in time. Quinn has promised to send a plane down to bring him home, even if he's in the middle of the jungle, but we have to find him first."

Her stomach gave a strange little quiver at the idea of Quinn having planes at his disposal.

"I'll keep my fingers crossed," she said, then picked up

her bag and headed for the front door. Easton followed to let her out.

"Get some rest, honey," she said again. "I'll be back for the next round of meds around three. You'd better be asleep when I get back!"

"Yes, Nurse Ratched."

"I mean it."

Easton smiled a little, even past the lingering sadness in her eyes. "Thanks, Tess. For everything."

"Go to sleep," she ordered again, then walked out into the night, with that same curious mix of relief and disappointment that she had avoided Quinn, at least for a few more hours.

He awoke to the sound of a door snicking softly closed and the dimmer switch in the bathroom being turned up just enough to jar him out of dreams he had no business entertaining.

In a rather surreal paradigm shift, he went from dreaming about a heated embrace on a warm blanket under starry skies near the lake to the stark reality of a sickroom, where his foster mother lay dying.

Oddly, the same woman appeared in both scenes. Tess stepped out of the bathroom, looking brisk and professional in her flowered surgical scrubs.

He feigned sleep and watched her through his lashes as she donned a pair of latex-free gloves.

He could pinpoint the instant she saw him sprawled in the recliner, purportedly asleep. Her steps faltered and she froze.

Probably the decent thing would be to open his eyes and go through the motions of pretending to awaken. But he wasn't always crazy about doing the decent thing. Instead, he gave a heavy-sounding breath and continued to spy on her under his lashes.

She gazed at him for several seconds as if trying to ascertain his level of sleep, then she finally turned away from him and back to her patient with a small, barely perceptible sigh he wondered about.

For the next few minutes, he watched her draw medicine out into syringes, then she quietly began checking Jo's blood pressure and temperature.

Though her movements were slow and careful, Jo still opened her eyes when Tess put the blood pressure cuff on her leg.

"I'm so sorry to wake you. I wish I didn't have to," Tess murmured.

"Oh, poof," Jo whispered back. "Don't you worry for a single moment about doing your job."

"How is your pain level?"

Jo was silent. "I'm not going to tell you," she finally said. "You'll just write it down in your little chart and the next thing I know, Jake Dalton will be increasing my meds and I'll be so drugged out I won't be able to think straight. My Brant is coming home. Should be any day now."

As Jo whispered to her, Tess continued to slant careful looks in his direction.

"Easton told me earlier that he was on his way," she said in an undertone.

"They'll be good for Easton. The four of them, why, they were thicker than thieves. I can't tell you how glad I am they'll still have each other."

Quinn swallowed hard, hating this whole situation all over again.

Tess smiled, relentlessly cheerful. "It's a blessing, all right. For all of them and especially for your peace of mind."

He listened to their quiet conversation as Tess continued to take care of Jo's medical needs. He was still trying to figure out how much of her demeanor he was buying. She seemed to be everything that was patient and calm, a serene island in the middle of a stormy emotional mess. Was it truly possible that this dramatic change in her could be genuine?

He supposed he was a cynical bastard but he couldn't quite believe it. This could all be one big show she was putting on. He had only been here a few days. If he stuck around long enough, she was likely to revert to her true colors.

On the other hand, people could change. He was living testimony to that. He was worlds away from the bitter, hot-tempered punk he'd been when he arrived at the Winders' doorstep after a year in foster care and the misery that came before.

He pushed away the past, preferring instead to focus on today.

Tess finished with Jo a few moments later. After fluffing her pillow and tucking the blankets up around her, she dimmed the light in the bathroom again and moved quietly toward the door out into the hallway.

He rose and followed her, careful not to disturb Jo, who seemed to have easily slipped into sleep again.

"I'll walk you out," he said, his voice low, just as she reached the door.

She whirled and splayed a hand across her chest. She glared at him as she moved out of the room to the hallway. He followed her and closed the door behind him.

"Don't do that! That's the second time you've nearly scared the life out of me. How long have you been awake?"

"Not long. Here, let me help you with your coat."

He took it off the chair in the hallway where she had tossed it and stood behind her. Her scent teased him, that delectable peach and vanilla, that somehow seemed sweet and sultry at the same time, like a hot Southern night.

She paused for a moment, then extended her arm through the sleeve. "Thank you," she said and he wondered if he was imagining the slightly husky note to her voice.

"You're welcome."

"You really don't need to walk me out, though. I'm sure I can find the way to my car by myself."

"I could use the fresh air, to be honest with you."

She looked as if she wanted to argue but she only shrugged and turned toward the door. He held it open for her and again smelled that seductive scent as she moved past him on her way out.

The scent seemed to curl through him, twisting and tugging an unwelcome response out of him, which he did his best to ignore as they walked out into the night.

The moon hung huge over the western mountains now, the stars a bright glitter out here unlike anything to be found in the city.

The October night wasn't just cool now in the early morning hours, it was downright cold. This time of year, temperatures in these high mountain valleys could show a wide range in the course of a single day. Nights were invariably cool, even in summer. In spring and fall, the temperature dropped quickly once the sun went down.

His morning spent in the garden soaking up sunshine with Jo seemed only another distant memory.

"Gorgeous night, isn't it?" Tess said. "I don't ever get tired of the view out here."

He nodded. "I've lived without it since I left Cold Creek Canyon, but something about it stays inside me even when I'm back in Seattle."

She smiled a little. "I know I'm going to miss these mountains when I move to Portland in a few weeks."

"What's in Portland?" he asked, curious as to why she would pick up and leave after her lifetime spent here.

"A pretty good basketball team," she answered. "Lots of trees and flowers. Nice people, from what I hear."

"You know what I mean. Why are you leaving?"

She was silent for a moment, the only sound the wind whispering through the trees. "A whole truckload of reasons. Mostly, I guess, because I'm ready for a new start."

He could understand that. He had sought the same thing in the Air Force after leaving Pine Gulch, hadn't he? A place where no one knew his history in the foster-care system or as the rough-edged punk who had found a home here with Jo and Guff.

"Will you be doing the same thing? Providing end-of-life care?"

She smiled and in the moonlight, she looked fresh and lovely and very much like the teenage cheerleader who had tangled the hormones of every boy who walked the halls of Pine Gulch High School.

"Just the opposite, actually. I took a job in labor and delivery at one of the Portland hospitals."

"Bringing life into the world instead of comforting those who are leaving it. There's a certain symmetry to that."

"I think so, too. It's all part of my brand-new start."

"I suppose everybody could use that once in a while."

"True enough," she murmured, with an unreadable look in her eyes.

"Will you miss this?"

"Pine Gulch?"

"I was thinking more of the work you do. You seem…

very good at it. Do you give this same level to all your patients as you have to Jo?"

She looked startled at the question, though he wasn't sure if it was because she had never thought about it before or that she was surprised he had noticed.

"I try. Everyone deserves to spend his or her last days with dignity and respect. But Jo is special. I can't deny that. She used to give me piano lessons when I was young and I've always adored her."

Now it was his turn to be surprised. Jo taught piano lessons for many years to most of the young people in Pine Gulch but he had never realized Tess had once had the privilege of being one of her students.

"Do you still play?"

She laughed. "I hardly played then. I was awful. Probably the worst student Jo ever had, though she tried her best, believe me. But yes, I still play a little. I enjoy it much more as an adult than I did when I was ten."

She paused for a moment, then gave a rueful smile. "When he was…upset or having a bad day, Scott used to enjoy when I would play for him. It calmed him. I've had more practice than I ever expected over the years."

"You should play for Jo sometime when you come out to the house. She gets a real kick out of hearing her old students play. Especially the hard ones."

"Maybe. I'm worried her hearing is a little too fragile for my fumbling attempts." She smiled. "What about you? Did Jo give you lessons after you moved here?"

He gave a short laugh at the memory. "She tried. I'm sure I could have taught you a thing or two about being difficult."

"I don't doubt that for a moment," she murmured.

She gazed at him for a moment, then she shifted her gaze

up and he could swear he saw a million constellations reflected in her eyes.

"Look!" she exclaimed. "A shooting star, right over the top of Windy Peak. Quick, make a wish."

He tilted his neck to look in the direction she pointed. "Probably just a satellite."

She glared at him. "Don't ruin it. I'm making a wish anyway."

With her eyes screwed closed, she pursed her mouth in concentration. "There," she said after a moment. "That should do it."

She opened her eyes and smiled softly at him and he forgot all about the cold night air. All he could focus on was that smile, that mouth, and the sudden wild hunger inside him to taste it.

"What did you wish?" he asked, a gruff note to his voice.

She made a face. "If I tell you, it won't come true. Don't you know anything about wishes?"

Right now, he could tell her a thing or two about wanting something he shouldn't. That sensuous heat wrapped tighter around his insides. "I know enough. I know sometimes wishes can be completely ridiculous and make no sense. For instance, right now, I wish I could kiss you. Don't ask me why. I don't even like you."

Her eyes looked huge and green in her delicate face as she stared at him. "Okay," she said, her voice breathy.

"Okay, I can kiss you? Or, okay, you won't ask why I want to?"

She let out a ragged-sounding breath. "Either. Both."

He didn't need much more of an invitation than that. Without allowing himself to stop and think through the insanity of kissing a woman he had detested twenty-four hours earlier, Quinn stepped forward and covered her mouth with his.

Chapter 8

She gave a little gasp of shock but her mouth was warm and inviting in the cold air and he was vaguely aware through the haze of his own desire that she didn't pull away, as he might have expected.

Instead, she wrapped her arm around his waist and leaned into his kiss for more.

A low clamor in his brain warned him this was a crazy idea, that he would have a much harder time keeping a safe distance between them after he had known the silky softness of her mouth, but he ignored it.

How could he possibly step away now, when she tasted like coffee and peaches and Tess, a delectable combination that sizzled through him like heat lightning?

Her lips parted slightly, all the invitation he needed to deepen the kiss. She moaned a little against his mouth and he could feel the tremble of her body against him, the confused desire in the slide of her tongue against his.

The night disappeared until it was only the two of them, until he was lost in the unexpected hunger for this woman in his arms. Her kiss offered solace and surrender, a chance to put away for a moment his sadness and embrace the wonder of life in all its tragedy and glory.

He lost track of time there in the moonlight. He forgot about Jo and about his efforts to find his recalcitrant foster brother and his worries for Easton. He especially refused to let himself remember all the reasons he shouldn't be kissing her—how, as he'd told her, he wasn't even sure he liked her, how he still didn't trust that she wasn't hiding a knife behind her back, ready to gut him with it at the first chance.

The only thing that mattered for this instant was Tess and how very perfect she felt in his arms, with her mouth eager and warm against his.

A coyote howled from far off in the distance, long and mournful. He heard it on the edge of his consciousness but he knew the instant the spell between them shattered and Tess returned to reality. In the space between one ragged breath and the next, she went from kissing him with heat and passion to freezing in his arms like Windy Lake in a January blizzard.

Her arms fluttered away from around his neck and he sensed she would have backed farther away from him if she hadn't been pressed up against her car door.

Though he wanted nothing more than to crush her to him again and slide into that stunning heat once more, he forced himself to step back to give them both a little necessary space.

Her breathing was as rough and quick as his own and he could see the rapid rise and fall of her chest.

Despite the chill in the air, the night seemed to wrap around them in a sultry embrace. From the trees whispering in the wind to the carpet of stars overhead, they seemed alone here in the darkness.

Part of him wanted to step toward her and sweep her into his arms again, but shock and dismay began to seep through his desire. What kind of magic did she wield against him that he could so easily succumb to his attraction and kiss her, despite all his best instincts?

He shouldn't have done it. In the first place, their relationship was a tangled mess and had been for years. Sure, she had been great with Jo tonight and he had been grateful for her help on the horseback ride into the mountains. But one night couldn't completely transform so much animosity into fuzzy warmth.

In the second place, he had enough on his plate right now. His emotions were scraped raw by Jo's condition. He had nothing left inside to give anything else right now, especially not an unwanted attraction to Tess.

Maybe that's why he had kissed her. He needed the distraction, a few moments of oblivion. Either way, it had been a monumentally stupid impulse, one he was quite certain he would come to regret the moment she climbed into her little sedan and drove down Cold Creek Canyon.

She continued to gaze at him out of those huge green eyes, as if she expected him to say something. He would be damned if he would apologize for kissing her. Not when she had responded with such fierce enthusiasm.

He had to say something, though. He scrambled for words and said the first thing that came to his head.

"If I had known you were such an enthusiastic kisser, I wouldn't have worked so hard to fight you off in high school."

The moment he said the words, he wished he could call them back. The comment had been unnecessarily cruel and made him sound like an ass. Beyond that, he didn't like revealing he remembered anything that had happened in their long-ago past. Apparently she still tended to bring out the worst in him.

He couldn't be certain in the darkness but he thought she paled a little. She grabbed her car door and yanked it open.

"That's funny," she retorted. "If I had known you would turn out to be such a jerk, I wouldn't have spent a moment since you returned to Pine Gulch regretting the way I treated you back then."

He deserved that, he supposed. *Now* he wanted to apologize—for his words at least, not the kiss—but the words seemed to clog in his throat.

She slid into her driver's seat, avoiding his gaze. "It would probably be better for both our sakes if we just pretended the past few moments never happened."

He raised an eyebrow. "You think you can do that? Because I'm not at all sure I have that much imagination."

She cranked the key in her ignition with just a little more force than strictly necessary and he felt a moment's pity that she was taking out her anger against him on her hapless engine.

"Absolutely," she snapped. "It shouldn't be hard at all. Especially since I'm sorry to report the reality didn't come close to measuring up to all my ridiculous teenage fantasies about what it might be like to kiss the bad boy of Cold Creek."

Before he could come up with any kind of rejoinder—sharp or otherwise—she thrust her car into gear and shot around the circular driveway.

He stared after her, wondering why the cold night only now seemed to pierce the haze of desire still wrapped around him.

Her words about teenage fantasies seemed to echo through his head. He supposed on some level, he must have known she had wanted to kiss him all those years ago. She had tried it, after all. He could still remember that day in the empty algebra classroom when he had been so furious with her over the false cheating allegations and then she had made everything much worse by thinking she could reel him in with a few flirtatious words.

He had always assumed her fleeting interest in him, her attempts to draw his attention, were only a spoiled fit of pique that he didn't fall at her feet like every other boy in school. Now he had to wonder if there might have been something more to it.

Trust him to make a mess out of everything, as usual. She had been kind to Jo and he had responded by taking completely inappropriate advantage. Then he had compounded his sins by making a stupid, mocking comment for no good reason.

She was furious with him, and she had every right to be, but he couldn't help thinking it was probably better this way. He didn't like having these soft, warm feelings for her.

Better to remember her as that manipulative little cheerleader looking so sweet-faced and innocent as she lied through her teeth to their history teacher and the principal than as the gentle caregiver who could suppress her own fears about horseback riding to help a dying woman find a little peace.

Tess waited until she drove under the arch at the entrance to Winder Ranch and had turned back onto the main Cold Creek road, out of view of the ranch house, before pulling her car over to the side and shifting into Park with hands that still trembled.

She was such an idiot.

Her face burned and she covered her hot cheeks with her hands.

She couldn't believe her response to him, that she had kissed him with such heat and enthusiasm. The moment his mouth touched hers, she had tossed every ounce of good sense she possessed into the air and had fallen into his kiss like some love-starved teenage girl with a fierce crush.

Oh, mercy. What must he think of her?

Probably that she was a love-starved thirty-two-year-old who hadn't known a man's touch in more years than she cared to remember.

How had she forgotten that incredible rush of sensations churning through her body? The delicious heat and lassitude that turned her brain to mush and her bones to rubber?

She had nearly burst into tears at how absolutely perfect it had felt to have his arms around her, his mouth sure and confident on hers. Wouldn't *that* have been humiliating? Thank the Lord she at least had retained some tiny modicum of dignity. But she had wanted to lose herself inside that kiss, to become so tangled up in him that she could forget the hundreds of reasons she shouldn't be kissing Quinn Southerland on a cold October night outside Winder Ranch.

If I had known you were such an enthusiastic kisser, I wouldn't have worked so hard to fight you off in high school.

His words seemed to echo through her car and she wanted to sink through the floorboards in complete mortification.

What was she thinking? Quinn Southerland, for heaven's sake! The man despised her, rightfully so. If she wanted to jump feetfirst into the whole sexual attraction thing, shouldn't she *try* to have the sense God gave a goose and pick somebody who could at least stand to be in the same room with her?

The unpalatable truth was, she hadn't been thinking at all. From the first instant his mouth had touched hers with such stunning impact, she felt like that shooting star she had wished upon, bursting through the atmosphere.

She had been rocked to her core by the wild onrush of sensations, his hands sure and masculine, his rough, late-evening shadow against her skin, his scent—of sleepy male and the faint lingering hint of some expensive aftershave—subtle and sexy at the same time.

To her great shame, she had wanted to forget everything sensible and sound and just surrender to the heat of his kiss. Who knew how long she would have let him continue things if she hadn't heard the lonely sound of a coyote?

Blast the man. She had everything planned out so perfectly. Her new job, relocating to Portland. It wasn't fair that he should come back now and stir up her insides like a tornado touching down. She didn't need this sort of complication just as she was finally on the brink of moving on with her life.

She scrubbed at her cheeks for another moment, then dropped her hands and took a deep, cleansing breath. The tragic truth was, he wouldn't be around much longer and she wouldn't have to deal with him. Jo was clinging by her fingernails but she couldn't hold on much longer. When she passed, Quinn would return to Seattle and she would be starting her new life.

For a few weeks, she would just have to do her best to deal with this insane reaction, to conceal it from him.

He didn't like her and she would be damned if she would pant after him like she was still that teenage girl with a crush.

* * *

"Thanks a million for taking a look at the Beast," Easton said. "I really didn't want to have to haul it to the repair place in town."

Four days after his startling encounter with Tess, Quinn stood with his hands inside Easton's temperamental tractor, trying to replace the clutch. "No problem," he answered. "It's good to know I can still find my way around the insides of a John Deere."

"If Southerland Shipping ever hits the skids, you can always come back home and be my grease monkey."

He grinned. "It's always good to have options, isn't it?"

She returned his smile, but it faded quickly. "Guff wanted you to stay and do just that, didn't he? You could always find your way around any kind of combustion engine."

True enough. He never minded other ranch work—roundup and moving the cattle and even hauling hay. But he had always been happiest when he was up to his elbows in grease, tinkering with this or that machine.

"Remember that old '66 Chevy pickup truck you used to work on? The blue one with the white top and all those curves?"

"Oh, yeah. She was a sweet ride. I imagine Cisco drove her into the ground after I left for the Air Force."

Something strange flashed in her mind for a moment, before she blinked it away. "You could have stayed. You would have been more than welcome," Easton said after a moment. "But I knew all along you never would."

He raised an eyebrow. Had he been so transparent? "Pine Gulch is a nice place and I love the ranch. Why were you so certain I wouldn't stick around? I might have been happy running a little place of my own nearby."

She shook her head. "Not you. Brant, maybe. He loves his ranch, though you would have to use that crowbar in the toolbox over there to get him to admit it. But you and Cisco had wanderlust running through your veins even when we were kids."

Maybe Cisco, Quinn thought. He had always talked about all the places he wanted to see when he left Idaho. Sun-drenched beaches and glittering cities and beautiful, exotic women who would drop their clothes if you so much as smiled at them.

That had been Francisco Del Norte's teenage dream. Quinn had no idea how close he had come to reaching it, since the man was wickedly skillful at evading any questions about his wandering life.

Quinn had his suspicions about what Cisco might be involved with, but he preferred to keep them to himself, especially around Easton. While she might love him and Brant like brothers, he had always sensed her feelings for Cisco were far different.

"I haven't wandered that far," he protested, instead of dwelling on Cisco and his suitcase full of secrets. "Not since I left the Air Force, anyway. I've been settled in Seattle for eight years now."

"Your dreams were always bigger than a little town like Pine Gulch could hold. I think deep down, Guff and Jo knew that, even if they were disappointed you didn't come home after you were discharged."

"They didn't need me here. They always had you to run the ranch." He sent her a careful look. "I always figured you were just fine with that. Was I wrong? You left for a while there, but you came back."

She had that strange look in her eyes again when he mentioned the eight months she had moved away from the ranch after Guff died. She didn't like to talk about it much, other than to say she had needed a change for a while. He supposed, like Cisco, she had her share of secrets, too.

"Yes. I came back," she said.

"Do you regret that?"

She raised her eyebrows. "You mean do I feel stuck here while the rest of you went off and conquered the world?"

He made a face. "I haven't *completely* conquered it. Still have a ways to go there but I'm working on it."

She smiled, though her expression was pensive. "I can't deny that sometimes I wonder if there's something more out there for me than a cattle ranch in Pine Gulch, Idaho. But I'm happy here, for the most part. I can't bear the thought of selling the ranch and leaving. Where would I go?"

"You could always come to Seattle. The company could always use somebody with your organizational skills."

"That world's not for me. You know that. I'm happy here."

Even as she said it, he caught the wistful note in her voice and he wondered at it. It wouldn't be easy to just pick up and make a new start somewhere. As had been the case more often than he cared to admit, he couldn't help thinking about Tess. In a few weeks, she was off to make a new start somewhere away from Pine Gulch.

As he worked on the clutch, his mind replayed that stunning kiss a few days earlier: the taste of her, like coffee and cinnamon, the sweet scent of her surrounding him, the imprint of her soft curves burning through layers of clothing.

He could go for long stretches of time without thinking about it as he went about the routine of visiting with Jo, helping Easton with odd jobs and trying to run Southerland Shipping from hundreds of miles away.

But then something would spark a memory and he would

find himself once more caught up in reliving every moment of that heated embrace.

He let out a breath, grateful he had seen Tess just a few times since, when she came out to take care of Jo—and then only briefly, in the buffering presence of Easton or Jo. He had wanted to apologize but hadn't been alone with her to do it and hadn't wanted to bring up the kiss in the presence of either of the other women.

That hadn't stopped him from obsessing more than he should have about her when she wasn't around, wondering which was the real Tess—the selfish girl he remembered or the soft, caring woman she appeared to be now.

The sound of an approaching vehicle drew his attention from either the mystery of Tess or the tractor's insides.

"Looks like company." Through the wide doors of the ranch's equipment shed, he watched a small white SUV approach the house. "Isn't it too early in the afternoon for any caregivers? The nurse was just here."

Easton followed his gaze outside. "I don't recognize the vehicle. Maybe it's one of Jo's friends."

They watched for a moment from their vantage point of a hundred yards away as the door opened, then a tall, brown-haired man in uniform stepped out.

"Brant!" Easton exclaimed, her delicate features alight with joy.

With a resounding thud that echoed through the building, she dropped the wrench to the concrete equipment shed floor and ran full tilt toward the new arrival.

Quinn followed at an easier pace and arrived just as Brant Western scooped East into his arms for a tight hug.

"I'll get grease all over your pretty uniform," she warned.

"I don't care. You are a sight, Blondie."

"Back at you." She kissed his cheek and Quinn watched

her dash tears away with a surreptitious finger swipe. He remembered again the little towheaded preteen who used to follow them around everywhere. He couldn't believe her parents had let them drag her along on all their adventures but she had always been a plucky little thing and they had all adored her.

After another tight hug, Brant set her down, then turned to Quinn with a long, considering glance.

"Look at you. A few days back on the ranch and Easton has you doing all the grunt work."

He looked down at the oil and grime that covered his shirt. "I don't mind getting my hands a little dirty."

"You never did." Brant smiled, though his eyes were red-rimmed with exhaustion. He looked not just fatigued but emotionally wrung-out.

Quinn considered Brant and Cisco his best friends, his brothers in every way that mattered. And though they had never been particularly demonstrative with each other, he was compelled now to step forward and pound the other man's back.

"Welcome home, Major."

"Thanks, man."

"Now I'm the one who's going to get grease all over your uniform."

"It will wash." Brant stepped away and Quinn was happy to see he seemed a little brighter, not quite as utterly exhausted. "On the flight over, I was trying to remember how long it's been since we've been together like this."

"Five years ago January," Easton said promptly.

Quinn combed through his memory bank and realized that must have been when Guff had died of a heart attack that had shocked all of them. By some miracle, they had all made it back from the various corners of the world for his funeral.

"Too damn long, that's for sure," he said.

Brant smiled for a moment but quickly sobered. "Like the last one, I wish this reunion could be under happier circumstances. How is she?"

"Eager to see you." Easton slipped her arm through his. "She'll be so happy you could make it home."

"I can't stay long. I was able to swing only a week. I'll have my regular leave in January and will have a couple more weeks home then if I can make it back."

Jo wouldn't be around for that and all of them knew it.

Easton forced a smile. "A day or a week, it won't matter to Jo. She'll just be so happy she had a chance to see you one last time. Come on, I'll take you inside. I want to see her face when she gets a load of you."

"You two go ahead," Quinn said. "I'm almost done out here. Since I'm already dirty, think I'll finish up out here first and come inside in a few."

Brant and Easton both nodded and headed for the house while Quinn returned to the tractor. A few minutes later, he was just tightening the last nut on the job when he heard the front door to the house bang shut.

"Quinn! Come quick!"

He jerked his gaze toward the ranch house at the urgency in Easton's voice and his blood ran cold.

He dropped the wrench and raced toward the house. Not yet, he prayed as he ran. Not when Brant had only just arrived at Winder Ranch and when his people hadn't managed to find Cisco yet.

His heart pounded frantically as he thrust open the door to Jo's room. The IV pump was beeping and the alarm was going off on the oxygen saturation monitor.

He frowned. Jo was lying against her pillow but wild relief pulsed through him that her eyes were open and alert, though her features were pale and drawn.

Just now, Easton looked in worse shape than Jo. She stood by the bedside, the phone in her hand.

"I don't care what you say. I'm calling Dr. Dalton. You were unconscious!"

"All this bother and fuss," Jo muttered. "You're making me feel like a foolish old woman."

Despite her effort to downplay her condition, he could see the concern in the expressions of both Brant and Easton.

"She was out cold for five solid minutes," Easton explained to Quinn. "She was hugging Brant one moment, then she fell back against her pillows the next and wouldn't wake up no matter what we tried."

"I should have called to let you know I was on my way." Brant's voice was tight with self-disgust. "It wasn't right to rush in like that and surprise you."

"I wasn't expecting you today, that's all," Jo insisted. "Maybe I got a little excited but I'm fine now."

Despite her protestations, Jo was as pale as her pillow.

"The clinic's line is busy. I'm calling Tess," Easton declared and walked from the room to make the call.

"Tess?" Brant asked.

Just when his heart rate started to slow from the adrenaline rush, simply the mention of Tess's name kicked it right back up again.

"Tess Claybourne. Used to be Jamison. She's one of the hospice nurses."

The best one, he had to admit. After several days here, he knew all three of the home-care nurses who took turns seeing to Jo. They were all good caregivers and compassionate women but as tough as it was for him to swallow,

Tess had a knack for easing Jo's worst moments and calming everybody else in the house.

Brant's blue eyes widened. "Tess Jamison. Pom-pom Tess? Homecoming Queen? That Tess?"

Okay, already. "Yeah. That Tess."

"You're yanking my chain."

"Not this time." He couldn't keep the grimness out of his voice.

"She still hotter than a two-dollar pistol?"

"Brant Western," Jo chided him from her bed. "She's a lovely young woman, not some...some pin-up poster off your Internet."

When they were randy teenagers, Jo had frequently lectured them not to objectify women. Brant must have remembered the familiar refrain as well, Quinn thought, as the deep dimples Quinn despised flashed for just a moment with his smile.

"Sorry, Jo. But she was always the prettiest girl at PG High. I used to get tongue-tied if she only walked past me in the hall."

She was still the prettiest thing Quinn had seen in a long time. And he didn't even want to think about how delectable she tasted or the sexy little sounds she made when his mouth covered hers...

Easton walked in, jarring him from yet another damn flashback.

"I reached Tess on her cell phone. She's off today but she's going to come over anyway. And I talked to Jake Dalton and he's stopping by on his way up to Cold Creek."

Pine Gulch's doctor had been raised on a huge cattle ranch at the head of Cold Creek Canyon, Quinn knew.

"Shouldn't we take her to the hospital or something?" Brant asked.

Quinn and Easton exchanged glances since they had frequently brought up the subject, but Jo spoke before he could answer.

"No hospital." Jo's voice was firm, stronger than he had heard it since he arrived. "I'm done with them. I'm dying and no doctor or hospital can change that. I want to go right here, in the house I shared with Guff, surrounded by those I love."

Brant blinked at her bluntness and Quinn sympathized with him. It was one thing to understand intellectually that her condition was terminal. It was quite another to hear her speak in such stark, uncompromising terms about it. He at least had had a few days to get used to the hard reality.

"But it's not going to happen today or even tomorrow," she went on. "I won't let it. Not until Cisco comes home. I just need to rest for a while and then I want to have a good long talk with you about what you've been doing for the army."

Brant released a heavy breath, his tired features still looking as if he had just been run over by a Humvee.

Quinn could completely sympathize with him. He could only hope Jo held out long enough so his people could track down the last of the Four Winds.

Chapter 9

"What's the verdict?" Jo asked. "Is my heart still beating?"

Tess pulled the stethoscope away from Jo's brachial artery and pulled the blood pressure cuff off with a loud ripping sound.

She related Jo's blood pressure aloud to Jake Dalton, who frowned at the low diastolic and systolic numbers.

"Let's take a listen to your ticker," Pine Gulch's only doctor said, pulling out his own stethoscope.

Jo responded by glaring at Tess. "Dirty trick, bringing Jake along with you."

"I told you I called him," Easton said from the doorway of the room, where she stood with Quinn and the very solemn-looking Major Western. Tess purposely avoided looking at any of them, especially Quinn.

It was a darn good thing Jake wasn't checking her heart rate right about now. She had a feeling it would be galloping along faster than one of the Winder Ranch horses in an open pasture on a sunny afternoon.

Knowing Quinn was only a few feet away watching her out of those silver-blue eyes was enough to tangle her insides and make her palms itch with nerves.

"And I told you I don't need a doctor," Jo replied.

"Be careful or you'll hurt my feelings," Jake teased.

"Oh, poof. Your skin is thicker than rawhide."

"Yet you can still manage to break my heart again and again."

Jo laughed and Tess smiled along with her. Jake Dalton was one of her favorite people. He had been a rock to her after she moved back to Pine Gulch with Scott. Though her husband had a vast team of specialists in Idaho Falls, Jake had always been her first line of defense whenever she needed a medical opinion about something.

He was a good, old-fashioned small-town doctor, willing to make house calls and take worried phone calls at all hours of the day and night and treat all his patients like family.

She had been thrilled four years earlier when he married Maggie Cruz, a nurse practitioner who often volunteered with hospice. She now considered both of them among her dearest friends.

"This is all a lot of nonsense for nothing," Jo insisted. "I was a little overexcited when Brant arrived, that's all."

Jake said nothing, only examined her chart carefully. He asked Jo several questions about her pain level and whether she had passed out any other times she had neglected to tell them all about.

When he was finished, he smoothed a gentle hand over her hair. "I'm going to make a few changes in your meds.

Why don't you get some rest and I'll explain what I want to do with Tess, okay?"

Tess knew it was an indication of Jo's weakened condition that she didn't argue, only nodded and closed her eyes.

Jake led the way out into the hall where the others waited. He closed the door behind him and headed for the kitchen, which Tess had learned long ago was really Command Central of Winder Ranch.

"What's happening?" Easton was the first to speak.

Jake's mouth tightened and his eyes looked bleak. "Her organs are starting to shut down. I'm sorry."

Even though Tess had been expecting it for days now, she was still saddened by the stark diagnosis.

"Which means what?" Brant asked. He looked very much the quintessential soldier with his close-cropped brown hair, strong jaw and sheer physical presence.

"It won't be long now," Jake said. "A couple of days, maybe."

Easton let out a long breath that wasn't quite a sob but probably would have been if she had allowed it.

Tess reached out and gripped her hand and Easton clutched her fingers tightly.

"I think it's time to think about round-the-clock nursing," Jake said. "I'm thinking more of her comfort and, to be honest, yours as well."

"Of course," Quinn said. "Absolutely. Whatever she needs."

Tess's chest ached at his unhesitating devotion to Jo.

Dr. Dalton nodded his approval. "I'll talk to hospice and see what they can provide."

Tess knew what the answer would be. Hospice was overburdened right now. She knew the agency didn't have the resources for that level of care.

"I'll do it. If you'll let me."

"You?" Brant asked, and she gave an inward flinch at the shock in his voice. Here was yet another person who only saw her as the silly girl she had been and she wondered if she would ever be able to escape her past.

"Right now the agency is understaffed," she answered. "I know they don't have the resources to have someone here all the time, as much as they would like to. They're going to recommend hospitalization in Idaho Falls for her last few days."

"She so wants to be here." Easton's voice trembled on the words.

"Barring that, they're going to tell you you'll have to hire a private nurse. I'd like to be that private nurse. I won't let you pay me but I want to do this for Jo. I'll make arrangements for the others to cover all my shifts and stay here, if that's acceptable to you all."

Tess refused to look at Quinn as she made the offer, though she could feel the heat of his gaze on her.

Part of her wondered at the insanity of offering to put herself in even closer proximity with him, but she knew he would be far too preoccupied to spend an instant thinking about a few regrettable moments of shared passion.

"I think it's a wonderful idea, if you're sure you're up to it," Brant said, surprising her. "Quinn and Easton both tell me you're the best of her nurses."

"Are you sure?" Easton asked with a searching look.

"Absolutely. Let me do this for her and for you," she said to her friend.

"What do you think?" Easton turned to Quinn, and Tess finally risked a glance in his direction. She found him watching the scene with an unreadable expression in his silver-blue eyes.

"It seems a good solution if Tess is willing. Better than bringing in some stranger. But we *will* pay you."

She didn't argue with him, though she determined she would donate anything the family insisted on back to hospice, which had been one of Jo's favorite charities even before she had need of their services.

"I'll need a little time to make all the arrangements but I should be back in a few hours," she said.

"Thank you." Easton squeezed her fingers. "I don't know how we'll ever repay you."

"I'll see you in a few hours."

She said goodbye to Dr. Dalton and headed for the door. To her shock, Quinn followed her.

"I'll walk you out," he said gruffly, and her mind instantly filled with images from the last time he had walked her outside, when they had given into the intimacy of the night and the heat simmering between them.

She wanted to tell him she didn't need any more of his escorts, thanks very much, but she didn't want to remind him of those few moments.

"Why?" Quinn asked when they were outside.

She didn't need to ask what he meant. "I love her," she said simply.

His gaze narrowed and she could tell he wasn't convinced. "Have you done this before? Round-the-clock nursing?"

She arched an eyebrow. "You mean besides the six years I cared for my husband?"

"I keep forgetting that."

She sighed, knowing he was only concerned for his foster mother. "I won't lie to you, it's always difficult at the end. The work is demanding and the emotional toll can be great. But if I can bring Jo a little bit of comfort and peace, I don't care about that."

"I don't get you," he muttered.

"I'm not that complicated."

He made a rough sound of disbelief low in his throat. He looked as if he wanted to say more but he finally just shook his head and opened the car door for her.

Two hours later, Tess set her small suitcase down in the guest room on the first floor, right next door to Jo's sickroom.

"This should work out fine," she said to Easton. It was a lovely room, one she hadn't seen before, filled with antiques and decorated in sage and pale peach.

She found it restful and calm and inherently feminine, with the lacy counterpane on the bed and the scrollwork on the bed frame and the light pine dresser.

Where did the others sleep? she wondered. Her insides trembled a little at the thought of Quinn somewhere in the house.

Why did sharing a house with him feel so different, so much more intimate, than all those other days when she had come in and out at various hours to care for Jo?

"I hope I'm not kicking someone else out of a bed."

"Not at all." Easton smiled, though she wore the shadow of her grief like a black lace veil. "No worries. We've got room to spare. There are plenty of beds in this place, plus the bunkhouse and the foreman's house, which are empty right now since my foreman has his own place down the canyon."

"That's where you were raised, wasn't it? The foreman's house?"

Easton nodded. "Until I was sixteen, when my parents were killed in a car accident and I moved here with Aunt Jo and Uncle Guff. The boys were all gone by then and it was only me."

"You must have missed them."

Easton smiled as she settled on the bed, wrapping her arms around her knees. "The house always seemed too empty without them. I adored them and missed them like crazy. Even though I was so much younger—Quinn was five years older, Brant four and Cisco three—they were always kind to me. I still don't know why but they never seemed to mind me tagging along. Three instant older cousins who felt more like brothers was heady stuff for an only child like me."

"I was always jealous of my friends who had older brothers to look out for them," Tess said.

"I loved it. One time, Quinn found out an older boy at school was teasing me because I had braces and glasses. Roy Hargrove. Did you ever know him? He would have been a couple years younger than you."

"Oh, right. Greasy hair. Big hands."

Easton laughed. "That's the one. He used to call me some terrible names and one day Quinn found me crying about it. To this day, I have no idea what the boys said to him. But not only did Roy stop calling me names, he went out of his way to completely avoid me and always got this scared look in his eyes when he saw me, until his family moved away a few years later."

Easton smiled a little at the memory. "Anyway, there's plenty of room here at the house. Eight bedrooms, counting the two down here."

Tess stared at her friend. "Eight? I've never been upstairs but I had no idea the house was that big!"

"Guff and Jo wanted to fill them all with children but it wasn't to be. Jo was almost forty when they met and married and she'd already had cancer once and had to have a hysterectomy because of it. I think they thought about adopting but they ended up opening the ranch to foster children instead, especially after Quinn came. His mother and Jo were cousins, did you know that? So we're cousins by marriage, somehow."

"I had no idea," she exclaimed.

"Jo and his mother were good friends when they were younger but then they lost track of each other. From what I understand, it took Jo a long time to get custody of him after his parents died."

"How old were you when they moved here?"

"I was almost ten when Quinn came. He would have been fourteen."

Tess remembered him, all rough-edged and full of attitude. He had been dark and gorgeous and dangerous, even back then.

"Brant moved in after Quinn had been here about four months, but you probably already knew him from school."

She knew Brant used to live on a small ranch in the canyon with his family. He had been in her grade and Tess always remembered him as wearing rather raggedy clothes and a few times he had come to school with an arm in a sling or bruises on his arms. Just like Quinn, Brant Western hadn't been like the other boys, either. He had been solemn and quiet, smart but not pushy about it.

She had been so self-absorbed as a girl that she hadn't known until years later that the Winders had taken Brant away from his abusive home life, though she had noticed around middle school that he started dressing better and seemed more relaxed.

"And then Cisco moved in a few months after Brant." Easton spoke the words briskly and rose from the bed, but not before Tess caught a certain something in her eyes. Tess had noticed it before whenever Easton mentioned the other man's name but she sensed Easton didn't want to discuss it.

"Jo and Guff had other foster children over the years, didn't they?"

"A few here and there but usually only as a temporary stopping point." She shrugged. "I think they would have had more but...after my parents died, I was pretty shattered for a while and I think they were concerned about subdividing their attention among others when I was grieving and needed them."

Her heart squeezed with sympathy for Easton's loss. She couldn't imagine losing both parents at the same time. Her father's death a few years after Scott's accident had been tough enough. She didn't know how she would have survived if her mother had died, too.

"They have always been there for me," Easton said quietly.

Tess instinctively reached out and hugged her friend. Easton returned the embrace for only a moment before she stepped away.

"Thank you again for agreeing to stay." Her voice wobbled only a little. "Let me know if you need anything."

"I will. Right back at you. Even just a shoulder to cry on. I might be here as Jo's nurse but I'm your friend, too."

Easton pulled open the door. "I know. That's why I love you. You're just the kind of person I want to be when I grow up, Tess."

Her laugh was abrupt. "You need to set your sights a little higher than me. Now Jo, that's another story. There's something for both of us to shoot for."

"I think if I tried the rest of my life, I wouldn't be able to measure up to her. She's an original."

Chapter 10

The entire ranch seemed to be holding its collective breath.

Day-to-day life at the ranch went on as usual. The stock needed to be watered, the human inhabitants needed food and sleep, laundry still piled up.

But everyone was mechanically going through the motions, caught up in the larger human drama taking place in this room.

Forty-eight hours later, Tess sat by the window in Jo's sickroom, her hands busy with the knitting needles she had learned to wield during the long years of caring for Scott. She had made countless baby blankets and afghans during those years, donating most of them to the hospital in Idaho Falls or to the regional pediatric center in Salt Lake City.

Jo coughed, raspy and dry, and Tess set the unfinished blanket aside and rose to lift the water bottle from the side of the bed and hold the straw to Jo's mouth.

Her patient sipped a little, then turned her head away.

"Thank you," she murmured.

"What else can I get you?" Tess asked.

"Cisco. Only Cisco."

Her heart ached for Jo. The woman was in severe pain, her organs failing, but she clung to life, determined to see her other foster son one more time. Tess wanted desperately to give her that final gift so she could at last say goodbye.

A few moments later, Jo rested back against the pillow and closed her eyes. She didn't open them when Easton pushed open the door.

Tess pressed a finger to her mouth and moved out into the hall.

"I came to relieve you for a few moments. Why don't you go outside and stretch your legs for a while? Go get some fresh air."

She nodded, grateful Easton could spell her for a few moments, though she had no intention of going outside yet. "Thanks. I'll be back in a few moments."

"Take your time. I'm done with the morning chores and have a couple hours."

When Easton closed Jo's door behind her, Tess turned toward the foyer. Instead of going outside, though, she headed up the stairs toward the empty bedroom Quinn had taken over for an office while he was in Pine Gulch.

She approached the open doorway, mortified that her heart was pounding from more than just the fast climb up the stairs.

She heard Quinn's raised voice before she reached the doorway, sounding more heated than she had heard him since that long-ago day she had accused him of cheating.

He sat with his back to the door at a long writing desk near the window. From the angle of the doorway, she could see a laptop in front of him with files strewn across the surface of the desk.

He wore a soft gray shirt with the sleeves rolled up and she could see his strong, muscled forearm flex. His dark hair looked a little tousled, as if he had run his fingers through it recently, which she had learned was his habit.

She wasn't sure which version of the man she found more appealing. The rugged cowboy who had ridden to Windy Lake, his hands sure and confident on the reins and his black Stetson pulled low over his face. The loving, devoted son who sat beside Jo's bedside for long hours, reading to her from the newspaper or the Bible or whatever Jo asked of him.

Or this one, driven and committed, forcing himself to put aside the crisis in his personal life to focus on business and the employees and customers who depended on him.

She gave an inaudible sigh. The truth was, she was drawn to every facet of the dratted man and was more fascinated by him with every passing hour.

Jo. She was here for Jo, she reminded herself.

"Look, whatever it takes," he said into the phone. "I'm tired of this garbage. Find him! I don't care what you have to do!"

After pressing a button on the phone, he threw it onto the desk with such force that she couldn't contain a little gasp.

He turned at the sound and something flared in his eyes, something raw and intense, before he quickly banked it. "What is it? Is she…"

"No. Nothing like that. Was that phone call about Cisco?"

"Supposed to be. But as you can probably tell, I'm hitting walls everywhere I turn. That was the consulate in El Salvador. He was there a few weeks ago but nobody knows where he is now. I have tried every contact I have and I can't manage to find one expatriate American in Latin America."

She walked into the room, picking her words carefully. "I don't think she's going to be able to hang on until he gets here, though she's trying her best."

"I hate that I can't give her this."

"It's not your fault, Quinn." She curled her fingers to her palm in an effort to fight the impulse to touch his arm in comfort, as she would have done to Easton and even Brant, who, except for those first few moments when he arrived, had treated her with nothing but kindness and respect.

Quinn was different. Somehow she couldn't relax in his company, not with their shared past and the more recent heat that unfurled inside her whenever he was near.

She let out a breath, wishing she could regard him the same as she did everyone else.

"Sometimes you have to accept you've tried your best," she said.

"Have I?" The frustration in his voice reached something deep inside her and this time she couldn't resist the urge to touch his arm.

"What else can you do? You can't go after him."

He looked down at her pale fingers against the darker skin of his arm for a long moment. When he lifted his gaze, she swallowed at the sudden intensity in his silver-blue gaze.

She pulled her hand away and tucked it into the pocket of her scrubs. "When you've done all you can, sometimes you have no choice but to put your problems in God's hands."

His expression turned hard, cynical. "A lovely sentiment. Did that help you sleep at night when you were caring for your husband?"

She drew in a sharp breath then let it out quickly, reminding herself he was responding from a place of pain she was entirely familiar with.

"As a matter of fact, it did," she answered evenly.

"Sorry." He raked a hand through his hair again, messing it further. "That was unnecessarily harsh."

"You want to fix everything. That's understandable. It's what you do, isn't it?"

"Not this time. I can't fix this."

The bleakness in his voice tore at her heart and she couldn't help herself, she rested her fingers on his warm arm again. "I'm sorry. I know how terribly hard this is for you."

He looked anguished and before she quite realized what he was doing, he pulled her into his arms and clung tightly to her. He didn't kiss her, only held her. She froze in shock for just a moment then she wrapped her arms around him and let him draw whatever small comfort she could offer from the physical connection with another person. Sometimes a single quiet embrace could offer more comfort than a hundred condolences, she knew.

They stood for several moments in silence with his arms around her, his breath a whisper against her hair. Something sweet and intangible—and even tender—passed between them. She was afraid to move or even breathe for fear of ruining this moment, this chance to provide him a small measure of peace.

All too soon, he exhaled a long breath and dropped his arms, moving away a little, and she felt curiously bereft.

He looked astonished and more than a little embarrassed.

"I… Sorry. I don't know what that was about. Sorry."

She smiled gently. "You're doing your best," she repeated. "Jo understands that."

He opened his mouth to answer but before he could, Brant's voice sounded from downstairs, loud and irate.

"It's about damn time you showed up."

Tess blinked. In her limited experience, the officer was invariably patient with everyone, a sea of calm in the emotional tumult of Winder Ranch. She had never heard that sort of harshness from him.

In response, she heard another man's voice, one she didn't recognize.

"I'm not too late, am I?"

Quinn's expression reflected her own shock as both of them realized Francisco Del Norte had at last arrived.

Quinn took the stairs two at a time. She followed with the same urgency, a little concerned the men might come to blows—at least judging by Brant's anger and that hot expression in Quinn's eyes as he had rushed past her.

In the foyer, she found Brant and Quinn facing off against a hard-eyed, rough-looking Latino who bore little resemblance to the laughing, mischievous boy she remembered from school.

"Where the hell have you been?" Quinn snapped.

Fatigue clouded the other man's dark eyes. Tess wasn't sure she had ever seen anyone look so completely exhausted.

"Long story. I could tell you, but you know the drill. Then I'd have to kill you and I'm too damn tired right now to take on both your sorry asses at the same time."

The three men eyed each other for another moment and Tess held her breath, wondering if she ought to step in. Then, as if by some unspoken signal, they all moved together and gave that shoulder-slap thing men did instead of hugging.

"Tell me I'm not too late." Cisco's voice was taut with anguish.

"Not yet. But she's barely hanging on, man. She was just waiting to say goodbye to you."

Tears filled Cisco's eyes as he uttered a quick prayer of gratitude in Spanish.

She was inclined to dislike the man for the worry he had put everyone through these past few days and for Jo's heartache. But she couldn't help feeling compassion for the undisguised sorrow in his eyes.

"They didn't... I didn't get the message until three days ago. I was in the middle of something big and it took me a while to squeeze my way out."

Brant and Quinn didn't look appeased by the explanation but they didn't seem inclined to push him either.

"Can I see her?"

Both Brant and Quinn turned to look at Tess, still standing on the stairs, as if she was Jo's guardian and gatekeeper.

"Easton's in with her. I'll go see if she's awake."

She turned away, but not before she caught an odd expression flicker across his features at the mention of Easton's name.

She left the three men and walked down the hall to Jo's bedroom. When she carefully eased open the door, emotions clogged her throat at the scene she found inside.

Easton was the one asleep now, with her head resting on the bed beside her aunt. Jo's frail, gnarled hand rested on her niece's hair.

Jo pressed a finger to her mouth. Though she tried to shake her head, she was so weak she barely moved against the pillow.

"It's not time for more meds, is it?" she murmured, her voice thready.

Though Tess could barely hear the woman's whisper, Easton still opened her eyes and jerked her head up.

"Sorry. I must have just dozed off."

Jo smiled. "Just a few minutes ago, dear. Not long enough."

"It's not time for meds," Tess answered her. "I was only checking to see if you were awake and up for a visitor."

Though she thought she spoke calmly enough, some clue in her demeanor must have alerted them something had happened. Both women looked at her carefully.

"What is it?" Easton asked.

Before she could answer, she heard a noise in the doorway and knew without turning around that Cisco had followed her.

Easton's features paled and she scrambled to her feet. Tess registered her reaction for only an instant, then she was completely disarmed when the hard, dangerous-looking man hurried to Jo's bedside, his eyes still wet with emotion.

The joy in Jo's features was breathtakingly beautiful as she reached a hand to caress his cheek. "You're here. Oh, my dear boy, you're here at last."

Quinn and Brant followed Cisco into the room. Tess watched their reunion for a moment, then she quietly slipped from the room to give them the time and space they needed together.

Chapter 11

The woman Quinn loved as a mother took her last breath twelve hours after Cisco Del Norte returned to Winder Ranch.

With all four of them around her bedside and Tess standing watchfully on the edge of the room, Jo succumbed to the ravages cancer had wrought on her frail body.

Quinn had had plenty of time to prepare. He had known weeks ago her condition was terminal and he had been at the ranch for nearly ten days to spend these last days with her and watch her inexorable decline.

He had known it was coming. That didn't make it any easier to watch her draw one ragged breath into her lungs, let it out with a sigh and then nothing more.

Beside him, Easton exhaled a soft, choked sob. He wrapped an arm around her shoulder and pulled her close, aware that Cisco, on her other side, had made the same move but had checked it when Quinn reached her first.

"I'll call Dr. Dalton and let him know," Tess murmured after a few moments of leaving them to their shared sorrow.

He met her gaze, deeply grateful for her quiet calm. "Thank you."

She held his gaze for a moment, her own filled with an echo of his grief, then she smiled. "You're welcome."

He had fully expected the loss, this vast chasm of pain. But he hadn't anticipated the odd sense of peace that seemed to have settled over all of them to know Jo's suffering was finally over.

A big part of that was due to Tess and her steady, unexpected strength, he admitted over the next hour as they worked with the doctor and the funeral home to make arrangements.

She seemed to know exactly what to say, what to do, and he was grateful to turn these final responsibilities over to her.

If he found comfort in anything right now, it was in the knowledge that Jo had spent her last days surrounded by those she loved and by the tender care Tess had provided.

He couldn't help remembering that embrace with Tess upstairs in his office. Those few moments with her arms around him and her cheek resting against his chest had been the most peaceful he had known since he arrived at the ranch.

He had found them profoundly moving, for reasons he couldn't explain, anymore than he could explain how the person he thought he despised most in the world ended up being the one he turned to in his greatest need.

He was lousy at doing nothing.

The evening after Jo's funeral, Quinn sat at the kitchen table at the ranch with a heaping plate of leftovers in front of him and an aching restlessness twisting through him.

The past three days since Jo's death had been a blur of

condolence visits from neighbors, of making plans with Southerland Shipping for the corporate jet to return for him by the end of the week, of seeing to the few details Jo hadn't covered in the very specific funeral arrangements she made before her death.

Most of those details fell on his shoulders by default, simply because nobody else was around much.

He might have expected them to all come together in their shared grief but each of Jo's Four Winds seemed to be dealing with her death in a unique way.

Easton took refuge out on the ranch, with her horses and her cattle and hard, punishing work. Brant had left the night Jo died for his own ranch, a mile or so up the canyon and had only been back a few times and for the funeral earlier. Cisco slept for a full thirty-six hours as if it had been months since he closed his eyes. As soon as the funeral was over earlier that day, he had taken one of the ranch horses and a bedroll and said he needed to sleep under the stars.

As for Quinn, he focused on what work he could do long-distance and on these last few details for Jo. Staying busy helped push the pain away a little.

He sipped at his beer as the old house creaked and settled around him and the furnace kicked in with a low whoosh against the late October cold. Forlorn sounds, he thought. Lonely, even.

Maybe Cisco had the right idea. Maybe he ought to just get the hell out of Dodge, grab one of the horses and ride hard and fast into the mountains.

The thought did have a certain appeal.

Or maybe he ought to just call his pilot and move up his departure. He could be home by midnight.

What would be the difference between sitting alone at his house in Seattle or sitting alone here at Winder Ranch?

This aching emptiness would follow him everywhere for a while, he was afraid, until that inevitable day when the loss would begin to fade a little.

Hovering on the edge of his mind was the awareness that once he left Winder Ranch this time, he would have very few reasons to return. With Jo and Guff gone, his anchor to the place had been lifted.

Easton would always be here. He could still come back to visit her, but with Brant in the military and Cisco off doing whatever mysterious things occupied his time, nothing would ever be the same.

The Four Winds would be scattered once more.

Jo had been their true north, their center. Without her, a chapter in his life was ending and the realization left him more than a little bereft.

He rose suddenly as that restlessness sharpened, intensified. He couldn't just sit here. He didn't really feel like spending the night on the hard ground, but at least he could take one of the horses out for a hard moonlit ride to work off some of this energy.

The thought inevitably touched off memories of the other ride he had taken into the mountains just days ago—and of the woman he had been doing his best not to think about for the past few days.

Tess had packed up all the medical equipment in Jo's room and had left the ranch the night Jo died. He had seen her briefly at the funeral, a slim, lovely presence in a bright yellow dress amid all the traditionally dark mourning clothes. Jo would have approved, he remembered thinking. She would have wanted bright colors and light and sunshine at her funeral. He only wished he'd been the one to think of it and had put on a vibrant tie instead of the muted, conservative one he had worn with his suit.

To his regret, Tess had slipped away from the service before he had a chance to talk to her. Now he found himself remembering again those stunning few moments they had shared upstairs in his office bedroom, when she had simply held him, offering whatever solace he could draw from her calm embrace.

He missed her.

Quinn let out a breath. Several times over the past days, as he dealt with details, he had found himself wanting to turn to her for her unique perspective on something, for some of her no-nonsense advice, or just to see her smile at some absurdity.

Ridiculous. How had she become so important to him in just a matter of days? It was only the stress of the circumstances, he assured himself.

But right now as he stood in the Winder Ranch kitchen with this emptiness yawning inside him, he had a desperate ache to see her again.

She would know just the right thing to say to ease his spirit. Somehow he knew it.

If he just showed up on her doorstep for no reason, she would probably think he was an idiot. He couldn't say he only wanted her to hold him again, to ease the restlessness of his spirit.

His gaze fell on a hook by the door and fate smiled on him when he recognized her jacket hanging next to his own denim ranch coat. He had noticed it the day before and remembered her wearing it a few nights when she had come to the ranch, before she moved into the spare room, but he had forgotten about it until just this moment.

If he gave it a moment's thought, he knew he would talk himself out of seeing her while his heart was still raw and aching.

So he decided not to think about it.

He shrugged into his own jacket, then grabbed hers off the hook by the door and headed into the night.

The nature of hospice work meant she had to face death on a fairly consistent basis but it never grew any easier— and some losses hit much harder than others.

Tess had learned early, though, that it was best to throw herself into a project, preferably something physical and demanding, while the pain was still raw and fresh. When she could exhaust her body as much as her spirit, she had half a chance of sleeping at night without dreams, tangled-up nightmares of all those she had loved and lost.

The evening of Jo's funeral, she stood on a stepladder in the room that once had been Scott's, scraping layers of paint off the wide wooden molding that encircled the high ceiling of the room.

Stripping the trim in this room down and refinishing the natural wood had always been in her plans when she bought the house after Scott's accident but she had never gotten around to it, too busy with his day-to-day care.

She supposed it was ironic that she was only getting around to doing the work she wanted on the room now that the house was for sale. She ought to leave the redecorating for the new owners to apply their own tastes, but it seemed the perfect project to keep her mind and body occupied as best she could.

The muscles of her arms ached from reaching above her head but that didn't stop her from scraping in rhythm to the loud honky-tonk music coming from her iPod dock in the corner of the empty room.

She was singing along about a two-timin' man so loudly

she nearly missed the low musical chime of her doorbell over the wails.

Though she wasn't at all in the mood to talk to anyone, she used any excuse to drop her arms to give her aching muscles a rest.

She thought about ignoring the doorbell, certain it must be her mother dropping by to check on her. She knew Maura was concerned that Jo's death would hit her hard and she wasn't sure she was in the mood to deal with her maternal worry.

Her mother would have seen the lights and her car in the driveway and Tess knew she would just keep stubbornly ringing the bell until her daughter answered.

She sighed and stepped down from the ladder.

"Coming," she called out. "Hang on."

She took a second before she pulled open the door to tuck in a stray curl slipping from the folded bandanna that held her unruly hair away from her face while she worked.

"Sorry, I was up on the ladder and it took me a minute…"

Her voice trailed off and she stared in shock. That definitely wasn't her mother standing on her small porch. Her heart picked up a beat.

"Quinn! Hello."

"Hi. May I come in?" he prompted, when she continued to stare at him, baffled as to why he might be standing on her doorstep.

"Oh. Of course."

She stepped back to allow him inside, fervently wishing she was wearing something a little more presentable than her scruffiest pair of jeans and the disreputable faded cropped T-shirt she used for gardening.

"Were you expecting someone else?"

"I thought you might be my mother. She still lives in

town, though my father died a few years back. He had a heart attack on the golf course. Shocked us all. Friends have tried to talk my mother into moving somewhere warmer but she claims she likes it here. I think she's really been sticking around to keep an eye on me. Maybe she'll finally move south when I take off for Portland."

She clamped her mouth shut when she realized she was babbling, something she rarely did. She also registered the rowdy music coming from down the hall.

"Sorry. Let me grab that music."

She hurried back to the bedroom and turned off the iPod, then returned to her living room, where she saw him looking at the picture frames clustered across the top of her upright piano.

He looked gorgeous, she thought, in a Stetson and a denim jacket that made him look masculine and rough.

Her insides did a long, slow roll but she quickly pushed back her reaction, especially when she saw the slightly lost expression in his eyes.

"I'm sorry," she said. "I was stripping paint off the wall trim in my spare bedroom. I...needed the distraction. What can I do for you?"

He held out his arm, along with something folded and blue. "You left your coat at the ranch. I thought you might need it."

She took it from him and didn't miss the tiny flicker of static that jumped from his skin to hers. Something just as electric sparked in his eyes at the touch.

"You didn't need to drive all the way into town to return it. I could have picked it up from Easton some other time."

He shrugged. "I guess you're not the only one who needed a distraction. Everybody else took off tonight in different directions and I just didn't feel like hanging around the ranch by myself."

He didn't look at her when he spoke, but she recognized the edgy restlessness in his silver-blue eyes. She wanted to reach out to him, as she might have done with anyone else, but she didn't trust herself around him and she didn't know if he would welcome her touch. Though he had that day at the ranch, she remembered.

"How are you at scraping paint?" she asked on impulse, then wanted to yank the words back when she realized the absurdity of putting him to work in her spare room just hours after his foster mother's funeral.

He didn't look upset by the question. "I've scraped the Winder Ranch barn and outbuildings in my day but never done room trim. Is this any different?"

"Harder," she said frankly. "This house has been through ten owners in its seventy-five years of existence and I swear every single one of them except me has left three or four layers of paint. It's sweaty, hard, frustrating work."

"In that case, bring it on."

She laughed and shook her head. "You don't know what you're getting into, but if you're sure you're willing to help, I would welcome the company."

It wasn't a lie, she thought as she led him back to the bedroom after he left his jacket and hat on the living-room couch. She had to admit she was grateful to have someone to talk to and for one last opportunity to see him again before he left Pine Gulch.

"You don't really have to do this," she said when they reached the room. "You're welcome to stay, even if you don't want to work."

Odd how what she had always considered a good-size space seemed to shrink in an instant. She could smell him, sexy and masculine, and she wished again that she wasn't dressed in work clothes.

"Where can I start?"

"I was up on the ladder working on the ceiling trim. If you would like to start around the windows, that would be great."

"Deal."

He rolled up the sleeves of his shirt that looked expensive and tailored—not that she knew much about men's clothes—and grabbed a paint scraper. Without another word, he set immediately to work.

Tess watched him for a moment, then turned the music on again, switching to a little more mellow music.

For a long time, they worked without speaking. She didn't find the silence awkward in the slightest, merely contemplative on both their parts.

Quinn seemed just as content not to make aimless conversation and though she was intensely aware of him on the other side of the room, she wasn't sure he even remembered she was in the room until eight or nine songs into the playlist.

"My father killed my mother when I was thirteen years old."

He said the abrupt words almost dispassionately but she heard the echo of a deep, vast pain in his voice.

She set down her scraper, her heart aching for him even as she held her breath that he felt he could share something so painful with her now, out of the blue like this.

"Oh, Quinn. I'm so sorry."

He released a long, slow breath, like air escaping from a leaky valve, and she wondered how long he had kept the memories bottled deep inside him.

"It happened twenty years ago but every moment of that night is as clear in my mind as the ride we took to Windy Lake last week. Clearer, even."

She climbed down the ladder. "You were there?"

He continued moving the scraper across the wood and tiny multicolored flakes of paint fluttered to the floor. "I was there. But I couldn't stop it."

She leaned against the wall beside him, hesitant to say the wrong word that might make him regret sharing this part of his past with her.

"What happened?" she murmured, sensing he needed to share it. Perhaps this was all part of his grieving process for Jo, the woman who had taken him in and helped him heal from his ugly, painful past.

"They were fighting, as usual. My parents' marriage was...difficult. My father was an attorney who worked long hours. When he returned home, he always insisted on a three-course dinner on the table, no matter what hour of the day or night, and he wanted the house completely spotless."

"That must have been hard for a young boy."

"I guess I was lucky. He didn't take his bad moods out on me. Only on her."

She held her breath, waiting for the rest.

"Their fighting woke me up," Quinn said after a moment, "and I heard my dad start to get a little rough. Also usual. I went down to stop it. That didn't always work but sometimes a little diversion did the trick. Not this time."

He scraped harder and she wanted to urge him to spare himself the anguish of retelling the story, but again, she had that odd sense that he needed to share this, for reasons she didn't understand.

"My dad was in a rage, accusing her of sleeping with one of the other attorneys in his firm."

"Was she?"

He shrugged. "I don't know. Maybe. My father was a bastard but she seemed to delight in finding and hitting every one of his hot buttons. She laughed at him. I'll never forget the sound of her laughing, with her face still bruised and red where he had slapped her. She said she was having a torrid affair with the other man, that he was much better in bed than my father."

She drew in a sharp breath, hating the thought of a thirteen-year-old version of Quinn witnessing such ugliness between his parents.

"I don't know," he went on. "She might have been lying. Theirs was not a healthy relationship, in any sense of the word. He needed to be in control of everything and she needed to be constantly adored."

She thought of Quinn being caught in the middle of it all and her chest ached for him and she had to curl her fingers into her palms to keep from reaching for him.

"My father said he wasn't going to let her make a fool out of him any longer. He walked out of the room and I thought for sure he was going to pack a suitcase and leave. I was happy, you know. For those few moments, I was thinking how much better things would be without him. No more yelling, no more fights."

"But he didn't leave."

He gave a rough laugh and set the scraper down and sat beside her on the floor, his back against the wall and their elbows touching. "He didn't leave. He came out of the bedroom with the .38 he kept locked in a box by the side of his bed. He shot her three times. Twice in the heart and then once more in the head. And then he turned the gun on himself."

"Oh, dear God."

"I couldn't stop it. For a long time, I kept asking myself if I could have done something. Said something. I just stood there."

She couldn't help herself, she covered his hand with hers. After a long moment, he turned his hand and twisted his fingers with hers, holding tight. They sat that way, shoulders brushing while the music on her playlist shifted to a slow, jazzy ballad.

She kept envisioning that rough-edged, angry boy he had been when he first came to Pine Gulch. He must have been consumed with pain and guilt over his parents' murder-suicide. She could see it so clearly, just as she saw in grim detail her own awful behavior toward him, simply because he had refused to pay any attention to her.

"I am so, so sorry, Quinn," she murmured, for everything he had survived and for her own part in making life harder for him here.

"The first year after was…hellish," he said, his voice low. "That's the only word that fits. I was thrown into the foster-care system and spent several months bouncing from placement to placement."

"None of them stuck?"

"I wasn't an easy kid to love," he said. "You knew me when I first came to Pine Gulch. I was angry and hurting and hated the world. Jo and Guff saw past all that. They saw whatever tiny spark of good might still be buried deep inside me and didn't stop until they helped me see it, too."

"I'm so happy you found each other."

"Same here." He paused, looking a little baffled. "I don't know why I'm telling you this. I didn't come here to dump it all on you. The truth is, I don't talk about it much. I don't think I've ever shared it with anybody but Brant and Cisco and Easton."

"It's natural to think about the circumstances that brought you into Jo's world. I imagine it's all connected for you."

"I was on a path to nowhere when Jo finally found me up in Boise and petitioned for custody. I was only the kid of a cousin. I'd never even met her but she and Guff still took me on, with all that baggage. She was a hell of a woman."

"I'm going to miss her dearly," Tess said quietly. "But I keep trying to focus on how much better a person I am because I knew her."

Their hands were still entwined between them and she could feel the heat of his skin and the hard strength of his fingers.

"I don't know what to make of you," he finally said.

She gave a small laugh. "Why's that?"

"You baffle me. I don't know which version of you is real."

"All of it. I'm like every other woman. A mass of contradictions, most of which I don't even understand myself. Sometimes I'm a saint, sometimes I'm a bitch. Sometimes I'm the life of the party, sometimes I just want everybody to leave me alone. But mostly, I'm just a woman."

"That part I get."

The low timbre of his voice and the sudden light in his eyes sent a shower of sparks arcing through her. She was suddenly intensely aware of him—the breadth of his shoulder nudging hers, the glitter of silvery-blue eyes watching her, the scent of him, of sage and bergamot and something else that was indefinable.

Her insides quivered and her pulse seemed to accelerate. "I don't regret many things in my life," she said, her voice breathy and low. "But I wish I could go back and change the way I treated you when we were younger. I hate that I gave you even a moment's unhappiness when you had already been through so much with your parents."

His shoulder shrugged beside her. "It was a long time ago, Tess. In the grand scheme of life, it didn't really mean anything."

"I was so awful to you."

"I wasn't exactly an easy person to like."

"That wasn't the problem. The opposite, actually. I... liked you too much," she confessed. "I hated that you thought I was some silly, brainless cheerleader. I wanted desperately for you to notice me."

His mouth quirked a little. "How could I help it?"

"You mean, when I was getting you kicked off the baseball team for cheating and then lying to my boyfriend and telling him you did something I only *wanted* you to do?"

"That's why Scott and his buddies beat me up that night? I had no idea."

"I'm so sorry, Quinn. I was despicable to you."

"Why?" he asked. "I still don't quite understand what I ever did to turn your wrath against me."

She sighed. "Every girl in school had a crush on you, but for me, it went way past crush. I didn't know your story but I could tell you were in pain. Maybe that's why you fascinated me, more than anyone I had ever known in my sheltered little life. I guess I was something of a healer, even then."

He gazed at her as the music shifted again, something low and sultry.

"I was fiercely attracted to you," she finally admitted. "But you made it clear you weren't interested. My pride was hurt. But I have to say, I think my heart was a little bruised, too. And so I turned mean. I wanted you to hurt, too. It was terrible and small of me and I'm so, so sorry."

"It was a long time ago," he said again. "We're both different people."

She smiled a little, her pulse pounding loudly in her ears. "Not so different," she murmured, still holding his hand. "I'm still fiercely attracted to you."

Chapter 12

Her breath snagged in her throat as she waited for him to break the sudden silence between them that seemed to drag on forever, though it was probably only several endless, excruciating seconds.

She braced herself, not sure she could survive another rejection. Nerves shivered through her as she waited for him to move, to speak, to do *anything*.

Just when she thought she couldn't endure the uncertainty another moment and was about to scramble away and tell him to ignore every single thing she had just said, he groaned her name and then his mouth captured hers in a wild kiss.

At that first stunning brush of his lips, the slick texture of his mouth, heat exploded between them like an August lightning storm on dry tinder. She returned his kiss, pouring everything into her response—her regret for the hurt she had caused him, her compassion for his loss, the soft tenderness blooming inside her.

And especially this urgent attraction pulsing to every corner of her body with each beat of her heart.

This was right. Inevitable, even. From the moment she heard him ring the doorbell earlier, some part of her had known they would end up here, with his arms around her and his heartbeat strong and steady under her fingers.

She wanted to help him, to heal him. To soak his pain inside her and ease his heart, if only for a moment.

She wrapped her arms more tightly around his neck, relishing the contrast between her curves and his immovable strength, between the cool wall at her back and all the glorious heat of his arms.

"While we're apologizing," he murmured against her mouth, "I'm sorry I was such an idiot the last time I kissed you. I don't have any excuse, other than fear."

She blinked at him, wondering why she had never noticed those dark blue speckles in his eyes. "Of what?"

"This. You." His mouth danced across hers again and everything feminine inside her sighed with delight.

"I want you." His voice was little more than a low rasp that sent every nerve ending firing madly. "I want you more than I've ever wanted another woman in my life and it scares the hell out of me."

"I'm just a woman. What's to be scared about?"

He laughed roughly. "That's like a saber-toothed tiger saying I'm just a nice little kitty. You are no ordinary woman, Tess."

Before she could figure out whether he meant the words as a compliment, he deepened the kiss and she decided she didn't care, as long as he continued this delicious assault on her senses.

He lowered her to the floor and she held him tightly as all the sleepy desires she had buried deep inside for years bubbled to the surface. It had been so long—so very, very long—since she had been held and cherished like this and she wanted to savor every second.

The taste of him, the scent of him, the implacable strength of his arms around her. It all felt perfect. *He* felt perfect.

She supposed that was silly, given the slightly unromantic circumstances. Instead of candlelight and rose petals and soft pillows, they were on the hard floor of her spare room with bright fluorescent lights gleaming.

But she wouldn't have changed any of it, especially at the risk of shattering this hazy, delicious cocoon of desire wrapped around them.

Okay, she might wish she were wearing something a little more sensual, especially when his hands went to the buttons of her old work shirt. But he didn't seem to mind her clothing, judging by the heavy-lidded hunger in his eyes after he had worked the buttons free and the plackets of her shirt fell away.

She should have felt exposed here in the unforgiving light of the room. Instead, she felt feminine and eminently desirable as his eyes darkened.

"You're gorgeous," he murmured. "The most beautiful thing I've ever seen."

"I'm afraid I'm not the tight-bodied cheerleader I was at sixteen."

"Who wants some silly cheerleader when he could have a saber-toothed tiger of a woman in his arms?"

She laughed but it turned into a ragged gasp when he slowly caressed her through the fabric of her bra, his fingers hard and masculine against her breast.

He groaned, low in his throat, and his thumb deftly traced the skin just above the lacy cup. Everything tightened inside her, a lovely swell of tension as he worked the clasp free, and she nearly arched off the floor when his fingers covered her skin.

He teased and explored her body while his mouth tantalized hers with deep, silky tastes and her hands explored the hard muscles of his back and the thick softness of his hair.

"This is crazy," he said after long, delirious moments. "It's not what I came here for, I swear."

"Don't think about it," she advised him, nipping little kisses down the warm column of his neck. "I know I'm not."

His laugh turned into a groan as she feathered more kisses along his jawline. "Well, when you put it that way..."

She smiled, then gasped when he began trailing kisses down the side of her throat. Every coherent thought skittered out of her head when his mouth found her breast. She tangled her hands in his hair, arching into his mouth as he tasted and teased.

Oh, heaven. She felt as if she had been waiting years just for this, just for him, as if everything inside her had been frozen away until he came back to Pine Gulch to thaw all those lonely, forgotten little corners of her heart.

She thought again how very perfect, inevitable, this was as he pulled her shirt off and then removed his own.

He was beautiful. The rough-edged, rebellious boy had grown into a hard, dangerous man, all powerful muscles and masculine hollows and strength. She wanted to explore every single inch of that smooth skin.

She would, she vowed. Even if it took all night. Or several nights. It was a sacrifice she was fully willing to make.

Again she had that sense of inescapable destiny. They

had been moving toward this moment since that first night he had startled her in the hallway of Winder Ranch. Longer, even. Maybe all that dancing around each other they had done in high school had just been a prelude to this.

A few moments later, no clothing barriers remained between them and she exulted in the sheer delicious wonder of his skin brushing hers, his strength surrounding her softness.

He kissed her and a restless need started deep inside her and expanded out in hot, hungry waves. She couldn't get enough of this, of him. She traced a hand over his pectoral muscles, feeling the leashed strength in him.

And then she forgot everything when he reached a hand between their bodies to the aching core of her hunger. She gasped his name, shifting restlessly against his fingers, and everything inside her coiled with a sweet, urgent ache of anticipation.

She felt edgy, panicky suddenly, as if the room were spinning too fast for her to ride along, but his kiss kept her centered in the midst of the tornado of sensation. She wrapped her arms around his neck, her breathing ragged.

He kissed her then, his mouth hot, insistent, demanding. That was all it took. With a sharp cry, she let go of what tiny tendrils of control remained and flung herself into the whirling, breathtaking maelstrom.

Even before the last delicious tremors had faded, he produced a condom from his wallet and entered her with one swift movement.

Long unused muscles stretched to welcome him and he groaned, pressing his forehead to hers.

"So tight," he murmured.

"I'm sorry."

His laugh was rough and tickled her skin. "I don't believe I was complaining."

He kissed her fiercely, possessively, and just like that, she could feel her body rise to meet his again.

With her hands gripped tightly in his, he moved inside her and she arched restlessly against him, her body seeking more, burning for completion. And then she could sense a change in him, feel the taut edginess in every touch. Her mouth tangled with his and at the slick brush of his tongue against hers, she climaxed again, with a core-deep sigh of delight.

He froze above her, his muscles corded, and then he groaned and joined her in the storm.

He came back to earth with a powerful sense of the surreal. None of this seemed to be truly happening. Not the hard floor beneath his shoulders or the soft, warm curves in his arms or this unaccustomed contentment stealing through him.

It was definitely genuine, though. He could feel her pulse against his arm where her head lay nestled and smell that delectable scent of her.

"How could I have forgotten?" she murmured.

He angled his head to better see her expression. "Forgotten what?"

She smiled and he was struck again by her breathtaking beauty. She was like some rare, exquisite flower that bloomed in secret just for him.

"This radiant feeling. Total contentment. As if for a few short moments, everything is perfect in the world."

He smiled, enchanted by her. "You don't think everything would be a tad more perfect if we happened to be in a soft bed somewhere instead of on the bare floor of your ripped-apart spare room? I think I've got paint chips in places I'm not sure I should mention."

She made a face, though he saw laughter dancing in her eyes. "Go ahead. Ruin the moment for me."

"Sorry. It's just been a long time since I've been so... carried away."

"I know exactly what you mean."

He studied her. "How long?"

Her lovely green-eyed gaze met his, then flickered away. "Since the night before Scott's accident. So that would be eight years, if anyone's counting."

"In all that time, not once?"

As soon as his shocked words escaped, he realized they weren't very tactful, but she didn't seem offended.

"I loved my husband," she said solemnly. "Even if he wasn't quite the man I expected to spend the rest of my life with when I married him, I loved him and I honored my wedding vows."

He pulled her closer, stunned at her loyalty and devotion. She had put her life, her future, completely on hold for years to care for a man who could never be the sort of husband a young woman needed.

Most women he knew would have felt perfectly justified in resuming their own lives after such a tragic accident. They might have mourned their husband for a while but would have been quick to put the past behind them.

He thought of his own mother, selfish and feckless, who wasn't happy unless she was the center of attention. She wouldn't have had the first idea how to cope after such a tragedy.

Not Tess. She had stayed, had sacrificed her youth for her husband.

"Scott was an incredibly fortunate man to have you."

Her eyes softened. "Thank you, Quinn." She kissed him gently, her mouth warm and soft, and he was astonished at the fragile tenderness that fluttered through him like dry leaves on the autumn wind.

"Can I stay?" he asked. "It's…harder than I expected to hang out at the ranch right now."

She smiled against his mouth and her kiss left no question in his mind about what her answer would be.

"Of course. I would love you to stay. And I even have a bed in the other room, believe it or not."

He rose and pulled her to her feet, stunned all over again at the peace welling inside him. He didn't think he had come here for this on a conscious level, but perhaps some part of him knew she would welcome him, would soothe the ache in his heart with that easy nurturing that was such a part of her.

"Show me," he murmured.

Her smile was brilliant and took his breath away as she took him by the hand and led him from the room.

She was having a torrid affair.

Two days later, Tess could hardly believe it, even when the evidence was sprawled beside her, wide shoulders propped against her headboard, looking rugged and masculine against the dainty yellow frills and flowers of her bedroom.

The fluffy comforter on her bed covered him to the waist and she found the contrast between the feminine fabric and the hard planes and hollows of his muscled chest infinitely arousing.

She sighed softly, wondering if she would ever get tired of looking at him, touching him, laughing with him.

For two days, they hadn't left her house, except for

sneaking in one quick trip to Winder Ranch in the middle of the night for him to grab some extra clothes and toiletries.

What would the rest of the town think if news spread that the sainted Tess Claybourne was engaged in a wild, torrid relationship with Quinn Southerland, the former bad boy of Pine Gulch?

Enthusiastically engaged, no less. She flushed at the memory of her response to him, of the heat and magic and connection they had shared the past few days. The sensual, passionate woman she had become in his arms seemed like a stranger, as if she had stored up all these feelings and desires inside her through the past eight years.

She didn't know whether to be embarrassed or thrilled that she had discovered this part of herself with him.

"You're blushing," he said now with an interested look. "What are you thinking about?"

"You. This. I was thinking about how I had no idea I could…that we could…"

Her voice trailed off as she struggled with words to finish the sentence. Her own discomfort astounded her. How could she possibly possess even a hint of awkwardness after everything they had done together within these walls, all the secrets they had shared?

He didn't seem to need any explanation.

"You absolutely can. And we absolutely have."

He grinned, looking male and gorgeous and so completely content with the world that she couldn't help laughing.

This was the other thing that shocked her, that she could have such fun with him. He wasn't at all the intense, brooding rebel she had thought when they were younger. Quinn had a sly sense of humor and a keen sense of the ridiculous.

They laughed about everything from a silly horror movie

they watched on TV in the middle of the night to the paint flecks in her hair after they made one half-hearted attempt to continue working on the trim in the guest room to a phone call from Easton the day before, wondering if Tess had kidnapped him.

And they had talked, endlessly. About his memories of the other Four Winds, about growing up on the ranch, about her friends and family and the miracle of how she had been led to become a nurse long before Scott's accident when those skills would become so vital.

They had also talked a great deal about his foster mother and also about Guff. He seemed to find great comfort in sharing memories with her. That he would trust her with those memories touched and warmed her, more than she could ever express. She hoped his sorrow eased a little as he brought those events and people to life for her.

"I wish it didn't have to end," she murmured now, then wished she could recall the words.

No regrets, she had promised herself that first night. She intended only to seize every ounce of happiness she could with him and then let him go with a glad heart that she had this chance to share a few wonderful days with him.

He traced a hand along her bare arm. "I wish I could put off my return to Seattle. But I've been away too long as it is. My plane's coming tomorrow."

"I know."

Her smile felt tight, forced, as she fought to hide the sadness hovering just out of reach at his impending departure.

How had he become so very important to her in just a few short weeks? Even the idea of moving to Portland, starting over with new friends and different employment challenges, had lost much of its luster.

Ridiculous, she told herself. She couldn't let herself fall

into a funk over the inevitable end of a passionate, albeit brief, affair, even one with the man who had fascinated her for two decades.

"We should do something," he said suddenly.

She took in the rumpled bedclothes and the hard muscles of his bare chest. "I thought we *had* been doing something."

His sensual smile just about took her breath away. "I meant go to dinner or something. It's not fair for me to keep you chained up in the bedroom for two days without even offering to feed you."

"We haven't tried the chained-up thing."

"Yet."

Her insides shivered at the single word in that low growl of a voice.

"We could go to The Gulch," he suggested, apparently unaffected by the same sudden vivid fantasies that flashed across her mind.

She pushed them away, wondering what the regulars or Lou and Donna Archuleta would think if she showed up in the café with Quinn looking rumpled and well-loved. What did she care? she thought. She deserved some happiness and fun in her life and if she found that with Quinn, it was nobody's damn business but theirs.

"What about the others?" she asked. "Easton and Brant and Cisco? Don't you think you ought to spend your last night in town with them?"

He made a face, though she thought he looked struck by the reminder of his friends and the shared loss that had brought them all together.

"I should," he finally admitted. "I stayed an extra few days after the funeral to spend time with them but I ended up a little...distracted."

She pulled away from him and slipped her arms through her robe. "I should never have monopolized all your time."

"It was a mutual monopoly. I wanted to be here."

"If you want to spend your last evening at the ranch with them, please don't feel you can't because of me. Because of this."

"Why do I have to choose? We should all go to dinner together."

She frowned. "I'm not one of you, Quinn."

"After the past two weeks, you feel as much a part of the family as any of us."

She wanted to argue that the others would probably want him to themselves and she couldn't blame them. But she had discovered she had a selfish streak hiding inside her. She couldn't give up the chance to spend at least a few more hours with him.

Chapter 13

In her heart, Tess knew she didn't belong here with the others but she couldn't remember an evening she had enjoyed more.

Several hours later, she sat at the table in the Winder Ranch dining room and sipped at her wine, listening to the flow of conversation eddy around her.

When they weren't teasing Easton about something, they were reminiscing about some camping trip Guff took them on into Yellowstone or the moose that chased them once along the shores of Hayden Lake or snowmobiling into the high country.

In every word and gesture, it was obvious they loved each other deeply, despite a few rough moments in the conversation.

Most notably, something was definitely up between Easton and Cisco, Tess thought. Though outwardly Easton treated him just as she did Brant and Quinn, with a sisterly sort of affection, Tess could sense braided ropes of tension tugging between the two of them.

They sat on opposite sides of the table and Easton was careful to avoid looking at him for very long.

What was it? she wondered. Had they fought about something? She had a feeling this wasn't something recent in origin as she remembered Easton's strange reaction whenever Cisco's name had been mentioned, before he made it back to the ranch. Obviously, her feelings were different for him than for Brant and Quinn and Tess wondered if anybody else but her was aware of it.

They all seemed so different to her and yet it was obvious they were a unit. Easton, who loved the ranch and was the only one of the Four Winds not to wander away from it. Brant, the solemn, honorable soldier who seemed to be struggling with internal demons she couldn't begin to guess at. Cisco, who by his demeanor appeared to be a thrill-seeking adventurer type, though she sensed there was much more to him than he revealed.

And then there was Quinn.

Around the others, these three people who were his closest friends and the only family he had left, he was warm and affectionate as they laughed and talked and shared memories and she was enthralled by him all over again.

She was the odd person out but Quinn had insisted she join them, even after Easton suggested they grill steaks at the ranch instead of going out to dinner.

The ranch house seemed empty without Jo. She wondered how Easton endured it—and how her friend would cope when she was alone here at the ranch after the men went their respective ways once more.

"Do you remember that snow prank?" Cisco said with a laugh. "That was classic, man. A masterpiece."

"I still can't believe you guys drove all the way into Idaho Falls just to rent a fake snow machine," Easton said, still not looking at Cisco.

"Hey, I tried to talk them out of it," Brant defended himself.

Quinn gave a rough laugh. "But you still drove the getaway car after we broke into the gymnasium and sprayed the Sweetheart Dance decorations with six inches of fake snow."

Tess set down her fork and narrowed her gaze at the men. "Wait a minute. That was you?"

"Uh-oh. You are so busted." Easton grinned at Quinn.

"I worked on that dance planning committee for weeks! I can't believe you would be so blatantly destructive."

"We were just trying to help out with the theme," Quinn said. "Wasn't it something about snuggling in with your sweetheart for Valentine's Day? What better time to snuggle than in the middle of a blizzard and six inches of snow?"

She gave him a mock glare. "Nice try."

"It was a long time ago. I say we all forgive and forget," Brant said, winking at Tess.

"Do you have any idea how long it takes to clean up six inches of snow from a high-school gymnasium?"

"Hey, blame it all on Quinn. I was an innocent sophomore he dragged along for the ride," Cisco said with a grin.

"You were never innocent," Easton muttered.

He sent her a quick look out of hooded dark eyes. "True enough."

Tess could feel the tension sizzle between them, though the other two men seemed oblivious to it. She wondered if any of them saw the anguished expression in Easton's eyes as she watched Cisco.

The other woman suddenly shoved her chair away

from the table. "Anybody up for dessert?" she asked, a falsely bright note to her voice. "Jenna McRaven owed me a favor so I talked her into making some of her famous turtle cheesecake."

"That would be great," Brant said. "Thank you."

"Quinn? Cisco?"

Both men readily agreed and Easton headed for the kitchen.

"I'll help," Tess offered, sliding her chair away from the table. "But don't think I've forgotten the snow prank. As to forgiving, I don't believe there's a statute of limitations on prosecution for breaking the spirit of the high-school dance committee."

All three of the men laughed as she left the room, apparently unfazed by her empty threat.

In the kitchen, she found Easton reaching into the refrigerator. She emerged holding a delectable-looking dessert drizzled in chocolate and caramel and chopped nuts.

"All right, out with it," Easton said as she set the cheesecake on the counter, and Tess realized this was the first chance they'd had all evening to speak privately.

"With what?" Tess asked in as innocent a voice as she could muster, though she had a feeling she sounded no more innocent than Cisco had.

"You and Quinn. He's been gone from the ranch for two entire days! What's going on with you two?"

She turned pink, remembering the passion and fun of the past two days.

"Nothing. Not really. We're just… He's just…"

"You're right. It's none of my business," Easton said as she sliced the cheesecake and began transferring it to serving plates. "Sorry I asked."

"It's not that, I just… I can't really explain it."

Easton was silent for a long moment. "Are you sure you know what you're dealing with when it comes to Quinn?" she finally asked with a searching look. "I wouldn't be a friend if I didn't ask."

"He's leaving tomorrow. I completely understand that."

"Do you?"

Tess nodded, even as her heart gave a sad little twist. "Of course. These past few days have been…magical, but I know it's only temporary. His life is in Seattle. Mine is here, at least for the next few weeks until I move to Portland."

"Seattle and Portland aren't so far apart that you couldn't connect if you wanted to," Easton pointed out.

She wouldn't think about that, especially after she had worked so hard to convince herself their relationship was only temporary, born out of shared grief and stunning, surprising hunger.

"I care about you," Easton said when Tess didn't answer. "We owe you so much for these past weeks with Aunt Jo. You carried all of us through it. I mean that, Tess. You always knew exactly what to say and what to do, no matter what was happening, and I'll be forever grateful to you for all you did for her. That's why I'll be absolutely furious if Quinn takes advantage of your natural compassion and ends up hurting you."

"He won't. I promise."

Easton didn't look convinced. Not surprising, she supposed, since Tess couldn't even manage to convince herself.

"It's just…he doesn't have a great track record when it comes to women," her friend said quietly.

Tess tried hard to make her sudden fierce interest in that particular subject seem casual. "Really?"

"I love him like a brother and have since he came to the ranch. But I'm not blind to his faults, especially when it comes to women. I don't think Quinn has ever had a relationship that has lasted longer than a few weeks. To be honest, I'm not sure he's capable of it."

"Never?"

"I can't be certain, I suppose. He's been away for a long time. But every time I ask about his social life when we talk on the phone or email, he mentions he's dating someone new."

"Maybe he just hasn't met anyone he wants to get serious with. There's nothing wrong with that."

"I think it's more than that, Tess. If I had to guess, I would assume it has something to do with his parents' marriage. He didn't have an easy childhood and I think it's made him gun-shy about relationships and commitment."

"I'm sure it did. He told me about his parents and his messed-up home life."

Surprise flashed in her blue eyes. "He did?"

She nodded. "It can't be easy getting past something like that."

"When we were kids, he vowed over and over that he was never going to get married. To be honest, judging by his track record, I don't think he's changed his mind one bit. It broke Jo's heart, if you want the truth. She wanted to see us all settled before she died, but that didn't happen, did it?"

Tess forced a smile, though the cracks in her own heart widened a little more. "Easton, it's okay. I'm not interested in something long-term right now with Quinn or anyone else. We both needed…peace for a while after Jo's death and we enjoy each other's company. That's all there is to it."

Easton didn't look at all convinced and Tess decided to change the uncomfortable subject.

"What time does Cisco leave tomorrow?" she asked.

The diversion worked exactly as she hoped. Easton's

expression of concern slid into something else entirely, something stark and painful.

"A few hours." Her hand shook a little as she set the last slice of cheesecake on a small serving plate. "He's catching a plane out of Salt Lake City to Central America at noon tomorrow, so he'll be leaving in the early hours of the morning."

Tess covered her hand and Easton gave her an anguished look.

"Without Jo here, I don't know if he'll ever come back. Or Quinn, for that matter. Brant at least has his own ranch up the canyon so I'm sure I'll at least see him occasionally. But the other two…" Her voice trailed off. "Nothing will be the same without Aunt Jo."

Tess pulled Easton into a hug. "It won't be the same," she agreed. "But you're still here. They'll come back for you."

"I don't know about that."

"They will." Tess gave her friend a little shake. "Anyway, Jo would be the first one to tell you to seize every moment. They might not be back for a while but they're here now. Don't sour the joy you can find tonight with them by stewing about what might be coming tomorrow."

"You must be channeling Jo now. I can almost hear her in my head saying exactly those same words."

"Then you'd better listen." Tess smiled.

Easton sighed. "We'd better get this cheesecake out there before they come looking for us."

"Can you give me a minute? I need some water, but I'll be right out."

Easton gave her a searching look. "Are you sure you're all right?"

Tess forced a smile. "Of course. You've got three men waiting for dessert out there. You'd better hurry."

After a pause, Easton nodded and carried the tray with the cheesecake slices out to the dining room.

When she was alone in the bright, cheery kitchen, Tess leaned against the counter and fought the urge to cover her face with her hands and weep.

She was a terrible liar. Lucky for her, Easton was too wrapped up in her own troubles to pay close attention.

She absolutely *wasn't* okay, and she had a sinking feeling she wouldn't be for a long, long time.

I'm not interested in something long-term right now with Quinn or anyone else.

It was a wonder Jo didn't rise up and smite her for telling such a blatant fib in the middle of her kitchen.

Finally, she admitted to herself the truth she had been fighting for two days. Longer, probably. The truth that had been hovering just on the edges of her subconscious.

She was in love with him.

With Quinn Southerland, who planned to blow out of her life like the south wind in the morning.

She loved the way his mouth quirked up at the edges when he teased her about something. She loved his tender care of Jo in her final days and his deep appreciation of the family and home he had found here. She loved the strength and honor that had carried him through incredible trauma as a boy.

She loved the way he made her feel, cherished and beautiful and *wanted*, and the heat and abandon she experienced in his arms.

And she especially loved that he knew the very worst parts of her and wanted to spend time with her anyway.

Whatever was she going to do without him in her world? Just the thought of going through the motions after he returned to Seattle left her achy and heartsore.

She knew she would survive. What other choice did she have?

That didn't mean she wanted to. Hadn't she faced enough heartache? Just once in her life, couldn't things work out the way she wanted?

Fighting back a sob, she moved to the sink and poured a glass of water so she could convince herself she hadn't completely prevaricated to Easton.

She thought of her advice to her friend a few moments earlier.

Don't sour the joy you can find in today by stewing about what might be coming tomorrow.

She couldn't ruin these last few hours with him by anticipating the pain she knew waited for her around the corner.

Something was wrong.

He never claimed to be the most perceptive of men when it came to the opposite sex, but even *he* could tell Tess was distracted and troubled after dinner when he drove her back from the ranch to town.

She said little, mostly gazed out the window at the lights flickering in the darkness, few and far between in Cold Creek Canyon and becoming more concentrated as he approached the town limits.

He glanced over at her profile, thinking how serenely lovely she was. He supposed her pensiveness was rubbing off on him because he still couldn't quite process the surreal twist his life had taken these past few days.

If Brant or Cisco—or Easton, even—had told him before he came back to town that he would wrap up his visit to Pine Gulch in Tess Jamison Claybourne's bed, he would have thought it was some kind of a strange, twisted joke.

Until he showed up at the ranch a few weeks ago, he honestly hadn't thought of her much in years. He was too busy working his tail off building his business to waste much time or energy on such an unimportant—though undeniably aggravating—part of his past.

On the rare occasions when thoughts of her did filter through his mind for whatever reason, they were usually tainted with acrimony and disdain.

In these past weeks, she had become so much more to him.

Quinn let out a breath. He had tried to avoid examining those fragile, tender feelings too carefully. He appreciated her care for Jo, admired the strength she had demonstrated through her own personal tragedy, found her incredibly sexy.

He didn't want to poke and prod more deeply than that, afraid to unravel the tangled mess of his feelings.

He did know he didn't want to leave her or the haven he had found in her arms.

His hands tightened on the steering wheel as he turned down the street toward her house. For two weeks, his associates had taken the helm of Southerland Shipping. Quinn ought to be ecstatic at the idea of jumping right back into the middle of the action. Strategizing, making decisions, negotiating contracts. It was all in his blood, the one thing he found he was good at, and he had certainly missed the work while he had been at Winder Ranch.

But every time he thought about saying goodbye to Tess, he started to feel restless and uneasy and he had no idea why.

He pulled into the driveway and turned off the engine to his rented SUV.

"You probably want to be with the others," she said, her voice low. "I don't mind if we say goodbye now."

Something remarkably like panic fluttered through him. "Are you that anxious to be rid of me?"

She turned wide green eyes toward him. "No. Nothing like that! I just... I assumed you would want to spend your last few hours in town with your friends," she said, a vulnerable note to her voice that shocked him.

Though he had already said his farewells to the others when he left the house, with lots of hugs and backslapping, he considered taking the out she was offering him. Maybe he ought to just gather his few belongings from her house and head back to bunk at the ranch for the night. That made perfect sense and would help him begin the process of rebuilding all those protective walls around his emotions.

But he had a few more hours in Pine Gulch and he couldn't bear the thought of leaving her yet.

"I'd like to stay."

He said the words as more of a question than a statement. After an endless moment when he was quite certain she was going to tell him to hit the road, she nodded, much to his vast relief, and reached for his hand.

A soft, terrifying sweetness unfurled inside him at the touch of her hand in his.

How was he going to walk away in a few hours from this woman who had in a few short weeks become so vitally important to him? He didn't have the first idea.

Chapter 14

She didn't release his hand, even as she unlocked her door to let them both inside. When he closed the door behind him, she kissed him with a fierce, almost desperate, hunger.

They didn't even make it past her living room, clawing at clothes, ripping at buttons, tangling mouths with a fiery passion that stunned him.

They had made love in a dozen different ways over the past few days—easy, teasing, urgent, soft.

But never with this explosive heat that threatened to consume them both. She climaxed the instant he entered her and he groaned as her body pulsed around him and followed her just seconds later.

He kissed her, trying to memorize every taste and texture as she clutched him tightly to her. To his amazement, after just a few moments, his body started to stir again inside her and he could feel by her response that she was becoming aroused again.

He carried her to the bedroom and took enough time to undress both of them, wondering if he would ever get enough of her silky curves and the warm, sweet welcome of her body.

This time was slow, tender, with an edge of poignancy to it that made his chest ache. Did she sense it, too? he wondered.

They tasted and touched for a long time, until both of them were breathless, boneless. She cried out his name when she climaxed and he thought she said something else against his shoulder but he couldn't understand the words.

When he could breathe again and manage to string together two semicoherent thoughts, he pulled her close under the crook of his arm, memorizing the feel of her—the curves and hollows, the soft delight of her skin.

"I wish I didn't have to go," he murmured again.

Instead of smiling or perhaps expressing the same regret, she froze in his arms and then pulled away.

Though her bedroom was well-heated against the October chill, he was instantly cold, as he watched her slip her slender arms through the sleeves of her silky green robe that matched her eyes.

"Are you lying for my sake or to appease your own guilt?" she finally asked him.

He blinked, disoriented at the rapid-fire shift from tender and passionate to this unexpected attack that instantly set him on the defensive.

"Why do I have to be lying?"

"Come on, Quinn," she said, her voice almost sad. "We both know you're not sorry. Not really."

He bristled. "When did you become such an expert on what's going on inside my head?"

"I could never claim such omnipotent power. Nor would I want it."

Okay. He absolutely did not understand how a woman's mind worked. How could she pick a fight with him after the incredible intensity they just shared? Was she just trying to make their inevitable parting easier?

"If you could see inside my head," he answered carefully, "you would see I meant every word. I *do* wish I didn't have so many obligations waiting for me back in Seattle. These past few days have been…peaceful and I don't have much of that in my life."

She gazed at him, her features tight with an expression he didn't recognize. After a moment, her prickly mood seemed to slide away and she smiled, though it didn't quite push away that strange, almost bereft look in her eyes.

"I'm happy for that, Quinn. You deserve a little peace in your life and I'm glad you found it here."

She paused and looked away from him. "But we both knew from the beginning that this would never be anything but temporary."

Whenever he let himself think beyond the wonder of the moment, the shared laughter and unexpected joy he found with her, he had assumed exactly that—this was supposed to be a short-term relationship that wouldn't extend beyond these few magical days.

Hearing the words from her somehow made the reality seem more bluntly desolate.

"Does it have to be?"

"Of course," she answered briskly. "What other option is there?"

He told himself that wasn't hurt churning through him at her dismissal of all they had shared and at the potential for them to share more.

"Portland is only a few hours from Seattle. We could certainly still see each other on the weekends."

She tightened the sash on her robe with fingers that seemed to tremble slightly. From the cold? he wondered. Or from something else?

"To what end?" she asked. "Great sex and amusing conversation?"

Despite his turmoil, he couldn't resist arching an eyebrow. "Something wrong with either of those?"

Her laugh sounded rough. "Not at all. Believe me, I've become a big fan of both these past few days."

She shoved her hands in the pockets of her robe and drew in a deep breath, as if steeling herself for unpleasantness. "But I'm afraid neither is enough for me."

That edgy disquiet from earlier returned in full force and he was aware of a pitiful impulse to beg her not to push him from her life.

He wouldn't, though. He had a sudden, ugly flashback of his mother at the dinner table trying desperately to catch his father's attention any way she could. New earrings, new silverware, a difficult new recipe. Only until she managed to push one of his father's hot buttons would he even notice her, and then only to rant and rail and sometimes worse.

He pushed it away. He certainly wasn't his mother trying desperately in her own sick way to make someone care who wasn't really capable of it. Tess was not like his father. She had a deep capacity for love. He had seen it with Jo, even Easton and Brant and Cisco.

Why else would she have stayed with an invalid husband for so long?

But maybe she couldn't care for *him*. Maybe he didn't deserve someone like her...

"I want more," she said quietly, interrupting the grim

direction of his thoughts. "All I wanted when I was a girl was a home and a family and a husband who cherished me. I wanted what my parents had. They held hands in the movies and whispered secrets to each other in restaurants and hid love notes for each other all around the house. My mom's still finding them, years after Dad died. That's what I wanted."

He was silent. If not for the years he spent with Jo and Guff seeing just that sort of relationship, he would have had absolutely no frame of reference to understand what she was talking about, but the Winders had shared a love like that, deep and rich and genuine.

"I thought I found that with Scott," Tess went on, "but fate had other plans and things didn't turn out quite the way I dreamed."

"I'm sorry." He meant the words. He hated thinking of her enduring such loss and pain as a young bride.

"I'm sorry, too," she said quietly. "But that time in my life is over. I'm ready to move forward now."

"I can understand that. But why can't you move forward with me? We have something good here. You know we do."

She was silent for a long time and he thought perhaps he was making progress on getting her to see his point of view. But when she spoke, her voice was low and sad.

"Easton told me tonight that when you were younger, you vowed you were never getting married."

"What a guy says when he's fifteen and what he says when he's thirty-four are two very different things," he said, though he had said that very same sentiment to Jo in the garden at Winder Ranch just a few weeks ago.

She sat on the bed and he didn't miss the way she was careful to keep plenty of space between them. "Okay, tell me the truth. Say we continue to see each other for those weekends you were talking about. Look ahead several months, maybe a year, with a few days a month of more of that great sex and amusing conversation."

"I can do that," he said, and spent several very pleasant seconds imagining kissing her on the dock of his house on Mercer Island, of taking her up in his boat for a quick run to Victoria, of standing beside the ocean on the Oregon Coast at a wonderfully romantic boutique hotel he knew in Cannon Beach.

"So here it is a year in the future," she said, dousing his hazy fantasies like a cold surf. "Say we've seen each other exclusively for that time and have come to...to care about each other. Where do you see things going from there?"

"I don't know. What do you want me to see?"

"Marriage. Family. Can you ever even imagine yourself contemplating a forever sort of relationship with me or anyone else?"

Marriage. Kids. A dog. Panic spurted through him. Though Jo and Guff had shared a good marriage and he had spent a few years watching their example, for most of his childhood, marriage had meant cold silences alternated with screaming fights and tantrums, culminating in terrible violence that had changed his world forever.

"Maybe," he managed to say after a moment. "Who's to say? That would be a long way in the future. Why do we have to jump from here to there in an instant?"

Her sigh was heavy, almost sad. "I saw that panic in your eyes, Quinn. You can't even consider the idea of it in some long-distant future without being spooked."

"That could change. I don't see why we have to ruin this. Why can't we just enjoy what we have in the moment?"

She didn't answer him right away. "You know, brain injuries are peculiar, unpredictable things," she finally said, baffling him with the seemingly random shift in topic.

"Are they?"

"The same injury in the same spot can affect two people in completely different ways. For the first two or three years after Scott's accident, all the doctors and specialists kept telling me not to give up hope, that things would get better. He could still improve and start regaining function some day."

Through his confusion, Quinn's heart always ached when he thought of Tess facing all that on her own.

"I waited and hoped and prayed," she went on. "Through all those years and promises, I felt as if I were frozen in the moment, that the world went on while I was stuck in place, waiting for something that never happened."

She paused. "He did improve, in minuscule ways. I don't want you to think he didn't. Near the end, he could hold his head up for long periods of time and even started laughing at my silly jokes again. But it was not nearly the recovery I dreamed about in those early days."

"Tess, I'm very sorry you went through that. But I don't understand your point."

She swallowed and didn't meet his gaze. "My point is that I spent years waiting for reality to match up to my expectations, waiting for him to change. Even being angry when those expectations weren't met, when in truth, he simply wasn't capable of it. It wasn't his fault. Just the way things were."

He stared. "So you're comparing me to someone who was critically brain-injured in a car accident?"

She sighed. "Not at all, Quinn. I'm talking about myself. One of the greatest lessons Scott's accident taught me was pragmatism. I can't hang on to unrealistic dreams and hopes anymore. I want marriage and children and you don't. It's as simple as that."

"Does it have to be?"

"For me, yes. Your views might change. I hope for your sake they do. Caring for Scott all those years taught me that the only way we can really find purpose and meaning in life is if we somehow manage to move outside ourselves to embrace the chances we're offered to care for someone else."

She lifted moist eyes to his. "I hope you change your mind, Quinn. But what if you don't? Say we see each other for six months or a year and then you decide you're still no closer to shifting your perspective about home and family. I would have spent another year moving further away from my dreams. I can't do that to myself or to you."

That panic from before churned through him, icy and sharp. He didn't want to lose what they had shared these past few days.

Or maybe it didn't mean as much to her. Why else would she be so willing to throw it all away? Maybe he *was* just like his mother, trying desperately to keep her from pushing him away.

No. This wasn't about that. The fear and panic warring inside him took on an edge of anger.

"This is it, then?" His voice turned hard, ugly. "I was here to scratch an itch for you and now you're shoving me out the door."

Her lovely features paled. "Not fair."

"Fair? Don't talk to me about fair." He jumped out of the bed and reached for his Levis, still in a heap on the floor. He couldn't seem to stop the ugly words from spilling out like toxic effluent.

"You know what I just realized? You haven't changed a bit since your days as Queen Bee at Pine Gulch High.

You're still the spoiled, manipulative girl you were in high school. You want what you want and to hell with anybody else and whatever they might need."

"This has nothing to do with high school or the person I was back then."

"Wrong. This has *everything* to do with Tess Jamison, Homecoming Queen. You can't have what you want, your little fantasy happily-ever-after, and so kicking me out of your life completely is your version of throwing a pissy little temper tantrum."

His gazed narrowed as another repugnant thought occurred to him.

"Or wait. Maybe that's not it at all. Maybe this is all some manipulative trick, the kind you used to be so very good at. Don't forget, I had years of experience watching you bat your eyes at some poor idiot, all the while you're tightening the noose around his neck without him having the first clue what you're doing. Maybe you think if you push me out now, in a few weeks I'll come running back with tears and apologies, ready to give you anything you want. Even that all-important wedding ring that's apparently the only thing you think matters."

"You're being ridiculous."

"You forget, I was the chief recipient of all those dirty tricks you perfected in high school. The lies. The rumors you spread. This is just one more trick, isn't it? Well, guess what? I'm not playing your games now, any more than I was willing to do it back then."

She stood on the other side of the room now, her arms folded across her chest and hurt and anger radiating from her.

"You can't get past it, can you?" She shook her head. "I have apologized and tried to show you I'm a different person than I was then. But you refuse to even consider the possibility that I might have changed."

He had considered it. He had even believed it for a while.

"Only one of us is stuck in the past, Quinn. Life has changed me and given me a new perspective. But somewhere deep inside you, you're still a boy stuck in the ugliness of his parents' marriage."

He stared at her, angry that she would turn this all back around on him when she was the one being a manipulative bitch.

"You're crazy."

"Am I? I think the reason you won't let yourself have more than casual relationships with women is because you're so determined not to turn into either one of your parents. You're not about to become your powerless, emotionally needy mother or your workaholic, abusive father. So you've decided somewhere deep in your psyche that your best bet is to just keep everyone else at arm's length so you don't have to risk either option."

He was so furious, he couldn't think straight. Her assessment was brutal and harsh and he refused to admit that it might also be true.

"Now you're some kind of armchair psychiatrist?"

"No. Just a woman who…cares about you, Quinn."

"You've got a hell of a way of showing it by pushing me away."

"I'm not pushing you away." Her voice shook and he saw tears in her eyes. Either she was a much better actress than he could possibly imagine or that was genuine regret in her eyes. He didn't know which to believe.

"You have no idea how hard this is for me," she said and one of those tears trickled down the side of her nose. "I've come to care about you these past few weeks. Maybe I always did, a little. But as much as I have loved these past few days and part of me wants nothing more than to continue seeing you after I move to Portland, it wouldn't be fair to either of us. You can't be the kind of man I want and I'm afraid I would eventually come to hate you for that."

His arms ached from the effort it took not to reach for her but he kept his hands fisted at his sides. "So that's it. See you later, thanks for the good time in the sack and all that."

"If you want to be crude about it."

He didn't. He wanted to grab her and hang on tight and tell her he would be whatever kind of man she wanted him to be. He had discovered a safety, a serenity, with her he hadn't found anywhere else and the idea of leaving it behind left him hollow and achy.

But she was right. He couldn't offer her the things she needed. He could lie and tell her otherwise but both of them would see through it and end up even more unhappy.

"I suppose there's nothing left to say, then, is there?"

She released a shuddering kind of breath and he supposed he should be somewhat mollified that her eyes reflected the same kind of pain shredding his insides.

"I'm sorry."

"So am I, Tess."

He grabbed his things and walked out the door, hoping despite himself that she would call him back, tell him she didn't mean anything she'd said.

But the only sound as he climbed into his rental car was the mournful October wind in the trees and the distant howl of a coyote.

Tess stood at the window of her bedroom watching Quinn's taillights disappear into the night.

She couldn't seem to catch her breath and she felt as if

she'd just been bucked off one of the Winder Ranch horses, then kicked in the chest for good measure.

Had she been wrong? Maybe she should have just taken whatever crumbs Quinn could offer, to hell with the inevitable pain she knew waited for her in some murky future.

At least then she wouldn't have this raw, devastating feeling that she had just made a terrible mistake.

With great effort, she forced herself to draw in a deep breath and then another and another, willing her common sense to override the visceral pain and vast emptiness gaping inside her.

No. She hadn't been wrong, as much as she might wish otherwise. In the deep corners of her heart, she knew it.

She wanted a home and a family. Not today, maybe not even next year, but someday, certainly. She was ready to move forward with her life and go on to the next stage.

She had already fallen in love with him, just from these few days. If she spent a year of those weekend encounters he was talking about, she wasn't sure she would ever be able to climb back out.

Better to break things off now, when she at least had half a chance of repairing the shattered pieces of her heart.

She would survive. She had been through worse. Scott's death and the long, difficult years preceding it had taught her she had hidden reservoirs of strength.

She supposed that was a good thing. She had a feeling she was going to need all the strength she could find in the coming months as she tried to go on without Quinn.

Chapter 15

"Tess? Everything okay?"

Three months after Jo Winder's death, Tess stood at the nurses' station, a chart in her hand and her mind a million miles away.

Or at least several hundred.

She jerked her mind away from Pine Gulch and the tangled mess she had made of things and looked up to find her friend and charge nurse watching her with concern in her brown eyes.

"I'm fine," she answered Vicki Ballantine.

"Are you sure? You look white as a sheet and you've been standing there for at least five minutes without moving a muscle. Come sit down, honey, and have a sip of water."

The older woman tugged her toward one of the chairs behind the long blue desk. Since Vicki was not only her friend but technically her boss, Tess didn't feel as if she had a great deal of choice.

She sipped at the water and crushed ice Vicki brought her in a foam cup. It did seem to quell the nausea a little, though it didn't do much for the panic that seemed to pound a steady drumbeat through her.

"You want to tell me what's bothering you?" Vicki asked.

She drew in a breath then let it out slowly, still reeling from confirmation of what she had begun to suspect for a few weeks but had only just confirmed an hour ago on her lunch break.

This sudden upheaval all seemed so surreal, the last possible development she had expected to disrupt everything.

"I don't... I haven't been sleeping well."

Vicki leaned on the edge of the deck, her plump features set into a frown. "You're settling in okay, aren't you? The house you rented is nice enough, right? It's in a quiet neighborhood."

"Yes. Everything's fine. I love Portland, you know I do. The house is great and everyone here at the hospital has been wonderful."

"But you're still not happy."

At the gentle concern in her friend's eyes and the warm touch of her hand squeezing Tess's arms, tears welled up in her eyes.

"I am," she lied. "I'm just..."

She couldn't finish the sentence as those tears spilled over. She pressed her hands to her eyes, mortified that she was breaking down at work.

Only the hormones, she assured herself, but she knew it was much, much more. Her tears stemmed from fear and longing and the emptiness in her heart that kept her tossing and turning all night.

Vicki took one look at her emotional reaction and pulled

Tess back to her feet, this time ushering her into the privacy of the empty nurses' lounge.

"All right. Out with it. Tell Auntie Vick what's wrong. This is about some man, isn't it?"

Through her tears, Tess managed a watery laugh. "You could say that."

Oh, she had made such a snarled mess of everything. That panic pulsed through her again, harsh and unforgiving, and her thoughts pulsed with it.

"It always is," Vicki said with a knowing look. "Funny thing is, I didn't even know you were dating anybody."

"I'm not. We're…" Her voice trailed off and she drew in a heavy breath. Though she wanted to protect her own privacy and give herself time to sort things out, she was also desperate to share the information with *someone*.

She couldn't call her mother. Oh, mercy, there was another reason for panic. What would Maura say?

Her mother wasn't here and she wasn't anywhere close to ready to tell any of her friends in Pine Gulch. Vicki had become her closest friend since moving to Portland and on impulse, she decided she could trust her.

"I'm pregnant," she blurted out.

Vicki's eyes widened in shock and her mouth made a perfect little *O* for a moment before she shut it with a snap. She said nothing for several long moments.

Just when Tess was kicking herself for even mentioning it in the first place, Vicki gave her a careful look. "And how do you feel about that?"

"You're the one who said I'm pale as a sheet, right? That's probably a pretty good indication."

"Your color's coming back but you still look upset."

"I don't know how I feel yet, to tell you the truth," she admitted. "I just went to the doctor on my lunch hour to verify my suspicions. I…guess I'm still in shock. I've wanted a child—children—for so long. Scott and I talked about having several and then, well, things didn't quite work out."

Though she didn't broadcast her past around, she had confided in Vicki after her first few weeks in Portland about the challenging years of her marriage and her husband's death.

"And the proud papa? What's his reaction?"

Tess closed her eyes, her stomach roiling just thinking about how on earth she would tell Quinn.

"I haven't told him yet. Actually, I…haven't talked to him in three months."

"If my math is right, this must be someone from Idaho since you've only been here for two months."

She sighed. "His foster mother was my last patient."

"Did you two have a big fight or something?"

She thought of all the accusations they had flung at each other that night. *You can't have what you want, your little fantasy happily-ever-after, and so kicking me out of your life completely is your version of throwing a pissy little temper tantrum.*

Now she was pregnant—*pregnant!*—and she didn't have the first idea what to do about it. She cringed, just imagining his reaction. He would probably accuse her of manipulating the entire thing as some Machiavellian plot to snare him into marriage.

Maybe you think if you push me out now, in a few weeks I'll come running back with tears and apologies, ready to give you anything you want. Even that all-important wedding ring that's apparently the only thing you think matters.

She pushed away the bitter memory, trying to drag her attention back to the problem at hand, this pregnancy that had completely knocked the pins out from under her.

She didn't even know how it had happened. Since hearing the news from her doctor, she had been wracking her brain about their time together and she could swear he used protection every single time. The only possibility was one time when they were in the shower and both became a little too carried away to think about the consequences.

She had been a nurse for ten years and she knew perfectly well that once was all it took but she never expected this to happen to her.

"You could say we had a fight," she finally answered Vicki. "We didn't part on exactly amiable terms."

"If you need to take a little time, I can cover your shift. Why don't you take the rest of the day off?"

"No. I'm okay. I just need a moment to collect my thoughts. I promise, I can put it out of my head and focus on my patients."

"At least take a quick break and go on out to the roof for some fresh air. I think the rain's finally stopped and it might help you clear your head."

She wanted to be tough and insist she was fine. But the hard truth was she felt as if an atomic bomb had just been dropped in her life.

"Clearing my head would be good. Thanks."

When she rose, Vicki gathered her against her ample breasts for a tight hug. "It will be okay, sweetheart. If this is what you want, I'm thrilled for you. I know if anyone can handle single motherhood, you can."

She had serious doubts right now about her ability to handle even the next five minutes, but she still appreciated the other woman's faith in her.

As she walked outside into the wet and cold January afternoon, she gazed out at the city sprawled out below her. So much for the best-laid plans. When she left Pine Gulch, she had been certain that she had everything figured out. Her life would be different but she had relished the excitement of making changes and facing new challenges.

In her wildest dreams, she never anticipated this particular challenge.

She pressed a hand to her abdomen, to the tiny life growing at a rapid pace there.

A child.

Quinn's child.

Emotions choked her throat, both joy and fear.

This pregnancy might not have been in her plans, but no matter what happened, she would love this child. She already did, even though she had only known of its existence for a short time.

She pressed her hand to her abdomen again. She had to tell Quinn. Even if he was bitter and angry and believed she had somehow manipulated circumstances to this end, she had to tell him. Withholding the knowledge of his child from him would be wrong, no matter how he reacted.

She only hoped she could somehow find the courage.

Two weeks later, she was still searching desperately for that strength. With each day that passed, it seemed more elusive than sunshine in a Portland winter.

Every morning since learning she was pregnant, she awoke with the full intention of calling him that day. But the hours slipped away and she made excuse after excuse to herself.

He was busy. She was working. She would wait until evening. She didn't have his number.

All of them were only pitiful justification for her to give in to her fears. That was the hard truth. She was afraid, pure and simple. Imagining his response kept her up at night and she was quite certain was contributing to the nausea she faced every morning.

That she continued to cater to that fear filled her with shame. She wasn't a weak woman and she hated that she was acting like it.

The night before, she had resolved that she couldn't put it off any longer. It was past time for her to act as the pregnancy seemed more real each day. Already, she was beginning to bump out and she was grateful her work scrubs had drawstring waists, since all her other slacks were starting to feel a little snug.

No more excuses. The next day was Saturday and she knew she had to tell him. Though she wanted nothing more than to take the coward's way out and communicate via phone—or, even better, email—she had decided a man deserved to know he was going to become a father in person.

But figuring out how to find the man in Seattle was turning into more of a challenge than she expected.

She sat once more on the rooftop garden of the hospital on her lunch break, her cell phone in her hand as she punched in Easton Springhill's phone number as a last resort.

Easton's voice rose in surprise when she answered. "Tess! I was just thinking about you!"

"Oh?"

"I've been meaning to check in and see how life in the big city is treating you."

She gazed out through the gray mist at the buildings and neighborhoods that had become familiar friends to her during her frequent rooftop breaks. "Good. I like it here. I suppose Pine Gulch will always be home but I'm settling in."

"I'm so glad to hear that. You deserve some happiness."

And she would have it, she vowed. No matter what Quinn Southerland had to say about their child.

"How are you?" she stalled. "I mean really."

Easton was silent for a moment. "All right, I guess. I'm trying to stay busy. It's calving time so I'm on the run all the time, which I suppose is a blessing."

"I'm sorry I haven't called to check on you before now. I've thought of you often."

"No problem. You've been busy starting a new life. By the way," Easton went on, "I checked in on your morning coffee klatch crowd the other day and they all miss you like crazy. I never realized old Sal Martinez had such a thing for you."

She laughed, thinking of the dearly familiar old-timers who could always be counted on to lift her spirits. "What can I say? I'm pretty popular with eighty-year-old men who have cataracts."

Maybe she was making a mistake in her decision to stay in Portland and raise her baby. Moving back to Pine Gulch would give her child structure, community. Instant family. She had time to make that particular decision, she told herself. First things first.

"Listen, I'm sorry to bother you but I'm trying to reach Quinn and I can't find his personal contact information."

"You can't?" Easton's shock filtered clearly through the phone and Tess winced. She had never told her friend that she and Quinn had parted on difficult terms. She supposed she had assumed Quinn would have told her.

"No. I tried to call his company and ended up having to go through various gatekeepers who weren't inclined to be cooperative."

"He can be harder to reach than the Oval Office sometimes. I've got his cell number programmed on mine so I don't have it memorized but hang on while I look it up."

She returned in a moment and recited the number and Tess scribbled it down.

"Can you tell me his home address?" she said, feeling awkward and uncomfortable that she had to ask.

Easton paused for a long moment. "Is something wrong, Tess?"

If you only knew the half of it, she thought.

"Not at all," she lied. "I just... I wanted to mail him something," she improvised quickly.

She could tell her friend didn't quite buy her explanation but to her vast relief, Easton recited the address.

"You'll have to find the zip code. I don't know that off the top of my head."

"I can look it up. Thanks."

"Are you sure nothing's wrong? You sound distracted."

"Just busy. Listen, I'm on a break at the hospital and really need to get back to my patients. It was great talking to you. I'll call you next week sometime when we both have more time to chat."

"You do that."

They said their goodbyes, though she could still hear the questions in Easton's voice. She was happy to hang up the phone. Another moment and she would be blurting it all out. Easton was too darned perceptive and Tess had always been a lousy liar.

She certainly couldn't tell Easton about her pregnancy until she'd had a chance to share the news with Quinn first.

She gazed at the address in her hand, her stomach tangled in knots at the encounter that loomed just over the horizon.

Whatever happened, her baby would still have her.

* * *

Talk about acting on the spur of the moment.

Quinn cruised down the winding, thickly forested street in Portland, wondering what the hell he was doing there.

He wasn't one for spontaneity and impulsive acts of insanity, but here he was, trying to follow his GPS directions through an unfamiliar neighborhood in the dark and the rain.

She might not even be home. For all he knew, she could be working nights or even, heaven forbid, on a date.

At the thought, he was tempted to just turn his car around and drive back to Seattle. He was crazy to just show up at her place out of the blue like this. But then, when it came to Tess and his behavior toward her, sanity hadn't exactly been in plentiful supply.

He felt edgy and off balance, as if he didn't even know himself anymore and the man he always thought he'd been. He was supposed to be a careful businessman, known for his forethought and savvy strategizing.

He certainly *wasn't* a man who drove a hundred and fifty miles on a whim, all because of a simple phone call from Easton.

When she called him he had just been wrapping up an important meeting. The moment she said Tess had called her looking for his address and phone number, his brain turned to mush and he hadn't been able to focus on anything else. Not the other executives still in the room with him or the contract Southerland Shipping had just signed or the route reconfiguration they were negotiating.

All he could think about was Tess.

His conversation with Easton played through his mind now as he followed the GPS directions.

"Something seemed off, you know?" she had said. "I

couldn't put my finger on it but she sounded upset. I just wanted to give you a heads-up that she might be trying to reach you."

As it had then, his mind raced in a hundred different directions. What could be wrong? After three months of empty, deafening silence between them, why was she suddenly trying to make contact?

He only had the patience to wait an hour for her call before he couldn't stand the uncertainty another moment.

In that instant, as he made the call to excuse himself from a fundraiser he'd been obligated to attend for the evening, he had realized with stark clarity how very self-deceptive he had been for the past three months.

He had spent twelve weeks trying to convince himself he was over Tess Claybourne, that their brief relationship had been a mistake but one that he was quite certain had left no lasting scars on his heart.

The moment he heard her name, a wild rush of emotion had surged through him, like water gushing from a dam break, and he realized just how much effort it had taken him to shove everything back to the edges of his subconscious.

Only in his dreams did he let himself remember those magical days he and Tess had shared, the peace and comfort he found in her arms.

He had definitely been fooling himself. Their time together had had a profound impact on his world. Since then, he found himself looking at everything from a different perspective. All the things he used to find so fulfilling—his business pursuits, his fundraising engagements, boating on the Sound—now seemed colorless and dull. Tedious, even.

Southerland was expanding at a rapid pace and he should have been thrilled to watch this company he had created begin at last to attain some of the goals he had set for it. Instead, he found himself most evenings sitting on his deck on Mercer Island, staring out at the lights reflecting on the water and wondering why all the successes felt so empty.

No doubt some of the funk he seemed to have slipped into was due to the grieving process he was still undergoing for Jo.

But he had a somber suspicion that a large portion of that emptiness inside him was due to Tess and the hole she had carved out in his life.

He sighed. Might as well be completely frank—with himself, at least. Tess hadn't done any carving. He had been the one wielding the butcher knife by pushing her away the first chance he had.

He couldn't blame her for that last ugly scene between them. At least not completely. At the first obstacle in their growing relationship, he had jumped on the defensive and had been far too quick to shove her away.

In his business life, he tried to focus most on the future by positioning his company to take advantage of market trends and growth areas. He didn't like looking back, except to examine his mistakes in an effort to figure out what he could fix.

And he had made plenty of mistakes where Tess was concerned. As he examined what had happened three months earlier in Pine Gulch, he had to admit that he had been scared, pure and simple.

He needed to see her again. He owed her an apology, a proper goodbye without the anger and unfounded accusations he had hurled at her.

That's why he was here, trying to find her house in the pale, watery moonlight.

His GPS announced her address a moment later and he pulled into the driveway of a small pale rose brick house, a strange mix of dread and anticipation twisting around his gut as he gazed through the rain-splattered windshield.

Her house reminded him very much of the one in Pine Gulch on a slightly smaller scale. Both were older homes with established trees and gardens. The white shutters and gable gave it a charming seaside cottage appeal. It was surrounded by shrubs and what looked like an extensive flower garden, bare now except for a few clumps of dead growth.

He imagined that in the springtime, it would explode with color but just now, in early February, it only looked cold and barren in the rain.

He refused to think about how he could use that same metaphor for his life the past three months.

Smoke curled from the chimney and lights gleamed from several windows. As he parked in the driveway, he thought he saw a shadow move past the window inside and his breathing quickened.

For one cowardly moment, he was tempted again to put the car in Reverse and head back to Seattle. Maybe Easton had her signals crossed and Tess wasn't really looking for him. Maybe she only wanted his address to send him a kiss-off letter telling him how happy she was without him.

Even if that was the case, he had come this far. He couldn't back out now.

The rain had slowed to a cold mist as he walked up the curving sidewalk to her front door. He rang the doorbell, his insides a corkscrew of nerves.

A moment later, the door opened and the weeks and distance and pain between them seemed to fall away.

She looked fresh and bright, her loose auburn curls framing those lovely features that wore an expectant look—for perhaps half a second, anyway, until she registered who was at her doorstep.

"Quinn!" she gasped, the color leaching from her face like old photographs left in the desert.

"Hello, Tess."

She said nothing, just continued to stare at him for a good thirty seconds. He couldn't tell if she was aghast to find him on her doorstep or merely surprised.

Wishing he had never given in to this crazy impulse to drive two and a half hours, he finally spoke. "May I come in?"

She gazed at him for another long moment. When he was certain she would slam the door in his face, she held it open farther and stepped back so he had room to get through. "I… Yes. Of course."

He followed her inside and had a quick impression of a warm space dominated by a pale rose brick fireplace, blazing away against the rainy night. The living room looked comfortable and bright, with plump furniture and colorful pillows and her upright piano in one corner, still covered with photographs.

"Can I get you something to drink?" she asked. "I'll confess, I don't have many options but I do have some wine I was given as a housewarming gift when I moved here."

"I'm fine. Thanks."

The silence stretched out between them, taut and awkward. He had a sudden vivid memory of lying in her bed with her, bodies entwined as they talked for hours.

His chest ached suddenly with a deep hunger to taste that closeness again.

"You're pale," he said, thrusting his hands in the pockets of his jacket and curling them into fists where she couldn't see. "Are you ill? Easton said you called her and she was worried."

She frowned slightly, as if still trying to make sense of

his sudden appearance. "You're here because Easton asked you to check on me?"

For a moment, he thought about answering yes. That would be the easy out for both of them, but he couldn't do it.

Though he had suspected it, he suddenly knew with relentless clarity that *she* was the reason for the emptiness of the past three months.

He had never felt so very solitary as he had without Tess in his world to share his accomplishments and his worries. To laugh with, to maybe cry with. To share hopes for the future and help him heal from the past.

He wanted all those things she had talked about, exactly what she had created for herself here.

He wanted a home. He wanted to live in a house with carefully tended gardens that burst with color in the springtime, a place that provided a warm haven against the elements on a bitter winter night.

And he wanted to share that with Tess.

He wanted love.

Like a junkie jonesing for his next fix, he craved the peace he had found only with Tess.

"No," he finally admitted hoarsely. "I'm here because I missed you."

Chapter 16

She stared at him, her eyes wide and the same color as a storm-tossed sea. "You...what?"

He sighed, cursing the unruly slip of his tongue. "Forget I said that. Yeah, I'm here because Easton asked me to check on you."

"You're lying." Though the words alone might have sounded arrogant, he saw the vulnerability in her eyes and something else, something that almost looked like a tiny flicker of hope.

He gazed at her, his blood pulsing loudly in his ears. He had come this far. He might as well take a step further, until he was completely out on the proverbial limb hanging over the bottomless crevasse.

"All right. Yes. I missed you. Are you happy now?"

She was quiet for a long moment, the only sound in the house the quiet murmuring of the fire.

"No," she finally whispered. "Not at all. I've been so miserable, Quinn."

Her voice sounded small and watery and completely genuine. He gave a low groan and couldn't take this distance between them another second. He yanked his hands out of his pockets and reached for her and she wrapped her arms fiercely around his neck, holding on for dear life.

Emotions choked in his throat and he buried his face in the crook of her shoulder.

Here. This was what he had missed. Having her in his arms again was like coming home, like heaven, like everything good he had ever been afraid to wish for.

How had he ever been stupid enough to push away the best thing that had ever happened to him?

He kissed her and a wild flood of emotions welled up in his throat at the intense sweetness of having her in his arms once more.

"I'm sorry," he murmured against her mouth. "So damn sorry. I've been a pathetic wreck for three lousy months."

"I have, too," she said. "You ruined *everything*."

He gave a short, rough laugh. "Did I?"

"I had this great new job, this new life I was trying to create for myself. It was supposed to be so perfect. Instead, I've been completely desolate. All I've been able to think about is you and how much I…" Her voice trailed off and he caught his breath, waiting for her to finish the sentence.

"How much you what?" he said when she remained stubbornly silent.

"How much I missed you," she answered and he was aware of a flicker of disappointment thrumming through him as he sensed that wasn't what she had intended to say at all.

He kissed her again and she sighed against his mouth, her arms tight around him.

Despite the cold February rain, he felt as if spring was finally blooming in his heart.

"Everything you said to me that last night was exactly right, Tess. I've given the past too much power in my life."

"Oh, Quinn. I had no right to say those things to you. I've been sorry every since."

He shook his head. "You were right."

"Everyone handles their pain differently. The only thing I know is that everyone has some in his or her life. It's as inevitable as…as breathing and dying."

"Well, you taught me I didn't have to let it control everything I do. Look at you. Your dreams of a happily-ever-after came crashing down around you with Scott's accident. But you didn't become bitter or angry at the world."

"I had my moments of despair, believe me."

His chest ached for her all over again and he cringed at the memory of how he had lashed out at her their last night together in Pine Gulch, accusing her of being the same spoiled girl he had known in high school.

He hadn't meant any of those ugly words. Even as he had said them, he had known she was a far different woman.

He had been in love with her that night, had been probably since that first moment she had sat beside him on the floor of her spare room and listened to him pour out all the ugly memories he kept carefully bottled up inside.

No. Earlier, he admitted.

He had probably been a little in love with her in high school, when he had thought he hated her. He had just been too afraid to admit the truth to himself.

"But despite everything you went through, you didn't let your trials destroy you or make you cynical or hard," he said gently, holding her close. "You still open your heart so easily. It's one of the things I love the most about you."

* * *

Tess stared at him, her heart pulsing a crazy rhythm in her chest. He couldn't have just said what she thought he did. Quinn didn't believe in love. But the echo of his words resounded in her head.

Still, she needed a little confirmation that she wasn't completely hearing things.

"You...what?"

His mouth quirked into that half grin she had adored since junior high school.

"You're going to make me say it, aren't you? All right. That's one of the millions of things I love about you. Right up there at the top of the list is your big, generous, unbreakable heart."

"Not unbreakable," she corrected, still not daring to believe his words. "It has felt pretty shattered the past three months."

He let out a sound of regret just before he kissed her again, his mouth warm and gentle. At the devastating tenderness in his kiss, emotions rose in her throat and her eyes felt scratchy with unshed tears.

"I'm sorry," he murmured between kisses. "So damn sorry. Can you forgive me? I've been a stupid, scared idiot."

He paused, his eyes intense. "You have to cut me a little slack, though."

"Do I?"

Her arch tone drew a smile. "It's only fair. I'm a man who's never been in love before. If you want the truth, it scares the hell out of me."

I'm a man who's never been in love before.

The words soaked through all the pain and loneliness and fear of the past three months.

He loved her. This wasn't some crazy dream where she would wake up once more with a tear-soaked pillow wrapped in her arms. Quinn was standing here in her living room, holding her tightly and saying things she never would have believed if she didn't feel the strength of his arms around her.

He loved her.

She pulled his mouth to hers and kissed him hard, pouring all the heat and joy and wonder spinning around inside her into her kiss. When she at last drew away, they were both breathing raggedly and his eyes looked dazed.

"I love you, Quinn. I love you so much. I wanted to make a new life for myself here in Portland, a new start. But all I've been able to think about is how much I miss you."

"Tess—" He groaned her name and leaned down to kiss her again but she gathered what tiny spark of strength remained and stepped slightly away from him, desperate for a little space to gather her thoughts.

"I love you. But I have to tell you something…"

"Me first." He squeezed her fingers. "I know you think we want two different things out of life. I'll admit, it would probably be a bit of a stretch to say I've had some sudden miraculous change of heart and I'm now completely ready to rush right off to find a wedding chapel."

Well, that would certainly make what she had to tell him a little more difficult. Some of her apprehension must have showed in her eyes because he brought their clasped fingers to his mouth and pressed a kiss to the back of her hand.

"But the thought of being without you scares me a hell of a lot more than the idea of hearts and flowers and wedding cake. I want everything with you. I know I can get there with your help. It just might take me a few months."

"We have a few months."

"I hope we have a lot longer than that. I want forever, Tess."

She gazed at him, dark and gorgeous and male, with clear sincerity in his stunning eyes. He meant what he said. He wasn't going to use his past as an excuse anymore.

She couldn't quite adjust to this sudden shift. Only an hour ago, she had been sitting at her solitary dining table with a TV dinner in front of her, lonely and achy and frightened at the prospect of having to face his reaction the next day to the news of the child they had created together.

And here he was using words like *forever* with her.

She still hadn't told him the truth, she reminded herself. Everything might change with a few simple words. And though she wanted to hang on to this lovely feeling for the rest of her life, she knew she had to tell him.

Though it was piercingly difficult, she pulled her hands away from his and crossed her arms in front of her.

"I need to tell you something first. It may…change your perspective."

He looked confused and even a little apprehensive, as if bracing himself for bad news. "What's wrong?"

"Nothing. At least I don't think so. I hope you don't, either."

She twisted her fingers together, trying to gather her nerves.

"Tell me," he said after a long pause.

With a deep breath, she plunged forward. "I don't know how this happened. Well, I know how it happened. I'm a nurse, after all. But not *how* it happened, if you know what I mean. I mean, we took precautions but even the best precautions sometimes fail…" Her voice trailed off.

"Tess. Just tell me."

"I'm pregnant."

The words hung between them, heavy, dense. He said nothing for a long time, just continued to stare at her.

She searched his gaze but she couldn't read anything in his expression. Was he happy, terrified, angry? She didn't have the first idea.

She pressed her lips together. "I know. I was shocked, too. I only found out a few weeks ago and I've been trying to figure out how to tell you. That's why I called Easton for your address. I was going to drive to Seattle tomorrow. I've been so scared."

That evoked a reaction from him—surprise.

"Scared? Why?"

She sighed. "I didn't want you to think it was all part of some grand, manipulative plan. I swear, I didn't expect this, Quinn. You have to believe me. We were careful. I know we were. The only thing I can think is that...that time in the shower, remember?"

Something flickered across his features then, something that sent heat scorching through her.

"I remember," he said, his voice gruff.

He didn't say anything more and after a moment, she wrapped her arms more tightly around herself, cold suddenly despite the fire blazing merrily in her hearth.

"I know this changes everything. You said yourself you're not ready quite yet for all of that. I completely understand. I don't want you to feel pressured, Quinn. But I... I love her already. The baby and I will be fine on our own if you decide you're not ready. I'll wait as long as it takes. I have savings. I won't ask anything of you, I swear."

Again, something sparked in his gaze. "I thought you said you love me."

"I did. I do."

"Then how can you think I would possibly walk away now?"

His eyes glittered with a fierce emotion that suddenly took her breath away. Hope began to pulse through her and she curled her fingers into fists, afraid to let it explode inside her.

"A baby." He breathed out the word like a prayer or a curse, she couldn't quite tell. "When?"

"Sometime in early July."

"An Independence Day baby. We can name her Liberty."

Her laugh was a half sob and she reached blindly for him. He swept her into his arms and pulled her close as that joy burst out like fireworks in the Pine Gulch night sky.

"Liberty Jo," she insisted.

His eyes softened and he kissed her with more of that heart-shaking tenderness. "A baby," he murmured after a long while. His eyes were dazed as he placed a hand over her tiny bump and she covered his hand with hers.

"You're not upset?" she asked.

"*Numb* is a better word. But underneath the shock is… joy. I don't know how to explain it but it feels right."

"Oh, Quinn. That was my reaction, too. I was scared to death to find out I was pregnant. But the idea of a child—*your* child—filled me with so much happiness and peace. That's a perfect word. It feels *right*."

"I love you, Tess." He pressed his mouth to hers again. "You took a man who was hard and cynical, who tried to convince himself he was happy being alone, and showed him everything good and right that was missing in his world."

He pressed his mouth to hers and in his kiss she tasted joy and healing and the promise of a brilliant future.

* * * * *

Michelle Major grew up in Ohio but dreamed of living in the mountains. Soon after graduating with a degree in journalism, she pointed her car west and settled in Colorado. Her life and house are filled with one great husband, two beautiful kids, a few furry pets and several well-behaved reptiles. She's grateful to have found her passion writing stories with happy endings. Michelle loves to hear from her readers at michellemajor.com.

Books by Michelle Major

Harlequin Special Edition

Crimson, Colorado

Anything for His Baby
A Baby and a Betrothal
Always the Best Man
Christmas on Crimson Mountain
Romancing the Wallflower
Sleigh Bells in Crimson
Coming Home to Crimson

HQN

The Magnolia Sisters

A Magnolia Reunion
The Magnolia Sisters
The Road to Magnolia
The Merriest Magnolia

Visit the Author Profile page
at Harlequin.com for more titles.

COMING HOME TO CRIMSON

Michelle Major

To Jan and Suzanne:
Thank you for being the best aunties a girl
(or her kids) could ever imagine!!

Chapter 1

Unfaithful dirtbag. Cheating scum ball. Two-timing lowlife. *Idiot.*

A slew of descriptive and mainly colorful phrases pinged through Sienna Pierce's mind. That last word, though, she reserved for herself as she sped along the two-lane highway toward Crimson, Colorado. She'd left the ritzy mountain town of Aspen, and her boyfriend—ex-boyfriend now—in her rearview mirror.

She was an idiot for not seeing the signs earlier. Kevin's late nights at the office, the last-minute business trips, the fact that they hadn't had sex in... Well, she should have guessed something was wrong between them.

But he fit her world—her mother's world. Kevin was her stepfather's heir apparent at the investment firm. She never thought he'd jeopardize his future this way. Although what did it say about their relationship that she'd believed their strongest bond was his career aspirations?

Another wave of humiliation washed over her, bringing with it a mix of sweat and nausea. Interesting that embarrassment and anger were the most prevalent emotions right now. Her stomach churned, but her heart remained relatively untouched.

Did that prove she deserved the ice princess accusations Kevin had hurled at her across the hotel room as he'd rushed to pull up his boxers, while the woman in his bed hid under the Egyptian cotton sheets at the five-star hotel?

She adjusted the temperature inside the Porsche, cold air blasting from the vents in the dash. Perspiration continued to bead all over her body, droplets snaking down her spine. Her long hair clung to her neck, and she pulled it over one shoulder.

The weather on this June morning was perfect, the sky overhead an expansively brilliant blue she rarely saw in downtown Chicago. Mountains rose up to meet the sky to the west, their massive rocky peaks reminding her that she was just a speck on the earth in comparison. Sunlight beat down on the cherry-red sports car, the glimmering reflection mocking both her mood and the fact that at twenty-seven years old, she seemed to be having a premature hot flash.

With one hand on the steering wheel, she tried to shrug out of her tailored Calvin Klein suit jacket, the one that had always made her feel both powerful and sexy, like she could handle anything. Until forty-five minutes ago, when her professional attire and meticulously straightened hair had somehow given the appearance that she was trying too hard compared to the effortlessly seductive woman she'd caught glimpses of in that hotel room.

Nothing in her life was right at the moment, especially when one of her arms got tangled between the jacket's sleeve and the seat belt. The car swerved as she yanked her arm, and she forced a deep breath. Oncoming traffic was pretty much nonexistent between the two towns, which was a bonus since the last thing she needed was to cause an accident.

Pull it together, she told herself as she lifted her foot from the gas pedal. How fast had she been driving anyway?

The answer to that question came as she glanced into the rearview mirror and saw red and blue lights flashing behind her. She let out a little growl, the thought of a speeding ticket fueling her temper.

This was Kevin's fault, too. At least Sienna blamed him. She blamed him for everything.

Dust billowed around the Porsche as she pulled onto the shoulder and parked. She unfastened the seat belt and shrugged out of her jacket. It felt like shedding a thousand-pound wool coat.

Knuckles rapped on the window, and she pressed the lever at the same time she leaned closer to the air vents.

"I'm sorry, officer," she said automatically, fanning her hand in front of her face. "I was having a bit of trouble taking off my jacket around the seat belt. I'll be more careful."

"License and registration, ma'am."

The rumbly voice gave her pause and she sat back, glancing up into the face of a man who could have been the direct descendent of some Wild West lawman. The firm set of his jaw and rugged good looks seemed like a throwback to the era of John Wayne, although he wore a modern law enforcement uniform of a beige button-down and black tie, khaki pants and a gun clearly tucked into the holster at his waist.

The button clipped above his shirt pocket read Sheriff. Okay then, the real deal.

And not feeling all that friendly, if the tight line of his

mouth was any indication. She couldn't see his eyes behind the mirrored aviator sunglasses but imagined he was glaring at her.

"Of course," she said and pulled her wallet out of the Louis Vuitton purse on the passenger seat.

"You know texting and driving is against the law," he said as she handed him her driver's license.

"I was having some sort of bizarre hot flash," she blurted. "Not texting." Even now she could feel the silk tank top clinging to her skin. "Anger induced, not hormonal," she felt compelled to add, her cheeks flaming.

One thick brow lifted above the frame of his sunglasses, and Sienna resisted the urge to fidget.

"You were also driving twenty miles above the speed limit."

"I certainly was not." Sienna rolled her eyes. "I'd never drive that fast."

"Ma'am—"

She pointed a finger at him. "I don't like your tone when you call me ma'am."

"I clocked you at eighty-five and it's a sixty-five mile an hour zone that drops to forty-five as you come into town." He paused, then added, "Ma'am."

Sparks raced across Sienna's skin. Somehow his tone had gone from patronizing to sexy-as-hell in one word. She had no idea what had possessed her to try to goad this small-town sheriff into a reaction, but her body's response to him was totally unexpected.

And bothersome.

"I'm sorry," she repeated. "This isn't my car so I'm not used to how it drives." The truth was she'd been too preoccupied with mentally trash-talking her cheating ex-boyfriend to realize she was driving recklessly. Kevin's fault, as well.

"Who does the car belong to?"

"I don't know." She flipped open the glove compartment. "I assume it's a rental. I took it from my ex-boyfriend."

The sheriff leaned forward, his hands resting above the driver's side window. The fabric of his shirt pulled tight across his arms, revealing the outline of corded muscles. "As in you stole it?"

"No," she answered immediately. "I... It wasn't quite like that." She closed her eyes and drew in a breath. In fact, it was exactly like that.

She'd taken a private shuttle from the Aspen airport to the upscale hotel where Kevin had made a reservation. She'd originally been scheduled to come on this trip with him, three days in the mountains of Colorado with a few meetings thrown in to make it a legitimate business expense. Sienna hadn't been back to Colorado in almost two decades, and to make a trip so soon after her estranged brother's visit to Chicago last year... Well, it had been too much to even consider.

Yet in the end, she couldn't stay away. Kevin had acted so disappointed she wasn't coming, dropping subtle hints that he'd planned to pop the question in Aspen. So she'd taken a red-eye into Denver, then a commuter plane to Aspen, thinking how fun it would be to surprise him.

She'd surprised him all right, in bed with another woman. Could it get more clichéd than that? Her life had been reduced to a cliché.

"How about we start with the registration?" the sheriff asked, his voice gentling as if somehow he could sense what a mess she was on the inside.

That infuriated her even more. Sienna didn't do vulnerable. People around her saw what she wanted them to see, and the thought that this mountain-town Mayberry lawman could see beyond her mask made her want to lash out at someone. Anyone. Sheriff Hot Pants, for one.

She dipped her chin and looked up at him through her lashes, flashing a small, knowing smile. "How about I write a healthy-size check to the police foundation or your favorite charity…" She winked. "Or you for that matter and we both go on our merry way?"

"Are you offering me a bribe?"

She widened her smile. "Call it an incentive."

The sheriff took off his sunglasses, shoving them into his front shirt pocket. His eyes were brown, the color of warm honey, but his gaze was frigid. "How's the thought of being arrested as an incentive for you to hand me the registration?"

He smiled as he asked the question. His full lips revealed a set of perfectly straight teeth in a way that made him look like some sort of predator. "Or perhaps you'd like to step out of the car and I'll handcuff you? Another viable option, *ma'am*."

Blowing out a breath, Sienna grabbed the stack of papers from the glove compartment. She hated that her fingers trembled as she leafed through to find the registration card.

She held it up without speaking, and the sheriff plucked it from her fingers.

"Do you have anything else you'd like to say before I run your information?" he asked conversationally.

"I might like to call my lawyer in Crimson," she answered automatically. It would be just her luck that Kevin the scumbag had reported his rental car as missing after she'd convinced the bellman to release it to her. It had felt like a tiny sliver of retribution for what he'd done but now it was coming back to bite her in—

"You have an attorney in Crimson? I find it hard to believe you have ties to anyone in my town."

"*Your* town," she muttered. "Like you own it."

"Ma'am." This iteration was a warning.

"I do know an attorney," she snapped before he could say anything more. "Jase Crenshaw."

The sheriff laughed. "*You* know Jase?"

The way he asked the question made her feel two inches tall. As if Jase Crenshaw wouldn't want anything to do with a woman like Sienna. Which was both ridiculous and possibly true at this point.

But she didn't let him see her doubt. Never show anyone the doubt.

Instead she flashed another smile. "I certainly hope I know Jase. He's my brother."

Cole Bennett blinked. Once. Twice. He rubbed a hand over his jaw, then pulled the sunglasses out of his pocket and returned them to his face.

If the gorgeous and obviously high-strung blonde in the Porsche had told him her brother was the President, he wouldn't have been more surprised.

He patted his open palm on the top of the car. "Sit tight."

"Are you going to call Jase?" she asked, her voice suddenly breathless.

"I'm going to run your plates and make sure this car hasn't been reported stolen."

She snorted, a strangely appealing sound coming from a woman who looked so uptight he guessed she'd never made a noise that wasn't appropriate for a luncheon at a ritzy country club. Living in the mountains of Colorado,

Cole had little use for anything fancy, even with Aspen an easy thirty-minute drive down the road.

"My cheating, dirtbag, sleazeball ex is probably too busy entertaining his mistress to even realize the car is gone."

Cole was amused despite himself. "And when he does?"

She rolled her pale blue eyes. "I *borrowed* the car. I'm planning to return it."

"I gather you recently discovered the cheating, dirtbag, sleazeball side of him."

"Along with a view of his saggy, naked butt in bed with another woman—that part I could have done without."

"How long did you date?"

"A little over two years."

"And his saggy butt came as a surprise?"

She laughed, low and husky, and he felt it all the way to his toes. "I got good at not looking. He had other redeemable qualities."

"Fidelity wasn't one of them?"

He regretted the question when the corners of her mouth turned down. He liked seeing her smile and got the impression she didn't do it half as much as she should.

"Apparently not."

"Do I need to confiscate the keys so you don't take off?" he asked conversationally. "I'm not in the mood for a car chase today."

She met his gaze, her blue eyes sparking with some emotion he couldn't name but that resonated deep in his gut. "Do I look like a flight risk?"

"You look like ten kinds of trouble," he answered, then turned and headed for the Jeep he drove while on duty. Cole Bennett didn't need trouble in his life, no matter how appealing a package it came wrapped in.

Both the car and the woman checked out fine, but Cole

didn't trust that things wouldn't go south when the ex-boyfriend realized the car was gone. Maybe she was indeed going to return it, or maybe she was going to do something stupid that would end up bad for all of them.

Cole prided himself on his ability to read people and situations. It was a skill he'd learned first in the army and then through a more recent career in law enforcement. But Sienna Pierce was an enigma.

On the surface, she was a perfect, polished society type—the kind of woman he would have looked right through on any given day. But a current of something more ran just below the surface—a feral energy he didn't quite understand but that drew him despite his better judgment.

He glanced through the front window of the Jeep to the Porsche and sighed. He could call Jase and dump this problem onto his friend's doorstep. There was no doubt Sienna was going to be a problem. Jase rarely talked about the sister who'd left with their mother when they were kids.

But Cole knew his friend had received a letter from his estranged mother last fall. It had pushed his recovering alcoholic father, Declan, off the wagon in a tumble that had almost cost Jase the town's mayoral election and the woman he loved.

Jase was a good man, honest and loyal. Cole understood better than most how much that meant and what a rare commodity it could be. No matter what Sienna's intentions were, her brother would give her the benefit of the doubt and open his home and heart to her. Cole wasn't convinced she deserved that chance.

Sometimes people were too kind and they got hurt because of it. His mother had been one of those gentle-hearted souls. Jase likely was, as well, although his wife, Emily, was tough enough for the both of them. Either way, Cole would do his best to protect his friend. He made his decision, called the station to tell the department's secretary his plans and got out of the car.

Sienna turned her head as he approached. She'd put on tortoise-framed sunglasses in the interim so her eyes were hidden from view. Also hidden—or at least ruthlessly tamped down—was any of the wild spirit he'd sensed in her earlier. The woman frowning up at him was so cold she could make a polar bear shiver.

"It's your lucky day, ma'am," he told her, handing back her license and registration.

Her rosy lips pressed together. "Is that so?"

"You've earned yourself a sheriff's escort."

"Was the car reported stolen?" she asked with much less concern in her voice than he would have expected. "Are you arresting me?"

"The car's fine," he answered. "For now. I'm going to make sure it stays that way. We're heading back to Aspen, Ms. Pierce, to return the Porsche."

"I don't need your help with the car."

"Good." He leaned a little closer. "Because it's not you I'm helping. It's your brother I care about."

Chapter 2

Kevin stood on the sidewalk under the hotel's blue awning, obviously arguing with one of the valets, as Sienna pulled the Porsche to the curb.

"You stole my car," he yelled as she got out, stalking toward her. "What the hell were you thinking?"

She took a moment to adjust her skirt and ran a hand through her hair, then tossed the keys to the relieved young man in the valet uniform gaping at them both.

"What were *you* thinking?" she countered, strangely empty of emotion at the moment. Her heels made a soft clicking noise on the pavement as she moved to stand in front of him.

"Come in the hotel, Sienna. We'll work this out."

"There's nothing left to work out." She reached in her purse and handed the valet a twenty-dollar bill. "Thank you," she told him with a serene smile. From the corner of her eye, she saw Cole Bennett climb out of the Jeep that had the words Crimson County Sheriff emblazoned across the side.

Under normal circumstances, Sienna loathed drawing attention to herself. Right now she couldn't find the energy to care.

"Don't be ridiculous," Kevin snapped. "I made a mistake. It was one night. I didn't even know her."

"That doesn't make it any better," Sienna said through clenched teeth.

"Ready to head out?" Cole asked as he came to stand beside her.

"Who the hell are you?" Kevin demanded.

Cole flashed an aw-shucks grin that would have done Andy Griffith proud and pointed to the badge on his chest. "Good morning to you, too, buddy. I gather you can read as well as cheat on your girlfriend?"

Kevin narrowed his eyes as he gave Cole the once-over. "A cop," he muttered.

"Sheriff," Cole corrected.

"I want this woman arrested." Kevin pointed toward Sienna. "For grand theft auto."

Sienna felt her body go rigid, then Cole put a hand on her back, whether as comfort or as a silent reminder not to flee, she couldn't tell.

"A fan of video games, I take it," Cole said conversationally. "'Grand Theft Auto' is good but I prefer 'Call of Duty' myself."

Kevin's hands clenched into fists. "This isn't a damn joke."

"I borrowed the car because I needed to compose myself," Sienna said, forcing her voice to remain calm. "Then I returned it."

"She has a witness," Cole added. He pointed to the young valet. "You saw her return it."

The gangly teen swallowed. "Yes, sir."

Kevin lifted a brow. "Come with me and work this out, and we'll let it go. Otherwise, you're going to have to explain to your parents why you were arrested for stealing a car. Mommy won't like it when that hits the news cycle, and what a blow after she just finished chemo."

He reached for her, but Cole moved forward, effectively blocking his access. "The only thing you're letting go of is Sienna," he said, all trace of civility gone from his tone. Sienna had a sudden twinge of sympathy for whatever bad guys were lurking around this section of the Rocky Mountains. Cole Bennett was clearly not a lawman to tangle with.

"This is none of your business, Sheriff."

"Are you joking?" Cole threw up his hands. "You're going to force me to use the 'I'm making it my business' line? I try not to veer into TV cop stereotypes, but if that's what it takes..."

Sienna raised a hand to her mouth, stifling a giggle. The situation was no laughing matter and Kevin had the right of it with his implied threat about her parents. Both her mom and stepdad assumed her marriage to Kevin was a done deal, the engagement just a box to check off the official wedding to-do list.

Maybe she was light-headed from lack of oxygen at this altitude, but she realized she not only had other options in life but wanted to explore them. To see who she could have become without the rigid constraints of the life her mom had orchestrated. Her mother had gone through her own emotional journey during her battle with cancer, one that had culminated with reuniting with the son she'd left behind. But Sienna wasn't on the path of reconciliation, and certainly not with Kevin.

She pointed at her ex-boyfriend. "You have a saggy butt."

The valet snickered as Kevin's mouth dropped open.

Cole turned to her, one corner of his gorgeous mouth twitching with amusement. His honey-brown gaze held hers for a moment. "You went there," he muttered. "Really?"

"I deserve better than you," she continued, moving around Cole to go toe-to-toe with Kevin. "I deserve better than how you treated me."

"Keep telling yourself that," he said, and she wondered why she'd never noticed that when he smiled it looked more like a sneer. "If you weren't such a stuffy prude, I wouldn't have had to find another woman to warm the bed. This is your—"

His head snapped back as her fist connected with his nose. She yelped, as surprised by the fact that she'd punched him as she was by the pain in her knuckles. Kevin cried out, covering his face with his hands.

"You saw her. Assault and battery," he shouted through his fingers.

"I'll keep that in mind," Cole promised. He gestured to the valet. "Get him a towel and some ice." Then he grabbed Sienna's arm. "I think you're done here."

"I didn't mean—"

"No more talking," he told her, half leading and half dragging her across the street to his Jeep. "Let's just get out of this town before you cause an even bigger scene."

She stopped a few feet from the car. "Are you going to make me sit in the back seat?"

"I should after that stunt," Cole said but opened the passenger door for her. "Get in. Your saggy bottomed ex has gone into the hotel. We should be gone by the time he comes out again."

Neither of them spoke as Cole drove out of Aspen. The upscale shops and restaurants housed in historic brick buildings gave way to apartment complexes and other, newer structures and finally changed to open meadows as he took the turn onto the highway that led to Crimson. It was the third time today she'd driven this stretch of road.

As they passed a herd of cattle grazing in a field behind a split-rail fence, Sienna searched for the mama and baby she'd spotted earlier this morning. The young calf, which couldn't have been more than a few weeks or months old, had been glued to its mother's side as if that was the safest place in the world to be.

Sienna wished she could relate to that feeling.

"I don't make scenes," she said, finally breaking the silence.

Cole's fingers tightened on the steering wheel. "Then you do a great imitation of someone who does."

"It's not my fault he cheated," she whispered.

Cole glanced over at her. "Say it like you mean it, sweetheart."

"I do. I want to." She clasped her hands tight in her lap. "He was right about one thing. My mother is going to be irked by this situation."

"The part where he cheated or the part where you broke up with him because of it?"

"We were supposed to get engaged on this trip," she said because she wasn't ready to answer his question out loud.

"Then I'd say you dodged a bullet."

She held on to that comment for a moment, cupped it between her hands—like a kid would with a firefly late on a summer night—and found she liked the light shining from it. So she tucked that light inside herself, the way she'd learned to do with anything that made her happy but would have disappointed her mother.

Sienna had learned early how to pick her battles with Dana Crenshaw Pierce, and most of them weren't worth waging.

"Did you grow up in Crimson?" she asked, needing a break from talking about her own messed-up life.

It was a simple enough question but Cole tensed like she'd just requested he recount his first sexual encounter in graphic detail, then broadcast the story across his cruiser's radio.

"No."

"Somewhere in Colorado?"

"No."

"Okay then." When he didn't add anything more, she threw up her hands. "I'm going to assume you're some sort of super secret law enforcement guy and you've had your past wiped out by the covert government agency that basically owns you and if you breathe one word of where you came from or who you used to be, everyone in your family will die."

"They're already dead," he said quietly.

"Oh." She reached out a hand, placed it on his arm. "I'm sorry."

He swerved off the highway to the shoulder, braking hard. The Jeep's tires crunched in the dirt and gravel. Sienna tried to catch her breath as she was jostled in her seat.

"Let's get a few things straight." Cole's voice was as jarring as fingernails on a chalkboard. "I don't need or want your pity."

"I wasn't—" she began, but he held up a hand.

"We're not friends," he continued. "We're not *going* to

be friends. You were a mess this morning and I was taking care of my friend by taking care of you. If the ex-boyfriend is any indication, you need serious help with your taste in men. Maybe you need help in general." He jabbed a finger toward her, then back at himself. "I'm not going to be the one to give it. I'm dropping you off at the rental car agency, and we're done. Is that clear?"

"Crystal," she said, feeling as if she had ice forming inside her veins. She straightened her skirt, wishing it were a few inches longer so her legs weren't exposed to Cole's gaze. She could feel him watching her, although she refused to make eye contact.

She sat tall, shoulders back, her posture impeccable—the way she'd been taught in the five years of ballet classes her mother had wrenched out of her after Dana had married Craig Pierce and had the money to reinvent herself. To recreate both of their lives—a do-over of monumental proportions and one Sienna had never wanted.

Eventually Cole blew out a long breath, then started driving again. Sienna didn't so much as twitch until he pulled into a rental car parking lot that was part of a strip mall a mile past the Crimson city limits sign. The rental car place shared the space with a grocery store, a hair salon and a sandwich shop.

As soon as the Jeep stopped, she unfastened her seat belt and opened the door.

"Thank you for the ride," she mumbled over her shoulder, because along with perfect posture, good manners had been drilled into her. Oddly, she felt almost as angry with Cole as she was with Kevin, which was stupid because the sheriff didn't owe her anything. He'd done her a favor this morning, but they weren't friends. He was nothing to her, so why had her chest ached when he'd told her exactly that?

"Sienna." He reached for her arm but she shrugged away from his touch.

"We're done, Sheriff." He winced slightly, as if he didn't appreciate having his words thrown back at him. "I can handle things from here."

She slammed the door shut and walked toward the building, telling herself she was glad to be leaving behind Sheriff Cole Bennett and this whole humiliating morning.

Fifteen minutes later, Cole pushed through the door of the mayor's office on the second floor of the county courthouse. "Where's Jase? He's not answering his phone."

"Good morning to you, too." Emily Crenshaw inclined her head, then turned her attention to the computer screen. "Help yourself to fresh coffee. Not sure what's got your boxers in a bunch today." Her gaze flicked back to him. "Or is it boxer briefs? You look like a boxer brief type of guy, Sheriff. Definitely not tighty-whities, something for which we can all be grateful."

"Emily."

"Either way, grab a cup of coffee, then come back and I'll give you a do-over on this conversation." She lifted a brow. "I learned that trick from my job at the front desk of the elementary school. Some kids need help learning how to appropriately greet people. I guess you didn't get that lesson or you've forgotten." She flashed a wide smile. "I'm here to help."

Cole felt his mouth drop open and quickly closed it again. What was it about this day and sassy blondes? But Emily Crenshaw was a force to be reckoned with and currently sat in the computer chair normally occupied by Jase's sweet-tempered secretary, Molly.

Cole was developing a new appreciation for sweet-tempered.

He grabbed a mug from the cart positioned along the far wall and poured himself a steaming cup of coffee. "Good morning, Emily," he said as he took a drink. "You're filling in for Molly today?"

"Just for the morning." Emily pushed away from the computer and smiled. "She had to take her mom to a doctor's appointment, and Davey is in a Lego camp this week. It's always a challenge to keep a first-grade boy occupied during the summer."

"I can imagine," he said even as he thought of how he and his brother, Shep, had run wild through the various army bases around the world where his dad had been stationed back in the day.

"Thank you for the pleasantries," Emily told him. "Jase had a meeting with the city finance director, so I doubt his phone is on. They're on the first floor, so he should be back soon."

"I'll wait."

"What's going on, Cole?" Emily's big eyes narrowed. She looked a little bit like Sienna, now that he thought about it. Blond hair, blue eyes, beautiful with that certain shine that time spent in a big city gave to women. Sienna was a couple inches taller, her face more heart-shaped with delicate features.

Emily was a Crimson native who'd moved away, then back with her young son early last year. She was different from Sienna in one major way—Emily radiated happiness. It had been hard earned, he knew, and was glad that she and Jase had worked out their issues.

She stood, and he was reminded of another significant difference between the two women. Emily was seven months pregnant, which made her seem somehow more intimidating than usual. Give Cole a bar fight to break up or even an underground drug bust rather than be stared down by a heavily pregnant woman.

He shrugged and gave her his don't-mess-with-me law enforcement face. "I need to talk to him. Sheriff's office business."

She crossed her arms over her chest, resting them on her round belly. "Do I look stupid?"

So much for intimidation. "Um…no."

"It seems like somebody's in trouble with my better half."

Cole turned, profoundly grateful to see Jase Crenshaw standing in the door to the outer office, one side of his mouth curved as he looked between Cole and Emily.

"The sheriff wants to talk to you," Emily told her husband.

"Okay," Jase answered and walked forward, leaning over the receptionist desk to kiss her, while gently placing a hand on her baby bump.

Cole quickly turned and refilled his coffee mug, uncomfortable with the easy show of affection.

"But he's acting suspicious." Emily frowned at Cole. "Something's up and I want to know what it is."

"It's nothing," Cole insisted and flicked a help-me glance to Jase.

"You might as well say it." Jase shrugged. "If she doesn't find out now, I'll have to tell her later."

"What if it's confidential?"

Emily sniffed. "I'm his *wife*. He tells me everything."

Jase nodded. "It's true. I'm not an expert on marriage, but I do understand that honesty is a pretty important foundation."

Anger spiked in Cole's chest, familiar to him as his face in the mirror. Not at Jase or Emily but at memories of his own father's lies and deceptions—the ones that had torn apart his family.

He blew out a breath, forcing his emotions under control. "I clocked a woman driving twenty miles over the speed limit coming into Crimson this morning."

"An out-of-towner, I assume?" Jase asked.

Emily scrunched up her nose. "What does that have to do—?"

"Her name was Sienna Pierce," Cole interrupted.

Emily immediately placed a hand on Jase's arm, almost the same way Sienna had done with Cole in the car earlier. He'd overreacted to the gesture but couldn't seem to stop himself from freaking out any time he was forced to talk about his family.

It was one of the reasons he'd first applied as a sheriff's deputy in Crimson five years ago. No one knew him here and it was easy to keep his conversations about his past vague—just the way he liked it.

"You gave my sister a speeding ticket?" Jase asked, his tone almost unnaturally calm.

"Not exactly," Cole answered. He'd planned to share with Jase the details of his morning run-in with Sienna but now the words wouldn't come. As reserved as she pretended to be, he knew Sienna had been humiliated by her cheating ex-boyfriend. He doubted that was information she'd appreciate being used as her calling card in Crimson. "More like a warning."

Emily raised a brow at Cole as her hand tightened on Jase's arm. "Is that what this is?"

"I thought you'd want to know she was here," Cole told his friend. "I got the impression she hadn't called first."

"Hardly," Jase said with a small laugh. "I haven't talked to Sienna since the night my mom drove away with her."

"Because she refused to see you when you visited your mom last Christmas." Emily came around the desk and laced her fingers through Jase's. "She made it clear she wanted nothing to do with you."

"I wonder what changed," Jase murmured, almost under his breath.

Her whole world from the looks of it, Cole wanted to answer. It's what he should have shared. But instead he only shrugged. "I don't know her plans but thought you'd want to know, and your dad…"

Jase groaned. "This is going to rock his world."

"She has no business showing up out of the blue." Emily reminded Cole of an Amazon warrior getting ready for battle or a grizzly mama standing between a pack of coyotes and one of her cubs. "If she upsets Declan—"

"I'll take care of it." Jase wrapped an arm around her shoulder. "Don't get riled up, Em."

Emily only rolled her eyes. "I love you, Jase Crenshaw, but you know me better than that. Telling me not to get riled up is like telling a retriever not to fetch the ball."

Cole laughed, then tried to cover it with a cough when Emily gave him one of her looks. "Sorry," he mumbled. "But you compared yourself to a dog."

"No more free coffee for you," she said, but her lips twitched as she said it.

"Thank you, Cole," Jase said. "I appreciate the heads-up."

"You bet. I've got to check in at the station. Call if you need anything."

He placed his mug on the cart and walked out of the office, rubbing a hand over his jaw as he stepped into the warm June sunshine. Several people waved and Cole forced himself to smile and greet them in return, even though the sick pit in his stomach was growing wider by the second.

He didn't owe Sienna Pierce a thing. So why did he feel like she was the one who needed protecting in Crimson? Jase had Emily and his dad and the whole town in his corner. From what he could tell, Sienna had no one.

Cole could relate, and the strange connection he'd felt to her this morning had somehow taken root inside him and refused to let go.

Ten kinds of trouble, he'd told her, but wondered if he'd underestimated even that.

Chapter 3

Sienna stared at the house tucked amid the pine trees, then checked the GPS on her phone one more time. She'd made a reservation at The Bumblebee Bed and Breakfast at 1 Ivy Lane on a whim after picking up an adorable business card at the counter of the grocery store next to the rental car agency.

Normally Sienna stuck to luxury hotel chains. She gravitated toward sleek decor and modern conveniences. But something about the colorful flowers and cheerful bees drawn on the card appealed to her. She needed some color and cheer in her life.

But she also wanted a hot shower and a toilet that flushed. Nothing about the plumbing van sitting in the driveway of the dilapidated house at the end of the long, winding drive gave her confidence she'd find either at The Bumblebee.

If her mother were here, she would have been happy

to enumerate the ways Sienna had managed to mess up her life—all of them in one day. Dana Pierce loved making lists.

The only thing on Sienna's to-do list right now was getting back in the compact car she'd rented and finding a decent hotel.

"Sienna!"

She turned back toward the house, surprised to hear her name shouted out like a long-lost friend had just spotted her.

"You're Sienna, right?" A tiny pixie of a woman ran toward her, appearing from the trees like a woodland sprite. "I've been waiting for you." The woman stopped, clasped a hand over her mouth. "Scratch that last part. It sounds like the start of some creepy horror movie." She waved her hands in the air as dark curls bounced around her face. "I've been waiting for you," she repeated in a deep, melodramatic voice. "You know what I mean, though. I'm excited you found us...me, rather... The Bumblebee, that is."

"You must be Paige," Sienna said, reaching out a hand.

"Who else?" the woman asked, bypassing her outstretched hand to give Sienna a tight hug. The innkeeper might be small, but she was strong, practically squeezing all the air out of Sienna's lungs. "You're my first guest. We're going to have the best week."

"This isn't summer camp," Sienna said quietly, making Paige laugh.

"I know, silly. But I just got the sign up today." She pointed behind her to a hand-painted piece of cardboard that read The Bumblebee B&B. It leaned against the edge of the porch rail. "Not quite up," Paige admitted. "But you still found me." She scrunched her winged brows, emerald green eyes zeroing in on Sienna. "How did you find me anyway?"

"The business cards you left at the grocery."

"I remember now." Paige nodded. "I picked them up from the post office on my way to buy food for dinner. I told Rodney—he's the manager at the Shop & Go—not to put them out until next week."

"Apparently he did anyway."

Paige squeezed Sienna's arms like they were best friends. "Lucky for both of us."

"Are you sure?" Sienna inclined her head toward the plumbing truck in the driveway, then pointed to the various pieces of furniture sitting in the front yard. "It looks like you might need a bit more time to get ready."

Paige gave her a brilliant smile. "I'm as ready as I'll ever be."

Terrifying, Sienna thought to herself.

"Then why the plumber?"

"A leak in the first-floor bathroom," Paige said, spacing her first finger and thumb a tiny width apart as she held them up to her eye. "But your bedroom is upstairs."

"That's good."

"Only now," Paige said, wrinkling her nose, "I'll be sharing it because mine is downstairs."

"Not so good." Although Sienna had a brother right here in Crimson, most of her life she'd been an only child. Her mother liked to tell her she wasn't good at sharing, and Sienna had no reason not to believe it because she'd never had to.

"It will only be for a day or two." Paige flashed a bright smile that only wavered slightly. "Maybe."

"I don't mind finding a normal—I mean regular—hotel in town."

"Good luck with that. The rodeo's at the county fairgrounds this weekend. Everything's booked from here to Grand Junction. Unless you want to stay in Aspen."

Sienna shook her head. "I don't."

"Huh. No offense, but you look like the Aspen type. Other than the mustard stain on your blouse."

"Why would I take offense to that?" Sienna picked at the dried mustard on the front of her shirt.

"Did you get a hot dog at the Shop & Go?" Paige asked instead of answering the question. "They're yummy."

"It was tasty," Sienna admitted. The hot dog had been the best thing she'd eaten in ages. Normally she stuck to a high protein, low-carb, all organic and very little fun diet. The hot dog had been another small act in the process of reclaiming her life. Or claiming it for the first time, since it had never truly felt like hers.

"Do you have luggage?"

"Yes, but not here." Sienna had left her suitcase with the hotel's bellman in Aspen this morning. She supposed it was still there and figured she'd have to drive back over at some point to retrieve it. But she wasn't ready for another potential confrontation with Kevin. "I picked up toiletries at the grocery store."

"I can lend you some clothes."

"That would be interesting." Paige was at least four inches shorter than Sienna and curvy like some throwback pinup girl from the forties. "Since you're new at this whole innkeeper thing, I should tell you that in normal circumstances you wouldn't offer your clothes to a paying guest."

"Not to assume too much," Paige said, inclining her head, "but do you think these are normal circumstances for either of us?"

Sienna blew out a breath. "No."

"Please stay," Paige said, then gave a nervous laugh.

"That sounded desperate. I don't mean it like that." She laughed again. "Except I sort of do. This was my grandma's house." She gestured to the ramshackle but still charming lodge with faded rough-sawed logs notched together and deep green shutters bordering the windows on the front. "My mom inherited it when Grammy died last year, and I convinced her to let me get it up and running again."

"I'm sorry for your loss," Sienna said automatically.

"Thank you," Paige whispered. "It's beautiful out here… but also quiet."

Sienna nodded, looking around the cul-de-sac. There were a few houses at the top of the street, where she'd turned onto Ivy Lane, but The Bumblebee's property was clearly the largest and most private.

"Grammy had five acres," Paige said, as if reading her thoughts. "It borders the old ski resort in back. We even have a view of the main chairlift. It hasn't operated for years, although some developer bought the property recently. My grandma fought like crazy with the old owner about selling this place and making it part of the resort. I'm hoping the new owner will be more friendly and that The Bumblebee will be in the right place to cater to skiers or families vacationing in Crimson."

"Smart move," Sienna murmured.

Paige beamed at her. "Thank you for saying that. My family thinks I'm crazy. I'm not exactly following the path they expected me to take."

There was something in the woman's gaze—a combination of hope and fear with a healthy dose of uncertainty and pride mixed in—that Sienna imagined she might see in her own eyes when she looked in the mirror.

"I'll stay," she said. If Sienna was going to forge her own way in life, she had to start taking some risks in order to figure out what she wanted that life to be. Somewhere between Kevin's butt and the ride in Cole's Jeep, she'd decided the time had come to take charge of her life on her own terms.

And Colorado, far away from her mother, seemed like a better place to spread her wings than in Chicago, tethered by the constraints of her regular life. Maybe she'd actually forge a relationship with her dad and brother instead of the awkward face-offs she imagined. The thought made panic spike in her belly, and she pressed a hand to her stomach. One step at a time.

Whether a risk or an adventure, coming to Crimson as the inaugural guest at The Bumblebee B&B seemed like the right move on her new journey. It would be interesting to see where it took her.

"One more refill."

Sienna grabbed the red plastic cup from Paige's hand and filled it to the brim.

"Too much." Paige grimaced, shaking her head. "You could put a Russian under the table with the amount of vodka in that."

"It's mainly lemonade," Sienna argued, then hiccuped. "I swear."

Paige rolled her eyes but took a sip. "It's good."

"Told you so." Sienna took a long drink from her cup. "An added bonus is that it makes this place look a lot better."

"True," Paige agreed and both women turned from the long butcher-block island in the kitchen to survey the house.

The kitchen opened onto a cozy family room in which all the furniture was shoved up against one wall. Half the wood floor had been ripped up after the plumber found a slow leak that had caused damage to the foundation. The Bumblebee's minor plumbing project now looked like it would stretch out at least a week, if not longer.

Paige had immediately started hyperventilating when she'd been given the news this afternoon. Sienna had shoved the novice innkeeper into a chair, found a paper bag for her to breathe into, then gotten a contractor recommendation from the plumber.

"You're the guest," Paige had said, wheezing into the bag. "You shouldn't be—"

"I'll manage," Sienna assured her. Besides, the more she focused on Paige's problems, the less time she had to think about her real reason for this impulsive trip to Crimson—confronting her dad after twenty years of no contact between them.

Plumbing issues were way less trouble than family drama.

Once Paige had calmed down, she'd insisted on making dinner, which consisted of an array of surprisingly delicious frozen appetizers heated in the oven. Sienna had searched through the cabinets until she'd found a decent bottle of vodka.

"Grammy liked a little nip before bed," Paige explained.

Sienna had concocted a hard lemonade drink, and no matter how much vodka she added it still seemed to go down far too easily.

They'd watched a few episodes of a reality TV show about pampered pets, then Paige had pulled a disco ball strobe light out of a closet.

"Dance party!" she'd shouted and Sienna had been too blissfully numb to argue.

They'd danced for what seemed like hours, avoiding the caution tape that roped off the hole in the floor. When

Sienna realized she was a sweaty and thirsty mess, she made another pitcher of hard lemonade. She smiled as she watched the bright flashes of color on the bumblebee wallpaper in the kitchen.

"This has been the funnest night ever," Paige said, then yawned.

"Ever," Sienna agreed without hesitation. She'd never had a night like this, one filled with laughing and dancing and ignoring all of her worries. Paige had asked a few subtle questions about what brought Sienna to Crimson but hadn't seemed to mind Sienna's vague answers.

Both women jumped when a loud knock sounded on the front door.

"Stupid neighbors," Paige muttered, stumbling a little as she hopped off her stool. "I bet they called the cops again."

"The cops?"

"The grumpy couple down the street has the local department on speed dial. If I so much as put my trash out too early, they report me. I'm guessing they think colored lights from a disco ball are the devil's handiwork."

A sinking pit opened in Sienna's stomach. It was highly unlikely Cole would be the one to respond to a call like this but with the way her luck was running...

"I'm going to head upsta—"

She got up from her stool just as Paige turned toward her. Sienna's arm jostled the cup Paige held, and vodka lemonade splashed all over the front of Paige's pajamas.

"Yuck," Paige cried. "I'm going to be a sticky mess. You get the door while I change."

"I can't—"

Paige's eyes widened. "Don't make me answer it when I'm practically bathed in vodka. A plumbing problem is bad enough. Who wants to stay at a B&B where the lady who runs it is a stinking drunk?"

The knock sounded again, more forcefully this time.

"It's not like potential guests will hear about it," Sienna protested, shaking her head.

"This is Crimson." Paige threw up her hands. "Everyone will know." She made a kissing sound toward Sienna. "I'll be back in a jiffy."

Sienna sighed as Paige disappeared into her bedroom. She turned down the music, flipped off the disco light and padded to the door, trying to ignore both her hammering heart and the fact that she was wearing a set of Paige's tie-dyed pajamas.

She wet her lips with her tongue, said a silent prayer that some low-level officer had gotten stuck with this call and opened the door.

Cole Bennett stood on the other side.

Chapter 4

"Seriously?"

Sienna's blue eyes burned like the center of a flame as she glared at him.

"The neighbors called," he said, like he owed her some sort of explanation. "Mrs. Morrison saw lights flashing through the trees while she was walking her dog before bed tonight. She was convinced they were a result of some sort of unlawful activity."

"I heard about the neighbors," Sienna muttered. "Paige and I were having a dance party." She glowered at him like he'd put the older couple up to making the complaint. As if he didn't have anything better to do than show up to check out the situation—like he'd been looking for an excuse to see her again. The latter might be slightly true, even though he'd never admit it.

"Don't you have deputies or something?" she demanded, crossing her arms over the faded tie-dyed tank top she wore. She had matching pajama pants, and with her blond hair tumbling over her shoulders and the pink glow to her cheeks, she was even more beautiful now than she'd been earlier that morning.

"I wanted to check on you." The fact that he admitted it obviously surprised her as much as it did him.

"How did you know I was here?"

She moved back and he stepped into the house, gently closing the ancient screen door behind him. He didn't bother with the front door. It was a perfect Colorado night, about ten degrees cooler than it had been when the sun was out, and Cole needed the fresh air to remind him to keep his self-control in place.

"Rodney mentioned you picked up one of the business cards for The Bumblebee. There aren't many open rooms in town because of the rodeo, so I assumed this is where you ended up. Once the call came in, I had no doubt you were here." He inclined his head. "You and trouble and all that."

"I don't get into trouble," she insisted, narrowing her eyes.

"Other than speeding and stealing a car and—"

"I didn't steal the car."

"You stole a car?"

Cole looked up as Paige Harper rushed into the room. "That's crazy in an awesome *Thelma and Louise* kind of way. Hey, Sheriff."

"Evening, Paige."

"Sorry about the music."

"It was more the lights this time. They worried Mrs. Morrison."

"Of course they did. She's probably jealous that she has no reason to turn on disco lights." Paige nudged Sienna. "If you want to be Thelma, I can be Louise. Or we can trade roles. I'm more of a Thelma anyway, I think. Sheriff, do you have an opinion on that?"

"Uh, no," Cole admitted, not sure what the bubbly innkeeper was talking about. But it didn't matter because he saw the start of a smile curve Sienna's full mouth and felt suddenly grateful for Paige Harper and her ramshackle inn.

Even though she seemed tough, he had a feeling Sienna was more vulnerable in Crimson than she'd ever let on. If Jase's wariness and Emily's underlying temper were any indication, she might need a friend during her time in town. Paige would be the perfect ally.

"I'm not Thelma *or* Louise," Sienna said. "I borrowed a car from my ex-boyfriend this morning and then I returned it. The sheriff was a witness. I'm not planning on causing trouble. Pierce women don't *do* trouble."

"You're a Crenshaw here in Crimson," Cole felt compelled to point out. "And the Crenshaw family has a long history of trouble in this town."

"Jase Crenshaw is the family you're in town to visit?" Paige asked, wide-eyed.

Sienna nodded tightly. "Jase and my dad."

"Why didn't you say so in the first place? Jase is a great guy. I'm new enough to Crimson that I don't know much about anyone's past history, but I can almost guarantee Jase isn't involved in any kind of trouble. He's too good for that."

"How do you know my brother?" Sienna asked quietly, shifting away from Paige and closer to Cole. He had the ridiculous urge to wrap an arm around her shoulder but managed to keep his hands at his sides.

"Well, he's the mayor so everyone knows him. But I met him personally at a town council meeting when I first started working on The Bumblebee. He was really helpful and supportive of my ideas for the inn. Everyone in Crimson loves Jase."

"Of course they do." Sienna's shoulders sagged.

Cole realized she had no reason to know that her brother was the town's favorite son. Jase had been through plenty—overcoming his family's less-than-stellar reputation and taking care of his father during the years Declan couldn't pull himself out of the bottle. But now Jase was universally liked and well respected, both in Crimson and throughout the network of high-country towns in this part of Colorado.

Cole wasn't sure why this knowledge seemed to affect Sienna like the sharp point of a pin to a balloon, but he could almost see her deflating before his eyes.

"You should invite Jase and Emily to the inn for dinner. They can bring Davey, too. He's a sweet kid."

"Davey?"

"Emily's son," Paige clarified. "You haven't met him?"

Sienna shook her head.

"What about Emily?"

"His wife?" Sienna asked Cole.

"They got married last year," he confirmed.

Sienna looked at Paige again. "Jase and I aren't exactly close."

"When was the last time you saw him?"

"Um...about twenty years ago."

Paige whistled softly. "We're going to need more vodka for this story."

"No more vodka," Cole said at the same time as Sienna.

"Or disco lights," Cole added, pointing at each of the women.

Paige pressed two fingers to her forehead. "Probably a good idea. I can already feel a headache brewing. I'm going to go to bed. Sienna, you can give me the fascinating details of your family history over coffee and muffins in the morning."

"There's nothing fascinating about me."

Paige darted a glance toward Cole, as if she knew he wanted to argue.

"I'll get going then," he said instead. "Keep the music down and pull the shades if you want to turn on the disco lights."

"Sienna will walk you to your car," Paige offered. "'Night, you two." She turned, then looked back over her shoulder. "By the way, there's something fascinating about everyone. Some of us just need to figure out what it is."

"Let's go," Sienna said, starting to move past him.

He placed a hand on her arm, not surprised to find her skin hot to the touch. As much as he might want to deny it, it seemed neither of them could ignore the flame of attraction that burned between them. "You don't need to walk me."

"Come on, Sheriff," she answered, shrugging off his touch.

He followed her onto the porch, the light above the door-frame casting a pale glow. He was used to people calling him Sheriff, and normally he liked it. At times his job felt like the only thing that defined him. But coming from Sienna, the word was wrong. He wanted to hear his name on her lips, preferably whispered over and over as he drove her crazy with desire.

No doubt he should have had a deputy answer this call tonight.

"I'm guessing you didn't contact Jase or Declan yet," he said into the silence.

She grabbed the porch railing, as if to steady herself—a result of the alcohol or the mention of her dad and brother, he couldn't tell which. "I wanted a day to get settled. Today wasn't exactly filled with shining star moments for me."

"Except maybe a pajama dance party. That's the stuff of shining moments, not to mention male fantasies everywhere."

She laughed softly, and once again he felt it all the way to his toes. The sound was low and husky, like she was as out of practice with laughter as he was. Holding out her arms, she spun in a small circle on the gravel driveway. "This outfit isn't the stuff of anyone's fantasy."

"You have no idea."

"How long have you lived in Crimson?" she asked suddenly, a variation of the line of questioning he'd reacted to so badly earlier.

He wanted to keep it together tonight. They'd made it to his Jeep, the Crimson County Sheriff's emblem emblazoned across the side and illuminated in the moonlight.

"I came here a few years back for a deputy position. There were some shake-ups within the department and Jase convinced me to run for sheriff in the last election. That was two years ago."

"You and Jase are close," she whispered.

"Yeah. Your brother is a good man, Sienna."

"My brother," she repeated as if she couldn't quite grasp the meaning of the word, then turned so she was facing Cole. "Did you tell him I was here?"

"Yes."

She sucked her bottom lip into her mouth and bit down. Cole's knees went weak.

"I should probably leave in the morning. Coming to Crimson seemed like a great idea when I was all fired up this morning, but now—"

"Don't go." He reached out, tucked a stray lock of hair behind her ear.

"I can't believe Jase would want me here. He came to visit our mom last winter. I wasn't exactly…cordial."

"Emily mentioned that."

"The wife. Is she going to be a problem for me?"

"Emily is protective of Jase. He's sometimes too nice for his own good. His dad…your dad has needed a lot of caregiving through the years. There were some dark days, most of them before I got to town, but Declan has stumbled even recently. Sobriety is a harsh mistress for him sometimes."

"I remember the drinking." Her eyes closed, and he watched her chest rise and fall as she sucked in a deep breath. "I don't remember much, maybe because that's the way Mom wanted it. We barely spoke about Jase or my dad once we left Crimson. But the smell of whiskey brings back snippets of memory. Most of them I should probably forget. My parents weren't exactly kind to each other when they drank."

"That's fairly common. Alcohol doesn't bring out the best in anyone."

She blinked, her blue eyes clear as a mountain lake as she looked up at him. "My mom hasn't taken a drink, not even a sip of champagne at a wedding, since she left here. Even though she wouldn't talk about it, I always got the impression she blamed the town for her downward spiral as much as she did my dad."

"I'm sorry she had to break ties with Colorado so dramatically, but this town isn't to blame for the troubles she had. It's a great community."

"You're the sheriff," she said with a smile. "Of course you think that. Everyone has to be nice to you. They'll end up in jail otherwise."

He laughed. "Not exactly."

"Do you have a girlfriend, Sheriff?"

Cole, he wanted to shout, suddenly desperate to hear her say his name.

"Nope. Work keeps me too busy."

"Lame excuse. I bet there is a line of women hoping you'll notice them."

"Hardly."

"How many times a week does some generous citizen…" She leaned in closer and he caught the light floral scent of her shampoo. "Some *female* citizen," she clarified, "bring fresh muffins by your office?"

"Only on Fridays," he admitted, then shrugged when Sienna looked confused. "Our office manager went low-carb last year. Marlene limits the baked goods to once a week."

Sienna shook her head, another smile playing around the corners of her mouth. "My mom only referred to Crimson as 'that place,' but I always imagined it as some sort of high-altitude version of Sodom and Gomorrah." Her smile widened. "It's more like mountain Mayberry."

"I'm not Andy Griffith," Cole argued, annoyed by the implied comparison.

"If you start whistling—"

He leaned in and kissed her, somehow wanting to prove that he wasn't the easygoing, small-town lawman she presumed him to be. At least that's the reason he gave himself. The truth was he couldn't resist her one more second. Her smart mouth and sassy attitude. All the ways she tried to pretend she wasn't hurting.

The fact that he recognized the loneliness in her gaze because he saw the same thing in his own eyes every time he looked in the mirror.

She stilled for a moment, then sighed and sank into the

kiss. It wasn't the reaction he'd expected and the surprise of it made his body burn. He'd figured she would snap at him or give him a swift punch to the gut. But she seemed to need the touch as much as he did.

He moved closer, still touching her with only his mouth, but close enough that he could feel her heat. Her mouth was soft under his, sweet and pliant. She made another sound, a soft moan, and swayed closer. Cole reached out a hand and gently gripped the graceful column of her neck.

The contact was enough to break the spell between them. Sienna stepped back, away from his grasp, her fingertips pressing against her swollen lips.

"Why did you do that?" She seemed more confused than angry, which was a small victory in Cole's mind.

"I needed to know if your mouth was as soft as it looks."

She gathered her long blond hair and flipped it over her shoulder, rolling her eyes at him. "I don't think I've ever been described as soft."

"You're soft," he assured her. "At least when you're not being disagreeable and argumentative."

"I don't argue and I can be agreeable when I want to." She no longer looked dazed. Instead the spark had returned to her gaze. He liked it there. "I don't need to prove anything to anyone."

He shrugged. "Except maybe yourself."

"You shouldn't kiss me again."

"Do you want to argue about it?"

She narrowed her eyes. "Good night, Sheriff."

"Call me Cole," he said, unable to stop himself from making the request.

She stared at him so long he wasn't sure she'd answer, then whispered, "Good night, Cole," and turned for the house.

He watched her walk away until the front door clicked shut behind her. Crickets chirped from the bushes and an owl in a tree at the edge of the forest gave a mournful hoot.

Cole had come to Colorado as an escape, running from the scandal and tragedy that surrounded his parents' deaths.

He'd found refuge in small-town life and in serving and protecting the people who made this town their home. But he wasn't a part of the fabric of Crimson's community in the same way as Jase. Growing up an army brat, Cole had become an expert at making connections without truly allowing himself to bond to anyone or anything. Hell, he'd never even owned a dog, which was practically a requirement in Colorado.

Sienna made him feel different. Maybe because she was also so obviously alone. He could allow himself this connection with her—but whether it was real or imagined he couldn't quite say.

Did it really matter? Cole knew that along with emotional ties came the very real possibility of someone getting hurt. He'd had a ringside seat to watch his mom unravel after his father's death until her heart had literally given out. He didn't want any part of that kind of pain, either for himself or anyone around him.

Marlene down at the department liked to tease him about the parade of women who made excuses to stop in. But Cole wasn't interested in getting close to a woman, even to an almost irresistible blonde who took his breath away every time he looked at her.

At least that's what he tried to convince himself of as he climbed in his truck and drove through the quiet streets of the town he'd made his home. Attraction was one thing, but he wouldn't let it go any further.

Chapter 5

Sienna couldn't have said how long she'd been sitting in her rental car outside the tiny brick duplex the next morning, but her backside was numb and her throat had gone dry from the air conditioner blowing through the vents in the dash.

She'd turned the car on and off at least a dozen times, psyching herself up for approaching the modest home. Within those walls lived a man she hadn't seen in two decades but who was never far from her mind, no matter how hard she tried to forget him.

A knock on the driver's side window made her jerk around so fast she banged her forehead into the glass. She let out a sound somewhere between a scream and a groan, blinking away tears of fear, frustration and pain. Her gaze focused on the gray-haired man standing next to the car, and her stomach dipped.

The years hadn't been kind to Declan Crenshaw, but

Sienna knew the signs of age had as much to do with the choices he'd made as the passage of time.

She looked at him through the glass, half tempted to throw the car into Drive and speed away from everything this moment represented.

For his part, her dad looked like he could wait all day for her to decide whether to acknowledge him. It was that air of serene patience that made her punch down the window button.

"I thought you might run out of gas idling at the curb so long," he said conversationally.

"It seemed like a good idea to sneak up on me?" she shot back, pressing her fingers to the goose egg quickly rising on her forehead.

He ran a hand over his face, where at least a day of salt-and-pepper whiskers shadowed his jaw. "Figured you'd drive off if I came at you through the front door."

She wouldn't tell him he'd been right. There was no way she'd admit that he had any sort of insight into her behavior. "You don't seem surprised to see me."

"Jase called yesterday." He inclined his head. "Damn, you look like your mother."

"So I'm told."

"You have softer features, though. And straighter hair."

Sienna huffed out a small laugh. It was the second time in less than twenty-four hours she'd been described as soft, after a lifetime becoming reconciled to her hard edges.

"How's your mother doing?"

"You can't expect me to answer that," she said, not bothering to hide the snap in her tone. No matter the issues Sienna had with her mom, Dana was the one who'd chosen her at least. She owed her mother some loyalty.

Declan stared, as if weighing her answer...as if weighing her. Then he asked, "How are you?"

He had no right to know anything about her life after all these years. Except she was the one who'd sought him out.

Sienna and her mother had left Crimson years ago, and not once had her father contacted her. He hadn't so much as sent a birthday card. How was she ever supposed to put aside the pain of rejection that was woven into every inch of the woman she'd become?

"I can't do this," she whispered, glancing up at him.

Something flashed in his blue eyes, but he didn't argue. There was no fight, no begging her to stay. He simply stepped back from the car as she rolled up the window, and watched her drive away.

Tears streamed down her face as she turned the corner. Had she really expected him to fight for her? Did her arrival in town mean anything to him? Jase had told him she'd come to Crimson, but neither man had sought her out. They had their lives here, and Sienna had stopped being a part of them a long time ago.

Why should that change now? Growing up without a real father might have defined her, but it clearly had very little impact on the man who'd let her go.

When her vision blurred to the point she couldn't see the road in front of her, she pulled off to the side, jolting as the car's tire scraped the edge of the curb. Where had these tears come from? Declan Crenshaw wasn't worth crying over—that's what her mother would say.

She took several deep breaths, took a wad of napkins from the glove compartment and wiped her face. Grabbing her cell phone from the passenger side seat, she punched in a number and hit the speaker button.

"You've been avoiding my calls." Her mother's crisp tone fairly dripped with censure.

"I have bad service up here," Sienna lied and heard Dana's disapproving tsk across the miles. Felt the subtle reprimand to her core.

"Kevin spoke with your father this morning. He mentioned you had a spat."

"It was more than a *spat*." Sienna drummed her fingers against the steering wheel. "I broke up with him."

A soft hiss from Dana.

"I found him in bed with another woman," Sienna added before her mother could tell her she was making a mistake.

"These things happen," Dana said quietly, her lack of emotion communicating far too much for Sienna's taste. "You'd do well to give him a bit of warning when he isn't expecting you."

"You can't be serious," Sienna said through her teeth before remembering that her mother was always serious. "He cheated on me and somehow it's my fault because I surprised him at the hotel?"

"I didn't say that," Dana insisted in her usual measured tone. "Not exactly. Kevin is important to your father's business, Sienna. Especially with him heading up the merger. You know it's scheduled to go through in a month. He can't afford to have you disrupting the status quo. Remember your place."

"My place." Sienna raised a hand to her head, pressing fingertips against the bump there and trying to pretend that the headache was the reason she felt like crying again. "Craig Pierce isn't my father, Mom. Let's not act like—"

"He raised you from the time you were a girl."

"He tolerated me because he wanted you," Sienna clarified. There had never been any question as to her value with her stepfather. Mostly she hadn't minded. Dana had made sure she understood they were to be grateful for Craig's largesse and the opportunities being part of the powerful Pierce family opened to them.

"You never wanted for anything," Dana insisted, the words coming out fast and with traces of the Alabama accent she'd tried so hard to erase. As far as Dana was concerned, she didn't have any past before meeting Craig Pierce. It was as if she'd been sprung fully formed as a society wife out of the mold Craig created.

But Sienna remembered the months before her mother had met Craig, when she'd managed to secure a job as a hostess in one of the toniest restaurants in Chicago. It was the type of stuffy, wood-paneled spot where local businessmen came for power lunches and drinks after work. Dana had spent hours with old magazines and CDs she'd borrowed from the library, studying Jackie Kennedy and Grace Kelly, modeling her appearance, the way she dressed and even her mode of speaking after the two women.

Within weeks, all traces of Dana Crenshaw, hard-living party girl had been wiped away. Sienna remembered being mesmerized by her mother's transformation. Back in Crimson, she'd always been vaguely embarrassed by her parents—Declan and Dana were too loud, hanging all over each other when they weren't fighting in a way most parents didn't. Plus they'd lived in the shabbiest trailer in the trailer park, when Sienna's classmates came from town or the outlying ranches around Crimson.

So it had been true that she'd never wanted for anything material once her mother met and quickly married Craig. But love and acceptance were another story, one Dana had shoved onto a high shelf to gather dust in the pristine mansion they'd moved into with Craig. Out of necessity, Sienna had quickly forced herself to forget where she'd come from and anything else but that gratitude she was meant to feel for her new life.

"I saw him today," she said suddenly.

From her mother's sharp intake of breath, she knew Dana understood whom she meant.

"You need to come home," her mother said after a weighted pause. "You don't belong there."

"That's kind of the problem." Sienna swallowed against the emotion that threatened to choke her. "I don't belong anywhere."

She drove around for hours, up and down the streets of Crimson and out toward the mountain pass and the farms and ranches that surrounded the town. There was the turn-off for Crimson Ranch, a property she knew was owned by some famous actress. She'd read about it in a magazine a few years ago, and the casual mention of her hometown had been the thing to reawaken her curiosity about where she'd come from and the father and brother still there.

Even with that curiosity, she'd kept herself distant when Jase had come to visit their mother last year after Dana had finished her cancer treatments. Much like today, the reality of her past and her present colliding had been too much for Sienna.

She'd hidden out in her apartment for an entire weekend, as if she'd spontaneously stumble upon him at one of her favorite neighborhood haunts. Which was stupid because Chicago was enormous.

Unlike Crimson. She was tired and hungry and had squatted to go to the bathroom on the side of a deserted Forest Service road because she was too scared to even run into the local gas station and take the chance on an encounter with Jase.

She could return to The Bumblebee. Paige had told her she planned on painting one of the upstairs bedrooms today. No doubt her new friend would be happy to see her and to hear all about how the meeting with Declan had gone.

Which was what kept Sienna from going back. How could she admit that she'd run away after only a few words with him? She hated that he'd surprised her instead of the other way around. He'd known she was in town to see him, and for some reason that seemed to take away the power she'd expected to feel in the moment.

As she did another loop through downtown Crimson, past painted Victorian houses that had been converted into businesses and the tourists milling along the picturesque shop fronts, she spotted a white Jeep parked at the curb, the words Crimson County Sheriff emblazoned on the side.

Her frustration coalesced into anger in an instant. She should be able to approach her father and brother in her own time, on her own terms. But that choice had been taken away from her because they'd been warned about her. *Warned*.

As if she were some criminal or loose cannon intent on trouble.

Cole Bennett had called her a troublemaker, and obviously he believed it because he'd taken it upon himself to tell Jase she was in town. He'd stripped her of the only power she had in this situation, and for that all of her wrath narrowed with laser precision to focus on him.

She parked the rental car on a side street and stepped out, surveying the block where Cole's Jeep was parked. There was a florist on one side and a toy store next to that. Several gift shops had wares displayed out on the sidewalk, displays of home goods or racks of colorful T-shirts.

About halfway down the block, she saw the sign for Life is Sweet bakery and started walking. Cops and doughnuts might be a stereotype, but she figured a coffee shop was as good a place as any to start her search.

She pushed open the door, ignoring the way her stomach growled at the mouthwatering scent of yeasty dough and sugar that enveloped her.

A woman from behind the counter called out a greeting, but Sienna ignored her. She stalked toward the table at the far side, where a man sat, his caramel-colored hair tousled. His shoulders were so broad under his sheriff's uniform, they made him look almost out of place at one of the small café tables in the cheery space.

"You did this to me," she said, her voice trembling slightly.

Cole looked up like he didn't have a care in the world, arched a brow. "There are a lot of things I'd like to do to you, sweetheart. Care to elaborate on what you're talking about at the moment?"

Butterflies zipped through her stomach at the intensity in his gaze, and she hated him even more for being able to so casually defuse her righteous anger. Now she was distracted by him—his brown eyes studying her, the shadow of stubble that covered his jaw, his big hand holding tight to a thin ballpoint pen. He looked strong and sure, and Sienna craved that like she imagined her father still wanted a drink, despite his sobriety.

It made her feel weak and unsteady, one more reminder that the mask of confidence and poise she'd worn all these years was nothing but her pretending to be someone she wasn't.

"You told them I was coming." She lifted a hand, jabbed a finger at him. "You *warned* them."

He wrapped his giant hand around hers, folding her fingers into her palm, then gently tugged her into the seat across from him.

She didn't fight because she was suddenly weary to the bone and grateful for the chair. The other customers had turned to stare, obviously curious about the crazy woman who'd go toe to toe with the hulking sheriff.

Cole pasted on a casual, good ol' boy type of smile, although his eyes told a different story. "Katie, would you mind sending over one of those amazing chicken salad sandwiches and a couple of lemonades?" He turned toward the counter. "Looks like I'm here for lunch after all."

"Sure thing, Sheriff," the pretty brunette at the cash register answered. "Chips or pasta salad on the side?"

Cole tossed a questioning gaze at Sienna. "Pasta salad," she mumbled after a moment and Cole put in the request.

"But I don't want anything," Sienna insisted, even though she could feel her hands trembling due to hunger. "I can handle myself just fine without your help."

"Marlene," Cole began conversationally. "She's my office manager and pretty much runs everything at the department. I might have mentioned her before?"

Sienna narrowed her eyes.

"Right." Cole sat back and studied her for a long moment. "Marlene is an undisputed genius and normally easy as pie to get along with. But if she gets too hungry... Well, she has a term for it. She calls it hangry." He inclined his head. "It's a mix of hungry and angr—"

"I know what hangry is," Sienna said, irritated that her snappish tone made her sound even hangrier than she was. "I had oatmeal for breakfast. I'm fine."

"What time did you eat breakfast?"

"Seven."

"That's five hours ago."

"A lawman and a mathematician. You really are all that and a bag of chips."

"Chips are good, but you made the right choice with pasta salad. It's homemade, along with the chicken salad. This place only recently started serving lunch. Katie Crawford, the owner, bakes all the bread herself. The fact that she's serving lunch has been kind of a game changer around here."

Cole Bennett was the biggest game changer Sienna had ever met. She'd come into the bakery to tell him off and somehow now they were having a casual conversation about food and hunger. She crossed her arms over her chest, unwilling to allow herself to be distracted any longer. She had business in Crimson, and she was done with the town's hottie sheriff inserting himself into it.

"I don't know—"

"Here's your sandwich. Hope you enjoy."

Sienna glanced up at the woman who'd approached the table, ready to snap out a scathing reprimand for being interrupted. One of the first things Craig Pierce had drilled into her was that good waitstaff should know their place. And interrupting a customer's conversation was tantamount to spitting in the food as far as her stepfather was concerned.

Sienna had never bought into the idea and had always been polite to everyone she met. Even though she'd been a "have" for over half her life, she never forgot what it felt like to be a "have not." But her temper was practically boiling over, and she didn't much care who bore the brunt of it.

Except all she could do when she turned to Katie Craw-ford was offer a small smile and a muttered "thank you."

Cole chuckled, as if he knew what she'd intended and was amused that she couldn't lash out at the bakery owner. But to unleash her temper on Katie would have been like kicking a week-old puppy. Maybe it was because she'd grown up in a big city, but Sienna didn't think she'd ever seen someone who oozed sweetness and inner goodness the way Katie did. It was a wonder she didn't have tiny blue-birds flitting around her head chirping a merry tune and anointing Katie with a crown of woven flowers.

"What's so funny about my chicken salad?" the woman asked Cole, hands on hips.

"Nothing at all," Cole said quickly. "Your food is always delicious and everyone in town knows it."

Katie beamed at Cole, then stuck out her hand toward Sienna. "Maybe not someone new to town. I'm Katie Craw-ford."

"Sienna Pierce."

"Nice to meet you, Sienna. What brings you to Crim-son? How do you and Cole know each other? Can I bring you dessert for later?"

"That's a lot of questions," Sienna said, her stomach growling as she inhaled the delectable scent of tangy chicken salad and fresh bread.

Katie's smile widened even farther. "My husband says I'm too curious for my own good, but it's part of owning a business." She scrunched up her pert nose. "Plus we have a little one at home now, so work hours are about all the time I get to socialize."

"I saw the other ladies at monthly Mexican a couple of weeks ago," Cole said. "Noticed you weren't part of the group."

"Willow had a bad cold," Katie told him. "Noah was on an overnight doing trail maintenance on the other side of the pass, and I didn't want to get a sitter."

Sienna took a big bite of the sandwich, moaning softly at the explosion of flavors that hit her tongue. She listened absently as Katie and Cole discussed Willow's cold and the various remedies Katie had tried to make her better.

"She's finally sleeping through the night again," Katie reported, then glanced toward Sienna. "Do you like it?"

"There aren't words," Sienna said around a mouthful, "for how much."

"I'll bring you a brownie for later. I don't think you ever mentioned what brought you to Crimson."

Sienna placed the uneaten portion of sandwich on the plate, then wiped her mouth with a napkin. "I'm visiting family."

"That's great." Katie clapped her hands together. "Anyone I know?"

Sienna shrugged and shot a look toward Cole.

"Katie is married to Emily's brother," he told her.

Her stomach pitched. "Of course she is." She closed her eyes for a moment, then forced herself to meet Katie's friendly gaze. "Jase is *my* brother."

She waited for Katie's expression to change, but if anything it gentled even more. "It's good to have you back in town. It can't be easy after all this time, but family is important no matter how much water has passed under the bridge."

Sienna opened her mouth to argue but found she couldn't. Although it was silly, the simple blessing from a relative stranger meant something to her.

"Isn't that right, Cole?" Katie asked quietly, and for the first time Sienna saw the unflappable sheriff look rattled.

"Sure, Katie. I'll have an iced tea if you don't mind?"

"Coming right up," Katie answered and turned away.

"You're hiding something," Sienna said, leaning forward across the table. "And Little Mrs. Sunshine knows what it is."

Cole made a dismissive sound low in his throat. "I'm not hiding anything." He snagged the remaining half a sandwich. "I also appreciate that you look less like you're going to claw my eyes out now that you've had something to eat. Want to tell me how that started?"

She picked up a fork and stabbed a piece of pasta. Her body was no longer bristling with anger now but the reminder of why she'd come in here in the first place made her chest ache.

"I saw Declan."

"It didn't go well?"

She took another bite of pasta salad, stared out the window of the bakery as she chewed, then turned back to Cole. "Before I could gather my courage to approach the door, he saw me. Went out the back door and slipped around my car to knock on the driver's side window." She blew out a breath. "Scared me half to death."

"Sounds like Declan. How did the conversation go?"

"Terrible. I freaked out. I wasn't ready. But he knew to expect me." She pointed a finger at Cole. "Because you warned Jase."

He closed his eyes for a moment, then said quietly, "I'm sorry, Sienna."

"Are you?"

"Jase is my friend," he told her as if that explained everything.

But the words only fueled her temper again. Jase was

his friend. Katie was his friend. Crimson was his home. And Sienna was nothing.

It shouldn't surprise her or hurt her feelings, but it did. To the point that the pain and loneliness were like a tidal wave, crashing over and pulling her under. She couldn't breathe. She certainly wouldn't stay here and casually enjoy the food he'd ordered because he could read her better than anyone had done in ages.

Like that meant something. Like she meant something.

"Stay out of my business," she said, pushing back from the table. "My time in Crimson has nothing to do with you, Sheriff." She purposely used his title instead of his name, watching his eyes snap in response.

A tiny victory, but she'd take anything she could get at this point. She walked out of the bakery and away from Cole before she could change her mind.

Chapter 6

"It's bad in there."

Cole nodded as he tightened his flak vest. "You don't have to go in, Grant. Melody and the kids—"

His top deputy snorted. "Don't do that, boss. I knew the risks of this job when I took it, and so did Mel. You can't treat me like I'm a rookie."

Turning toward the darkened warehouse that sat on an abandoned property outside of town, Cole shook his head. "This is Crimson," he said, anger making his voice low. "We shouldn't have to be dealing with scumbags like this up here."

Grant shrugged. "The town is growing, and the world is changing. Big cities don't have the market cornered on lowlife drug dealers."

"It's a small operation." Cole inclined his head toward JJ Waring, a second deputy who stood about twenty feet from them, camouflaged by an overgrown bush and the darkness of the hour. "Waring and I can handle it."

"I'm fine, Sheriff." Grant moved so he was standing in front of Cole. "Elaina is fine."

Cole blew out a breath. Last fall, Grant's young daughter had gotten caught in the middle of an incident with a tweaked-out petty criminal who'd had too many run-ins with the department to count. But on that night, the man had gone too far, and Elaina had ended up hospitalized from a knife wound. Grant and his wife, Melody, had witnessed the whole thing.

Although everyone from Grant to Marlene to Jase had insisted it wasn't Cole's fault, he couldn't help but blame himself. There had been something about the man that had reminded Cole of his brother, Shep. The brother he hadn't seen in close to seven years. Cole had gone easy on the guy too many times, and his drug use and subsequent bad behavior had escalated.

Cole took his responsibilities as sheriff seriously, but his duty to the men and women who worked for him was even more important. He knew that each of them understood the risks involved but that didn't stop him from wanting to protect them, along with every person who lived under his jurisdiction.

Since that night last fall, he'd made it his personal mission to take down the underground drug ring that had spread its slimy tentacles up from Denver and into several of the high mountain communities.

It went beyond the legal marijuana that had become so popular in Colorado in the past few years. The stuff these guys were manufacturing was hard-core, and the bigger operations in the city had set up satellite sites in rural areas where there was more room and less monitoring by local law enforcement.

Not in Crimson if Cole had anything to do about it.

He unholstered his gun and nodded at Grant. "Glad to have you by my side," he said, and together they slipped into the shadows.

Sienna blinked awake, then glanced at the clock. Two in the morning.

She sighed and sat up, the sheets and comforter twisted into a ball at the foot of the bed. Maybe a glass of water would help—or warm milk. Anything to stop her from tossing and turning, sleep remaining elusive as her mind spun in a dozen different directions.

She went to the bedroom window, unlatched it, then pushed it open. Cool air was good for sleeping, too. Her gaze snagged on the familiar white Jeep parked at the curb in front of The Bumblebee. Was there something wrong in this quiet neighborhood to bring out Crimson's finest at this late hour?

The SUV was dark, no motor running. She couldn't see the driver but knew without a doubt that Cole was behind the wheel.

She hadn't seen him since yesterday at the bakery, and tried to ignore the thrill that zipped along her skin at the mere thought of him now.

After walking away from him, she'd planned to march down the street to the mayor's office in the county courthouse, a redbrick historic building situated across the park that made up the center of downtown Crimson.

But the thought of facing her brother made her break out in a cold sweat, heart pounding and hands trembling. Why was it so difficult to face Jase or her father?

Her mother had been the one to take her away from Crimson, but Sienna still felt the painful sting of rejection from being let go so easily. The argument could be made that her life had been better far away from the turmoil of her alcoholic father—she knew her mother would contend that Sienna had been given many more opportunities in Chicago than she ever would have had in Crimson.

That didn't matter either. She'd felt expendable. Even though they'd both been kids, Jase had stayed in Crimson because Declan had needed him, not Sienna. The two Crenshaw men were a pair, and she was an outsider in the town where she'd been born.

Not allowing herself to think too much about her actions, she padded downstairs, slipped on a pair of shoes and let herself out the front door. The driver's side window lowered as she rounded the front of the Jeep.

"Is there a problem, Sheriff?" She wrapped her arms around her waist, still surprised by the nip in the air. The temperature in the mountains dipped every night when the sun went down, so different from the Midwest, where it often stayed within a few degrees of the sweltering heat and humidity of daylight hours.

"No." The one syllable was a low rumble. Cole's face remained in shadow, but something was different tonight. The invisible current that seemed to connect them was still there, but there was an unusual charge to it.

"Was my restless sleep disturbing the neighbors tonight?"

"I didn't get a call from the neighbors."

She stepped closer to the SUV. "Then why are you—" She sucked in a breath. "What happened? You're hurt."

He was leaning back against the headrest and shifted to meet her gaze fully. "I'm fine. Just not ready to go home."

"The bandage on your shoulder doesn't look fine," she insisted, reaching for the door. "Oh, my God, Cole. Were you shot?"

He didn't argue when she reached around him to unfasten the seat belt. He wore a white T-shirt with one sleeve bunched above the bandage that covered the upper part of his arm. "You said my name again." One side of his mouth curved. "It sounds good coming from your lips."

"You're delirious. We need to get you to the hospital."

"I'm fine. Bullet grazed me."

"Who shot you?" she demanded, tugging him from the Jeep.

"Bad guy," he muttered.

"There's a cut on your forehead."

"It's only a scratch. I chased him through the woods."

She took his hand and led him up the flagstone walkway toward the house. Paige was a deep sleeper, so Sienna didn't think the inn owner would wake up, but she climbed the stairs to her bedroom quietly, Cole following behind her.

She pushed him toward the bed. "Sit down," she ordered. "I'm going to get something to clean out that cut."

"Scratch," he insisted.

"Tomato, to-mah-to," she shot back and hurried toward the bathroom at the end of the hall. She found a bottle of hydrogen peroxide, cotton balls and a small box of bandages, returning to the bedroom to find Cole sprawled across the bed.

He glanced at her as she moved toward him. "Nice wallpaper," he said, circling a finger in the air.

A rose-hued paper with a pattern of red and pink roses covered the walls. The queen-size bed had a wrought-iron frame in a delicate design with filigree decorating the end of each post. There was a tall chest of drawers against one wall, and a shorter, longer dresser on the opposite wall. Both were covered with lace doilies and vases of dried flowers.

It was like a throwback to an inn of a hundred years ago, and Sienna had immediately appreciated all the homey touches. It was a feminine space, but even on his back, Cole looked ridiculously masculine in it.

"Tell me what happened." She sat on the edge of the bed, placing the supplies on the nightstand.

"Drug bust," he said tightly. "More guys than we anticipated."

"A drug bust in Crimson?" She soaked a cotton ball with hydrogen peroxide. "That seems hard to believe."

"I only wish our mountain Mayberry, as you call it, was safe from the issues people associate with big cities. But drugs are an insidious problem. Maybe not to the level other places find, but we deal with our share of bad here, Sienna."

"Was it a success?"

He nodded, then hissed out a breath when she dabbed the cotton ball against his broken skin. "Did you ever consider a career as a nurse?"

She smiled sweetly and pressed harder against the cut. "I should take you to the hospital."

He gave a small laugh. "Spent some time there earlier and not going back. One of my deputies shot a guy who was fleeing the scene. He'll live, but his leg needed some attention." He moved his arm, then groaned. "The doc wrapped up my shoulder so I know it's fine."

"Was anyone…?"

"Killed? No, thankfully. But we arrested four of them and shut down the local operation. It was a good night."

She took a bandage strip from the box and unpeeled the wrapper. "So why are you here?"

"I really am sorry," he said quietly. "Not that I told Jase about you being in town, but that he and Declan knowing seems to be messing with your head."

"My head is fine," she whispered, covering his cut with the bandage.

"Your head is gorgeous," he countered, "just like the rest of you. I didn't intend to hurt you, Sienna."

"The road to hell…" she said, making her voice light.

Pretending it didn't mean anything to her that he'd come here tonight.

Not fooling either of them.

He encircled her wrist with his big hand. "I'm sorry."

She nodded, ignoring the butterflies fluttering through her chest. "I probably would have freaked out either way. Somehow the idea of facing Jase and my dad is way different than the reality of it."

"But you're still here."

"Call me a glutton for punishment, but I'm not ready to give up quite yet."

"Good."

She tugged out of his grasp, stood and walked to the window. "You're in my bed," she told him, stating the obvious.

He flashed a wry smile, sat up and placed his feet on the floor. "I should go."

"You can stay," she blurted, feeling color flood her cheeks as he arched a brow.

"Sienna."

"I don't mean I'm going to sleep with you." She pressed her fingers to her flaming cheeks. "Or I guess I do mean sleep. But nothing else. No hanky-panky."

"Hanky-panky," Cole murmured.

She rolled her eyes, walking to the opposite side of the bed. "I remember my… Declan using that term when Jase and I were little, before Mom and I left, of course. There was a young couple that moved into the trailer next to ours for just a few months, but they were quite enamored of each other. When Jase asked why they turned off the lights and went to bed so early every night, Declan answered 'hanky-panky.'" She reached down and smoothed a hand over the pillowcase. "I didn't even understand what he meant, but the phrase stuck with me."

"It's strange the things we remember from childhood."

"Tell me something funny from when you were a kid," she said, slipping between the cool sheets and leaning back against the headboard.

Whether from her proximity or the thought of having to share something personal, she saw Cole's shoulders stiffen. Maybe he'd shut her out, as he had the other night. But she wouldn't regret her curiosity. He was like a puzzle she couldn't stop trying to solve.

He straightened from the bed, massaged the back of his neck with one hand. "We moved every couple of years because of my dad's career in the army. Me and my twin brother, Shep—"

"You have a twin brother?" she asked, stunned. "I thought you said your family was gone."

His jaw clenched. "They are. My parents are dead, and Shep could be for all I know. We haven't spoken in years, and he seemed hell-bent on destruction before he left. I don't even know where he is at this point."

"But you could—"

"Do you want the funny story or not?"

She clamped her mouth shut and nodded.

"Shep and I are identical, so we did a lot of pretending we were each other, especially when we first got to a new school. Fourth grade in Germany, we spent an entire semester taking tests for each other because we were in different classes. They wanted to suspend both of us but couldn't prove anything."

Sienna gave a small laugh. "Was your mom mad?"

"She dragged us down to a local barber and flipped a coin to decide which one of us had to have our head shaved." As he spoke, he toed off first one boot, then the other. Sienna's heart raced in response. "From that day on, we weren't allowed to have the same haircut because she never wanted us to be able to play that kind of trick again."

"I bet you found other ways to be bad."

"Plenty of them."

"I was a good girl," she blurted as he moved toward the door and flipped off the lights, plunging the room into darkness.

"I never had a doubt," he told her, and she could hear the humor in his voice, "despite the speeding and the car-borrowing and all the other trouble I'm sure you're going to cause while you're in town."

She pulled the covers tighter around her. "I meant what I said, Cole."

"God, it kills me when you say my name." The mattress dipped as he lowered himself to the bed again.

"Should I stick to 'Sheriff'?"

"You know the answer to that, and I know the no hanky-panky rule." He shifted, stretching out on his back. "But I'm tired as hell after the night I had, Sienna, so I'm going to take you up on the offer of sleeping together." He smiled. "Emphasis on sleeping."

"You're laying on top of the covers," she pointed out.

"Safer this way, sweetheart." She heard him yawn and turned on her side. It was a crazy offer she'd made and even crazier that he'd taken her up on it, but there was something comforting about Cole's big body next to her on the bed. She felt less alone, safer—although she had no reason not to feel safe. But she'd been off-kilter since the moment she'd arrived in Colorado.

Now she took a deep breath and closed her eyes, her weary body practically melting into the soft mattress.

"Good night, Cole," she whispered.

"Good night, Sienna. Sweet dreams."

Chapter 7

Cole winced as the second stair from the bottom squeaked under his foot. It was five in the morning, and he was working on three hours of sleep—albeit the best sleep he'd had in years. He'd drifted off almost as soon as he closed his eyes, then woken a few minutes ago with Sienna snuggled tight against his chest, his arm wrapped around her waist.

He'd wanted to run his hands along her curves, to kiss the sweet spot at the base of her neck, to press himself into her—all those things and more. But she'd said no "hanky-panky" and he was going to honor that request, even if it killed him. So he'd gingerly climbed out of bed, grabbed his boots and let himself out of her bedroom without waking her.

He sure as hell didn't need any early morning runners to notice his patrol Jeep in front of The Bumblebee and start asking questions. Crimson was a small town and a close-knit community and gossip traveled faster than a prairie fire across the drought-plagued plains.

"Coffee, Sheriff?"

He cursed under his breath, then pasted on a smile as he turned to meet Paige's questioning gaze. "I'll get some at the station later."

"You must have arrived late last night," she said conversationally, sipping from a mug that said *I drink coffee for your protection.* "Now you're heading out before sunrise."

"This is not what it looks like," he said through clenched teeth.

"Is that so?" She scrunched up her nose. "Because despite the fact that you seem a little worse for wear with those bandages, it looks like a booty call."

"Nothing happened between Sienna and me." He ran a hand through his hair, unable to figure out how to explain why he'd parked in front of the inn last night in the first place. Not when he barely understood the reasons himself. "I was here but we slept. Not together. Next to each other. That's all."

She studied him for a moment, then nodded. "Okay."

"Okay? Just like that?"

"I don't know you well, Sheriff, but you don't strike me as a liar. Plus, I think you like Sienna." She wiggled her eyebrows. "You really like her."

He didn't bother to deny it. "It doesn't matter how I feel about her. She's here temporarily. She could leave town at any time."

"Even she isn't sure how long she'll stay," Paige agreed. "I guess it depends on how things go with Jase and her dad, whenever she actually has a real conversation with either of them." She shook her head. "Family stuff is always more complicated than you want it to be."

Cole thought of his parents and his brother, of the lies

and drama that tore apart his family. His biggest regret in life was being unable to fix what his father broke.

"Yeah. Would you mind not mentioning me being here to anyone? I don't want…"

"You like her," Paige told him. "That matters. She needs someone in her corner."

Cole blew out a breath. How could he be in Sienna's corner and still remain loyal to his friendship with Jase? But he couldn't deny the connection he felt to her.

"I've got to go. Thanks for understanding."

She smiled. "I don't understand it, but I don't need to. Just don't hurt her and we'll have no problems."

"I'll do my best," he promised with a low chuckle, then let himself out the front door. It was funny to think of the petite inn owner, with her bohemian dresses and crazy curly hair, giving him an implied threat. He couldn't imagine what kind of problem Paige could possibly create for someone like him, but he still appreciated her loyalty.

He glanced at Sienna's bedroom window as he climbed into the Jeep and turned the key in the ignition, his shoulder still aching. Where did last night leave the two of them? As he drove through town toward his house on the other side of Crimson Creek, those late-night hours spent in Sienna's bed felt more and more like a dream.

He showered, grabbed a stale bagel from the cabinet, then headed to the station. He checked in with a couple of his deputies, then called the county jail to get an update on the men they'd arrested. There was a mountain of paperwork to process, and he was on his fourth cup of coffee when a knock sounded on the door to his office.

"You got a minute?" Jase asked, peering in. "I brought muffins from Life is Sweet if that makes a difference."

"Katie's muffins make all the difference." Cole sat back,

stretched his arms over his head and then winced at the pain in his arm. "Come on in and have a seat."

"I heard last night was intense."

"Yeah."

"But you took down Elton's operation." Jase set the brown bag from the bakery on Cole's desk, then folded his tall body into a chair.

Cole inclined his head. "For now. The guys running the bigger operation in Denver will have another lackey in place within months. We need to make sure we don't let down our guard."

"It was still a win," Jase insisted. "Can you ever just take credit for something and bask in the glory for a day?"

"There's no glory in what we did last night. But I'm grateful my men came out unscathed."

"What about your shoulder and face?"

"Minor."

"Of course."

Cole reached in the bag and pulled out a blueberry muffin, his favorite. "Did you come here for an official report on last night?" He took a big bite, tossing the remainder of his bagel in the trash as he did.

Jase gripped the arms of the chair, his shoulders stiffening. "She saw my dad."

"Her dad, too," Cole said quietly, choosing not to mention he knew all about Sienna's encounter with Declan. It would reveal too much when he wasn't sure yet what Jase wanted from him.

"Apparently she sat in her car in front of his duplex."

"No law against that."

Jase blew out a breath. "Dad noticed and walked out to talk to her. But she took off right after. Now he's worked up that he scared her away and wants me to reach out."

"Okay."

"Not okay," Jase countered. "I don't know what to say to her. I have no idea what she wants or why she's still in town when she hasn't talked to either of us."

"Maybe she's getting her bearings," Cole suggested.

"What does that mean?"

"We both know she didn't plan this trip. She might need some time to figure out exactly what she wants from a relationship with you and Declan."

"I don't believe she wants any kind of relationship." Jase shook his head. "I think she's hanging around to stir the pot. I get the feeling she's angry with both of us, although I can't figure out why. Hell, she was the one who got out. I stayed behind and dealt with Dad's demons while Sienna lived the good life in Chicago."

Cole concentrated on pulling the wrapper from the oversize muffin. He took another bite, then a long drink of coffee. He'd hoped Jase would just continue his rant, but obviously he wanted Cole's take on the situation.

"You chose to stay."

"It wasn't much of a choice," Jase muttered.

"But you got to make it. Maybe the life you had was difficult, but it was yours. Your mom took Sienna. She had no choice."

"Are you telling me I got the better deal spending my childhood trying to keep Declan away from the bottle— unsuccessfully for years as everyone knows? I went to my mom's house last year when I was in Chicago. Remember the movie *Home Alone*?"

Cole nodded.

"They live around the corner from the house where it was filmed. It's a hell of a nice neighborhood. That's where Sienna grew up. She went to great schools, played tennis and rode horses if the framed photos our mom has displayed are any indication. Am I supposed to feel sorry for her?"

"You know a bunch of material crap doesn't necessarily make for a happy childhood."

"You're defending her."

"There's nothing to defend, Jase." Cole blew out a breath. "I'm telling you that from what I gather, the grass wasn't always green for Sienna, despite where she was raised."

"I need her gone," Jase said suddenly.

"Why?"

"It's not the right time. We're about to have a baby. Em is worried about how Davey is going to take to having a little sister or brother. He seems excited by it now, but it's going to be a lot of work."

Cole knew that Emily's son from her first marriage had Asperger's syndrome, and helping him manage social situations and interactions with other people had been Emily's priority for years.

"Work is crazy busy," Jase went on. "Did you hear a private equity group out of California bought the old ski resort?"

"Seriously?"

Jase nodded. "Colorado has had some great ski seasons the past few years, but the popular places are getting too crowded. There aren't too many independently owned mountains left, but if these people get the resort and the lifts operational again, it would be a game changer for the town."

"That's great, I guess," Cole said, although he thought Crimson was just fine the way it was. "But none of what you've told me has anything to do with Sienna."

"It's not her exactly," Jase said with a sigh. "It's everything—the baby, working with the resort's new owner, plus my dad. Mainly my dad. He's been doing great since we moved him into his new house. But the last time he fell off the wagon, it was after he got the letter from Mom. Now Sienna shows up here and he's worked up about it." He rubbed a hand across his jaw. "I know his issues aren't her fault, but the timing of her coming back into his life…"

"Why are you telling me all this?"

"You know her."

"She's been in town less than a week."

Jase lifted a brow. "Katie told Emily you bought her lunch the other day."

"People around here talk to each other entirely too much."

"True," Jase agreed. "But maybe you can help with Sienna. I don't want to set her off—"

"You're not at all interested in having a relationship with her?"

"I'm not against it. But I'm not sure I trust her motivation. My mom reached out to me last year, and I saw her in Chicago. She was going through cancer treatments and her desire to reconnect with me seemed genuine. Then she let it slip that her husband was brokering some big merger at work and couldn't have any whiff of scandal attached to his name."

"How are you a scandal?"

"It was during the mayoral election, and the other company was headquartered in Denver. I'm not sure what was going into the deal or why her background mattered to anyone. But it was like she was trying to acknowledge she had a past in Colorado while still making sure it didn't affect her current life."

"That's cold."

"Don't get me wrong, we had a fine visit. She genuinely feels guilty about ripping apart our family the way she did.

I also think she'd do anything to protect the life she has now. Maybe it was more like she was putting her affairs in order, although now that she's in remission I haven't heard from her. Bottom line is it all felt too coincidental in timing, like there was an underlying agenda I wasn't privy to."

Jase shrugged. "I don't know Sienna, but it makes sense that she'd be cut from the same cloth. Will you talk to her?"

Cole wanted to agree to help. He didn't have family in his life, and his friends meant all the more to him because of it. But he couldn't make his mouth form the words. Not after spending the wee hours last night with Sienna tucked against his body, even with the bedclothes separating them.

"I can't get involved like that."

Jase stared at him for a long moment, then closed his eyes and let out a soft laugh. "She's more like my mother than I even realized."

"What does that mean?"

"I heard a ton of stories growing up about my dad's side of the family. The Crenshaws are infamous around Crimson as a bunch of hard-drinking, hard-living hooligans. It took a lot of work to make people in this town believe I wasn't like that."

"You do look remarkably like your great-great grandfather."

Among a group of pictures that displayed life in the early days of Crimson was a sepia-colored photo in the county courthouse of a man sitting in the original town jail. A man who happened to be Jase's forefather. Cole had been shocked when he'd first met Jase at his resemblance to "Black Jack" Crenshaw.

"Trust me, I know." Jase blew out a breath. "But I also heard plenty of stories about my mother—how pretty she was, how she could have had any man in town when she arrived here with her family from Alabama. People couldn't seem to stop speculating on why she'd chosen my father. Of course, no one was surprised when their marriage fell apart. But Sienna must take after her in some ways if she already has you wrapped around her finger."

Cole bristled at the implied accusation. "I'm not wrapped around her finger," he shot back, "but I get what it's like to be alone."

"She's not alone," Jase countered.

"She is," Cole insisted. "And whatever her reasons are for coming here, she's not looking to cause trouble for you." It was funny he could assure Jase with no reservations, even though Sienna was the most troubling thing that had hit his life in years.

"I hope not." Jase ran a hand through his hair and stood. "At least keep an eye on her. That shouldn't be too difficult."

"Give her a chance, Jase."

"Maybe I will," his friend agreed as he backed toward the door. "I just hope you don't give her too big of one."

Chapter 8

Later that morning, Sienna walked into Life is Sweet, her stomach in knots. Pretending like she belonged in Crimson seemed to be almost as difficult as gathering the courage to talk to her father or brother.

But she couldn't spend her day holed up at the inn, especially with Paige dropping not-so-subtle hints about Cole. Sienna still wasn't sure what she'd been thinking inviting him into the house—and into her bed. All she knew was she'd slept better in those hours she was next to him than she had in ages.

Paige wasn't much for subtlety, so as soon as Sienna had walked down the stairs, the innkeeper handed her a cup of coffee and a box of condoms.

"Here at The Bumblebee," she'd said with a smile, "we like to make sure our guests haven't forgotten anything they might need during their stay."

"It wasn't like that," Sienna had insisted.

"Then you're not as smart as you look. That man is gorgeous and I'll tell you if a hot guy ended up in my bed—no matter the reason—I wouldn't squander my opportunity."

Sienna wasn't sure what kind of opportunity she wanted with the town's sexy sheriff, but she knew she wasn't ready to talk about it. She'd taken the condoms and the coffee and returned to her room with the excuse of having to call her office in Chicago.

That part wasn't a lie. Before she left for Aspen, she'd been working on a big ad campaign for a multinational telecommunication company ready to roll out its latest device. Although her extended stay in Colorado complicated things, she could do most of the work remotely.

She'd sent out a round of emails to her team, then tweaked a presentation her assistant had sent her the night before. Her boss was being patient because he needed Sienna's reputation and the relationships she'd cultivated with their client base, but she knew that wouldn't last forever.

The hotel in Aspen had delivered her luggage, and while her clothes weren't perfect for Crimson's casual vibe, at least they were hers. Now she had to come up with a plan for her time in Crimson and figure out how long she was planning to stay. For that, she needed more coffee and one of the muffins she'd seen in the glass display counter of the bakery.

Katie, the bakery's owner, was nowhere in sight as Sienna approached the counter, and a strange sense of disappointment washed over her. The woman had been friendly, even after Cole explained who she was. Sienna secretly looked forward to another conversation with someone who didn't seem either fascinated by or skeptical of her past in Crimson.

She ordered a coffee and muffin, then turned to find a beautiful and very pregnant woman staring at her.

"Even if I hadn't Googled you, I'd know who you are," the woman told her, one hand coming to rest on her belly in an oddly protective gesture. "You and Jase must have looked like twins as kids."

"I don't have photos," Sienna answered automatically, then took her drink as the barista placed it on the counter. She didn't need to ask the woman's identity. This had to be Emily, her brother's wife. Sienna's sister-in-law. The thought of it was both strange and oddly appealing.

At least it would have been in a perfect world. But not with how Emily was glaring at her. This was one confrontation Sienna knew she wouldn't be able to get out of so easily.

"Your dad does." Emily's eyes narrowed. "In fact, a framed photo of you has pride of place on the mantel in his new house. Maybe you would have found that out if you hadn't run off like a big chicken when he spoke to you."

Sienna heard the sharp intake of breath from the woman behind the counter. She turned and took the bag with the muffin the woman handed her, offering a smile and ignoring the fact that her fingers trembled. *Big chicken.* Good to know Emily Crenshaw didn't hold back.

Sienna had spent a lifetime tiptoeing around difficult conversations. Her mother preferred the don't ask/don't tell school of thought for any topic thornier than which strand of pearls to wear to the country club for her weekly ladies' luncheon.

So the issues and questions Sienna had throughout her childhood consumed her body from the inside out. And with that one snappish comment, Emily set lighter fluid to the flame and Sienna's entire being was engulfed. The mask she'd worn for years burned to ash, leaving her true self standing raw and new. Somehow it was a liberating sensation.

She straightened her shoulders and inclined her head. "I was seven when my mother put me in that car and drove away. For years, I waited for a letter or phone call from my dad. Every birthday, each Christmas. I wanted him to care that I was gone. I wanted him to find me. But he never did. He never even tried."

"You don't know what—"

Sienna held up a hand. "He had Jase because Jase was the one he needed. So if you think I'm going to go all misty-eyed and sentimental over the fact that he still has a left-behind picture of me on display, think again."

Suddenly she understood why she couldn't force herself to confront her father or brother. The pain might pour out, and then they'd see—everyone would see—how much it hurt her to be taken away from her life in this town.

Even though her childhood had been far from perfect, she'd belonged, unlike the way she'd been raised in Chicago, where she was constantly reminded of how grateful she should be for the advantages her mother's marriage to Craig Pierce had given both of them.

But to Sienna, those advantages had felt like a straitjacket. Having Emily try to confront her was like breaking free, and the tumble of emotions was overwhelming and devastating. She no longer cared who heard their conversation.

Sienna was done hiding her crazy.

"How about the years in between and the memories that could have—should have—been captured? Maybe I'm more interested in the things in my life he missed." She leaned in slightly. "But I'm sure not interested in being lectured on how I handle myself now. So back off, sister-in-law."

Emily's blue eyes widened slightly, but she didn't back down. "I won't let you hurt my family."

"Is that why you think I'm here?"

"If you're anything like your mother," Emily said, arching an eyebrow, "then yes."

"I'm nothing like her," Sienna said, but she couldn't be sure that was true. Dana had tried her best to mold Sienna into her own image. Sienna had followed along because she hadn't felt like there was another choice. How much of it had become embedded into the fiber of who she was remained to be seen away from her mother's influence.

Her comment seemed to surprise Emily, and she nodded slightly. "We'll see about that. Come to dinner tonight."

Sienna felt her mouth drop open. "You just read me the riot act about not messing with you, and now you're inviting me to dinner? Are you nuts?"

"Rhetorical question," a voice chimed in and both women turned to see Katie standing behind the cash registers. "Don't question how Emily's mind works. It's a mystery to us all."

"Very funny," Emily muttered, but Sienna felt an easing in the tension rolling off her brother's wife. She expected nothing less from the sweet-tempered bakery owner. Katie Crawford could likely tame a grizzly bear by whispering lullabies into its furry ear.

"Not as funny as most of my customers watching this little exchange with great fascination." Katie inclined her head. "I'm pretty sure Mrs. Wasinski recorded the whole thing on her new smartphone. If we're lucky, she'll upload the video to Facebook and tag you both." Saccharine-sweet sarcasm dripped from her tone.

Emily whipped around and pointed at an elderly woman in a lavender tracksuit and thick hiking boots. "Delete it, Mrs. W., or I'm going to take Ruby for an after-dinner walk every night this month and let her poop in your rosebushes."

"You wouldn't dare," the woman said, looking shocked. "My roses took first place in the county fair last year."

"Then you probably don't want extra fertilizer on them."

"I assume Ruby is your dog," Sienna said, "and not your daughter."

"Best dog ever," Emily confirmed. She patted her belly. "My girl is on the way."

Mrs. Wasinski messed with her phone for several seconds before looking up again. "I don't care what Jase has done for this town, the Crenshaws have always been trouble, whether they grew up in Crimson or married into the family."

"Thanks for your opinion," Emily said sweetly as the older woman hurried out of the bakery.

"You're chasing off my customers now," Katie said with a groan.

Emily rolled her eyes. "She'll be back. No one can stay away from here for long." She turned her full attention on Sienna again. "Dinner at six tonight."

"I don't think—"

"You don't have to think. Just show up. If you're not here to make trouble, that's fine. If you are, we need to deal with it sooner than later because when this baby comes I need Jase's full attention."

Sienna glanced at Katie, who shrugged. "She won't take no for an answer at this point."

"Will you and your husband be there?" Sienna asked Katie.

"You need a buffer between yourself and your family?" Emily demanded.

Sienna winced slightly but nodded. "It can't hurt."

"Noah and Katie will be there then. I'll call my brother and tell him the good news," Emily said. "He's got dinner plans."

"I'll bring dessert," Katie offered.

"Make it chocolate," Emily said, then added, "Please." She pulled a small notepad from her purse, scribbled something on it and handed a sheet of paper to Sienna. "Here's our address. See you tonight."

"Um…thanks."

With a sharp nod, Emily turned and walked out of the bakery. Sienna let out a long breath as she stared at the address written on the slip of paper. Family dinner.

"Here you go." She looked up to find that Katie had walked around to the front of the counter. She handed Sienna another brown paper bag. "It's banana nut to go with your blueberry. I figure after that it could be a two-muffin morning."

"Thanks." Sienna took the bag. "Is she always so intense?"

"More so with the pregnancy. She really loves your brother."

"My brother," Sienna repeated softly. "Family dinner at my brother's house."

"Ready or not," Katie told her, as if reading Sienna's mind.

"Ready or not," Sienna agreed.

"I'm coming," Cole called, muting the baseball game he'd been watching and straightening from the couch. "No need to break down the door."

The pounding at his front door stopped as he approached it. Through the gauzy curtains he hadn't bothered to change when he bought the house last year, he saw the outline of a slender woman, her blond hair pulled back in a low ponytail.

"How did you find out where I live?" he asked as he opened the door.

Sienna stood on the front porch, her arms wrapped tightly around her waist. "Is it a secret? Do you call it the Sheriffcave?"

"Not quite," he said, trying to get his bearings. He still felt off-kilter from spending the night with her, and having her so close made him remember all the things about the previous night he'd been trying to force himself to forget. The warmth of her body, the scent of her hair as it tickled his cheek, how soft her skin was at the crook of her neck.

"Are you going to invite me in then?" One delicate brow lifted. "Because that would be the polite thing to do."

"Yeah, I'm real concerned about good manners," he said with a laugh but stepped back so she could walk past him into the house. She wore a pale pink scoop neck cotton shirt and slim jeans that grazed her ankles. As he'd come to expect, her makeup was minimal, and he had the urge to trace his finger along her cheek to feel its softness. She didn't yet look at home in Colorado but seemed less buttoned-up than she had that first day she'd arrived in town. As if the casual vibe of Crimson was slowly rubbing off on her.

An emotion he didn't recognize flared low in his belly as he watched her examine the space. He'd never brought a woman to his house. Hell, his dating life had been almost nonexistent since he'd moved to Crimson. Cole was dedicated to his job, and up until the past few days, that had been enough.

"Did you just move in?" she asked, her gaze snagging on a stack of cardboard boxes pushed against one wall.

"About a year ago," he admitted. "I've been too busy to deal with unpacking everything."

She inclined her head toward the muted television and the half-empty beer bottle and bag of chips on the coffee table. "Clearly."

"What's going on?" he asked. "Or did you stop by for the sole purpose of critiquing my interior decorating skills?"

"I need you to go to dinner with me," she blurted.

"Okay," he said slowly. "Did you have someplace special in mind?"

"I met my sister-in-law today," she continued. "She invited me to dinner. I'm supposed to be there in..." She glanced at the chunky silver watch that encircled her wrist. "Ten minutes."

"Emily invited you for dinner?" Cole tried to hide his shock, especially after Jase had told him he didn't trust Sienna. "And you want me to go with you?"

"Katie and her husband will be there, too." She walked forward and ran a hand along the back of his leather couch. "But they're Team Jase. I need someone on my side."

"You think that's me?" Pride and disbelief warred inside him at the idea that he was the one she'd come to for support. He realized she knew very few people in town, but still—

"You're all I've got," she muttered, then made a face. "Sorry. I didn't mean it to come out that way."

"You know Jase is my best friend," he said. "I'm the one who told him you'd come to town. You might remember raking me over the coals in the bakery."

"So all of this is really your fault." She flashed a smile

that was more like a baring of teeth from a grizzly bear facing off with a mountain lion. "You have to go."

"What if I have plans?"

She glanced at the television, then back at him. "Are they important?"

"Give me a minute to change clothes."

"Thank you," she said softly, her gaze dropping to the ground as if she couldn't bear to make eye contact. He wondered what he'd see in her beautiful blue gaze right now. Unable to resist, he moved toward her and placed a finger under her chin, tipping it up until she looked at him.

It was all there—pain, loneliness, vulnerability and the smallest sliver of hope. As much as she pretended otherwise, Sienna wanted things to work out with Jase and her father. This night meant something to her. More than she probably knew.

Cole felt the heavy weight of responsibility settle on his shoulders, but to his surprise, he didn't immediately want to shrug it off. He had no problem with work responsibility but kept his personal life clean and simple because it was easier that way—no chance for mess or for anyone to get hurt. But he couldn't seem to keep Sienna at arm's length, and the more time he spent with her, the more he wanted to pull her in closer.

"It's going to be fine," he told her and brushed his lips across hers.

"Only if we're not late," she said, her breath tickling his skin.

He drew back, dropped a quick kiss on her nose and headed toward his bedroom.

Chapter 9

"We should have sex."

Sienna threw a sidelong glance at Cole. Her stomach flipped up and down after she made the suggestion, like she was being pummeled by a tropical storm.

He stopped dead in his tracks, staring at the cobblestone walkway before them, and massaged a hand over the back of his neck. "Uh...do you have any context you want to offer with that suggestion?"

They were standing at the edge of sidewalk in front of Jase and Emily's house. Sienna was about to spend an evening with her father and brother for the first time in twenty years. The thought made her terrified, and fear made her say stupid things.

"You want to, right?" she demanded, turning to face Cole.

He looked down, desire and amusement both clear in his gaze. "Yes, but I don't think that's the point at the moment."

"No one has seen us yet. We could turn right around and drive back to your house." She held up her hands like she was showing off the grand prize in a game show contest. As if she were the prize, when they both knew she was anything but at the moment.

The words coming out of her mouth sounded crazy to her own ears, but she couldn't stop them. "Or we could get a hotel room. Not The Bumblebee. That would be weird with Paige there. Does Crimson have any rent-by-the-hour motels?"

He shook his head. "Not as far as I know."

"Your place then." She grabbed his hand and turned for the truck he drove when he wasn't on duty.

Cole didn't budge, and trying to get him to move was like tugging on a mountain.

"Sienna."

"Is it yes or no?" She tried to pull her hand away from his when it was clear he wasn't moving, but he held tight. "Because I could find someone else."

She gave a little yelp as she was suddenly plastered against the hard front of Cole's body. "No one else," he said, his voice a gravelly purr. "But right now we're having dinner at Jase's house. A dinner you invited me to about eight minutes ago. We couldn't be late and all that."

"Changed my mind."

"No."

"Yes," she insisted, letting her tone become peevish. "It's my mind and I get to do with it what I want. Along with my body."

"Duly noted," he said, infinitely patient. "I told you, tonight is going to be fine."

She bit down on her lip when a whimper threatened to escape. She swallowed and shook her head. "It's not going to be fine. I shouldn't be here. I should never have come in the first place. If they'd wanted to see me, they would have. It's been two decades and—"

"Jase said he came to Chicago last year. You didn't see him."

She spread her fingers out along his chest, letting the heat of his body seep into her palms. Wanting to curl against him but forcing herself to take a step back in case anyone inside the house was looking. "He was there because my mom summoned him. No one refuses Dana Pierce."

She sighed when Cole grimaced.

"I know I sound harsh," she told him. "But that's how my mom is about things. She's in remission now, and I'm grateful but I couldn't be a part of it at that time. And now..."

"Now is your chance."

"These aren't my people," she said, feeling miserable and alone.

"I'm your person."

"You're Jase's friend," she countered, refusing to allow herself to hold on to his words the way her heart wanted to. "You said so yourself."

"Tonight I'm yours." He laced his fingers with hers and started forward. "I've got your back."

She allowed him to lead her, knowing she wouldn't be able to make her legs move if he wasn't next to her.

"You ring the bell," he told her when they were on the porch.

She knocked instead, earning a smile from Cole. "A rebel at heart," he murmured. "You'll fit in just fine, sweetheart."

The door opened to reveal Jase Crenshaw standing on the other side. He was taller than Cole, probably close to six foot four, lanky and handsome and familiar to Sienna even as much as he was a stranger.

"I wasn't expecting to see you tonight," he said to Cole, looking more confused than surprised. "How many times have you been invited over but always managed not to make it?"

Cole flinched but covered it with a small laugh. "I made it tonight."

"I invited him," Sienna offered.

Jase raised a brow. "I'm glad you *both* could make it."

"Your wife didn't seem like she was going to take no for an answer."

"That's Emily," he agreed, smiling.

Sienna glanced over her shoulder toward Cole's truck. "I brought a bottle of wine but left it in the truck. I'll go—"

"I'll get it," Cole offered and jogged down the walkway toward the street before she could argue.

"Is wine okay?" she asked, turning back to Jase. "I forgot about your dad being sober and—"

"It's fine. And he's your dad, too," Jase added quietly. "He's doing well right now, but sobriety and Declan are fickle companions."

"I'm not going to do anything to sabotage him." Sienna clasped her hands in front of her stomach. "I just want you to know I'm not here to cause trouble for either of you."

"I'd ask why you are here," Jase said, stepping back into the house and gesturing for her to follow, "but I suppose you'll let us know that in your own time."

"Do you remember me?" she asked suddenly. "From when we were kids."

Jase frowned. "Yes. You're my sister."

He said the words with such certainty, it made Sienna's chest tighten. "I can picture the night we left," she told him. "I remember turning around in the back seat and watching you get smaller, then disappear in the darkness as Mom drove away." She shook her head. "But nothing else in any detail."

"There wasn't much worth remembering," Jase said with a small laugh.

"It was the first seven years of my life," Sienna countered. "And it's all a jumble to me."

"Is that part of what upsets you?" He studied her, his gaze intense, and a whisper of familiarity brushed over her like the touch of a feather. She could see in her mind the image of a solemn boy putting a bandage on her knee as she wiped away tears after a fall.

"I think so," she admitted. "Although I didn't realize I cared until I came to Colorado. Did you teach me to ride a bike?"

"Maybe you remember more than you think," Jase said.

"Here's the wine," Cole said as he came through the front door. "Everything okay?"

He pressed his fingers to the small of Sienna's back, handing Jase the bottle of wine. The light touch was more comforting than she could have imagined.

"It's fine," she said.

"Come into the kitchen," Jase told them both. "We'll eat soon."

Cole kept his hand on her back as they walked, reminding Sienna that she didn't have the option to run away, even if her hammering heart told her that would be the smart thing to do.

She heard voices and laughter as they walked toward the back of the house, but silence descended over the group as she entered the bright and airy kitchen.

Jase and Emily's house was an old Victorian, but the inside had been remodeled recently. The kitchen had white craftsman-style cabinets with dark soapstone countertops over them. The floors looked original in a deep mahogany stain. There was a vase of fresh flowers on the island and framed photos and kids art decorated the walls.

Emily, Katie and a friendly looking man who Sienna guessed was Noah Crawford all glanced between her and Cole, but it was Declan Crenshaw who moved forward.

"Isn't she the spitting image of your mother back in the day?" he asked Jase. "She even has Dana's eyes." He stopped when he was directly in front of Sienna. "You gonna take off again if I talk to you tonight?"

She shook her head, ignoring her sweaty palms and pounding heart.

"Good," he said, "because I got plenty to say."

"Dad, let's eat first." Jase's voice was gentle.

"It's been twenty years," Declan argued. "Food can wait."

"I'm hungry now," a small voice said from behind Sienna.

A young boy scooted past, keeping his hands at his sides so he wouldn't brush against her. A fluffy dog followed, wagging its tail and sniffing at Sienna and Cole before trotting forward to greet everyone else.

"Davey, we have people here for dinner," Emily said.

"I know," the boy answered, glancing at his mother before dropping his gaze back to the ground. He held out one hand and the dog immediately moved to his side, tucking herself against his leg. "I want a hot dog."

"Dogs and burgers are almost ready to come off the grill," Noah said. "I just checked them."

Jase touched Davey's shoulder. "Do you want to say hello to our guest?"

"Hi," the boy muttered but didn't make eye contact.

Everyone else seemed to take the behavior in stride.

Katie and Noah both greeted Davey and the adorable baby Noah held smiled widely.

Paige had told Sienna that Emily's son from a previous marriage had Asperger's, which explained the way he interacted with everyone. She looked toward Emily, who lifted her chin as if in challenge. Clearly, Jase's wife had been through some battles defending her boy.

Sienna didn't have much experience with kids, and certainly not special needs children, but she felt a new respect for Emily. "Why don't we talk over dinner?" she said to Declan. "Davey's not the only one who's ready to eat."

She saw Emily let out a breath, and Jase gave her an approving nod. "Davey, get a plate from your mommy," he told the boy, setting the wine on the counter, "and you can help me with the burgers and hot dogs."

"I'm Noah Crawford," Katie's husband said as he stepped forward. "This is little Willow."

"Nice to meet you," Sienna said, smiling.

She could feel her father's intense gaze on her and was relieved when Cole turned and engaged Declan in conversation. Emily handed Sienna a bowl of salad across the counter. "Would you bring this to the patio?"

"Sure." The nerves in Sienna's stomach began to settle slightly. Other than her dad's behavior, the evening felt almost normal. Better than normal even. Most of the social events she attended, even the casual summer get-togethers, involved catered food, cloth napkins and usually some kind of dress code. "No formal seating chart, right?" she asked Katie as they stepped outside.

Katie chuckled. "You really did grow up a world away from Crimson."

They took seats around the wrought-iron table on the large patio that overlooked a lovely yard with a swing set in one corner. Sienna made sure she was at the opposite end from Declan. Something about the way he kept staring at her, like she was a ghost, made her uncomfortable. She'd come to Crimson to face her past but hadn't considered the fact that her dad might have his own ideas about their relationship.

She'd assumed he wouldn't care about seeing her. That she could say her piece, once she figured out what it was, then leave again and return to her old life or start creating a new one, since a big part of who she'd been was the next Mrs. Kevin Patterson.

She didn't have to say much during the meal. The others fell into an easy discussion about the upcoming July Fourth celebration in town and how elaborate the fireworks display over Crimson Mountain was going to be this year.

Sienna forced a smile at the same time she suppressed a shudder. She'd never liked fireworks. The high-pitched whistle and reverberating boom that followed made her edgy, heart hammering and breath coming in shallow pants like she was some kind of scared animal or soldier back from the front lines.

Her reaction had been a constant embarrassment to her mother. Each year, their country club hosted a big Fourth of July soiree, where everyone dressed in patriotic shades of red, white and blue, and the annual member photo would be displayed on the wall of the clubhouse. It was a point of pride for Sienna's mother that Craig's family had been one of the founding members of the club, which meant that the Pierces were guaranteed a front-row seat for the evening fireworks display, always spectacular and set to classical music.

The first year they'd attended, Sienna had puked all over the manicured lawn when her mother refused to excuse her as the display started. After that, it had been a battle of wills each summer and Sienna's fear of the noise and scent of sulfur had only increased.

"You remember," Declan shouted suddenly, pointing a bony finger at Sienna. "And it still gets to you."

All eyes turned to Sienna, other than Davey, who continued to pet Ruby, sitting loyally next to his chair.

Sienna swallowed. "I don't know what you mean."

"Dad, calm down." Jase shifted in his chair and put a hand out in what Sienna guessed was an attempt to quiet Declan.

But the older man shook him off, rising from the table and moving toward Sienna. Cole stood, as well, like he was ready to protect her if needed.

"Sit down, Declan," Cole said in a serious law enforcement tone. It sounded to Sienna like the sheriff had some experience with her father acting out.

"Turn your wrist over," Declan commanded, ignoring Cole. Sienna obeyed automatically. She hated that her first instinct was to obey without question, even though Cole had called her a rebel. What a joke.

"Don't touch her." Cole blocked Declan when the older man reached for Sienna.

"He's not going to hurt her," Jase said, frustration lacing his tone.

"What's for dessert?" Davey asked solemnly.

"In a minute, honey," Emily told him.

The questions and comments swirling around Sienna sounded distant and muffled, as if they were coming through a tunnel. She was alone on the other end, her attention focused on the crescent-shaped scar on the inside of her arm, just to the right of the center of her wrist. It had been there since she could remember and had grown so faint over the years she'd all but forgotten it.

But as her father stared at the same spot, a memory flickered to life in the back of her mind. Like a flame exposed to air, it grew. She saw herself as a young girl, sticky with cotton candy at a summer carnival with the massive outline of Crimson Mountain as a backdrop.

She held a sparkling wand in her hand, making big circles in the air and laughing at the trail of light and smoke her movements made. Her brother was next to her and a dozen more kids all around them. Suddenly a whistle and a thunderous boom sounded. People around them clapped, but the noise startled Sienna and she let the sparkler drop to her other wrist, then screamed as the tip of it burned her skin.

Tears had come hot and fast, and Jase had called for someone. Sienna would have expected a younger Dana to be the one to rush over, but she could see her mother enraptured by the fireworks display as she laughed with her friends nearby. Instead, Declan peeled away from the crowd. He plucked the sparkler from her fingers, then hefted her into his arms.

"It's all right, baby girl," he told her. "It's just a wee burn." She buried her face in her daddy's shirtfront, which smelled of beer and cigarettes—an oddly comforting combination to her little-girl senses.

"Make the noise stop," she'd said in a whimper. "The boom makes it hurt worse."

He'd carried her to the beer tent and taken a piece of ice from one of the kegs to rub over her red skin. She kept her eyes shut tightly, unwilling to look at the fireworks she blamed for her pain.

Now she glanced up to Declan's knowing gaze. "You remember," he repeated quietly and she gave a jerky nod.

"Remember what?" Cole demanded.

"Sienna got burned by a sparkler when she was little," Jase said before she had a chance to answer. "She never liked fireworks after that."

It shouldn't be a surprise that Jase could recount the story as easily as Sienna. He'd been the one to call for help. But the fact that her brother and father seemed to know more details of her early life than she could remember rocked her to her core just the same.

"I've got to go." Sienna pushed back from the table. "Thank you for dinner, Emily." She forced herself to smile as she glanced around the table. "Thanks to all of you for making me feel welcome."

She turned away and hurried into the house before anyone could stop her. Her biggest fear was that her dad would follow, forcing her to pull up more memories. Not that remembering the night she'd been burned was painful exactly, but she'd always told herself that neither Declan or Jase cared about her at all—that's the reason they let her go.

She'd never questioned why her early childhood memories were somewhat blank in her brain. She figured there was nothing good to remember about the years she'd lived in Crimson.

But she was quickly coming to realize that wasn't true. That knowledge seemed to change everything.

Chapter 10

Cole turned his truck off the road and rolled down the windows, gravel crunching under the tires as he pulled to a stop at the edge of the trees.

"Where are we?" Sienna asked, blinking like she was waking up from a dream. She'd been in her own world since they left Jase and Emily's, staring out the front window while she rubbed a finger over the tiny scar on her wrist.

They hadn't spoken because she seemed to need quiet and Cole respected that. He understood the need to process things and didn't want to push her too hard or fast. But he also wasn't willing to let her go just yet.

She might not realize it, but alone was the last thing Sienna needed to be at the moment.

"One of my favorite spots in Crimson." He turned off the truck and opened his door. "Come on."

"I should go home," she protested weakly.

He glanced over his shoulder, arching a brow in her direction. "Where is home for you right now?" he asked, not to be unkind but because he was truly curious how she would answer.

She tugged her bottom lip between her teeth and sucked in a breath. "Fine," she said after a moment, not answering his question. "Show me this special spot of yours."

He led her down the dirt path, holding back branches that hung across the trail, partially obstructing it and hiding it from plain sight. It was one of the things Cole liked best about this area—not many people knew it existed so even at the height of summer tourist season, it wasn't crowded.

The sun was just beginning to dip behind the peak, the evening light that played through the trees soft and warm.

"Watch your step," he told her as they navigated a rocky section of the trail.

A minute later, the forest ended and they emerged onto a grassy knoll with the river flowing in front of them. From the spot they were standing, there was a view of the tip of Crimson Mountain in the distance, along with a hillside covered in aspen trees and early season wildflowers on the other side of the bank.

"It's beautiful," Sienna whispered.

The look of wonder playing across her face was far more to Cole's liking than the confusion and pain in her gaze right before she'd rushed from the table at Jase's.

His heart skipped a beat, and he smiled. "The river is high right now because of runoff from the snow. It will be half this size by August if we have another dry summer."

"Look, there's deer over there." Sienna pointed to a spot in front of the trees near the bend in the river. "Those are the biggest deer I've ever seen."

"Because they're elk," Cole explained. "They come

down to the river this time of day. They'll go back up to higher ground as the weather gets warmer."

He stepped back and pointed to a bench tucked at the base of two pine trees about ten feet away. "Want to sit down?"

Sienna glanced between him and the rustic wooden bench. "Did you build that?"

"I wish I had that talent," he said, shaking his head as they moved toward the trees. "I found out about this place from one of the guys who ran the snowplow when I first got a job with the sheriff's department. Manny's retired now and moved to Pueblo last year to be closer to his daughter. He and his wife used to come out here so he could fish." Cole brushed a few pine needles off the bench, then took a seat next to Sienna on it. "He built this so his wife would have a comfortable place to sit and read while he did his thing."

"That's sweet," Sienna murmured.

"Yeah. There's a few popular fishing spots about a half mile down on either side, but not many people come right here because the trailhead isn't obvious."

"Do you fish?" she asked.

"Not nearly as much as I'd like," he admitted. He pointed to a section of the river where the current wasn't running so hard. "But that's about as perfect of a spot as you can get."

"My dad used to fish. I remember it now."

Sienna was back to worrying the tip of one finger against the scar on her wrist.

"He still does." Cole took her hand in his, lacing their fingers together. "Want to talk about earlier?"

"No."

He lifted her hand and grazed a kiss over her knuckles. "Talk to me anyway."

"I made them into the bad guys," she said after a moment. "They were the ones who didn't want me then. They wouldn't want me now." She swiped at her cheek with the hand he wasn't holding. "I never questioned why I couldn't remember any details from the time before Mom and I left Crimson. She'd barely talk about it or her reasons for leaving, so I think I made up a story in my mind about how bad it was."

"And maybe that wasn't the whole story?"

She looked over at him. "It wasn't great. My memories are hazy but coming back to me. You may not have been raised here, but you've heard plenty of Crenshaw stories, I'm sure."

"Yeah," he admitted. "The family track record is spotty at best."

"The Crenshaw track record is a mess of crater-size potholes and everyone knows it. I thought there was nothing more to my father. I wanted closure. I wanted him to admit that he didn't care enough to make my mom stay. He didn't fight or come after me."

She shook her head, and a lock of blond hair fell forward against her cheek. "If you'd asked me a week ago, I would have told you there was nothing Declan Crenshaw or even Jase could say that would make me forgive them for letting her take me."

"Even though your life might have been better away from here. The advantages and opportunities you had—"

"But it wasn't my life." She pulled her hand away from his, stood and paced to the edge of the river. He let her go, watched as she hugged her arms around herself. There were some things a person had to work out on their own, and Cole hoped the serenity of this space—the view of the mountains surrounding them and the sound of the river babbling over rocks—would help her calm the demons pulling at her.

He'd certainly come here often enough to soothe his own soul.

She turned back to him after a few minutes. "I know I sound like an ungrateful little princess," she said, her gaze pained. "I did have opportunities. I had stability and security. They sent me to the right schools and ballet and debutante balls. I went to cotillion and birthday parties where parents rented ponies and magicians and we vacationed to beaches and mountains and…"

She threw up her hands. "None of it mattered because it wasn't mine. My mom made the choice to reinvent herself, and she worked so hard to leave behind everything about her marriage and life before. But I was always there, a physical reminder of the mistakes she'd made."

"She couldn't have thought of you as a mistake," Cole argued, hating that she believed that about herself. "She's your mother."

Sienna gave a sharp bark of laughter. "Not all moms are created equal, Sheriff. It wasn't that I blamed her. I didn't think she had a choice. She made me think that. Now I know…"

She sat down again beside him. "Somehow I blocked the details before we left. But I remember…not all of it but enough. She left Jase behind because Dad needed him. He was always the strong one—the caretaker of all of us. I wasn't that important, so I got the ticket out of Crimson."

She held up her wrist, pale and delicate in the soft evening light. "I dropped a sparkler on myself at one of the Crimson Fourth of July festivals. Maybe I was five at the time. My dad took care of me. Granted, he got ice from a beer keg plus a refill at the same time, but he tried to make it better."

"Declan isn't a bad man," Cole told her. "He has issues, but he's also got a big heart."

"I wanted—needed—him to be the bad guy in this." She leaned forward and placed her elbows on her knees. "My brother taught me how to ride a bike. He sat with me instead of his friends on the bus home from school when I started kindergarten so I wouldn't get scared."

"You didn't remember any of this before tonight?"

"No. The only things Mom would ever discuss were the drinking and fighting between her and my dad. So those are the things I remember. Now I wonder which are mine and which are hers."

"I'm sorry, Sienna." He curled his fingers around her neck and massaged gently.

"But that doesn't give me an answer to the million-dollar question. Why did my dad let me go so easily?" She swayed toward him, and Cole looped an arm around her shoulder and pulled her close.

"I don't know, sweetheart. You'll have to ask him."

"I'm so afraid," she whispered, "of hearing the answer." She let out a choked sob that just about ripped open Cole's chest. He pressed a long kiss to the top of her head and smoothed a hand over her hair.

After a few minutes, she straightened, dabbed her fingers to the corners of her eyes and shifted to face him. "How did you lose your parents?" she asked, and he felt his head snap back like she'd punched him.

"We were talking about your messed-up family," he said, trying to keep his tone light. "Not mine."

"Change of subject."

He swallowed, ignoring the tightening in his gut. He

hated revisiting his past. Most people were shocked enough when he shared that his family had died that he could side-step giving any details. Leave it to Sienna to be different.

"My father killed himself," he said bluntly. "Mom had a heart attack six months later." He closed his eyes and added, "I'm pretty sure she actually died of a broken heart."

"Oh, Cole. Was your father… Did he… Were there drugs or alcohol involved?"

"Not a bit."

"Mental illness?"

He shook his head, feeling the suffocating band of anger and humiliation tighten around him. "He was a career army man, close to retirement age. They were based outside of DC at the time. My mom had her eye on an RV. She'd traveled the world but wanted to see the United States."

"That's sweet."

"Yeah," he agreed. "She was a sweetheart. The perfect army wife. She could make the most basic military housing feel like home. Then my dad was arrested."

"For what?"

"He was charged with conspiracy and bribery. There was a ring of officers being bribed by a defense contractor in the Middle East. They gave him classified and confidential information that he used to defraud the US military and he offered…" Cole paused, shook his head "…a lot of things in return. Apparently it had been going on for years, and he was one of the ringleaders. He denied everything, but the government had enough evidence."

Sienna placed a hand on his leg. His skin burned beneath the fabric of his jeans where the warmth of her seeped through.

"Mom posted bail, and he came home. The next week, he shot himself."

"No," Sienna whispered. "Did she—?"

"I found him," he said. "Mom had asked my brother and me to fly in. She thought seeing the two of us would bolster his spirits. She'd come to pick me up at the airport. Shep was arriving that night. There was a note on the door when we got back to the house that I should come in without her."

"I can't even imagine, Cole. I'm so sorry."

He shrugged, trying to stay strong. He'd become immune to sympathy in the weeks following his father's death because at that time the kind remarks were always laced with a trace of judgment.

Almost everyone in his parents' circle of friends was or had been military at some point. The accusations against his father, and the fact that his suicide seemed tantamount to admitting guilt, were a hard pill to swallow for some people. Most people.

The question of the kind of man his father truly was had driven a wedge between Cole and his twin. Shep had always been a free spirit, the family rebel and the brother who'd given their parents the most trouble growing up. He'd felt somehow justified in his choices after Richard Bennett's years of treachery had been revealed.

Cole, who at the time was stationed in Texas, proud to follow in his father's footsteps with his own military career, had been knocked so far off center he wasn't sure he'd ever right himself again. Despite the mountain of evidence, including emails and other correspondence that implicated Colonel Bennett, Cole still wanted to believe his dad could be innocent.

"The worst was mom's reaction," Cole told her, keeping his voice neutral as emotions buffeted him from every side. "She was his biggest supporter. She'd been so proud of his service. Even after the arrest, she insisted he'd been framed.

She wanted him to be the honorable man she'd married but would have stood by his side no matter the outcome."

"He didn't give her that choice," Sienna said quietly.

"She felt like he'd abandoned her. It didn't help that Shep was doing the 'I told you so' routine every waking minute. Her pain didn't seem to phase him at all."

She squeezed his leg. "That couldn't have gone over well with you. It's obvious you were protective of your mom."

"Picture the most generous, selfless, caring person you can imagine, then multiply by ten. That was my mom."

"You were lucky."

"So was Shep. I still don't get how we could have had the same parents, the same childhood, most of the same experiences and his take on everything was the polar opposite of mine."

"I can't answer that," Sienna said. "Jase and I obviously had different upbringings, at least for most of it. Did you finally get your brother to come around?"

Cole shook his head. "We got in a fight at Dad's funeral. Both of us ended up with black eyes, and he had a split lip to go with it. Never could block a shot. Mom blamed us both." He closed his eyes as memory and regret coalesced inside his chest. "Shep left that night. I haven't talked to him since."

"What about when your mom died?" Sienna asked.

He pressed his lips together, then said, "He didn't come back, and I did a private burial. Without Shep, it was only me there. I couldn't stand the idea of her family and friends judging her in death at a big service."

"You don't know—"

"I do," he insisted. "It was awful for her, and she had no one with Dad gone."

"She had you."

He stood, paced a few steps forward and plucked a stone from the creek bank, hurling it toward the river. It skipped across the water twice, then disappeared into the current with a plop.

He closed his eyes and listened to the water, hoping the bubbling sound would calm his tumultuous emotions as it had so many other evenings. This was the place he came when he needed to regroup—when the stress of work or the sting of the past got to be too much.

Before tonight, he'd always come here alone.

He felt more than heard Sienna come up behind him. She wrapped her arms around his waist and pressed her cheek to the center of his back. "Neither one of our fathers fought for us," she said into his shirt. "What a pair."

A pair.

Cole liked the sound of that. He liked the thought of not being alone, and especially of not being alone with Sienna. She softened his edges, dulling the throbbing pain inside his heart until it lessened to a manageable ache.

No one had ever been able to reach him that way before. Cole might be stubborn, but he wasn't stupid. What she gave to him was precious, a gift to be cherished even if only for a short time.

So he turned around, cupped her cheeks between his hands and kissed her.

Chapter 11

A tremor raced along Sienna's skin at the press of Cole's mouth to hers. Within seconds, he deepened the kiss, his tongue lacing with hers and their breath mingling until she wasn't sure where he ended and she began.

The emotions that assailed her from tonight still held on, but being with Cole had loosened their grip on her. They were distant now, brushing against her legs like tall grass in a summer field instead of making her feel like she was being sucked down into suffocating quicksand.

The longer they kissed, the more she lost herself in the moment—in the feel of Cole's strong body against hers, the way he held her face so tenderly.

It was as if he saw her for something more than she knew herself to be. Someone who could handle whatever life threw at her, even though she had so many doubts about herself. He'd trusted her with his own painful memories, and she had a suspicion that wasn't something he did lightly.

"Let's go…" She paused because what she wanted to say was "home" but she didn't have a home at the moment. Yes, her condo was waiting for her back in Chicago but the idea of returning there now felt foreign to her. She no longer belonged in her own life, but she didn't quite have a place in Crimson either. The Bumblebee was lovely, but only a temporary situation. Everything felt fleeting at the moment, and she desperately wanted to hold on to something sure.

"To my place?" Cole whispered against her mouth, and she nodded.

Not her home, but it would do for now.

He took her hand and they returned down the path toward the parking lot. Shadows fell over the trail and the air had already cooled several degrees.

A shiver passed through her as she climbed into the truck, and she wished she'd worn more to dinner than a thin T-shirt with her jeans. As if reading her mind, Cole reached into the back seat, then handed her a fleece pullover.

"This should help," he said as he turned the key in the ignition.

"I'm fine," she lied. It was obvious she was nowhere near fine. She slipped the soft fabric over her head, inhaling the scent of laundry soap and spice she would forever associate with her sexy sheriff.

Her sheriff.

Heart stuttering at that thought, she zipped up the fleece. Cole might not be hers forever, but she wasn't going to waste this chance with him.

"Do you want seat heat?" he asked.

She shook her head. "The jacket is plenty. Do you mind if I roll down my window?"

He gave her a confused glance out of the corner of his eye. "I saw you shiver."

"I'm warm now, and I love the smell of the forest." She

paused, then added, "I love the scent of pine. I didn't remember it until tonight, but there were woods at the edge of the trailer park where we lived. I used to build forts and secret hideaways in the trees. Sometimes when my mom and dad fought, I'd escape and pretend I lived in the woods by myself."

He depressed both of the window buttons, and a moment later cool air and the crisp scent of pine filled the truck. Sienna leaned back against the headrest and let her eyes drift closed. She was used to the hot, humid air of Midwestern summers and appreciated the freshness of the mountains in a way she couldn't have guessed before returning to Crimson.

"Actually," she said softly, glancing over at Cole, "an escape still sounds like a pretty good idea."

He chuckled and took her hand, enfolding it in his larger one. They didn't speak the rest of the drive back into town. Now that she was calmer, Sienna had a chance to process everything that had happened tonight and what she was about to do with Cole.

What going to his house with him meant. Nerves skittered along her skin, but she didn't consider changing her mind. She wanted him and for once she wasn't going to waste time second-guessing herself.

He parked the car in the driveway and came around to open her door. "I'm happy you're here," he said and leaned in to kiss her.

"Your neighbors might see," she said against his mouth, then pulled back.

"I don't want to hide anything."

She gave his arm a playful nudge as they walked toward the house. "Is the beloved town sheriff really allowed to bring a woman home for the night?"

They entered the house, cool and quiet in the evening

light. "This is nobody's business but ours," he said, dumping his keys onto a table next to the door.

She liked the sound of that—of having something here in Crimson that belonged only to her. It was doubtful Cole truly meant the words, but she still appreciated them.

She wrapped her arms around his neck and kissed him, letting everything else melt away in the heat of her desire. The kiss was slow and deep but quickly turned molten. Suddenly she couldn't wait any longer. There was nothing Sienna needed more than Cole—all of him with every part of her.

As if sensing the change in her, the consuming need pulsing through her, he lifted her into his arms. She held on tight, her legs encircling his hips as he moved from the family room down the hall.

He continued to kiss her as he moved, and she smiled against his mouth. "A man who can multitask. I like it."

"I aim to please," he told her, rounding the corner of what was obviously his bedroom. In the soft light coming from the window, she could see that the walls were painted pale gray and the furniture was dark wood, heavy and masculine. Perfect for Cole.

He pulled back the sheets and followed her down onto the mattress.

"Too many clothes." She pushed at his wide shoulders.

He laughed softly. "I thought we'd try a little foreplay first."

"Foreplay later," she countered. "Right now I need you." She leveled a look at him, hoping he'd get the message. "Right. Now."

Straightening, he flipped on the light next to the bed, then tugged his shirt over his head, revealing a broad, muscled chest that made her mouth go dry. The hard planes weren't a surprise, but the sight of his golden skin and the smattering of dark hair across his chest were the sexiest things she'd ever seen.

"Your pants, too," she demanded, pointing a finger at him.

One side of his mouth curved. "Do you want to check and make sure my butt passes the no-sag test?"

She shook her head. "I have no concerns about your butt."

His grin widened. "I hope you're not going to make me get naked alone." One finger traced the top button of his jeans. "I could move a lot faster with the right motivation."

Sienna wasn't totally inexperienced with men, but she couldn't remember a time when she'd had so much fun in the bedroom. And they hadn't even gotten to the good part yet.

She sat up, then undid the buttons on her cotton shirt. The soft fabric tickled her overly sensitive skin as it fell from her arms. She looked down at herself, then said a silent prayer of thanks that she'd worn a pretty bra tonight.

Reaching behind her back, she unfastened it and tugged the red straps off her shoulders.

"Is this what you had in mind?"

Cole's eyes had gone as dark as rich chocolate. His chest rose and fell like he was having trouble catching his breath. "I couldn't have imagined you in my wildest dreams."

The hoarse rasp of his voice sent another round of shivers skittering over her skin. She liked the power she felt in this moment, reveled in his reaction to her.

"Then you're going to love this," she told him and tossed the lacy bra in his direction.

In what seemed like one fluid movement, he caught it, tossed it aside and was stretched across her a moment later.

She gasped as his big hands covered her breasts, then arched into him when he captured one nipple in his mouth.

"So damn beautiful," he said and turned his attention to the other breast. Sensation spiked through her, making it feel like her whole body had gone liquid.

"I thought we agreed..." she paused to suck in a breath as his teeth grazed the tip of one breast "...to skip foreplay."

"This is too important," he said, then lifted his head. "You're too important to skip any part of it."

Emotion swept through her, even more overwhelming than the physical pleasure Cole was giving her. She raked her fingers through his hair, groaning when he shifted on the bed and undid her jeans, then tugged them, along with her panties, over her hips.

He straightened from the bed and undid his jeans, pushing them down and revealing himself to her. He was perfect...everywhere.

"Do you have...?" She glanced toward the nightstand.

"Yeah." The one word did crazy things to her body. How was it possible to feel so much when he'd barely touched her?

He stepped forward, opened the nightstand drawer and pulled out a condom, tearing open the wrapper with his teeth.

Automatically, Sienna reached for the light.

"Leave it on," Cole told her. "I want to see you."

He was on the bed a moment later, a perfect fit as he joined himself with her. She sucked in a breath as he entered her, wrapping her legs around his lean hips.

They moved together, slowly at first, the rhythm building as he kissed her like his life depended on it.

"You're perfect," he whispered, trailing kisses along her jaw.

"Hardly," she couldn't help but respond.

He stilled, and she could feel the tension in his body. "Perfect," he repeated, his gaze intense on hers.

She reached up and pulled his head down to hers, kissing him with all the emotion she wasn't willing to let him see in her eyes quite yet.

Pressure built inside her as they found a rhythm again and for the moment she let herself believe that she was perfect. That her life wasn't a total mess. She gave herself over to Cole and as soon as she did, it was like a million stars burst inside her.

She called out his name as pleasure washed over her, lifting her on a wave of sensation so strong it felt like she might never recover.

And in that instant, she realized she wouldn't recover from Cole Bennett. Because as much as she wanted to believe what was happening between them was just physical, to Sienna it was so much more.

His body tensed and he whispered her name like it was a prayer. After they'd both returned to earth, he held her tight, rolling over and taking her with him.

"Don't go anywhere," he told her like he thought she was some kind of flight risk.

Which could be the truth if she wasn't so boneless.

He took care of the condom, then returned to the bed, straightening the sheet and comforter over her and pulling her to his chest again.

"Perfect," he repeated, his tone gentle.

"Perfect," she agreed and let her eyes drift closed.

"Is it called the walk of shame even if you drove home?"

Sienna gasped and whirled around to find Paige leaning against the hallway doorframe.

"You practically scared the pants off me," Sienna said, clasping a hand to her chest.

Paige flashed a wide grin. "I think Cole took care of that last night."

Color rose to Sienna's cheeks and she forced herself not to look away. "No drive of shame this morning. I'm tired but not ashamed."

"Because you're so happy and satisfied?" Paige suggested. "Am I going to get all the naughty details?"

Sienna shook her head.

Paige made a face. "At least give me something. It's been a marathon dry spell around here. I need to live vicariously through someone."

"It was nice," Sienna said. "Now I need coffee. Do I smell banana bread?"

"Yes," Paige said, walking down the hall toward the kitchen with Sienna following. "But you can only have a piece if you tell me last night was the most amazing, life-changing experience you've ever had." She grabbed a mug from the counter and handed it to Sienna. "And that Sheriff Bennett is as thorough and capable as I'd imagine."

Sienna took the mug and moved toward the coffeepot.

"In case we haven't discussed it," Paige told her, "I have a very vivid imagination."

Sienna had a difficult time hiding her grin. "Yes."

"Yes?"

She kept her gaze on the mug as she poured coffee in it. "To all of it. Amazing, life changing, thorough and capable doesn't do him justice."

Paige squealed and did a little dance, coffee sloshing over the mug she held. "I knew it."

"That's all I'm going to say," Sienna added quickly. "No details."

"Fine," Paige said as she grabbed a paper towel from the rack attached to the underside of the cabinet. "I even kind of respect you for it. Although I wouldn't complain if you changed your mind."

Sienna shook her head. "What's going on around here?"

She gestured toward the living room, where there was still a gaping hole in the floor.

"The contractor is coming today to tell me how much money I don't have that it will take to fix everything."

"Sorry."

Paige shrugged. "I'll figure it out. I always do. What's next for you and Cole?"

"Nothing."

"Do we need to revisit amazing, thorough and more than capable?"

"It was great but I'm not here for that. I need to talk to my dad. We had a little incident last night."

"What does that mean?"

"I never remembered much about my life before we left Crimson. I'm starting to now. It's weird. The situation was so black-and-white to me, but there's more to it than I realized."

"There always is with family."

Sienna sipped at her coffee. "Do you need help with money for the repairs? I have some savings that—"

"No." Paige held up a hand. "You're a guest here—my only paying guest at the moment."

"That's not going to change," Sienna pointed out, "until the inn is up and running. Isn't summer the big tourist season in town?"

"Well, yes."

"So you need to get things moving."

"Are you trying to manage my life because it's easier to deal with than yours?"

Sienna sighed. "Maybe."

Paige sliced a piece of banana bread from the loaf cooling on the stove, placed it on a small plate and handed it to Sienna. "Eat some carbs, then go visit Declan. I'll let you know when I need help around here."

"Fine." Sienna popped a bite of the sweet bread in her mouth, then headed upstairs for a shower. The part of her night with Cole she hadn't shared was the fact that she'd rushed to get dressed and run out of his house while he was showering this morning. It was cowardly and stupid, but as close as she'd felt to him last night, she couldn't quite face him in the morning. There were way too many questions about where they went next that she wasn't ready to ask or to answer.

She got dressed in the clothes she'd worn her first day in Colorado—a silk shirt and pleated trousers far too formal for this town. She really needed to shop for something new, but that was one more item on her to-do list she was embarrassed to admit she couldn't handle at the moment.

Did she buy clothes appropriate for summer in Colorado or restock her wardrobe with items she'd be able to use back in her old life? It was hard to know when she was so unclear as to what was coming next.

She could hear Paige talking to someone when she came back downstairs and noticed an enormous truck parked at the curb with the words Travers Construction painted on the side.

Sienna slipped out the front door and headed for her rental car. Her phone rang just as she turned the key in the ignition.

"Did you forget something?" Cole's deep voice asked when she picked up.

She swallowed, butterflies taking flight in her belly just at the sound of his voice. "I don't think so."

"How about to say goodbye?" he suggested, and she could hear both amusement and frustration lacing his tone.

"You were in the shower."

"The bathroom door wasn't locked."

"Oh."

"Thank you for staying with me," he said gently. "Next time don't run off."

"Oh," she repeated, realizing she sounded like an idiot but unable to form better words.

"There *will* be a next time," Cole told her, once again displaying his uncanny ability to read her mind."

She licked her dry lips. "Okay."

He chuckled. "What are your plans today?"

"I'm going to see my dad. After last night, there are things he and I need to talk about."

"Memories?"

"I know my mom's side of the story." Sienna pushed her hair away from her face. "Why she left and why she took me and not Jase. I want to understand Declan's side."

"And?" Cole prompted.

"Why he never reached out to me," Sienna admitted.

"You have a right to answers."

"Thank you," she whispered. "I'll call you later."

She disconnected the call, took a deep breath and drove to her father's neighborhood on the other side of downtown.

It was another beautiful day in Crimson, the bright sun warming the air. The sky overhead was the brilliant blue she was quickly coming to associate with Colorado, and she realized now why she'd never quite grown accustomed to the gray skies that hung over Chicago at different times during the year. Some place inside her remembered the expansive swath of blue and the constant sun, because the warmth of the rays felt like a hug from a long-lost friend.

She didn't stop at Life is Sweet this morning, keeping her focus on her goal of meeting with Declan. Downtown was just beginning to wake up as she drove through, and she wondered if Jase was already at his office or still at home.

Did he find it as crazy as she did that she barely remembered anything about the first seven years of her life?

He'd seemed shocked at her reaction to the talk about fireworks. Maybe if things went well with her father, she'd go and see Jase next.

Maybe today would be the day she'd get closure on issues that had plagued her for decades. Maybe today she could finally move forward.

She got out of the car as soon as she parked, not letting her nerves get the better of her.

Declan opened the front door as she approached. He wore a black T-Shirt and faded Levis. So different from her stepfather, who favored monogrammed button-downs and crisp cotton pants even on the weekends. "I wondered if I'd see you this morning," he said, stepping back to let her into the space. "I wasn't sure after you took off last night."

"I didn't remember how I got the scar on my wrist," she admitted as she walked past him. "When I did, it threw me for a loop."

She blinked several times as she took in the interior of the small family room, her breath catching in her throat.

"Is that the same sofa you had in the trailer?" she asked in a whisper.

Declan let out a small laugh behind her. "That throwing you for a loop, too?"

"Maybe."

Definitely. She walked forward and placed a hand on the back of the worn fabric, a heavy plaid pattern that was faded and threadbare in some spots.

"Jase wanted me to get something new, but this is the most comfortable couch I've ever sat on. Besides, it's lucky."

"How do you figure?"

"I watched the Broncos win two Super Bowl rings on that couch. Look at this." He moved around to the front of the sofa and picked up one of the cushions, holding it up so she could see the underside of it. "See that stain?"

Sienna stifled a grimace. "Yes."

"You had reflux as baby," he told her with a grin. "Seemed like you threw up more formula than you kept down some days. That's from you."

"Oh." She had no idea how to respond to that or the pride in Declan's voice, like he should be awarded some kind of gold star for his knowledge of her.

"I understand things about you, baby girl." Her heart ached at the term of endearment. More memories whispered into her mind, hazy and fine like a wisp of smoke. She could make them out as if through a fog, smell them, taste the past on the tip of her tongue but if she reached for them, tried to hold them in her hands, they disappeared like mist.

In their place, anger rose like a wave inside her. "You don't know enough. You have this tiny scar, but Mom has the rest of me. She was the one who held back my hair when I got the flu and puked for three days."

She pressed a hand to her stomach. "Would you like to see the scar from when I had my appendix out senior year of high school? I sure don't remember you being in the hospital or sending a card."

"I didn't know," he said, placing the cushion back on the sofa.

"You don't know anything about me. Maybe you've convinced yourself you were a decent dad when I was young, but a good father wouldn't let his daughter go the way you did."

"Your mother didn't give me a choice," Declan argued, but his voice was weak, shaky.

"There's always a choice." Sienna paced to the far side of the room, drawn by the framed photographs displayed on the narrow bookshelf. One showed Emily's son, Davey, holding up a trout on a dock in front of a mountain lake.

One was a photo of Declan and Jase that looked like it had been taken at that same lake.

The third was Sienna as a toddler. She wore a pale yellow dress with a pattern of sunflowers across the front of it and her blond hair was pulled back into two pigtails. It was a photo she hadn't seen before. Her mother didn't have many pictures of Sienna before they moved to Chicago.

"That was your favorite dress," her dad said from behind her. "You'd wear it for days at a time before your mom would force you to take it off so it could be washed."

Studying the photo was almost like looking at a stranger, even though she clearly recognized herself. She squeezed her eyes shut and combed through her memories, trying to recall the dress.

"It doesn't matter," she said after a moment, more to herself than Declan. "You let me go." She whirled around to face him. "Why didn't you fight for me? I can't imagine I was so precious to you if you didn't even come after me when Mom moved away."

"She needed you," he said, holding up his hands. "I knew there was no way to make her stay with how unhappy she was here. I loved your mother, but we were toxic together."

"All you needed was Jase," she said, the words like sandpaper scraping across her tongue. "As long as you had him—"

"He chose to stay," Declan argued. "Dana would have taken him, too, but—"

"He was a kid," Sienna shouted. "Just like me. Neither of you had the right to make the choice you did for either of us."

"Your mother was the one to cut off communication. This is her fault."

"You didn't fight for me." Sienna pounded an open palm against her chest. "Because I wasn't worth it to you."

"Not true." Declan ran a hand through his hair. "I thought about you every day. I loved you."

"Don't say that. You don't get to use those words with me." The emotion she'd kept at bay for so many years poured forth. The walls she'd built around her heart bursting open. She wanted to hurt her father the way she'd been hurt.

"This was a mistake," she said, drawing in a deep breath. "I have nothing to say to you because you mean nothing to me. Less than nothing." She bit down on her bottom lip to keep from crying. That's how his tacit rejection had made her feel—less than nothing. For years, she'd taken scraps of affection from everyone around her because that's all she felt like she deserved.

She started toward the front door. Fresh air and sunshine would remind her that there was a big world still spinning despite the pinpoint of her own problems that seemed to be all she could see at the moment.

Her fingers had just gripped the knob when the crash had her spinning back around. Her breath caught as she saw Declan land on the floor, eyes closed and body limp. The lamp and side table he'd knocked over during his fall lay on the ground next to him.

"Dad!" she screamed, already reaching for her cell phone to dial 911.

Chapter 12

Cole took off his hat as he strode through the automatic doors of Crimson Community Hospital an hour later.

He'd been out near the county line when Marlene had radioed him to report that Declan Crenshaw was being rushed to the ER.

Marlene told him Jase was already on his way to the hospital, so Cole tried calling Sienna's cell but hadn't been able to reach her. He'd called Paige next, and his gut twisted when she'd explained in a frantic voice that Sienna hadn't returned after the visit with her father that morning.

He couldn't imagine a scenario where Sienna might have anything to do with Declan's condition, but the idea still scared the hell out of him. The last thing she needed was to deal with a health crisis surrounding her dad.

He scanned the waiting room and saw Emily and Noah next to each other on a small leather sofa.

"What happened?" he asked, moving toward them. "Is Declan okay?"

Emily shook her head. "We don't know. The doctor is with him now. They let Jase go back, but they're running more tests." She put a hand on her belly. "It was definitely his heart, but we don't know how serious it is yet."

Noah placed a hand on his sister's shoulder. "The old man is tough."

"Not like he used to be," Emily countered. "He puts on a good front, but all those years of drinking have taken their toll."

Cole ran a hand through his hair and glanced around the waiting room as if he could produce answers to take away some of Emily's anxiety. She and Jase had been through enough in the past year. They should be getting ready to come to the hospital for the happiest of reasons, not something like this.

"Has anyone talked to Sienna?"

Noah's lips pressed into a thin line, and Emily let out a muttered curse. "She was with him at the time," she said, meeting Cole's gaze. Her pale blue eyes were icy. "She rode here with him in the ambulance—called Jase on the way. But we haven't seen her."

Noah snorted. "At this point, all we know is she took off."

"You can't blame her," Cole said immediately.

"Where is she then?" Noah asked. "As usual, Jase is left to take care of his dad on his own."

"I'll find her." Cole stepped away and punched in Sienna's cell number again. The call went straight to voice mail so he sent a text. When a response didn't come immediately, he approached the reception desk.

"Hey, Dixie," he said with a small smile for the fifty-something woman behind the computer.

"Howdy, Sheriff." The woman fluffed her hair as she spoke. "Are you here checking on Declan? I hope it's not too serious, especially for Jase's sake. That boy has been through hell and back for his dad."

"Yeah," Cole agreed automatically. "I'm hoping you can help me with something. There was a woman who rode in the ambula—"

"The daughter," Dixie said in a scandalized whisper. "I'd heard she was back in town. Looks exactly like her mother did years ago. I used to see Dana Crenshaw in the grocery—do you remember that she was a checker down at the Shop & Go back in the day?"

"I don't," Cole admitted, mentally counting to ten. He'd learned quickly upon his arrival in Crimson that a small town moved at its own pace. Most people in Crimson were friendly to a fault, but they wouldn't be rushed in how they doled out their help.

"We all knew she'd taken a step back marrying Declan. It was obvious she didn't belong in that trailer park. Falling in love makes a woman do stupid things. She was half out of her mind most of the time, but sober she handled those groceries like she was the queen of England. People around here didn't see, but I knew she was destined for better things."

"You're a good woman, Dixie. As far as Sienn—"

"Do you think the daughter takes after her mom?" Dixie frowned, tapping a finger on her glossed lips. "It was hard to tell when they came through here. I gave her the paperwork to fill out for Declan, and she didn't say much. But the poor thing could have been in shock, you know? I remember when—"

"Have you seen her?" Cole interrupted, unable to be patient any longer. "I'm looking for Sienna."

"Well then." Dixie studied him for a few moments, her

brows raised. "She might have headed for the cafeteria." She pointed down the hall. "I think I mentioned that Tuesday is tomato soup day, since she was going to be waiting for her dad. People forget to eat in times of stress."

"Thanks, Dixie." Cole smiled again. "The hospital is lucky to have you."

"Of course they are," the woman agreed with a wink. "See you, Sheriff."

Cole glanced back to the waiting room, but Emily and Noah hadn't moved and Jase was still nowhere in sight. He made his way quickly to the cafeteria, scanning the tables until he saw a familiar cascade of blond hair near the far corner.

"Hey," he said as he came to stand next to her. "You doing okay?"

Sienna glanced up, then quickly away, her eyes round with what looked like residual shock. Her skin was pale, her shoulders slumped. Cole wanted nothing more than to gather her in his arms and tell her he'd make everything right again.

"I should never have come here," she told him, shaking her head.

"Don't say that." He pulled out the chair next to her, metal scraping against the floor.

"Why not? Everyone else will be." She stared directly in front of her, unwilling to look at him. "I could hear it in Jase's voice when I called him." She shuddered. "Do you know what he said? 'What did you do to him?' Like the cardiac arrest was my fault."

"It wasn't."

"You don't know that." She pressed a hand to her chest. "I don't know that. The woman at the front desk handed me all this paperwork like I can fill it out. As if I know

anything about my father's medical history or insurance."
She gave a short laugh. "I don't even know his birth date."

She grabbed the clipboard from the table, holding it so
tight her knuckles turned white. Cole placed a hand over
hers, willing her to relax.

"Look at me, Sienna. Tell me what happened."

She shook her head. "I went to his house, and we argued.
Or I argued. I yelled at him. So much anger came tumbling
out." Her gaze flicked to his. "He had a framed photo of
me as a girl, and it set everything off. He thinks he knows
me, but he doesn't. He couldn't possibly."

"You can change that."

"I've done a real bang-up job so far." She blew out a
breath. "I spent my first week in town hiding out only to
storm away from a family dinner. Then today—" Her voice
cut out on a choked sob. "What if Declan doesn't make it?
What if all those horrible things I said are his last memories of me?"

"It wouldn't matter." He lifted his free hand to the back
of her neck, gently massaging the tight muscles there. "Declan owns his mistakes, and he made some big ones with
you. That's on him, Sienna."

She leaned into his touch and let out a sigh. "How I
deal with him now is on me. I'm an adult. I have a life. My
daddy didn't want me when I was a girl. Big deal, right?"

Cole thought of his relationship with his own father.
Until his arrest, Richard Bennett had been a picture-per-
fect parent. He'd taught Cole and Shep to fish and hunt,
run alongside them when they'd learned to ride bikes. He'd
been to every football game and parent-teacher conference
he was in town for, and most of all he'd always made both
boys feel safe and loved. At least that's how Cole had seen
it. Shep had a different opinion—bristling against the strict
rules his father set in the house.

Cole's dad had been his idol, which was why his arrest and then shocking death had hit so hard. He still couldn't imagine how he would have felt growing up without his dad or believing he didn't want anything to do with him.

"Come back with me to the waiting area. Emily and Noah are there while Jase is in the room with Declan."

"Saint Jase," Sienna muttered.

"No one blames you."

She rolled her eyes. "Liar."

"It won't help to keep yourself separate from them."

"It'll help me," she said, her voice breaking, "not deal with the fact that I may have just killed my estranged father."

"Don't say that."

She lowered her head, tears dripping onto the hospital paperwork.

His heart ached, but clearly sympathy wasn't helping. "I never took you for a coward." He cringed inwardly when her shoulders stiffened.

A moment later, she looked up, her eyes blazing. If she could have killed him with a look, he'd be long gone. She swiped at her eyes. "Is this reverse psychology?" she asked, her tone menacing.

"You have to face this thing," he said instead of answering. "Or run back to Mommy and Stepdaddy and your little insulated world of privilege and first-world problems."

She barked out a laugh. "First-world problems. That's a good one."

"Where are you going to find the next candidate for a country club husband since the last one couldn't keep it in his pants?"

"I don't need another candidate."

She was angry now, every inch of her radiating temper. It was better than seeing her broken. He could take anything but that. "Maybe you should go for more of a father figure. Someone older, probably divorced and looking for wifey number two. You can try to work out some of the daddy issues you're too scared to face with your real father."

"Low blow, Sheriff," she said on a hiss of breath. "And rich coming from the man who hasn't talked to his twin brother in years. I'm not the only one who's messed up around here."

"You have no idea, sweetheart," he agreed. Somehow Sienna had worked her way past his defenses, and it scared the hell out of him how much her happiness mattered. If only he had something real to offer her. "Unlike you, I'm content with my mess. You came here to fix yours. Do you have the guts to do it?"

"You're a terrible man." She grabbed the clipboard and rose from the table. "You might be excellent in bed, but dealing with your head games is not worth the effort."

He followed as she stalked from the cafeteria. "You're moving," he told her, "toward the waiting room."

"Because you're a manipulative, jerky...jerk."

He kept his features schooled when she glanced over at him. "I'll take that."

"They don't want me here," she whispered as they drew closer to the hospital's main entrance.

"You're stronger than you realize, Sienna, even when you have to be bullied into admitting it."

"I'm not going to thank you for being mean," she said under her breath.

"Will you go out with me on a real date to make it up to you?"

She stopped in her tracks, took a deep breath and narrowed her eyes. "First you're rude and now you're trying to distract me before I go in front of the firing squad?"

"Or I'm just asking you out," he suggested with a wink.

"Definitely distraction," she agreed, then walked toward Emily and Noah.

"Any news on Declan?" Sienna kept her shoulders straight as she looked from Emily to Noah, proud her voice didn't falter.

"Where have you been?" Emily demanded, crossing her arms over her chest. "We've been here almost an hour and haven't seen you once."

"I needed some time to collect myself." There was no point in trying to act like she hadn't been deeply affected by watching her father almost die.

She'd started CPR immediately and the EMTs had arrived within minutes. They'd used a defibrillator to shock his heart into beating normally again, but he hadn't regained consciousness during the ambulance ride. No one would answer any of her questions about his condition and he'd been whisked behind the large metal doors that separated the exam and operating rooms from the public part of the hospital.

She'd been left standing in front of the reception desk, alone and scared half out of her mind. A woman had shoved the clipboard of paperwork into her hands and Sienna had rushed off to the women's restroom, shutting herself in a stall while she sucked in gasping breaths, fear and guilt and adrenaline pumping through her veins.

Don't die. Don't die. Don't die.

That was the refrain in her head, even though she hadn't spoken the words out loud. She hadn't trusted her voice, hadn't wanted to admit—even to herself—how much she couldn't stand the thought of losing him.

Yes, she'd been angry and about to walk out, but she still cared. Far too much. She always had.

"The last we heard," Noah said gently, as if he understood how difficult this was for her, "your father is stable."

"Thanks for calling Jase right away," Emily added, pulling her purse off the chair next to her. "Have a seat. It makes the baby nervous to have you looming over her like that."

"I wasn't exactly looming."

Cole gave her a small nod as she sat down. "I'm going to see if I can get more information."

"I'll go with you," Noah said and jumped out of his chair like he thought his sister and Sienna might get into a catfight right there in the middle of the hospital waiting room.

"He has to be okay," Sienna whispered when she and Emily were alone.

"Yes," Emily agreed. She reached for the clipboard. "Want me to work on the information you didn't know?"

"That's pretty much all of it," Sienna said with a sigh. "I'm useless."

"You got him here." Emily shrugged as she began filling in the little boxes. "That counts."

"But Jase is with him now. He doesn't need me."

"I don't know why either of your parents let things happen the way they did." Emily placed a hand on her round belly. "I'd never cut my daughter off from her father, and if I tried, Jase would fight me every step of the way. It's not fair that Declan didn't fight for you."

Sienna swallowed. "Yeah."

"I was married before I came back to Crimson and reconnected with Jase." Emily hugged the clipboard to her chest. "My first husband couldn't handle being a dad to a child with special needs. When I left the East Coast, he went on with life like Davey and I never existed. He doesn't call or check in. He's gotten remarried and had another baby. I wouldn't be surprised if he doesn't admit to having an older son."

"I'm sorry," Sienna whispered automatically.

"Me, too, but mostly for my ex-husband. I never want my son to feel like it was his fault that his daddy didn't want to be a part of his life."

"Sometimes you can't help that. What would you do if Davey wanted to pursue a relationship with his dad or if your ex tried to come back into his life?"

Emily inclined her head, as if weighing the question in her mind. "I'd allow it to happen, but I'd be there to support Davey and what he needed along the way."

"My mom can't stand the fact that I'm here." Sienna reached out a hand, placed it on Emily's arm and squeezed. "Your son is going to turn out great." She gave a small laugh. "Unlike me. It's obvious you want what's best for him, and he has Jase, too."

"You're doing okay," Emily answered.

"Other than the fact that I've upended your and Jase's lives and quite possibly put my father in the hospital."

"Other than that," Emily agreed and pain speared through Sienna's chest. "I'm joking," Emily added quickly. "But things definitely took a turn toward more complicated today. Don't let that scare you off."

"Complicated has never been my favorite thing," Sienna admitted.

"Stick around long enough and you'll learn to appreciate it."

Jase appeared in the waiting room at that moment. Emily set aside the clipboard and rose from her seat to move forward, throwing her arms around his neck. They stood together for several long moments, holding on to each other tight.

Sienna glanced over and met Cole's dark gaze as he and

Noah came to stand to one side of the couple. She could imagine holding on to him in that same way, and she felt a pang of envy that she might not get that chance.

"How is he?" she asked, rising from the chair.

"He's stable," Jase answered. He let go of Emily and moved toward Sienna. To her surprise, he leaned in for an awkward hug as relief filled her. "Thanks for getting help to him so quickly. The doctor says it might have saved his life."

Sienna felt her mouth drop open, unsure of what to say in response. "I thought you'd blame me." Immediately she knew that was the wrong response but couldn't retract it now.

Her brother only shook his head. "He's been on heart medicine for the past few years but isn't good about taking his pill every day."

He was giving her an out, but Sienna couldn't allow herself to take it. "I fought with him. He was angry and upset."

"You really must not remember much from our childhood," he said, one side of his mouth curving. "Arguing is Dad's love language. It would probably be easier if there was a bad guy in this situation, but we're just going to have to deal with things the hard way."

Emily peered around Jase's arm. "You could use a little work on accepting kindness," she told Sienna. "And not rushing off before dessert is served."

"I'll remember that for next time." Sienna returned Emily's smile, her heart swelling. The situation still wasn't perfect, but somehow it seemed like she might be able to forge a relationship with her estranged family after all.

"Can we see him?" Emily asked, taking Jase's hand in hers.

Jase shook his head. "He's resting now. The doctor expects him out of ICU by this afternoon. They think he'll only have to spend one night in the hospital, and we should be able to visit later today." He met Sienna's gaze again. "I'll call you when we know more"

She nodded, blinking back tears she didn't want anyone to see.

Cole stepped forward. "I'll give you a ride back to Declan's to pick up your car."

"I can take her," Jase said, shifting to block Cole from reaching for her.

"I've got it," Cole told him, confusion marring his movie-star features.

"I don't think so," Jase countered.

Sienna glanced at Emily and raised a brow.

"Okay, boys," the other woman said, moving between them. "Enough for now. Jase, we need to finish filling out paperwork and insurance forms. Cole, if you need to get back to work, I'm sure Noah can take Sienna."

"I'll take her," Cole repeated, his jaw clenched tight like he'd read something in Jase's expression that sat with him wrong.

"Text me later, Em," Noah said. He turned to Sienna and winked. "Welcome to having a big brother," he told her and walked away.

Emily put a hand on Jase's arm and pushed him toward the chairs where she'd left the clipboard. "We'll call you as soon as we know anything about your dad." Her tone was more chipper than Sienna had ever heard it.

"Let's go," Cole said and turned on his heel.

She stood where she was a moment longer, not sure what she was missing in the exchange between the two long-time friends.

"Did Jase do something to make you mad?" she asked as she caught up to Cole's long strides.

"No."

"Did you have an argument?"

"Nope." Cole didn't glance her way but held open the door as she passed through.

She turned and reached out, placing both her hands on his arms. "What happened? You two are best friends."

"He's stepping into the role of protective older brother." He looked past her, his eyes unreadable.

Sienna felt color flood her cheeks. "I find that hard to believe. He doesn't even want me here."

"Don't let him fool you. Jase cares." He opened the Jeep's door and she got in, fatigue coursing through her now that the adrenaline had worn off. "Are you okay?"

She nodded. "I'll be fine, although waiting for an update is going to drive me crazy."

He dropped a quick kiss on her lips, then walked around the front of the SUV and climbed in the driver's side. "Have dinner with me later," he said, pulling away from the curb.

"I'm not sure—"

"We can change plans if you hear from Jase." An unspoken promise flickered in his gorgeous brown eyes, and she tried not to moan out loud. "Give it a chance, Sienna. Just one date."

"One date," she agreed, tamping down the delight and uncertainty that warred inside her, not to mention the hallelujah chorus her lower half was singing.

She could totally handle dinner with Cole, sure and steady and able to make butterflies dance across her chest with one smoldering glance. She could handle anything, she told herself, then sent up a silent prayer of thanks when no bolt of lightning appeared to strike her down for the lie.

Chapter 13

"This is ridiculous," Sienna said. "The worst idea ever." She reached for the zipper on the back of the dress Paige had convinced her to wear to dinner with Cole.

"Don't you dare," Paige said, grabbing her arms and turning her until she faced the mirror. "That dress is amazing on you. Cole is going to lose his mind."

"That's not a good thing," Sienna said with a huff.

"It's great," Paige countered.

"How can I go out on a date with my father in the hospital? People will think I'm living up to my mom's awful reputation and only caring about myself."

"You have to eat dinner." Paige grabbed a bottle of perfume from the dresser in her room and spritzed Sienna. "You've talked to Jase twice since you got back here. He'll call you if anything changes with Declan's condition."

A loud hammering sounded from outside the bedroom window, and Paige made a face. "I hate construction," she said.

"How's it coming?"

"The contractor thinks he's got things under control, and I definitely appreciate that he's got the guys working late most nights to get the job done more quickly. But the water damage caused several floor joists to rot. Since the joists apparently hold up the actual floor, it's not good."

"Sounds expensive."

"Exactly," Paige agreed, then sighed. "And it's money I don't have. I'm going to have to call my mom and ask for a loan or tell her I'll be late on the mortgage payment for another month. I can't open for business without a floor and there's no money coming in without paying guests."

"I thought you were only going to share good news with your mom so she won't worry about you."

"That was the plan, but plans change. I'm not giving up on The Bumblebee. I just need to convince Mom not to give up on me."

"I hope she agrees."

"Yeah." Paige closed her eyes for a moment, then gave her head a little shake and opened them again. "But tonight is about you and our sexy sheriff. Do you think he carries handcuffs?"

"Only when I'm on duty."

Both women whirled around to find Cole standing at the bedroom door.

"I knocked," he said, holding up his hands, palms out, "but no one heard me over the hammering."

"You look quite handsome, Sheriff Bennett," Paige said with a wink. "Although the lack of handcuffs is a bit of a disappointment."

"We'll make do," Cole told her in his deep, rumbling voice.

Sienna was pretty sure she let out a whimper because Paige and Cole both turned to stare at her.

"It was my stomach growling," she lied, pressing a hand to her belly. "I'm hungry."

Paige grinned as she pushed Sienna toward Cole. "I just bet you are. Have a good night, you two. Be safe. Do lots of things I won't have a chance to."

"Thanks for letting me borrow the dress," Sienna said over her shoulder.

"Thank you *very* much," Cole echoed.

His whiskey-colored gaze burned into hers as he took her hand and lifted it, turning it over and placing a soft kiss on the inside of her wrist. "You're beautiful," he whispered and her knees felt like they were made of jelly.

"You, too," she blurted, then flashed a smile. "I mean, you look handsome tonight. Every night really. And during the day. But tonight especially, I guess."

"Maybe stop talking now," Paige called from behind her. Cole laughed and Sienna felt her cheeks go hot. What was it about this man that turned her into a babbling schoolgirl with her first crush?

He wore a pair of dark jeans and a crisp white buttondown that made his tanned skin look even more golden. The sleeves were rolled up to the elbows, and the hair that peppered his forearms was somehow the sexiest thing she'd ever seen.

"I'm pathetic," she muttered, and Cole grabbed her hand and squeezed.

He waved to one of the workers, then led her out of the house. As soon as the front door had closed behind them, he turned and claimed her mouth, the kiss gentle and intense at the same time.

Her eyes drifted shut as she lost herself in the feel of him. This was what she wanted, to forget everything in her life except the way Cole's touch made her body come to life.

All too soon, he pulled away. "Thank you," he whispered, pressing his forehead to hers.

"For kissing you?"

"For agreeing to go out with me."

She should tell him it didn't mean anything. She needed to eat and wanted a distraction while she waited for news on her dad. But she couldn't make her mouth form the words, because it *did* mean something to her.

Yes, Cole was handsome as sin, but her connection to him was way more than a physical attraction. She loved his honesty and integrity, the way he tried to take care of her even when she didn't need him to. She liked the person she was when they were together. He made her feel more confident because he expected more from her than anyone ever had.

"I'm glad you asked," she told him, then fused her mouth to his. By the time she pulled back, they were both breathing heavily and Sienna felt like her whole body was on fire.

"But we should get dinner," she added, not trusting herself to share her bone-deep yearning to be close to him. Sienna had always stayed emotionally distant from the people around her. It was a defense mechanism, something to ensure she wouldn't be hurt.

Cole made her want to throw caution and all her self-preservation instincts to the wind and open herself up completely. It was terrifying and exhilarating at the same time, like climbing the first hill on a roller coaster when the car was cresting the top and about to careen down the other side.

"You're too practical for your own good," he said with a low chuckle. "But let me ply you with food and spirits and then we'll see where this takes us."

"Romantic," she said, elbowing him as they walked to his truck.

"I have my moments," he told her with a wink.

"I just bet you do."

She climbed into the truck and fastened her seat belt, her insides still tingling from his kiss.

He pulled away from the curb, surprising her when he turned away from town.

"Where are we going?"

"It's a surprise."

She glanced at him out of the corner of her eye. "I hope this isn't some covert plan to dump me over the county line because I'm too much trouble."

He kept his eyes on the road in front of them. "Apparently I like trouble."

She tried—and failed—to hide her smile at his words.

A few minutes later, the truck's front dipped as he maneuvered onto a dirt road and drove over a deep rut. Sienna's stomach lurched in response.

She wasn't sure what to expect from this night. Her past dating experience had always been completely traditional and boring.

Dinner at a trendy restaurant, sometimes dancing at a nightclub or a round of tennis at the country club. After a few weeks, there would be the obligatory family get-together—usually Sunday brunch or happy hour with business colleagues. All of it on an appropriate timeline that showed interest—but not too much—and a sense of decorum that Sienna now recognized had been one of the things that had made her feel stifled and sick to death of her own life.

Everything with Cole felt new and exciting, and the unknown of it thrilled her.

"We're here," he said, pulling onto the narrow shoulder.

"Where's here?"

"Dinner," he answered. "Although with the way you look tonight, I'm second-guessing my plan."

"Do you have a plan?"

"You trust me, right?"

"Well, I trust that you're not a secret sheriff serial killer."

"Good to know," he said with a grin.

He got out of the truck and moved around to her side, opening the door for her. "We don't have to go far."

She nodded and stepped out, figuring she might as well be game for whatever adventure he had planned. At least it was taking her mind off her father and his condition.

She silently congratulated herself for choosing a pair of comfortable wedge heels from Paige's closet so she wasn't worried about breaking an ankle on the trail.

Cole took a cooler out of the truck's cargo bed and started up the path peeking out from the heavily wooded area.

They'd only walked about twenty-five feet when the forest opened into a picturesque meadow, complete with a view of the mountains and a rustic picnic table set up in the middle of the field.

She stepped into the clearing, then spun around in a slow circle, marveling at the quiet beauty around them. "Is there some manual they gave you when you moved here about hidden vistas in Crimson?"

He flashed a wide smile. "I talk to a lot of people in my line of work. I ask questions. Privacy is important to me, but I don't want to miss out on how great this area is because of it. I'll take the road or the picnic area less traveled when I can."

"I'm overdressed."

"You look perfect."

"It looks like the picnic table is already set."

He nodded, looking almost sheepish. "I came out earlier and got things ready."

She followed him to the center of the meadow. A linen covered the picnic table, which was set for two. "I hope you're not disappointed that we're not at a restaurant in town. It seemed like you might get a bunch of questions about your dad. I thought you could use a break, and we're closer to the hospital here than if we'd gone downtown."

"So you cooked?"

He placed the cooler on one of the long benches. "Not exactly," he told her, opening the lid. "But I'm great at ordering carryout." He took out several cardboard food containers. "There's a new Italian place on the way to Aspen. Best manicotti ever."

He placed the boxes on the table, then pulled out a bottle of wine and two glasses.

"You went to so much trouble," she murmured.

"We can hit the town next time if you want," he told her with a boyish smile that melted her heart.

"This is perfect." She leaned in to brush a kiss across his jaw. What she wanted to say was that Cole was perfect. Perfect for her. But she was afraid to reveal too much, terrified at how serious her feelings for him had become in such a short time.

He uncorked the wine and she held the glasses while he poured. They toasted to Declan's health and new beginnings, then Cole opened the containers and served them both crisp green salad and a scrumptious-smelling portion of pasta.

"It's amazing," she said after taking a bite, the combination of tangy sauce and rich cheese making her want to moan with pleasure.

"What's your favorite restaurant in Chicago?" he asked.

She smiled. "The shawarma food truck that parks around the corner from my condo. I'm not much of a cook either. I eat there at least twice a week."

"Do you miss the city?"

She forked up another bite but paused before putting it in her mouth. "Not really, which is strange. Everything in my regular life was so structured. I thought that's how I liked it, but now I see that it was also suffocating me."

"Structure isn't a bad thing," he said, taking a sip of wine.

She smiled. "So says the lawman with the military background. I wish I'd questioned things more when I was growing up, and even as an adult. My mom made it clear that I should be grateful for the life we had, and I was. But I didn't choose it. I never learned to figure out what I wanted. You'd think with the Crenshaw blood in me I would have rebelled or gone off the rails or something. Instead I was just a dutiful little sheep following the flock."

She put down her fork and picked up the wineglass. "I'm mostly disappointed in myself at this point for letting other people decide how I should live my life."

"You can always change that."

"What about you?" she asked, twirling the stem of the wineglass between her fingers.

"What about me?"

"Is there something you'd change about your—?"

"Nope. My life is just fine."

"What about your brother? Aren't you curious about where he is now? He's the only family you have, right?"

Cole's jaw clenched, but he nodded.

"You could reach out to him. Try to mend the rift—"

"I told you I don't even know if he's still alive."

"You're twins," she insisted. "I have to believe you'd know if something awful had happened."

"Yeah," he agreed reluctantly, running a hand over his jaw. "I'd know. But Shep made his choice after Dad died. The fact that he didn't come back for Mom's funeral... I can't forgive that."

"You could at least try to contact him."

"I have no idea where he is at this point."

"People have to work hard to hide in this day and age. One quick Google search and I bet—"

"I don't need him," Cole snapped. "I don't need anyone. My life is fine the way it is."

She forced herself to swallow the bite of pasta she'd just taken, even though it felt like it had turned to sawdust in her mouth. "Good to know."

Cole blew out a breath. "I didn't mean that the way it sounded."

"It's fine," she lied.

"Sienna, I'm—"

He broke off when both of their phones chirped wildly. Sienna grabbed hers from her purse as Cole pulled his from his back pocket.

"He's awake," she whispered, knowing that Cole would understand she was talking about her father. Jase had texted them both.

She let out a shuddery breath and pressed her fingers to her mouth when a sob threatened to emerge. Cole immediately stood and came around to her side of the table. He dropped down next to her and wrapped a hand around her shoulder.

She buried her face in the crook of his neck, breathing

in the strong, safe scent of him. He rubbed his open palm in wide circles on her back, murmuring soothing words against her ear.

"I'll take you to the hospital," he told her.

"We haven't finished dinner," she argued weakly. "Jase is there and—"

"It's okay," he promised. "We can take a rain check on dessert. You need to be with your family right now."

Family. It was still difficult to believe that just by coming to Crimson and inserting herself in their lives that Declan and Jase were her family. Not after so many years of absence from her life.

But that's how it felt. They were family. The bond between the three of them was fragile, but it tied them together nonetheless.

"Thank you for understanding," she said as he gathered their plates and leftover food.

They made quick work of putting away the picnic, then returned down the trail to the truck. They were only ten minutes to the hospital, but the drive seemed interminable to Sienna. She vacillated between guilt that she hadn't been there when Declan first woke to regret that she'd effectively ruined the perfect date Cole had planned. Once again, nothing she did was quite right.

"Do you want me to go in with you?" Cole asked, parking in front of the hospital's entrance.

"I should go on my own," she told him, then leaned across the console to give him a quick kiss. "Thank you again. Tonight was the best date I've ever had."

He traced a finger along her jaw. "And the shortest, I'm guessing."

"Rain check," she promised, giving him one last kiss before hurrying into the hospital.

Chapter 14

The swoosh of the elevator doors sounded particularly loud as Sienna exited. She checked in with the nurse at the charge desk, then walked down the hall toward her father's room.

She knocked softly and, with a deep breath, pushed open the door. Jase immediately straightened from a chair to one side of the bed, rubbing a hand over his eyes as he moved toward her.

"Sorry I wasn't here earlier." Her gaze tracked to Declan, lying in the hospital bed with his eyes closed and a sheet pulled up to just below his chest. He looked peaceful. Silver whiskers shadowed his jaw and a long tube peeked out from the gap in the front of the hospital gown, attached to a heart monitor next to the bed.

"Don't worry about it," he answered. "He only woke up for a few minutes, then drifted back to sleep."

"Is that good or bad?"

"The doctors believe he'll make a full recovery. They did an angioplasty for a blockage in one of his arteries and inserted a stent to keep it open long-term. He's going to need to finally take his diet more seriously, and we'll need to make sure he starts exercising regularly. But if we can convince him to give up the junk food and make his health a priority, he should be around to be a pain in the butt for a good while."

She laughed softly. "Cheese puffs," she murmured. "I remember him loving cheese puffs. He'd deny it, but his fingertips were always stained orange."

"Still loves them," Jase confirmed. He took a step back and looked her up and down. "You look nice."

She smoothed a self-conscious hand over the front of her dress. "I borrowed it from Paige. I had… I went out… I was having dinner when you texted."

"With Paige?" he asked, one thick brow lifting.

She shook her head but didn't give any more information.

"Then it must have been Cole." His tone was low and fairly disapproving.

"He's your best friend," she pointed out. "Is there some problem with me having dinner with him?"

"You're my sister," he answered, as if that explained everything.

It was odd but sweet to hear him refer to her in that way, sounding both overprotective and exasperated. It was clear Jase couldn't explain how they'd gotten to this place any more than she could.

She raised a brow. "From what I heard, not that long ago you wanted Cole close to me so he could make sure I didn't have any evil plans for my time in Crimson."

One side of his mouth curved. "Evil isn't quite the right

term. Things changed. I'm not trying to chase you away, Sienna, and Cole is a friend. But he's not a long-term bet for a woman."

"Who says I'm interested in that?"

"No one." He shook his head. "But I hope you're in our lives for the long term. It's taken too many years to get to this point, and I don't want anyone to mess that up. Dad can handle that all on his own."

"I'm stuck in this damn bed," a gravelly voice said, "and you're going to diss me."

"When did you start using the word *diss*?" Jase asked as they both turned to the bed, where Declan had propped himself up against the pillow.

"My neighbor has a twelve-year-old boy. He downloaded Urban Dictionary on that fancy phone you got me."

"Lord help us," Jase muttered.

Sienna moved to the side of the bed. "How are you feeling, Dad?"

Declan stared at her for a moment. "You called me Dad," he said, adjusting the sheet. "I should come close to dying more often."

"Don't even think about it," she countered.

"I'm fine, baby girl." He lifted one thin shoulder, then let it drop. "It takes more than a wee clogged artery to finish me off."

"I'm glad." She reached out and squeezed his hand. "You gave me quite a scare."

"Let's be clear." Declan looked between the two of them. "This episode had nothing to do with Sienna. It was me and the fact that I can barely remember to put the toilet seat down, let alone take my heart medication every day."

"I know," Jase told him, affection clear in his tone. "You were lucky Sienna was with you when it happened."

"True dat," Declan said, nodding.

Sienna stifled a laugh and glanced at Jase.

"Overmedicated," he said in a stage whisper.

Declan laughed. "No such thing."

Sienna felt a strange sense of happiness bubble up in her chest. It was surreal to be here with her dad and brother, a family gathered when someone needed help, making light of a situation that had clearly scared all of them.

"How do you feel?" She let go of his hand and moved the chair closer to the bed.

"Like a herd of cattle trampled over my chest." He shrugged. "Pretty normal."

"You shouldn't make light of it. Jase said they've talked to you about diet and exercise. You need to comply with the doctor's orders."

Declan looked past her to Jase. "Did you pay her to say all that?"

"She cares," Jase answered, "even though you probably don't deserve it."

"I definitely don't," her father agreed.

"I care," Sienna murmured, still surprised to find it was true. Not just because she felt guilty that she'd been arguing with her father when he collapsed. She wanted him to be well. She wanted a chance at some kind of relationship with both of these men. The feeling of abandonment that had been her companion for so long was slowly fading, replaced by the bright glow of her newly forged connection.

Her father met her gaze for a long moment, his blue eyes tired but tender as he seemed to drink her in.

"You two should go," he said gruffly. "You've seen that I'm gonna make it. Go home and get some rest."

"I'll stay for a bit," Sienna said immediately. "Jase can go. He's been here all day."

Jase rubbed a hand over his whiskered jaw. "Are you sure? I can—"

"Your sister will stay," Declan said, and Jase gave a small smile, seeming pleased by his father's use of the word *sister*.

Sienna was secretly pleased, as well. She appreciated this unfamiliar sense of belonging.

Jase gave her a short, somewhat less awkward hug than before, then squeezed his father's shoulder. "Rest," he said. "You've got a new granddaughter to meet in a few weeks, so you'll need plenty of energy."

"I promise," Declan answered, and Jase left the room.

"You want to talk more about all the things I did wrong?" her dad asked when they were alone.

"Of course not. You're in a hospital bed."

He raised a brow. "It's the perfect location. I can't leave and they've got paddles all over this place if things go south."

"That's morbid."

"And a joke."

"At least I know I didn't get my sense of humor from you." She adjusted her dress, then picked an invisible piece of lint from the fabric. "Thanks for not dying."

"Your sense of humor has hope after all." He waved a finger at her. "Why are you all dolled up tonight?"

"I was out to dinner when Jase texted to say you'd woken."

"With Cole Bennett?"

She shrugged. "I had to eat."

Declan tipped back his head and laughed. "Well played, baby girl. Not that I have any business doling out parental advice, but be careful with Cole. I have enough demons that I've gotten damn good at recognizing them in others. Our sheriff is a stand-up kind of guy, but he's got some of his own stuff to work through. I don't want you getting hurt."

"That sounded suspiciously like parental advice." She adjusted her position on the chair, settled in to the cushions. "I doubt anyone can top the issues I'm dealing with on my own."

Declan shook his head. "You're not like Cole. But you do what you need to. Jase and I are here now, and we'll catch you if you fall."

She swallowed against the emotion rising in her chest. Yes, she'd grown up with a mom and stepdad. She'd never been alone, but somehow she'd felt it all her life. The idea that there were now people in her corner made her heart sing.

Declan leaned back against the pillow, and she watched as his eyes drifted closed. Pretty soon he was softly snoring. She closed her eyes, feeling a greater sense of peace than she had in years.

It was still dark when Cole opened his front door, revealing Sienna standing on the porch.

"Did I wake you?" she asked, the corners of her mouth pulling down. She still wore the gorgeous dress from the night before, the fabric wrinkled in places. Her long hair was pulled back in a messy bun, and there were smudges under her eyes that looked like they'd come from lack of sleep. She remained the most beautiful woman he'd ever laid eyes on.

"It's ten minutes to five," he answered, stifling a yawn. He'd thrown on an old T-shirt and a pair of basketball shorts on the way to the door. "Even the birds aren't awake yet."

"Sorry," she murmured, taking a step back. "I'll go so you can—"

"Not so fast." He grabbed her arm and pulled her closer, lifting her over the threshold and swinging the door shut with his foot. "I'm awake now and damn glad to see you." Pressing a kiss to the top of her head, he breathed in the scent of her, his body revving to life in an instant. "Tell me about your dad."

"He's fine. I spent the night at the hospital."

"Big step."

"It felt right. He and Jase and I had…" she shrugged, as if not sure what words to choose "…a moment last night. It was like we were a family."

"You *are* family," he reminded her.

"But for the first time, I felt it."

"Good for you, Sienna."

"When I left the hospital, this was the only place I wanted to go."

"Good for me," he whispered.

She ducked her head, smoothed a loose strand of hair away from her face. "Any chance you've still got the brownies I spied earlier at the bottom of the cooler?"

He chuckled. "Now I understand why you're here. I'm playing second-string to Katie's brownies."

"Only a little," she admitted.

They walked to his kitchen and he handed her the box of brownies while he took a gallon of milk from the fridge. "Unless you want me to make coffee?"

"Milk is fine."

She lowered herself to one of the chairs at his kitchen table. His breath caught as he watched her in the simple task of unwrapping the sweet treat. Cole had been living alone for a lot of years, and he liked it that way. He was a solitary person by nature, but Sienna looked like she belonged in his house. She made it feel like a home, something Cole hadn't allowed himself to have in a long time.

He brought the milk and two glasses to the table and pulled out the chair next to her. She took a small bite of the brownie, her pink tongue darting out to catch a crumb that clung to her bottom lip.

She didn't say anything more about her dad, and Cole didn't ask, content to share these quiet minutes with her.

Content wasn't a word he normally associated with himself, but he was smart enough to appreciate the new sensation.

And when Sienna stood and took a step forward, so close the front of her legs brushed the inside of his thighs, he stayed perfectly still, not wanting to do anything to screw up the moment.

She bent forward and kissed him, tasting of chocolate, and right now Cole was the biggest sugar addict on the planet.

"Can we finish the rest of last night now?" she asked against his mouth. "Or do you have to get ready for work?"

"I'll make time for you whenever you want." He straightened, scooping her into his arms as he did. She felt right there, and his heart sang as she settled in against his chest.

His house was simple, a two-bedroom bungalow that hadn't been updated since the mid-seventies. He didn't care about much other than a clean set of sheets, a stocked fridge and a big-screen television. For a second, he wondered what Sienna thought of it. Clearly, she'd grown up in an affluent community in Chicago, and he guessed most of her previous boyfriends had fast cars and fancy houses.

"I love it here," she whispered, as if she could read his mind. "There's no place I'd rather be."

He walked into his bedroom and set her down, cupping

her cheeks between his palms. "I don't deserve you," he said, then inwardly cringed. Why the hell did he have to go and admit something like that?

Her eyes clouded, then she gave a small shake of her head. "You're a good man, Cole. Don't try to deny it."

Now that he'd said the words, he couldn't back down from them. "Jase was smart to warn you off of me. I don't want to hurt you."

"You won't."

The unwavering confidence in her tone did funny things to his insides, loosening parts of him that had been tightly caged for so long. The sensation was both exhilarating and disturbing, like he was a toy top spinning out of control. He held on to Sienna to ground him.

He breathed her in, then kissed her until his doubts had returned to the shadowed recesses where they lurked. She pressed closer, moaning softly when his palm grazed the underside of her breast.

"You're sure this is what you want?"

She took a few steps away, reaching her hands behind her back. The soft whir of a zipper being undone filled the quiet room. "Can I ask you a question?"

He sucked in a breath and nodded as the fabric of her dress dipped below her shoulders.

"Do you really think I came here for a brownie?" She wiggled a little and the dress pooled at her feet. She wore a black lace bra with matching panties and his knees threatened to give out. He already knew her body was perfection, but somehow this felt different. She was choosing him. Claiming him for her own.

He loved every second of it. Loved everything about this woman, not just her body but who she was on the inside—who he was when they were together. He paused as the implication of the emotions tumbling through him hit home. He couldn't *love* Sienna. He wouldn't let himself fall in love. Cole had seen how love could ruin a person. It had destroyed his mother, and he'd never make himself or anyone else that vulnerable.

He forced the breath in and out of his lungs, willing himself to stay in the present moment. Here with Sienna.

"Should I give you a hint as to the answer?" Color flooded her cheeks as she pulled out the elastic that held back her hair. Blond waves fell over her shoulders, and she tugged on her lower lip.

"I seriously do not deserve you," he whispered, "but I'm damn glad I've got you right now."

One side of her mouth kicked up. "So what are you going to do with me?"

"Everything," he answered as he shucked out of his shirt. He reached for her, and they fell to the bed together in a tangle of limbs. He nipped on her earlobe, and she skimmed her fingernails along his back.

He stood for a moment, pushing his boxers and shorts down over his hips.

"You're still wearing too much," he told her, arching a brow.

She lifted her back off the bed and unclasped her bra, letting the straps ease down her shoulders the same way the dress had earlier. This impromptu striptease was even sexier, and he reminded himself he was a lucky man to have this woman in his bed. In his life.

She reached for her panties, but he moved forward and brushed her fingers out of the way. "Allow me."

He tugged them over her hips, then pushed apart her legs, taking in the heavenly view he had of her body from this vantage point.

His hands moved along her thighs until he reached her center, and he almost lost himself when she arched off the bed, moaning as he touched her.

"Cole," she said, her voice hoarse, "I don't think—"

"That's right," he interrupted, "no thinking right now."

He couldn't resist following his fingers with his mouth and was rewarded with a soft cry and the word "Yes."

She continued to make the most beautiful little noises, finally crying out as he felt a tremor snake through her body. He reached into the nightstand drawer for a condom, then entered her in one swift thrust, unable to hold back any longer.

Sienna wrapped her arms around his neck, and they moved together, pressure building in Cole as she whispered his name. Pleasure burst over him like a shower of stars, brilliant and bright, and Cole never wanted the moment to end.

Chapter 15

"Where are you rushing off to?"

Sienna gave a weak smile as she fastened her bra, then reached for her dress, which was still in a crumpled pile on the floor next to the bed. It was remarkably difficult to get dressed while keeping the sheet around her body.

"I need to go home." She cleared her throat. "To the inn. I'm sure you need to get to work and…" She stretched out a toe, trying to inch the dress closer. "I should call the office. I've been missing a lot of client meetings so I check in with my assistant first thing in the morning. It makes me feel like I'm not totally out of touch."

Cole had been in the bathroom for a few minutes, which had given her much needed time to collect herself after the best two orgasms of her life. She'd never thought herself the kind of woman to be affected by great sex, although maybe that was because up until Cole, she'd only had mediocre intimate relationships. Mediocre at best, as the saying went.

"You're talking fast like you're uncomfortable," Cole said, bending forward and plucking her dress off the floor.

She sighed and reached out a hand. "Babbling," she muttered. "It's called babbling."

One corner of his mouth kicked up, then he dropped down next to her on the bed. He'd put on his boxers, although his bare chest was plenty distracting. She was currently dealing with something way more serious than physical attraction. She was falling hard and fast for Sheriff Cole Bennett.

Falling in love.

It was ridiculous and painfully ill-advised. Cole had all but admitted he was going to hurt her. Her brother had warned her. Her father had warned her.

Sienna might be new to having so many men who cared in her life, yet she wasn't a fool. She'd be an idiot to let herself fall in love with Cole, not when her time in Crimson might be temporary and he hadn't given her any sign he wanted anything long-term.

"I'm an idiot," she muttered, quickly ripping off the sheet and pulling up her dress. It had been easy to feel confident about her body when she was in the throes of passion. Now she felt too exposed.

"I like the babbling," Cole said, giving her arm a playful nudge.

She stood, turning away from him, and slipped her arms into the dress, struggling to tug the zipper all the way up. She felt his warm body at her back a moment later. With gentle fingers, he gathered her hair and draped it over one shoulder, then zipped up the dress.

"I know it's silly," she protested, "that I get nervous around you." She grabbed her shoes off the floor and forced herself to meet his gaze. "I'm sorry I'm bad at the morning-after stuff."

"Technically, it's still the morning of."

She groaned. Why couldn't she manage to act normal five minutes after the best sex of her life? "Even worse."

"You're cute." He dropped a kiss on the tip of her nose.

She wanted to splay her hands across his bare chest, push him back down on the bed and have her merry way with him.

"I *really* need to go," she said instead.

"Okay." He traced the tip of one finger along her jaw. "But promise me you won't let this freak you out. It's not a big deal."

If they gave out Academy Awards for keeping a poker face, Sienna would be a front-runner. It felt like Cole had just driven his fist into her chest. She could actually feel her heart shriveling as his words spread like a cancer through her.

"Of course," she agreed, forcing a bright smile. He frowned, as if he detected the hysterical edge to her voice but couldn't quite figure out what had caused it. "I'll catch you on the flip side, Sheriff." She placed a quick kiss on his mouth, then turned and gave what she hoped was a jaunty wave.

"I'll check in at the hospital later," he called, and she lifted her arm again, then pulled it tight to her side when she realized her fingers were shaking like an aspen leaf in the wind.

She grabbed her purse and quickly let herself out of Cole's house, only realizing as she stood on the front porch that she had no mode of transportation to get home. Not home. To the inn. She had no home at the moment.

Tears of pain and embarrassment pricked at the backs of Sienna's eyes. Afraid Cole would realize she'd taken an

Uber from the hospital to his house, she hurried down the sidewalk and around the corner. Still somewhat unfamiliar with Crimson's geography, despite the small-town flavor, she punched the B&B's address into the GPS on her phone and began walking the neighborhood streets in the direction it sent her.

The morning was lovely, as seemed to be the norm in Colorado. A chill hung in the air but the sun shining from a clear blue sky was quickly warming things. She held her heels in one hand, appreciating the feel of the sidewalk beneath her feet. The cool pavement acted to ground her, helping her to remember she was more than just her aching heart.

She waved to an older woman sweeping off her front walk. The woman stared for several seconds, then called, "Dana?"

"I'm her daughter," Sienna answered, slowing her pace.

The woman walked closer. "Of course. I heard you were in town. You really do look so much like her."

"I've been told that most of my life. Were you friends with my mother?" She suddenly had an urge to know more about her mom's time in Crimson. How did things get so far off track and why did Dana feel like she had no choice but to leave the way she did?

"Lordy, no." The woman gave a dismissive laugh. "She and Declan hung with a wild crowd. Always up to no good. It's a wonder you and your brother survived it."

"Oh." Not that Sienna necessarily denied the truth of the woman's words but that didn't make them any easier to hear.

"Those two were the most irresponsible, reckless—"

"Well, nice talking to you," Sienna interrupted. She couldn't stand to hear any more.

"Someone told me you were different," the woman continued, scrunching up her nose like she'd smelled something rotten. "More like your brother." Her gaze raked over Sienna, disapproval clear in her dull brown eyes. "But I doubt you put on that outfit this morning. It's clear the Crenshaw blood runs strong in you, missy."

Paige had joked about the walk of shame the first time Sienna spent the night at Cole's, but this woman wasn't making a joke.

"I take that as a compliment," Sienna said, despite the embarrassment washing over her. She had nothing to feel guilty about—spending the night in an uncomfortable hospital chair didn't constitute wild and reckless. She lifted her chin and adopted the haughty glare she'd watched her mother perfect over the years. "Have a lovely morning," she said in a clipped tone, then walked away without a backward glance.

It was another half mile to The Bumblebee, and Sienna walked it quickly, her gaze focused on the sidewalk in front of her. She passed several morning joggers but didn't bother greeting any of them. The woman's words had hit their mark. Was that the sort of judgment her mom had received from this small community? It left a sour taste in Sienna's mouth.

The front door of the inn was open and she called out a greeting to Paige as she entered the foyer. The sound of hammering had already started, and she hoped for her friend's sake the construction project would finish soon.

"Sienna, you're back." Paige rushed from the direction of the kitchen, curls bouncing.

"No 'walk of shame' comments," Sienna said with a dry laugh. "I've had enough—"

"I have another guest," Paige blurted. "She arrived this morning and insisted on taking the room across from yours. I told her she'd be more comfortable at one of the hotels in town, but—"

"Where have you been and why are you dressed like that?"

Sienna sucked in a breath, dropping the shoes she'd been holding to the wood floor with a thud. "Oh, no," she whispered under her breath.

"Oh, yes," Paige answered in a similar whisper.

"Mom, what are you doing here?"

Dana Pierce came down the steps as if she was being presented at a debutante ball, shoulders straight, chin lifted, two fingers gingerly skimming the wooden handrail. As if Sienna's mother needed support. Her blond hair was pulled back into a neat chignon, putting her elegant throat and the strand of pearls around her neck on full display. She wore an outfit Sienna had come to think of as her mother's uniform—slim trousers and a crisp button-down shirt, slightly fitted, with the collar starched so that it stood stiff like a soldier at boot camp.

Today's shirt was a shade of pale green, perhaps as a nod to the pine forests that surrounded Crimson. Matching the occasion was sort of a thing for Dana. Pink for Valentine's Day, yellow on Easter and a pattern of red and white stripes around the holidays. Festive but understated.

"You haven't called in several days," Dana said, as if that explained everything.

"So you flew to Colorado?" Sienna pressed a hand to her forehead.

"Coffee?" Paige asked.

Sienna nodded. "Yes, please."

"Mrs. Pierce?"

"Half a cup with a tablespoon of creamer." Dana pierced Paige with one of her laser-beam glares as she came to stand at the bottom of the stairs. "No more than a tablespoon."

"I'll measure," Paige offered quickly, then hurried toward the kitchen.

"You could have just asked for light creamer," Sienna said with an eye roll.

"How do I know what that woman considers light?" Dana swept an arm toward the front room, which was crowded with the furniture and knickknacks Paige had moved so the guys could work on the floor. "I appreciate details, and it doesn't seem like the innkeeper cares much for them. How does one expect to run a business like this?"

"The floor had water damage. She's having it repaired. Paige has done a great job refurbishing this place, and she's a fantastic cook and generous hostess. The Bumblebee will succeed." Sienna wasn't sure why she felt the need to defend Paige, but it was easier than talking about her mother's unexpected appearance.

Dana sniffed. "I didn't rearrange my schedule to come here and talk about a ramshackle bed-and-breakfast."

Sienna inclined her head to study her mother, thinking about her encounter with the woman on her way home from Cole's. "What happened to you in Crimson?"

"I don't know what you mean. I arrived this morning and—"

"When I was a kid," Sienna clarified. "I've talked to several people who remember you and—"

"I changed."

"That could be the understatement of the century. Going from brunette to redhead or having bangs cut is a change. You left Crimson a party girl and made yourself into some sort of Grace Kelly or Jackie O. wannabee."

"That's ridiculous. I never wanted to be anyone but myself."

"Who are you *really*?" Sienna stepped closer, and her mother looked away.

"I'm a woman who fell in love with the wrong man

and wanted to take my children away from the mess of our lives."

"You walked away so easily. You never drink and your idea of a party is a string quartet and cucumber sandwiches."

"This is who I am."

"But not who you were. I didn't realize the reputation you had here. I thought it was Dad."

Her mother's mouth pressed into a thin line. "Declan Crenshaw is your father by biology only. Do not call him *Dad* to me." She practically spit the word. "It's disrespectful to your stepfather, who's taken care of you all these years."

"Financially," Sienna muttered.

"Excuse me?"

"Craig Pierce has taken care of me financially, and I'm grateful to him. I always will be. But neither of us should pretend he has any real affection for me. He wanted you, and I was part of the package."

"That's not…" Her mother broke off because it was the truth and they both knew it. "Declan doesn't care about you either."

"He does," Sienna argued. "Jase, too. I was just never allowed to believe it."

"You don't know everything, Sienna."

"Because you'd never tell me anything. Dad has talked to me plenty, and he's apologized for the mistakes he made."

Dana let out a derisive laugh. "He hasn't told you the truth then."

Sienna threw up her hands. "Are you going to enlighten me?"

"I'm here to take you home." Her mother clasped her hands together in front of her chest. "We had dinner with Kevin the other night. He told us you'd moved your things out of the condo."

"I had Jennie do it. She's keeping them in her parents' garage until I get back."

"It was a hasty decision. Kevin wants another chance."

"He cheated on me," Sienna shouted. "Then blamed me for not being able to keep his junk in his pants."

"Don't be crude."

"You know what I discovered? It's not me. I'm not frigid. In fact, I had the best sex of my life just this morning and a big, fat…" She made the shape of an O with her fingers. "I had no complaints about my part in things."

"Sienna."

"It wasn't my fault," she yelled, then pressed a hand to her mouth. The hammering from the other room had stopped. Color flooded her cheeks as she imagined the workers listening to her outburst.

Paige breezed into the room, smiling widely but looking about as uncomfortable as Sienna felt at the moment. "Who's ready for coffee?" she asked brightly. "One tablespoon of creamer." She held out a mug to Sienna's mother. "Not a drop more."

Dana didn't take the mug. "I'm going to return to my room and gather my things," she said, her lips barely moving. "Paige, I believe you were correct in your assessment that I'd be better suited to a hotel in town. Sienna, we'll talk when you've calmed down. This behavior is unbecoming and not like you. Crimson has a bad effect on the women in our family. We leave for Denver the day after tomorrow. I'll have my travel agent make the flight arrangements."

Sienna clenched her hands into fists, focusing on drawing air in and out of her lungs. The hammering resumed, and her mother turned and walked up the stairs.

"Okay then," Paige said cheerily, moving into Sienna's line of sight. "I think that went well."

Chapter 16

The following morning, Cole sped along the winding road that led to Crimson's abandoned ski resort, the Jeep's lights flashing but its sirens silent. He was checking on a call the station had received that shots were being fired on the ski mountain.

It wasn't anywhere near ski season, not to mention no one in town had rights to be on that land anyway. Cole couldn't imagine the resort's new owner would want to hear about some crazy person popping off multiple rounds on private land.

Since the road was all but deserted this time of day, Cole kept the Jeep's siren off. If someone was trespassing or worse on resort property, he didn't want to warn them of his approach.

He parked in the lot, empty except for a gleaming black Porsche SUV near the far end. As he approached the vehicle, the distant sound of music wafted toward him. He shined his flashlight into the tinted windows, but the Porsche was empty.

He followed the sound of music—and more specifically *The Piña Colada Song*—up the stairs that led to the lodge's wraparound patio.

The ski resort had closed in the early nineties due to a bankruptcy filing and family disputes by the long-time owners. Some of the older deputies had shared that it used to be a popular spot for local teens right after it was abandoned, but that had changed in the ensuing years. Nowadays, he had someone check the property on a routine basis but not many people ventured out this way other than hikers or tourists who'd taken a wrong turn.

Beer cans lined the patio's wide rail, and Cole automatically put a hand on his weapon as he came around the corner.

A pair of long legs and expensive-looking sneakers came into view, and the next moment Cole let out a string of curses so vile it would have made his old army buddies blush. The man lounging in the chair was so similar to Cole in his features and build, it was almost like looking in a mirror. A mirror he wanted to punch with every fiber of his being.

"Hey, bro. I was wondering when you'd get here." Shep Bennett made a show of checking his watch, sun reflecting off the shiny face. "Twenty-four minutes from when I fired my first round. Not great response time, if you ask me." He hit a button on his phone to turn off the music, then picked up a .22 handgun from the arm of the weathered lounge chair where he was sitting and aimed at the beer cans.

"Don't you dare—"

Shep fired three shots and a trio of cans disappeared over the railing.

"Put it down and explain what the hell you're doing here."

Shep laughed as he placed the gun on the chair's arm again. "I'm letting off a little steam is all. You remember fun, don't you?"

Anger flooded through Cole, engulfing the relief he felt at seeing Shep safe after all these years. He grabbed the gun, unloaded the magazine and took the bullet out of the chamber. He stepped directly in front of his brother, blocking his view of the ski mountain. "Why does your idea of fun always involve being an idiot?"

Shep stood, walked to the patio's railing. "Guess I take after dad," he said and flicked the remaining beer can over the edge.

"You're going to clean all those up." Cole moved forward to stand next to his brother. "Then you can drive away from here—back to wherever life has taken you."

"That's a funny story," Shep muttered.

"Tell me you didn't steal the Porsche."

Shep turned, leaning a hip on the rail. "Give me a break, Cole. It's mine."

"Since when do you have that kind of money?"

"A lot can happen in seven years."

"Like Mom's funeral," Cole shot back. He saw pain flare in his brother's features before the smirk he remembered so well returned.

"You had to go there."

It wasn't just that Cole saw he'd upset Shep. He felt his brother's emotional pain, courtesy of the unexplainable connection he had with his twin. Shep might pretend he didn't care, but the truth was far more complicated.

"Where were you?" Cole asked.

Shep shrugged. "Arizona for a while. A few months in Mazatlán. Mainly I've been in California. The weather is—"

"February 12," Cole interrupted. "That was the day I buried her. By myself. It would have killed her how little you care."

"The heart attack beat me to it," Shep ground out between clenched teeth. "You know I loved her. She knew it. I was down in Mexico when she died and couldn't get back in time."

"You never even called."

"To say what?" Shep crossed his arms over his chest. "What did you want from me? Were we supposed to commiserate over our shared loss? As if being orphaned was going to bring us suddenly closer. Dad ruined all of our lives."

"She died of a broken heart," Cole murmured.

"There was nothing I could have done about it at the time."

"You could have helped me deal with things."

Shep barked out a harsh laugh. "Give me a break. You've never needed a moment's help in your whole life. The stronger twin. The alpha. That's what Mom always called you."

"Only so she'd have an excuse to baby you."

"Baby me? That's rich."

Cole pushed away from the railing and paced along the edge of the patio. Shep exasperated him, but Cole didn't want this kind of animosity. It did neither of them any good to fight. Cole prided himself on keeping his temper in check and blamed the shock of seeing his brother after so long on his behavior.

His first instinct, after wanting to berate Shep for the business with the gun and beer cans, had been to rush forward and throw his arms around his twin. It felt like he'd stumbled upon an appendage he hadn't realized he'd been missing. A part of him had come home.

But Crimson wasn't Shep's home, and the fact that he'd shown up without warning, clearly ready to antagonize Cole, didn't bode well for a brotherly reunion. Still, Cole felt like he had to try.

"It's good to see you despite everything."

"Liar." Shep flashed a small smile. "You always were a horrible liar. Half the time that's how Mom could tell us apart when we got into trouble."

"You were an expert," Cole agreed. "Yet somehow we both got into the same amount of trouble. Out with it, Shep. What are you doing here?" He held out his hands. "Why the big production to get me to this place? A phone call or a text would have worked fine."

"I figured it was time I visit my new home." Shep flashed a far too innocent smile. "Do you want to be the first person to welcome me to Crimson, Sheriff Bennett?"

Cole swallowed, feeling like he'd just downed a handful of sawdust. He and Shep were like oil and water, and Cole had made Crimson his own. It was one thing for his brother to pay an unexpected visit, but the thought that Shep might be in Colorado permanently was too much.

"Don't mess with me." He removed his sunglasses, made a show of cleaning them on his shirtfront. Trying to look casual. Trying to appear as if he wasn't losing his mind. "Crimson isn't your kind of place."

The town was Cole's place. He and his brother had never been good at sharing. Whether toys or friends or later women, if one twin claimed something or someone, there was an unspoken rule that the other let it go.

"I'm ready for a change." Shep lifted his arms and spun in a slow circle. "A new challenge."

"A development company bought the resort," Cole argued. "Even abandoned and in disrepair, the land is worth millions. Unless you've been running drugs for the past few years, there's no way you could do this on your own." He cursed, then added, "I sure as hell hope you're not running drugs."

"Dude, you've been binge-watching too many shows," Shep said, looking both amused and offended. "I'm the head of Trinity Development Company. Right after Dad died, I got lucky on a piece of land outside of Vegas. Turns out real estate development is a lot about luck."

"Our family never had much."

"Things change. I like to think it was the old man looking out for me from the great beyond." He tapped a finger on his chin. "Do you think he's upstairs or down below given the rat he turned out to be?"

"Shut up, Shep."

"Down below. That's what I think, too. But he's still taking care of me." He shrugged. "I only had to make half a deal with the devil in the process."

"What have you gotten yourself mixed up in now?"

"Success," Shep said, pointing a finger at Cole. "You're not the only one in this family who has something to offer."

"You know better than anyone that I'm no competition in the success game." Cole blew out a breath, rubbed a hand over his jaw. "I'm sheriff in a small town in the middle of the Rocky Mountains. I walked away from a career in the army because I didn't want to deal with Dad's legacy haunting me every step of the way. It works for me, but there's nothing about my life you need to envy."

"I don't envy you," Shep said tightly. "But those stupid two minutes you had on me at birth meant I had to spend my whole childhood in your shadow."

"Not tru—"

"I'm here, Cole. I'm not leaving."

The ridiculous old Western movie phrase "this town ain't big enough for the two of us" leaped into Cole's mind. He felt like he was six years old again, arguing over who got first dibs with their favorite Lego set. But this was his brother. Cole had learned as a kid that all he had to do was wait and Shep would get bored and move on to the next shiny toy.

Somehow Shep had gotten a burr up his backside to mess with Cole again, just when things were starting to feel like a decent fit. Cole wondered if it was that twin spidey sense at work. Shep had somehow recognized Cole's contentment and decided it was high time to crash it.

"Welcome to Crimson," Cole said, making his tone casual. "Folks around here are thrilled the resort's going to open again. It'll mean more jobs for locals and an influx of tourist dollars that the town can always use. A lot of people will be counting on you."

Shep blanched but didn't respond. He'd never been one for responsibility, and Cole knew it.

"You still have my cell number?"

"Yeah, I've got it."

"Give me a call later." Cole flashed a quick smile. "I'll introduce you to Jase Crenshaw, Crimson's mayor. I'm sure he'll want you involved in the local business owners' association right away."

"Sure," Shep agreed, but his voice wavered the tiniest bit.

"Do you have a general contractor lined up?"

Shep stared at him for a long moment, as if he couldn't quite figure out why Cole had changed tactics. Finally he said, "We have plans. Big ones."

"I bet."

"It's not a joke."

"I'm not laughing." Cole gestured to the darkened lodge. "I gather you're not staying here."

"Not yet," Shep admitted. "There's some work to do before the place is habitable again. And I have other…commitments right now."

"What's your time frame?"

"Six months."

"Are you joking? You'll never get things going again in that amount of time."

Shep bristled, as if Cole doubting him was a physical blow. "We're farther along than you think."

Cole ran a hand through his hair. "Why didn't you contact me earlier?"

"I like surprises," Shep said, his smirk firmly back in place.

"Don't cause trouble. This town means something to me, and I won't have you stirring things up around here."

"You sure do know how to make a man feel welcome. It warms my heart. Really."

Cole shook his head, both unable and unwilling to bridge the distance between him and his brother. "I'll see you later, Shep," he said and walked away.

Sienna heard a crash, then another, coming from the kitchen as she walked down the inn's staircase the next morning.

It was too early for construction workers, so she hurried toward the sound, calling out to Paige as she did.

She found the innkeeper grabbing pans and metal bowls from the pantry and slamming them onto the counter.

"Everything okay?"

"Coffee in the pot and French toast casserole on the stove," Paige said, her frenetic movements not stopping. "Do you want fresh squeezed orange juice to go with it?"

"Paige." Sienna put a hand on her friend's arm. "What are you doing?"

"Taking care of the only guest this place might ever see." Paige shook her head and pressed the back of her hand to her mouth when a small sob escaped.

"What are you talking about?"

"I called my mom this morning." Her voice was miserable. "I told you the house is in her name, and I've been trying to save money to buy it from her. I've also been paying the mortgage, and maybe I missed a couple of months because of other expenses I've had to shell out to maintain this place. Maybe I told her I'd miss this month, as well."

"Okay."

"Not okay," Paige countered. "At least that's what I realized. My mom is under contract to sell The Bumblebee."

"She can't do that," Sienna said immediately. "You've put so much time and effort into it. You're almost ready to open."

Paige gave a strained laugh and gestured to the mess of the living room floor. "Not quite almost, but I was getting there. I called to give her an update and talk about the construction expenses. She told me she was approached last week by a buyer out of California who wanted this property."

"Why The Bumblebee?"

"It's not just the house. The land borders the old ski resort. Apparently whoever bought the resort wants to make the inn part of that property. Grammy was always at odds with the former owner of the ski mountain, but I never thought it would be an issue for me."

"Your mom didn't bother to mention this to you?"

Paige sniffed and shook her head. "I made the mistake of calling her in a moment of weakness—when I was feeling overwhelmed. I might have cried and told her I wasn't sure I could handle the inn."

"Crying is okay and doubts are normal. It doesn't mean—"

"I was sick as a kid," Paige blurted. "Really sick."

Sienna felt her mouth drop open. "Are you sick now?"

Paige shook her head. "I had leukemia. I was in and out of the hospital my last two years of high school doing chemo and radiation. I've been fine for almost ten years, but after that phone call, my mom decided that the stress of opening and running an inn would be too much for me." She threw up her hands. "According to her, she's doing me a favor."

"We need to convince her to cancel the sale. When is the closing scheduled?"

"You have no idea what my mom is like when she sets her mind to something."

"Maybe not," Sienna agreed. "However, I'm familiar with overbearing mothers."

Paige gave a soft laugh. "I suppose you are. But you've made a success of yourself in your own right. You have that important job—"

"Which I don't miss."

"You lived with your boyfriend—"

"Who cheated on me," Sienna pointed out with a wince.

"There were some setbacks," Paige admitted. "But you've proven you can be an adult. Before I came to Crimson, I still lived with my mom. She said the house was too big for her to be there alone after my dad died, and she wasn't ready to sell it. The truth was she didn't trust me on my own. Do you have any idea what it's like when no one believes you can handle your own life? It's embarrassing, and now this happens."

Sienna could relate to Paige's dilemma. Maybe her life wasn't as sheltered, but she'd followed wherever her mom and stepdad had led her. Yes, she had a great job, but she'd gotten hired with the ad agency because her stepdad had been fraternity brothers with one of the senior partners. Her mom had basically set up her first date with Kevin through someone she'd met at a charity dinner.

Everything in Sienna's life had been arranged to follow the path that Dana deemed appropriate. As if Sienna couldn't be trusted to make her own decisions.

It wasn't until she'd arrived in Crimson that she'd tasted real freedom. Cole had been the first person to act like he believed she was strong enough to handle whatever life threw at her. No wonder she'd fallen for him so fast and hard. Butterflies flitted around her insides at the thought of him, but right now she needed to focus on seeing her friend through this mini meltdown.

"Your mom lives in Denver, right?" she asked.

"On the south end of town."

"Has she been up here to see what you've done with the place?"

"No. She hasn't been here since my grandma's funeral and the house was a mess at that point. When Grammy died, Mom wanted to sell the inn right away. I convinced her to let me try to make something of it."

"You have," Sienna said immediately, her heart aching to see the other woman so sad. In the past couple of weeks, Paige had become a true friend. They'd spent hours sitting on the front porch at night, and Paige had been infinitely patient listening to all of Sienna's worries. Paige had seemed so settled and sure, and it was a shock to hear about her illness and the uncertainty surrounding her mother and the inn.

"Not quite. I should have known better than to share my problems with her. She's always treated me like the sick girl I used to be, even after I wasn't sick anymore. It's part of the reason I wanted to open the inn. I wanted to prove to her and to myself that I could succeed in something big. I can work hard and it won't hurt me."

"You're doing great," Sienna insisted. "Invite your mom up, and we'll make sure she changes her mind."

"Maybe I can introduce her to your mother," Paige said with a slight smile. "They can compare notes on their wayward daughters."

Sienna grabbed a coffee mug from the counter. "My mom won't be here long enough for that."

"Are you going back to Chicago with her?"

"She definitely thinks so. I managed to convince her I couldn't leave until tomorrow at the earliest. But we both know I can't ignore my life forever."

"But this is your life, too." Paige handed her a carton of creamer as she poured coffee into the mug. "Maybe it's time to think of making some permanent changes. You have to claim the life you want to live."

Sienna lifted a brow. "Like you're going to claim the inn?"

Paige drew in a tremulous breath, like the question had knocked the wind out of her. Then she pulled two plates from a cabinet, porcelain clattering as she placed them on the counter with unsteady hands.

"French toast first," she said with a too-bright smile. "No one should take back her life on an empty stomach."

Sienna nodded. "I'll get the syrup."

Chapter 17

Sienna flipped the button on her phone to vibrate and shoved the device into her purse as she walked through the hospital doors later that morning.

Her mother had called earlier, but Sienna wanted to speak to her dad before facing Dana and her expectations that Sienna would be leaving Crimson.

She wasn't finished in this sweet little town. Despite her mixed emotions, Colorado was quickly beginning to feel like home. She wouldn't give that up without a fight.

She waved to Dixie at the receptionist's desk and headed for the elevators.

"Your mother hasn't aged a day since she left here," the older woman called. "I recognized her the minute she walked in."

Sienna spun on her heel. "In where?"

Dixie chuckled. "The hospital, of course. She got here about twenty minutes ago."

"Is Jase with her?" Sienna asked, already backing away.

"Haven't seen him."

Dana was alone with Declan. The implications screamed through Sienna's brain, as if she was standing too close to the tracks when a powerful freight train came speeding by. She bypassed the elevator and pushed open the stairwell door, taking the steps two at a time to the third floor.

It was difficult to tell whether her gasping breath was a result of racing up two sets of stairs at altitude or the overwhelming panic at the thought of her parents together.

The door to her father's room was open halfway, and she paused outside to catch her breath, gather her thoughts and try to discern whether any blood had been shed yet.

"We had an agreement, Dec. Nothing has changed."

The sharp edge in her mother's tone wasn't a surprise, but her words certainly were.

"She showed up here. That changed everything." Declan coughed, painful and raspy in a way that couldn't be good for his continued recovery. He sounded out of breath and agitated. Sienna started to interrupt the conversation but stopped as her father spoke again. "What was I supposed to do? Send her away? Reject her to her face?"

"Yes," her mother said, exasperation clear in her tone. "If you want to keep receiving the monthly check, then yes."

Sienna felt like she'd taken a punch to the gut. She reached out and put a hand on the wall to steady herself.

"Let him explain," a quiet voice behind her said.

She turned to find Jase standing a few feet behind her, Emily at his side. Her sister-in-law's gaze was gentle, and Sienna understood she'd been duped by everyone. As far as she'd seen, Emily wasn't one for sympathy...ever.

"I've got to get out of here," she muttered, but her legs were rooted to the polished linoleum floor.

"Sienna?" The door to the room opened to reveal her mother standing stiff as a statue, her mouth pressed into a tight line even as her gaze tracked wildly from Sienna to Jase.

"Baby girl, come in here," Declan called from over Dana's shoulder. "We need to talk."

"Did you pay him to stay away from me?" Sienna didn't move, ignoring her dad's request.

"I helped out with living expenses." Dana glanced at Jase again. "For your brother."

"Sienna!" Declan shouted. "Get her in here."

Dana gave a small nod. "We can discuss the details behind closed doors. No need for the entire hospital to overhear you."

But Sienna was beyond caring who knew this latest detail in their sordid family history. "Did your *help* include an agreement that he wouldn't try to contact me?"

Her mother tipped up her chin and gave Sienna the patented mom stare that used to shut her down when she asked questions about her dad and brother.

Sienna pressed her palm flat against the wall and stared back.

"Your father and I had an understanding. I never forbade him from contacting you."

"The hell you didn't, woman," Declan called from inside the room. "Now someone get me out of this dang bed."

"You had no right," Sienna whispered to her mother.

Dana's eyes narrowed. "He cashed the checks every month."

"Dad had some rough times," Jase explained, stepping forward. "He needed—"

"Did you know about this the whole time?" Sienna demanded, pulling her hand away from the wall and fisting it at her side.

"Not at first," Jase said after a moment. "But eventually I started managing the bank account."

"Inappropriate to put a child in that situation," Dana muttered.

Sienna felt like she was at the center of a tornado, all the parts of her life spinning around her in a whirlwind.

"Do you want to get a cup of coffee?" Emily asked. "A few minutes away might help you collect your thoughts."

"I don't need time." Sienna looked between the three people facing her. "My thoughts are clear. You've all lied to me. I want nothing to do with any of you."

Sienna paced back and forth in the corner office of the sheriff's department, anger and humiliation buzzing through her like a swarm of insects.

The friendly woman at the front desk had offered her a cup of coffee, then led her to Cole's office. He was on his way back to the station, she'd explained, and Sienna was welcome to wait.

The door burst open a few seconds later, and Cole appeared, his gaze frantic. "Marlene called me," he said, moving toward Sienna. "She said my girlfriend was in the office crying and that I'd better get my butt back here stat."

Sienna's cheeks grew warm as a thrill coursed through her at his casual use of the word *girlfriend*. Did that make her optimistic or pathetic? Probably a bit of both. "I hope she didn't actually use the word *stat*."

"She did," he confirmed. "Marlene's a big fan of medical shows. She's also happy to give an armchair diagnosis of any physical ailments you might have."

"I'll remember that." Sienna smoothed her fingers across

her cheeks. "For the record, I wasn't crying when I got here. I was totally composed when I walked into the station."

"But you'd been crying?" He didn't wait for an answer, only reached for her. His strong arms wound around her back as he pulled her against his chest.

She sucked in a shaky breath and let herself sag against him. They stood together for several minutes, Cole gently tracing circles on her back with his palm. She splayed her fingers across his shirtfront, feeling the steady beat of his heart. The sorrow that had tightened around her chest, ensnaring her heart like a vine, slowly subsided.

It was this moment more than any other that made her certain of her love for him. He felt like home, and she'd been yearning for a place to belong for as long as she could remember. She drew in her first normal breath since leaving the hospital, realizing she could handle anything with this man at her side.

"My mother went to visit my dad in the hospital this morning," she said, pulling away.

As reluctant as she was to leave Cole's embrace, she had to have a little distance to get the words out. She walked to the edge of the desk, ran her fingers along a deep scratch in the oak top.

"I take it things didn't go well."

"Not exactly. They argued over the money she'd been giving him all this time."

Cole's thick brows furrowed, but otherwise he didn't respond. She'd expected him to be as shocked as she was by the revelation so she didn't quite understand his calm reaction to the news.

Maybe he didn't understand the implication of what she was telling him. "Mom has been sending a monthly check to Declan for the past twenty years," she explained. "She tried to tell me it was for Jase, but obviously my brother is a grown man now and even when he was a kid…" She shook her head, confused that Cole still looked unsurprised. "They had an unspoken agreement that Declan wouldn't contact me. Jase knew about it. He'd started depositing the checks when Declan was having issues."

"That's a lot of pressure for a kid," Cole said quietly. "Your parents never should have made that arrangement."

"Yes," she agreed slowly, an uncomfortable feeling—an itch she couldn't quite reach—skittered along the back of her neck. "That's not the point. Jase knew and never mentioned it. My mom made me believe my dad wanted nothing to do with me. Declan took the money and was willing to stay out of my life to ensure it didn't stop. It's untenable that they'd all have kept this from me, even once I arrived in Crimson."

"I'm sorry, Sienna." He crossed his arms over his chest. "It was a bad situation all around. But you have to understand—"

"You knew." She lifted her arm, pointing a finger at him. It felt as though her hand wasn't connected to her body. She saw everything through the haze of heartache crashing over her once again. Only this time it was a pain she doubted she'd ever recover from. "You knew about the checks."

"Jase didn't like keeping it from you." Cole took a step forward but she stretched out her hand, palm out, to keep him from moving closer to her. "He was trying to figure out a way to tell you. He mentioned that Declan hadn't cashed the checks for a while, if that helps."

She felt her eyes widen. "You've discussed this with Jase."

"He needed to confide in someone," Cole said by way of explanation. "It was long before you and I were together."

"We're *not* together," she whispered, the words little pokes of a dagger. Her insides were raw at this point, battered and bloody, and yet the hits just kept on coming.

"Don't say that." He closed his hand around hers but she wrenched away, trying to gather herself. Trying to make sense of any of this. She felt the heat of his body behind her, although he didn't try to touch her again. "This can't come between us. Not now."

"I trusted you, Cole. I love you."

As soon as she said the words, she knew they were a mistake. His features went blank, as if he were suddenly made of stone.

"You must have heard I was a bad bet," he said with no inflection. "You should have listened."

She drew in a breath, squared her shoulders and met his dark gaze. "That's an excuse to keep yourself from being hurt, and we both know it."

"I care about you, Sienna." He shrugged, ran a hand through his hair. "That's all I have to give you."

Care. What an inconsequential word compared to the all-encompassing love she felt for him. Care was a nibble on a corner of stale bread and she was ready to offer the entire buffet—her heart and soul spread out before Cole. She'd wanted to give him everything.

"It isn't enough, and I don't believe it anyway. Not after everything—"

"Jase would have told you about the checks," he interrupted, a clumsy change of subject that made Sienna want to scream in frustration. "Eventually. Or made Declan do it. You shouldn't have found out the way you did."

"Thanks, Sheriff Obvious." Her anger was the rising tide at the beach on a hot summer day. She let it wash over her, obliterating her heartache—at least for the moment.

It was hard to see Cole as anything but the man she loved, so Sienna let anger surge through her heart. The less she allowed herself to feel right now, the more she could handle without a total breakdown.

"I'm sorry," he said, lifting a hand as if to reach for her again, then dropping it when she took another step away.

"Me, too," she whispered, her hand on the door to his office. "You'll never know how much."

"Make it right, Jase."

Cole didn't need to turn around on the barstool where he'd been planted for the past two hours to know his friend had arrived at Elevation Brewery, the most popular bar in Crimson. Guilt radiated from Jase, hot and sticky, scorching everything in its path.

"Tell me how." Jase took a seat next to him and inclined his head to the man behind the bar. "Hey, David. Gimme whatever the sheriff's drinking."

"Too much whiskey," David McCay, the bar's owner, said quietly.

Out of the corner of his eye, Cole saw Jase nod. "Sounds good to me."

David frowned but pulled a bottle of Jack Daniels from the shelf behind the bar. "Is there some high altitude apocalypse on the horizon?" he asked as he poured two fingers into a highball glass and set it in front of Jase. "Because it concerns me to see two of our top town leaders bellied up to my bar looking like they just got kicked in the family jewels."

"His fault." Cole hitched a thumb toward Jase. "He's a damn liar."

Jase grimaced. "Mind dialing down the volume? That's the last thing I need broadcast out to the town."

"A coward, too," Cole added, ratcheting up his voice another notch. "I'm only telling the truth here. You should try it sometime, Mr. Mayor."

"How much has he had?" Jase asked David.

"Enough that I'm cutting him off after that one."

Jase leaned toward Cole. "Ida Wasinski is devouring a plate of wings at the table to your left. She's the biggest gossip in Crimson, and she's watching you like you're covered in buffalo sauce."

"You can't cut me off." The burn of the alcohol was the only thing that could ease the stabbing pain in his heart. Cole drained his glass, then pushed it toward David. "You think I'm going to be arrested if I have another drink?"

David shook his head. "I think you're going to keep running your mouth, which might be worse."

"Bring the lawman a drink, barkeep."

Cole groaned as Shep slapped him on the shoulder.

David's eyes widened and he swore under his breath. Jase swiveled his seat so he was facing the two Bennett brothers.

"That must have been one hell of a pour," he said, glancing toward his empty glass. "Because I'm seeing double."

"Not for long," Cole muttered. "Get out of here, Shep."

"In your dreams." Shep settled on the barstool next to Cole. "I take it my brother the sheriff didn't spend his off-duty hours regaling you with clever anecdotes from our twinsie childhood."

"They know about you."

"Hypothetical knowing and real-life seeing are different things," Jase said, rubbing a hand over his eyes. "Put your faces next to each other's so I can compare your features."

Cole rolled his eyes. "Kiss my—"

"Another round for everyone," David said quickly. He

poured liquor into three glasses, then got called to the other end of the bar.

"My brother," Shep said, leaning back to speak directly to Jase, "never loses control."

Jase held up his glass as if he was toasting Cole's self-control. "He's a steady force in this community. A real prize."

"A prize," Cole muttered with a sharp laugh. "Gee, thanks."

"Which makes whatever's going on tonight all the more intriguing." Shep tapped a finger on his chin as if he was pondering the future of the world. Cole wanted to punch him.

"What brings you to Crimson, Shep?" Jase asked.

Cole might be damn angry with his best friend, but he could still appreciate that Jase was trying to distract Shep. Cole sure as hell didn't want to share anything about his feelings for Sienna with his twin. Even without details and not factoring alcohol into the equation, Shep had to be able to sense how upset Cole was and that meant giving his brother too much power.

"I bought some property here."

"A summer home?"

"Not exactly."

"The ski resort," Cole blurted, sick of Shep's weird little head games.

"Thanks, bro," Shep whispered.

"It's not like it's a secret."

Jase's mouth dropped open but he quickly closed it. "You're with the Trinity Development Company?"

"I'm the president."

"Well then, welcome to Crimson."

"You're the mayor, right?"

"I am."

"And friends with my brother."

"Yes," Jase said at the same time Cole mumbled, "We'll see."

"Trouble in paradise?" One side of Shep's mouth curved. "Did one of you lads break the bro code? Skim a little from the other's milk?"

"Shut up, Shep."

"Nothing like that," Jase clarified. "It's my sister."

"You dishonored a friend's sister?" Shep nudged Cole's shoulder. "I didn't think you had it in you, buddy."

"Do you ever get sick of being a jerk?" Cole asked his brother.

"Nope," Shep said with a laugh. "It's my superpower."

"A jerk is handling the reopening of the ski mountain?" Jase downed the remainder of his drink. "Perfect."

"Sienna is the only thing I care about right now." Cole leaned his elbows on the bar and bent his head forward. "You should have seen how she looked at me."

Jase sighed. "I know exactly how she looked at you because it was the same way with me."

"Not the same," Cole muttered. "You're not in love with her."

Shep whistled low under his breath.

"Hell, no, I'm not *in* love with her. She's my sis—" Jase stopped, sucked a breath. "Did you say you're in love with her? With my sister?"

"That explains everything," Shep said. He took another sip of whiskey. "If you love this chick, then of course you messed it up."

"She's not a chick," Cole snapped, then turned to his brother. "Don't call her that."

"Yeah," Jase agreed. "Show some respect."

Shep held up his hands. "Got it."

"What do you mean, of course I messed it up?"

"Tell me what happened."

Cole pressed his lips together. "There was something she didn't know that I knew and when she realized I knew before she knew—"

"He lied to her." Jase rose from his stool.

"I didn't lie," Cole countered. "I just didn't tell her that you'd lied."

"It was for her own good," Jase said, shaking his head.

"I thought so, too," Cole said.

"Like all of Dad's lies were for Mom's own good?" Shep asked.

Cole shook his head. "Don't go there."

"Isn't that what he told her?" Shep took another long drink. "That's what he told all of us." His tone was disgusted. "He ruined her." He tipped his glass toward Cole. "And this ch…woman probably got off easy. How long were you together anyway?"

"It doesn't matter," Cole said. "What matters is that I should have told her from the start."

"What was the big lie anyway?" Shep asked.

Cole glanced toward Jase, who shrugged.

"There was something she didn't know about the agreement her parents had for child support after they got divorced," Cole said.

Jase laughed softly. "You should be the politician. That was the biggest spin I've ever heard." He took a step toward Shep. "My mother moved away from Crimson with Sienna when we were kids. My dad was a mess. Mom sent him money, and it was understood that he wouldn't contact her or see my sister."

"Like a payoff?" Shep asked.

"Such an ugly word," Jase muttered.

"Exactly like a payoff," Cole admitted, even though he'd tried to convince himself it was something different when Jase had first told him about the arrangement.

"That's bad." Shep leaned forward over the bar. "Bartender," he shouted. "Another round for these two idiots and one for me, as well."

Cole looked to David and shook his head slightly. "No more for me." He glanced at his brother. "It's bad."

"Why didn't you tell her?"

"I'm an idiot," Cole muttered. "Just like you said."

"It's my fault." Jase shook his head. "I asked you not to say anything."

Shep gave a small laugh. "Bros before—"

"Sometimes I wish we were twelve again," Cole interrupted, "so I could tackle you to the ground. It's better this way. She got out early before I could hurt her even worse than I have. I'm my father's son after all."

"You don't actually believe that."

Cole glanced at his brother. "What are you talking about? We look just like him."

"I'm not debating paternity." Shep ran a hand through his hair. "But you aren't like him." He leaned in closer. "You are *not* our father."

"I lied to her," Cole whispered.

"Yes, and you'll have to fix the mess you're in. I recommend flowers and jewelry and a load of sappy, humiliating groveling. You can make this better. Hell, Cole, Dad could have made it better if he hadn't been such a coward."

"He was going to jail."

"Which didn't stop Mom from loving him. He gave up on her and on himself. That's the part I couldn't face. That's why I never came back. He was supposed to be the strongest man I knew, and he gave up. Don't be like him. Don't give up."

"I hate to side with your brother," Jase said, "but he's right."

"Hell, yeah, I am." Shep stood from his chair, pulled his wallet from his back pocket and threw a few crisp bills on the bar. "Do you know why?" He held up a hand before Cole could answer. "Because *you* are the strongest man I know. It sounds like this woman loves you, and there is nothing worth fighting for more important than that. Speaking of, I've actually got a lady waiting on me tonight. You two sad saps remind me I'd rather be with her."

"I thought you just got to town," Jase murmured. "You work fast."

Shep flashed a grin. "Something like that."

Cole met his brother's gaze, and it was like looking at a version of his own reflection. "I'm glad you're here," he said quietly, surprised to realize it had been true from the first moment he'd spotted Shep on the ski resort's patio. His brother might infuriate him, but their bond couldn't be broken.

"Besides..." Shep quickly drained the glass of whiskey David had set on the bar in front of him, then took two steps back. "If you don't handle it, I'm going to have to make myself available to help this poor girl get over you."

"Shut up."

"See ya, Cole." Shep turned with a laugh and walked out of the bar.

"Can I fix this?" Cole asked Jase a moment later.

His friend sighed. "I sure as hell hope so."

Chapter 18

Sienna looked up from the suitcase she was packing the next morning, shocked to see her father standing in the doorway of her room in the inn.

"You were discharged?" she asked, pressing a hand to her chest.

Declan shrugged. "AMA."

Sienna felt her mouth drop open. "Against medical advice? Dad, you can't do that. You have to go back. Let me take you back."

He inclined his head toward the window at the front of the house. "I'm paying the cabbie to wait. Johnny and me have been friends forever. He cleaned up his act a few years before me, but he understands what I'm trying to do here."

"Which is?" she asked slowly.

"Make things right," he answered, flashing one of his self-deprecating grins. The years might have been hard on her father but she could see the handsome man he must have been twenty years ago. It was no wonder her mother had found him irresistible. "Can I come in?"

"You need to be in the hospital."

"They were going to release me eventually." He lifted a brow. "This won't take long, baby girl, but you have every right to send me away if that's what you need to do. Lord knows I deserve it."

Sienna closed her eyes for a moment. A part of her wanted to refuse to hear him out. She had a flight booked to Chicago that afternoon, even though she didn't recognize the life she was returning to. Her mother had left Crimson last night. She'd tried to convince Sienna she'd sent the monthly checks for Jase's benefit and not to bribe Declan to stay out of Sienna's life. Sienna didn't believe it, but where else did she have to go at this point?

At least she had a history in Chicago. A job and friends... although the connections she'd made during her short time in Crimson felt just as strong as the relationships she'd had for years.

"I've got five minutes," she said, meeting her father's slate blue gaze.

"I only need four," he promised and stepped into the room.

He took a thick envelope from his back pocket and shoved it toward her. "Johnny ran me by the house before we came here," he explained. "This is for you."

She shook her head. "I don't want your money."

"Darlin', I don't have any money," he said, then laughed. "Just open the envelope. Please."

She took it, and they both ignored her trembling fingers.

"Why?" she whispered, glancing between her father and the thick stack of checks in the envelope. They were made out to Declan, written in her mother's precise script. Each one was dated for the first of the month, and they went back over ten years.

"Your mother sent them even after Jase graduated high school." He lifted one shoulder, let it drop like the weight on it was too much to sustain. "I was in pretty bad shape at that point, and she knew it. She sent a note—it was the first communication other than the checks I'd had with her since she left with you."

Despite Sienna's anger, the pain in her dad's voice tore at her heart. Was it any wonder she was so messed up in her own life when she had the parents she did? Declan and Dana made dysfunction anything but fun. "You don't have to share this with me." She didn't want to hear it. She didn't want to feel anything for this man.

"She told me to use the money to get my act together," he continued as if she hadn't spoken. Sienna got the impression he was saying the words as much for his own benefit as hers. "Because if you ever came looking for me, she wanted me to be around to deserve a second chance with you."

Sienna shook her head slowly. "I don't believe it." The checks felt like a flame in her hand. It burned through her skin, but she kept her fingers tight on the edge of the stack. She couldn't let go just yet. "She didn't want me to see you. She hated when I came here."

"Can you blame her?" he asked. "I don't. Of course your mom didn't want you anywhere near me, but she still wanted what was best for you."

"So why didn't you cash the checks?" She held up the envelope. "What's the point of saving them?"

"That note was a wake-up call." He scratched at the stubble that covered his jaw and smiled again. "Not that I was ready to wake up just then, but it resonated with me. I didn't want to owe getting clean to your mom. I wanted to earn my way back into your life on my own."

"But you never contacted me," she countered. "Even after you got sober."

"Letting you go was my greatest regret," he said quietly. "Don't think I didn't realize what kind of a father it made me, even if I could rationalize it at the time. I still don't deserve to be a part of your life, Sienna."

"Why did you let Jase stay?" It was the question that still plagued her. Why was her brother important enough to keep when she could be so easily discarded?

"He was different." Declan shrugged. "It's not logical, but the Crenshaws had been a family of boys for generations. Bad boys that turned into lousy men. I figured Jase could handle anything that came down the pike because it was in his blood. But you..." He sighed, his eyes drifting closed. "You were different. You were this bright, shiny thing in the cesspool of my life. A girl. The first one with the name Crenshaw in three generations. The thought of what could happen to you in this town..." He threw up his hands. "Your mom was right to take you away."

"I still don't believe that. Not the way she did it— letting me think you didn't want me." She took a breath, then added, "That you didn't love me."

"I always loved you," he said, moving forward. "I always will, baby girl. Whether you're in Crimson or Chicago or halfway around the world."

She bit down on the inside of her cheek to keep from crying. She *would not* cry.

"Do what you want with those checks," he said, covering her hand with his. "I never understood why I was saving them, but now I know it was to give them to you. You can hate me and refuse to speak to me but don't ever doubt that I love you." The corner of his mouth lifted. "In my own messed-up way."

She choked back a sob. "Is there any other way to love someone?"

He pulled her in for a tight hug. "Not in this family," he said.

After a moment, Sienna relaxed into him, and it felt like coming home.

Sienna watched the black Porsche tear into the ski resort's empty parking lot. Dust flew up around the SUV as it came to a quick stop in front of where she sat on the gravel.

She sucked in a breath as a man rushed from the vehicle, slamming shut the driver's side door and stalking toward her. Shep Bennett was indeed identical in looks to Cole, although Sienna would never confuse one brother for the other. She'd been shocked when Paige had told her Shep's company had bought the ski resort and that he was personally under contract to purchase The Bumblebee.

Of course, she couldn't call Cole to ask him about it because she wasn't speaking to Cole—wasn't sure if she'd ever speak to him again. She knew it didn't make sense, but the fact that he hadn't told her what he knew about her parents' arrangement felt like a bigger betrayal than her family lying to her all those years. Although she knew in her heart—her broken heart—the lie was just an excuse.

"You're trespassing, Sienna." He pointed a finger at her. "Not to mention making me think my resort was on fire and scaring the hell out of me."

Sienna looked up at the plume of smoke wafting into the air, then poked a stick at the smoldering logs in the metal fire pit she'd dragged from around the back of the lodge.

"You know who I am," she said quietly.

Shep nodded. "My brother is pretty much tied in knots over you. I'll admit I was curious, although he forgot to mention your pyromaniac tendencies. You know there's a fire ban around here?"

"That's why I'm in the parking lot, where there are no trees. It seemed safe." She glanced at Shep and raised a brow. "Are you going to call the cops?"

Shep blew out a breath. "Sadly, you don't look like a handcuffs type of girl."

"You have no idea what kind of woman I am."

"The kind my brother fell in love with, which says something about you."

"That I was crazy," Sienna muttered, "to get involved with him."

"Well, yes," Shep agreed, rubbing a hand over his jaw in a gesture so similar to Cole's that it made her heart ache. He glanced back at the SUV, then crouched down next to her. "What's with the fire?"

"Maybe I wanted to make s'mores."

"Or burn down the forest." He grabbed the stick from her hand. "Enough poking at it. You got your point across."

"Back off, Smokey Bear," she said under her breath.

Shep laughed. "I can see why Cole is so damn in love with you."

She leveled a glare at him. "Your brother said he *cares* about me, which is not the same thing as love."

"Not always silky smooth, that guy. I also heard he lied to you, although he wasn't forthcoming with much in the way of details."

"I've got the details right here." Sienna plucked another check out of the envelope she held between her knees, wadded it into a ball, then tossed it into the fire. The edges caught first, burning bright orange, then turning to black as the paper disintegrated in the heat of the fire.

She'd come out to the ski resort because she wanted to

be alone but didn't trust her rental car on the dirt roads that led into Forest Service land. The mountains were so close here it felt like they were embracing the valley, and it surprised her that no one had bought the property sooner.

Shep straightened when a noise came from the SUV. He jogged around the driver's side and Sienna heard a small cry, then the soft rumble of Shep making soothing sounds.

"Tell me you don't have a baby in that Porsche," she called as she stood.

"Rosie will actually be eighteen months next week," Shep said as he reappeared, a child snuggled to his chest. "She's officially a toddler."

Sienna felt her mouth drop open. "Where did you get her?"

"Aisle seven of the local grocery," Shep answered with a wink. "Near the canned peas."

"Shep."

He moved forward, smoothing fine, dark hair away from Rosie's face. "Rosie is my daughter."

"Does Cole know?"

Shep shook his head, his full lips thinning. "Not yet. Hell, I didn't even know about her until recently."

"You shouldn't curse in front of a child," Sienna said automatically.

"Thanks for the tip," Shep said tightly. "I'll add it to the list of things I need to learn about being a dad." He cupped a hand on the back of Rosie's head. "It's a long damn list."

"Shep."

He groaned. "No cursing. Right."

"Dada," Rosie said in a tiny voice. She tipped up her face to look at Shep. "Damn, Dada."

"I'm a bad daddy." Shep dropped a kiss on the tip of the young girl's nose. "I'll do better next time."

"That's why no cursing," Sienna told him, unable to hide her smile. "Hi, Rosie."

Rosie shifted in her father's arms, looked at Sienna, then buried her face in Shep's shirtfront.

"She's kind of shy," Shep offered. "Plus she fell asleep in the car, and it takes her a while to wake up from a nap. Takes after her daddy in that respect. This is Sienna," he explained to his daughter. "She's a friend of your uncle Cole's. I told you about him, remember? He looks like Daddy, only not as handsome."

After a moment, Rosie turned to look at Sienna again, her gaze wary. The girl was adorable, with big brown eyes and dark hair that curled above her ears. She wore a wrinkled pink dress and polka-dot socks on her feet.

"Is it just the two of you?" Sienna asked.

"I brought a nanny with us from California, but she took off this morning." Shep rolled his eyes. "Saw a bear on her run and freaked out."

"She just left?"

"So fast it would make your head spin."

"Jettie," Rosie said with a sniff.

"Jessie had to go back to Los Angeles," Shep said with a sigh. "Where there are way scarier things on the streets than bears if you ask me."

"You need help."

"No doubt," Shep agreed. "But the first thing I need is for you to completely put out that fire."

"Got it." Sienna picked up the bucket of water she'd set to one side of the fire pit. "I was prepared. I really wasn't trying to cause trouble." She closed her eyes for a moment as the memory of Cole teasing about her being a trouble-maker played through her mind.

Shep eyed the now empty envelope on the ground.

"What exactly were you doing? I can't imagine Cole writing love letters for you to burn."

The wood sizzled as she dumped the bucket of water over it, a huge rush of smoke pouring into the air.

Rosie covered her ears and shouted, "'Moke, Daddy."

"It's okay, sweethcart. I've got you." Shep stepped back toward the SUV.

When the smoke cleared, Sienna turned to Cole's brother. "Just getting rid of some old family drama."

"Cole and I have plenty of that ourselves," Shep told her. "Next time, drown your sorrows at a bar like he did. It's a lot safer for all of us."

She picked up the envelope and crumpled it into a ball as Shep opened the door and loaded Rosie into her car seat. "Cole had *sorrows* to drown?"

"Oh, yeah. He was a bad drunk and that *never* happens to my brother. I'm sure whatever he did to mess things up was bad, but I can guarantee he regrets it. I hope you give him another chance." He shut the door and flashed a wide grin. "I have a feeling he'll be a lot easier to deal with if you're a part of his life. I know I would be."

Sienna gave a small wave as Shep climbed in the Porsche and drove away. Her feelings were still jumbled enough that she wasn't sure she wanted another chance with Cole. She could easily forgive him for not telling her about the checks. But she'd told him she loved him and he'd offered her nothing in return.

After spending most of her life wondering if she was even worthy of love, Sienna had finally realized she deserved so much more than she'd ever believed. And she was no longer willing to settle for someone who'd give her anything less.

Chapter 19

"Isn't there some kind of limit on how many turns a person can take with this thing?" Cole climbed back onto the dunk tank platform at the Crimson Fourth of July Festival the following weekend, pushed sopping wet hair away from his face.

"It's for charity, boss," Marlene called from the ticket table she was manning next to the booth. She held up the cash box in his direction. "We're making lots of money for the community center."

"Yeah, Sheriff. Don't be a bad sport."

Cole glared at his brother, who was gleefully handing over another five-dollar bill to Marlene.

"I'm a great sport," Cole argued, gathering the hem of his uniform shirt in his hands to wring out the water. It had been Marlene's idea that he wear the uniform, but he'd refused the sign she'd tried to hand him that read Did I Give

You a Ticket? No sense in giving the festival-goers too much motivation.

He glanced up at the clear sky, grateful for another bluebird day in Colorado. At least he had the sunshine to warm him between dunks, although thanks to the ice-cold water in the tank, he was still shivering slightly. "But you're taking too much pleasure in soaking me."

"Just loosening up the arm," Shep said with a laugh, shifting his hold on Rosie. "You want to see Daddy dunk Uncle Cole again, sweetheart?"

Rosie clapped her chubby hands. "Dunk, Daddy!"

"Good idea." Cole pointed toward Shep through the bars of the dunk tank. "Why don't we change places?"

"Not a chance. Besides, the good people of Crimson want to see their fine, upstanding sheriff take the plunge, not his newcomer brother." Shep turned to the crowd that had gathered in front of the dunk tank, tossing a ball in the air. "Isn't that right, everyone?"

A round of cheers went up and Cole gave an obligatory smile and wave.

The festival was in full swing. Booths housing carnival games and food trucks lined the perimeter of the field next to the county fairgrounds outside of town. An oversize tent with picnic tables under it and a large stage were situated at one end of the festivities, and a three-piece bluegrass band played to an audience of older folks and families.

But the big draw this afternoon was the dunking booth, especially since Cole had climbed onto the platform thirty minutes ago. He'd replaced Jase, who'd only had a few people interested in dunking him. Cole, on the other hand, was a popular target.

First up had been Emily, then Katie Crawford, then Declan. Cole was pretty sure Sienna's father would have rather aimed the ball directly at Cole's head, but the old man managed to send him into the tank of freezing water on the first throw. Impressive for a man still recovering from a stint in the hospital.

Cole hadn't complained or tried to defend himself against Sienna's little posse of protectors. He wanted to fix the mess he'd made.

He'd even paid a visit to Declan's house after he'd learned Sienna had moved in to help take care of her father. Declan had seemed to take great pleasure in slamming the door shut in Cole's face. Cole hadn't slept in a week, had no appetite and could barely focus on work as his thoughts were consumed with Sienna and how to win her back. But earning a second chance was difficult when she apparently wanted nothing to do with him.

"I'd like to dunk the newcomer," a voice called out now, and Cole watched the sea of bystanders part to reveal Paige Harper glaring at Shep.

"It's about time," Cole muttered under his breath. "I need a break."

"I've got a baby in my arms," Shep said, glancing over his shoulder at Cole, then back to Paige. "Miss, I'm not sure what I've done to raise your ire, but I can assure you—"

"Save it, buddy." She plucked the ball from Shep's fingers. "Cute kid, by the way."

Cole couldn't help but smile at the shocked look on Shep's face as Paige leaned in to tickle Rosie's dimpled chin. The little girl, who was the shyest child Cole had ever encountered, giggled and reached for Paige.

"Stay with your daddy," Paige said, smoothing a hand across Rosie's soft hair. "I have business with your uncle Cole, too."

Rosie flashed a toothy grin, then shoved her fist into her mouth.

Cole had never seen his brother at a loss for words, but Shep stared at Paige like she was standing there juggling in nothing but her birthday suit.

Paige stepped forward, eyeing the ball in her hand. "How much for a guaranteed dunk?" she asked Marlene.

"That's not part of the deal," Cole shouted. "She has to hit the target."

"I'll hit it all right," Paige shouted back. "But I'll wish it were your face."

Shep let out a low moan. "A toddler whisperer with a temper? I think I've died and gone to heaven."

"I tried calling her but she won't answer," Cole said to Paige, leaning forward as if that would prevent the rest of the town from hearing his words. He'd made a habit of keeping his private life just that, but somehow everyone in Crimson seemed to know that things had gone south between Sienna and him. Hard to believe, when it had been only a few weeks since he'd stopped her on the road from Aspen, but that's how small towns worked. Nothing was private in Crimson. Not for long anyway.

"Ten dollars," Marlene told Paige, who quickly pulled a few bills from her purse.

"Done," she said, slapping them on the table, then stalking toward Cole. "You should try harder."

"Tell me how."

She gave a small shake of her head, curls bouncing. "You don't deserve to know. I told you she needed someone in her corner."

"I know you did." Cole swiped a hand across his eyes, sweat beginning to bead along his forehead despite the cool breeze whirling across the fairgrounds. "I should have been that person."

"But you weren't." Paige yelled the words despite the fact that she was standing right next to the dunk tank. "You broke her heart. You hurt her. Do you know that she almost—?"

"Paige."

The tiny woman clasped a hand over her mouth and turned as Sienna walked out of the crowd.

"Almost what?" Cole asked, leaning forward. He sucked in a breath as Sienna moved toward the dunk tank. She wore a red floral shirt with lace detailing around the neckline and slim denim jeans that molded over her curves in a way that made his mouth go dry. Her long hair was down, casually curling over her shoulders. She looked so beautiful, happy and at peace in a way he hadn't seen before.

Then she met his gaze and the pain in her eyes was like a gunshot to his heart because he knew he'd put it there.

"You don't have to do this," she said, her gaze gentling as she looped an arm around Paige's shoulder. "As much as I appreciate it—"

"I have pent-up aggression," Paige muttered, darting a glare toward Shep. "And I can't take it out on the brother holding the kid. Cole's an easier target."

"Literally," Cole said, then shrugged when both women turned to him. "I'm stuck in this cage and half the town has some sort of bizarre need to defend your honor."

"I'm heading to the beer tent," Paige said, giving Sienna a quick hug. "Meet me there."

Sienna nodded, then tipped up her chin as she focused on Cole once again. "I can take care of myself."

"I know you can," he whispered, loving how color flooded her cheeks even as she glared at him. Loving everything about her. Offering up a thousand silent prayers that she'd give him another chance—one he wouldn't squander.

"I almost left Crimson," she said, crossing her arms over her chest. "That's what Paige was about to tell you. As much as I wanted to, I didn't think I could stand to stay and risk running into you and pretend like things were right between us."

"I want us to be right."

She shifted to look back at the crowd of people watching them. His brother. Her brother and Emily. Declan. Marlene. A dozen other people he knew in some capacity. His most colossal mistake on display for everyone to witness, and he still had no idea how to make it better.

He met his brother's dark gaze, watching Shep's eyes widen as he inclined his head toward Sienna like he was trying to tell Cole something. Shep raised a hand and pointed a finger toward his eye then lowered it to his chest and finally leveled it at Cole.

Eye. Heart. You.

I love you.

Cole still hadn't said the words out loud, although he'd replayed them in his head countless times over the past week.

"Sienna."

She swiped a hand across her cheek. "I can't do this now," she said softly and took a step away.

"Wait." He leaned forward so fast he almost slipped off the platform. "Don't go. Please. I need to talk to you. I need to tell you I love you."

A chorus of cheers went up from the people watching, and Sienna froze. Cole waited for what seemed like an eternity until she finally lifted an arm, as if she were holding out her hand to him. Instead she reached forward and casually pressed the dunk tank lever.

Sienna watched Cole drop into the tank with a splash, droplets of frigid water hitting her face and shoulders.

He surfaced a moment later, sputtering and wiping water from his eyes.

"I tell you I love you," he said, coughing violently, "and you dunk me?"

She shook her head and took a step back. "I dunked you for breaking my heart in the first place."

He stilled for a moment, then grabbed onto the bars of the cage and pulled himself forward. "I'm sorry."

"Dunk him again," a man from the crowd shouted.

"Shut up, Shep," Cole shouted back, then unlatched the cage and started out of the tank.

"You have five minutes left on your time, Sheriff," Marlene called.

"I'll donate a hundred dollars to the community center as a forfeit," Cole said, hoisting himself over the metal side. Water sluiced from his body and his sheriff's uniform clung to the hard muscles of his chest and thighs. Sienna had a ridiculous thought of Poseidon emerging from the sea.

Cole was a god in that moment and she was a mere mortal and how could she resist a god? His words had cut through the newly built defenses she'd erected around her heart, and she automatically turned away, afraid of how much she wanted them to be true.

He circled her wrist with his hand. "Please don't go."

His fingers were icy cold, but she could still feel the heat of his body behind her, and she wanted nothing more than to turn and wrap herself around him and never let go.

"I'm staying because this is my home," she said, keeping

her gaze straight ahead. "I belong here. I made that decision for me and no one else."

He shifted his grasp on her arm, sliding his fingers across her hand and interlacing them with hers. "You're my home," he said quietly. "I belong anywhere you are, Sienna. I'm sorry I was too much of an idiot to tell you that when you needed to hear it."

"Me, too," she whispered.

Ignoring the crowd still watching them, he moved in front of her, keeping their hands linked together. "I'm saying it now, sweetheart. I love you with everything I am and if you give me another chance, I'll prove it to you every day for the rest of our lives. I know you don't need me. You're so damn strong, and I can't tell you how happy it makes me that you finally know it."

She drew in a breath. "You helped me understand that," she admitted. "I'm not sure I would have believed it about myself if you hadn't believed it first."

"There was never a doubt in my mind." He stepped closer, crowding her a little. "I know I hurt you, and I probably don't deserve your forgiveness. I'm not the sharpest knife in the drawer, but I can learn. I finally understand that I have to take some risks to get the life I want. A true home and a family—someone who will make my life complete. You, Sienna. I want you and I get that I have to be brave to earn my place at your side."

She laughed as hope filled her, making her feel lighter than she had in years. "You know how to be brave. You're the sheriff."

"Not with my heart," he told her. "Not until you. If you want me to walk away—"

She pressed her fingers to his lips. "Don't you dare."

"I'll never go far," he finished quickly. "There's no place

I can imagine being except by your side." He traced his thumb against the inside of her wrist, his touch sending shivers of awareness across her skin.

"I love you, Cole," she whispered, then yelped as he lifted her in his arms and gathered her close. "But you're a soaking wet mess."

"I'm your mess," he said. "Forever if you'll have me." He pressed his mouth to hers, the kiss at once tender and possessive. She was swept away on a wave of happiness so massive she wondered if she'd ever come back down to earth.

"I'll take you on, Sheriff," she whispered against his lips. "Forever."

He spun her in a circle as their friends and family cheered. Sienna grinned, realizing she'd found so much more than she'd ever expected in Crimson. A family. A home. And love. Whatever came her way, she could face it fully with Cole by her side. Forever.

* * * * *

SPECIAL EXCERPT FROM

◈ HARLEQUIN

SPECIAL EDITION

*Rosa Galvez's attraction to Officer Wyatt Townsend is as powerful
as the moon's pull on the tides. But with her past, Rosa knows
better than to act on her feelings. But her solo life slowly becomes
a sun-filled, family adventure—until dark secrets threaten to break
like a summer storm.*

*Read on for a sneak peek at
the next book in The Women of Brambleberry House miniseries,*
A Brambleberry Summer,
by New York Times *bestselling author RaeAnne Thayne.*

"Everyone has secrets, do they not? Some they share with those
they trust, some they prefer to keep to themselves."

He was quiet for a long moment. "I hope you know that if you
ever want to share yours, you can trust me."

She trusted very few people. And she certainly wasn't going to
trust Wyatt, who was only a temporary tenant and would be out of
her life in a few short weeks.

"If I had any secrets, I might do that. But I don't. I'm a completely
open book."

She tried for a breezy smile but could tell he wasn't at all
convinced. In fact, he looked slightly disappointed.

She tried to ignore her guilt and opted to change the subject
instead. "The lightning seems to have stopped for now. I am sure
the power will be back on soon."

"No doubt."

"Thank you again for coming to my rescue. Good night. Be careful going back down the stairs."

"I will do that. Good night."

He studied her, his features unreadable in the dim light of her flashlight. He looked as if he wanted to say something else. Instead, he shook his head slightly.

"Good night."

As he turned to go back down the stairs, the masculine scent of him swirled to her. She felt that sudden wild urge to kiss him again but ignored it. Instead, she went into her darkened apartment, her dog at her heels, and firmly closed the door behind her. If only she could close the door to her thoughts as easily.

Don't miss
A Brambleberry Summer *by RaeAnne Thayne,*
available July 2021 wherever
Harlequin Special Edition books and ebooks are sold.

Harlequin.com

HSEEXP40987MAX

Love Harlequin romance?

DISCOVER.

Be the first to find out about promotions, news and exclusive content!

f Facebook.com/HarlequinBooks

Twitter.com/HarlequinBooks

Instagram.com/HarlequinBooks

P Pinterest.com/HarlequinBooks

You Tube YouTube.com/HarlequinBooks

ReaderService.com

EXPLORE.

Sign up for the Harlequin e-newsletter and download a free book from any series at **TryHarlequin.com**

CONNECT.

Join our Harlequin community to share your thoughts and connect with other romance readers! **Facebook.com/groups/HarlequinConnection**

HARLEQUIN

Heartfelt or thrilling, passionate or uplifting—Harlequin is more than just happily-ever-after.

With twelve different series to choose from and new books available every month, you are sure to find stories that will move you, uplift you, inspire and delight you.

SIGN UP FOR THE HARLEQUIN NEWSLETTER

Be the first to hear about great new reads and exciting offers!

Harlequin.com/newsletters

HNEWS2021MAX